# Marigolds AND Murder

# Marigolds
## AND
# Murder

### A·K· IKEZOE

Starmist Press

Published by Starmist Press

An imprint of STARMIST PRESS LLC, Chicago, IL

https://www.starmistpress.com/

First Edition: June 2025

Book Cover by Holly Dunn Designs

ISBN 978-1-967332-01-4 (paperback)

Library of Congress Control Number: 2025905628

*To Daisy*
*For reading your war crimes textbooks to me*

"Down in our hearts we cried and cursed this government every time when we showered with sand. We slept in the dust; we breathed the dust; we ate the dust."

-Joseph Kurihara

# CHAPTER 1

# THE CLIENT

The jam in Philly wasn't made with Nisei strawberries. It would never taste right. Added sugar made it excessively sweet, like candy, and its vibrant red came from food dye. Kat had already sampled every jar in the city, but there was no better option. Nisei strawberries only grew on the West Coast, so the jam would never taste like home.

A heavy glob of the most tolerable strawberry jam Kat could find smothered her toast. She took an unsatisfying bite, keeping the crumbs off her desk. She had worked through lunch, but family dinner was in a couple hours. She only needed a snack to hold her over until then.

The radio droned on about that annoying Wisconsin senator that wouldn't shut up. Communists this or Shapeshifters that. Didn't matter who. All of them were Soviet spies infiltrating America. Nobody could trust their neighbors. Kat rolled her eyes at the idiocy. Five years since the war ended, and the government was pointing fingers again.

Kat switched off the radio. She would rather eat in silence than indulge in fearmongering. There was no point in going crazy again. Not when she had work to do. She flipped through the files on her desk as she verified for a third time that the background checks were perfect for her client.

Background checks were tedious and paperwork heavy, but they made up most of her job as a private detective. Kat had half a dozen regular clients who relied on her for employee background checks on their candidates. Her clients paid well, but the work was procedural. Was this new hire a criminal? Were they in contact with any competitors? Were they a bad employee at their previous job? Most of the time, the answer was no, and business carried on as usual.

On rare occasions, a file got flagged. Maybe the new hire was drunk and disorderly. Maybe she was from a competing company, seeking to steal secrets. Maybe he got fired from his last accounting firm for threatening to hex his entire department after—having eaten his coworker's lunch for weeks—his coworker planted a fake lunch laced with parsley-snapspolygon potion, which temporarily turned the candidate's face into cubic zirconia, thus exposing him as the culprit. Well, that only happened once. The rest were usually boring. At the end of the day, it was business. And businesses only wanted a yes or no.

Kat preferred when her clients had personal grievances. Yes, his girlfriend was cheating on him with his best friend. No, her husband was not cheating, but he had a very serious gambling addiction. Yes, her sister stole the inheritance from their dead mother, but in the process of reclaiming it, they discovered the sister murdered the mother too, so now the client gets the entire inheritance. Those were the cases Kat felt she could truly help with. She could prove she was a good person and give someone else closure.

While Kat had given up on finding closure in her own life, she could find it for others. The relief on their faces was enough for her. She would do anything to help someone in need, especially someone nobody else would help. Her compassion made her a good private detective. That was what her old colleagues said. Her compassion—and her innate intuition for cracking the final clue. Nobody suspected she used magic to solve her cases.

Kat finished her toast and took the plate to the kitchen. The floorboards in the hallway crackled under her feet. Each step sputtered in a cacophony of agony.

The house was old and in desperate need of repairs. The floorboards creaked and sagged. The water damage on the ceiling could qualify it as a mural. Some doors didn't close right, and the front porch was rotting. Kat's family was worried about the state of the building. Her uncle Tsukuru had hesitated to cosign the mortgage, but it was all Kat could afford then. It didn't matter how fancy it was. She'd just needed a starting point.

She had converted the sitting room and foyer into a lobby for her business, painting over the peeling wallpaper to make it more approachable for clients. She had even saved enough money to buy a front desk, which would be delivered in a few days. Then it would look more like a business lobby and less like a living room.

The kitchen had its own wall that separated it from the rest of the lobby. In it stood a tiny table with a wobbly wooden chair. All the cupboards were outdated and bland. Kat wanted to paint everything in bright pastels, but color wasn't a priority. She had at least updated her appliances to functional models. The brand-new stove sparkled as the old water kettle heated on it, steam spiraling from the spout. Unfortunately, the dented piece of metal heated the water just fine. She couldn't justify the expense of buying a new one.

The kettle whistled, and more steam rushed out of the funnel. Kat washed the plate and put it back in the cupboard with the rest of the mismatched dishware. The whistling grew louder. A figure crept past her.

Kat gasped and ducked. Her assistant stared at her, and

Kat took a breath. "Emrah, I'm putting a bell on you, I swear."

Emrah smirked as he adjusted his black-framed glasses. The chunky lenses magnified his blue eyes in a cartoonish way. "You'd get sick of it ringing every time I got more coffee," he said. Emrah spoke with the same city accent as everyone else in Philly. However, some of his words and phrases, such as "coffee," came out in a Slavic accent.

"Then I'll get bigger mugs, so you don't need a refill as often," Kat said. She stepped out of his way, and the floorboards squeaked. Emrah walked past her, taking uneven strides on his toes. Despite being several inches taller than her, he moved silently, finding quiet parts of the floor to step on. It hadn't taken him long to figure out how to navigate the floors. By the end of his first week, he'd already jump-scared her by noiselessly popping around a corner.

Emrah had a longer triangular face with narrow features and pale skin. He slicked his dirty-blond hair back and had recently started wearing clothes that fit him properly. Most of the time, Kat refrained from commenting on his attire. His button-down shirts were often untucked from his slacks. He never ironed his clothes either, but she could live with a few wrinkles. She only spoke up when he was going undercover as someone who would be better dressed. But in the few months he had been her assistant, he had shaped up a lot. She was glad she'd given him a second chance.

Kat stepped out of the kitchen. The front door opened, and a young woman came inside. Kat fixed her hair and smiled. The woman looked around, her tangled blonde hair attempting to conceal her gaunt face. Her pallid complexion contrasted her dark, oversized clothing. Baggy layers of fabric gave her an ambiguous body frame, but the floorboards barely squeaked under her weight when she stepped into the foyer. She limped forward, gripping a cane. Her fingers wrapped around the handle, her knuckles bulging.

"Good afternoon," Kat said. "How may I help you?"

The woman kept her head down. "Hello," she croaked, glancing around the room. Kat did her best to maintain a bright smile and not fear the woman's judgment of the state of her building. "I was told I could find a private investigator here." She had a thick French accent.

"Well, good news. You found me," Kat said. "Would you like to have a seat, so we can discuss matters?"

Her cane wobbled under her taut, white-knuckled grip. "I don't know if you can help me. Others declined."

"Well, there's no harm in a free consultation. What do you say?" Kat asked.

The woman looked up, and Kat noted her bloodshot, pale blue eyes. "Maybe a small meeting."

"Splendid. Right this way." Kat guided her down the hall. The floorboards creaked under Kat's weight but hardly made a sound when the woman walked. They entered her office, and Kat grabbed the stack of background checks off her desk. "Take a seat, and I'll be with you shortly." Kat left the room and rushed back to the kitchen.

Emrah poured foaming coffee from his copper džezva into his mug. The earthy aroma was almost tempting enough to crave. "New client?" Emrah asked. He set the copper pot on the stove next to the kettle, grabbed a sugar cube, and then dropped it into the frothing liquid.

"Hopefully," Kat said. She held out the folders to Emrah. "I need you to give these to Jerry if he comes by before I'm done."

Emrah raised an eyebrow. "You sure that's a good idea?" he asked, setting his mug down. "The guy hates me."

"Just try not to offend him."

"No promises."

She shoved the folders into his arms and scurried down the hall. The squeaking followed her until she hopped into her office and shut the door. The woman sat in the chair across from her desk. "Sorry about the wait." Kat sat at her desk and grabbed her notebook.

The woman stared at the name plaque on Kat's desk. "How do you say your name?"

One of the most common questions she got asked. "Katsumi Okazaki." The woman nodded. No further commentary was a relief. Kat smiled. "And what might your name be?"

The woman stared at her hands, clutching her cane. She wore an engraved silver band with a gorgeous diamond on her ring finger. Her gaze lingered for a moment before she answered. "Héloïse Keeler."

Kat dated the top of her notebook and wrote down the name. "It's nice to meet you, Héloïse. What brings you in here today?" Héloïse fiddled with her ring, twisting it back and forth. Was it a cheating husband? Unusual financial transactions? "Anything you say to me is confidential."

Héloïse looked up at her and took a breath. "I think my in-laws killed my fiancée." Kat's eyes widened, but she maintained her composure. "I have no proof. The police cannot help, and I've been turned away by other investigators," Héloïse said. "But I am not crazy. They are not acting right. I think they did something. Can you help me?"

"I can do my best," Kat said. "May I ask how this started?"

Héloïse sat up in her chair. "Last week, my fiancée had a fall at work. Broken neck." Her voice trembled and her breath shook. "Passed away on the 23rd."

Kat took notes while pushing the tissues closer. "I'm sorry for your loss. Where did he work? What was his job?"

Héloïse took a tissue and crumpled it in her hands. "My fiancée was a woman."

Kat clenched the pen in her hand. Her face grew hot as an ache spread in her chest. Two women could get married in Pennsylvania. It was legal, but not without challenges.

"Is that a problem?" Héloïse asked.

Kat blinked. "No, no, not at all." Her voice wavered as she searched for the right words. Héloïse looked at her skeptically. "I'm sorry. What was her name?"

"Serena." Héloïse eased in the chair. "Serena Line."

"Where did Serena work?" Kat asked. She cleared her throat, but her face was still flushed while she wrote the name down.

"At city hall. She was a . . . court reporter. A . . . stenographer. She was very good. Made her own money."

Serena would've been able to support them, but there were still potential legal restrictions.

"And you think her parents had something to do with her death?" Kat asked.

"I am not sure," Héloïse said. "Their behavior is strange. They ignore me. They won't answer the door. I spoke with Serena's aunt. They won't talk to her either. They refuse to hold a funeral." Her eyes welled with tears, and she took a breath.

People processed grief in different ways, but to refuse a funeral after a week indicated either a strong case of denial or indifference to their daughter. Then again, if they did have something to do with their child's death, complete apathy would be suspicious.

"Was Serena close with her parents?"

"Very much," Héloïse said. "We visited often. They were helping plan the wedding. We had dinner together every Sunday. Now they will not answer the door."

"Have you spoken to the rest of the family? You mentioned an aunt?"

"Yes, Serena was close with her too. Her aunt will hold a memorial lunch this Saturday for the family. I don't think Serena's parents will come." Héloïse's eyes watered, and she blotted her cheeks with the tissue. "I know this is not much proof, but it is strange. It is not right."

"I believe you, and I'll help you get to the bottom of this,"

Kat said, flipping to a new page. "When Serena fell, what happened? It was at work?"

Héloïse nodded. "She fell down the stairs. No one saw. The police said the stairs were wet, and she slipped. But something must be wrong."

If she slipped and broke her neck, then why would her parents change their attitude? "Did she have any health problems?" Kat asked. "Trouble walking or a history of fainting?" Héloïse shook her head. "Can you think of any other reason why her parents would act like this?"

Héloïse stared at her hands. "No, everything was good."

"Did Serena have any recent fights with her parents? Did they get into arguments of any kind?"

Héloïse shook her head again. "They were excited for the wedding."

Same-sex marriage had been recently legalized in Pennsylvania, but it wasn't perfect. Especially not for women. Unmarried women still didn't have the same financial privileges as men. Opening a bank account, buying property, or starting a business required a male cosigner. As if finding a male sponsor wasn't difficult enough, a lesbian couple also needed at least one of their fathers to approve the marriage license. Lack of an approving father—or lack of a living father—prevented two women from getting married.

"I have to ask," Kat said, "whose father approved the marriage license? Was it hers?"

"Her father would sign," Héloïse said. "It had to be him."

Kat nodded, flipping the pen between her fingers. "Was there any reason to suspect she didn't fall on accident? Was there a coroner's report that suggested she was pushed or had been drugged?"

Héloïse sat back in the chair, and tears fell from her face. "No," she whispered.

Kat stared at her notes. Not much of a case here. Not enough leads yet.

"I know what it sounds like," Héloïse said, "but I'm not crazy."

"I understand. However—"

"No." Héloïse hit her cane against the floor. "Something is wrong." Kat froze, staring at the woman's bloodshot eyes. "I thought it was a terrible accident at first. And when her parents refused to see me, I feared they never liked me after all. But they will not hold a funeral or speak to the rest of the family. There must be a reason. Please." Her blue eyes glistened with sorrow and desperation.

"I believe you," Kat said. Héloïse's eyes softened. "I want to help you, but investigations of this type tend to take time. The more you can tell me, the easier it'll be for me to find out what happened." Héloïse nodded, holding on to every word Kat said. "Is there *anything* else you can tell me? Any reason Serena's parents could have been upset with her, or perhaps something about the wedding? Anything about the extended family or Serena's work?"

Héloïse pressed her lips together and looked down at her cane as she stretched out her fingers. "Maybe, you should know . . ." Kat readied her pen on her notepad. "I am an Exalter."

The French accent.

As of today, there were four kinds of Exalters. Originally, only military personnel had the abilities. The Soviet Union developed Shapeshifting. The Nazis developed Telepathy. And the US developed Necromancy just before D-Day. The Nazis had been working on a fourth ability, but it became a calamity.

The catastrophic Munich Incident ended the war in an instant. The Nazis failed to create Material Phasing, an ability that would've made their soldiers immune to bullets. Something went awry at the Munich laboratory, and half of Europe paid the price. It was unclear how much of it had been accidental. Was it a mishap? Or had there been an undocumented attack on the lab that triggered the devastation? The Allies decided it was the Nazis' hubris. That was the story most people wanted to believe. But there were plenty of theories on what had *really* happened since nobody could confirm the truth. All documents and witnesses had been incinerated. Not even a Necromancer could resurrect survivors to interrogate. There were no bodies left. There was no city left.

After the war, newspapers printed aerial photos of what was left of Munich. Kat hadn't believed it was real at first. As if a meteor had struck down, gouging the city out of the earth. There was no rubble or debris or any indication a city had ever been there. Everything was reduced to a crater of blackened ash. But the damage didn't stop in Munich. The fallout infected people for hundreds of miles. The Alps contained the spread to the south, but neighboring countries in other directions were not protected. Many of those in the fallout zone—soldiers, civilians, men, women, children—became sick. Then the powers showed up. In the survivors.

According to the news reports, the infecteds' powers didn't work like the powers created by the military. They weren't as stable or controllable. Those closest to the epicenter became Material Phasers, but not many of them survived. Everyone else who was in the fallout zones, the majority of Germany and parts of neighboring countries, such as France, ended up with an unstable version of Telepathy. It wasn't as fatal as Material Phasing, but it had reportedly killed thousands.

After the war, the world powers signed the Munich Treaty, agreeing to disuse and heavily regulate magic. The US adapted some of the laws into domestic legislation. Exalters weren't allowed to use their abilities. But what if Héloïse did? What if she knew her in-laws were guilty because she'd used Telepathy? But she didn't have proof, which was why she needed a private detective, to find proof—

"Is this a problem?" Héloïse asked.

Kat snapped out of it. "I'm sorry?"

"Will you refuse my case because I am an Exalter?"

"No, no, not at all. Forgive me, I—you're a Telepath?"

Héloïse gave a bitter smile and clenched her hands around her cane. "No, a Material Phaser."

"Oh." Kat slumped in her chair and tossed her theory out of her mind.

"The cane steadies my atoms," Héloïse said. "It gives my hands focus, so I don't get out of place."

Héloïse wasn't transparent. But she barely made a sound on the floors, like she wasn't really there. "Sorry, I assumed with the French accent," Kat said while taking notes. She stopped writing. How had Héloïse gotten those powers? "You—" Kat cleared her throat. "Sorry, you were in . . . Germany?"

"It is not what you think," Héloïse said as she clenched her jaw. "The Third Reich took me. They thought I looked German enough for them." Her voice grew sharp. "I was in a boarding school when Munich happened." Héloïse's eyes glazed over, and her expression hardened. "I gave up on finding my family. I came to America alone." She cleared her throat. "Serena became my family."

Kat's chest tightened in pain. Her eyes stung, but she blinked to keep calm. "I'm sorry," she whispered. Hollow words that Héloïse had probably heard too many times. "I'll do my best to find out what happened."

Héloïse almost looked relieved. "Before we agree, I need to ask about costs." Kat nodded, and Héloïse rocked the cane back and forth. "I never married Serena. Her parents were the next of kin. I don't have much money. Some, but not much."

"It would be twenty dollars a day plus expenses," Kat said. Héloïse tightened her jaw. "Is that doable?"

"It . . . it's better than the other places. But I think I can afford . . . four days? Is that enough time?"

Kat glanced at her calendar. Four full days of investigation would take her to the end of Monday. She could get the background checks ordered now and have them ready tomorrow. Start surveillance on the parents. She could even attend the memorial. "That would be enough time. If I uncover something, we can discuss how to proceed later."

Héloïse sighed with relief, but sadness still loomed in her eyes. "Thank you. Thank you."

Kat nodded, but she couldn't smile. That pain in her chest didn't fade away. Instead, it crept into her throat. Héloïse deserved closure, even if Serena's death was an accident.

And accident or not, Kat's magic would soon let her know for certain.

# CHAPTER 2

# THE ASSISTANT

Kat finished taking down the rest of the details, and Héloïse paid the first half of the bill. They stepped out of Kat's office and into the hallway. Down in the lobby, Emrah was trying to hand off the background checks, but Jerry stood with his arms crossed.

Jerry was a burly, middle-aged gentleman who made Emrah appear short next to him. He wore navy suits every day, and his hair was slicked with so much oil it was reflective. Despite his abrasive personality and abhorrent handwriting, Kat was grateful for him. He was one of her first clients and had soon become a regular.

"I have another client here to attend to," Kat said to Héloïse as they walked down the hall, "but come by on Tuesday and we can discuss our findings."

When Kat led Héloïse into the lobby, the floorboards creaked. Jerry snapped his head in their direction. "Miss Okazaki, there you are." Between his thick city accent and a rusty voice from years of smoking, he always pronounced the vowels in her name harshly.

While Jerry wasn't looking at him, Emrah mouthed, "Help me."

"Hello, Mr. Morris," Kat said. She opened the front door, and Héloïse left.

"Mr. Stojanovic said you were busy," Jerry said. Emrah's eyes rolled to the back of his head as Jerry mispronounced the "j" and "c" in his name. He had given up correcting the man a while ago.

"I was in a meeting, but I have those background checks ready for you." Kat walked over and took the stack of folders from Emrah's hands. She held it out for Jerry.

Jerry took the files and started flipping through the pile. "Any delinquents to keep an eye on?" he asked.

"No, spick and span." Kat smiled. She had never considered herself short, but her head didn't even reach Jerry's shoulders.

"Check should be in the mail by Monday." Jerry clapped the stack against his hand, and it let out a sharp echo. Emrah flinched.

"It's always a pleasure doing business," Kat said.

Jerry nodded. "Right, I'll be needing more checks done sooner than expected," he said. "They opened that new office building and already want to start filling it."

"Wonderful," Kat said. "When can I expect the list of candidates?"

"I'll stop by either tomorrow or Monday. Can you handle that, or will you be stuck in more meetings?"

"That will be more than manageable," Kat said with a smile. "Thank you, Mr. Morris." Jerry gave her a nod, then glared at Emrah before he let himself out and slammed the door shut.

Emrah took a breath. "You see that? He wouldn't take the damn files from me. But the second you have them, he takes them!"

"Keep your voice down. He might hear you," Kat said as she grinned.

"He kept asking if I only had glasses on because I was

your secretary." Emrah threw his hands in the air. "The hell does that mean?"

Kat stifled a laugh. She didn't know the full extent of Emrah's problems, but his vision was bad enough he had partial night blindness. "Guess only secretaries can't see."

"I swear he hates me," Emrah grumbled.

"What are you talking about? It looked like you were best friends."

Emrah squinted at her. "You're hilarious."

"Of course I am."

"And now we'll see him again. And so soon!" Emrah sulked off to the kitchen, and Kat followed.

"Yeah, well, it means more money." Kat leaned against the wall.

Emrah grabbed his coffee and shrugged. "You've twisted my arm." He took a long sip. "Enough of him. There's a new client we're taking?"

"She suspects there's been a murder," Kat said.

Intrigue spread across Emrah's face. He grinned. "Murder? Like last time?"

"Technically, we didn't know it was murder when we started last time."

"But we do know it was murder this time?" he asked. "So why not go to the police?"

Kat swayed her head from side to side. "Client's fiancée passed away, and the police said it was an accident. But the client thinks the in-laws killed her."

Emrah tilted his head. "Killed who?" he asked.

"The fiancée." Kat kept her voice nonchalant. This topic of conversation had never come up with him before.

The gears were turning in his head. "Fiancée's a woman?"

Kat locked eyes with him and refused to blink. "They both are."

"Oh," he said and shrugged. "Good for them. The law changed—take advantage of it." He took another sip.

Kat eased up and hopped on top of the counter next to the sink. While she briefed him on the case, Emrah started the dishes.

Emrah was supposed to be Kat's office assistant. Tasks like dishes or cooking or groceries weren't part of his job description. But he insisted that he owed her. At first, she had tried to stop him. However, he had quickly convinced her once she'd tried his cooking. She hadn't known food could taste divine until he'd made her breakfast for the first time. She had long since forgiven Emrah, but he still insisted on helping her with every little thing. After all, she had given him a second chance.

Kat met Emrah just four months ago. Her business as a private investigator was gaining traction. She had just received her first high-stakes case and needed an assistant. Emrah conned her by impersonating a much more qualified candidate to get the job. Then he tampered with her files, burned her mail, and God knows what else to bury the truth. Despite the deception, he'd been vital in solving that case. But Kat couldn't trust him.

She fired him and nearly had him arrested, but he begged her for a second chance. He had only lied because he needed the money, and the job was too good an offer to pass up. And technically, it was *her* fault. *She* had gotten the interviews mixed up. He had just taken advantage of the opportunity.

Kat only gave him a second chance under the condition he wouldn't lie to her again. No matter the circumstances, no matter the severity, he had to be honest with her. He promised he could do that. Of course, Kat was reluctant to believe a liar. But she set a contingency in place that verified she could trust him. Unlike people, her magic didn't lie.

Keeping him around had paid off, and not just because of his cooking and cleaning skills. Emrah had grown up in Philly and knew the city better than Kat. He also was a young, Caucasian man, which always came in handy. And the skills from his previous employment, whatever it was, had useful crossovers. Such as his tendency to sneak around. Or his ability to look someone in the eyes and lie with a charming smile. Or the few nameless connections that could provide insight into contraband. Qualities that wouldn't make him citizen of the year but did make him a resourceful detective.

Kat and Emrah had an unspoken agreement. As long as he stayed honest with her, she wouldn't ask too many questions. Like why he was desperate for money or where he had learned how to pick locks.

By the time she finished debriefing him, Emrah had started drying the dishes. "What motivation would the parents have for killing her?" he asked.

Kat rested her head against the cupboards and dangled her feet over the counter ledge. "No idea," she said. "But they are acting strange. I'll give Héloïse that."

"Strange can mean a lot of things," Emrah said while he dried a plate. "It doesn't seem like they're mourning. But if I murdered my child, I wouldn't want to get caught. I would at least pretend to be sad."

Kat raised her eyebrows. "Murdering your own children is something you think of often?"

"You know it," Emrah said. "But if you plan on killing anyone, you include the aftermath in the plan. Like remembering to pretend to be sad when people ask about your dead daughter." He put the stack of plates back in the cabinet.

"What other reason would they be acting like this?" Kat asked.

"Don't know," he said. "Strong case of denial. The shock completely altered their brain chemistry. Or they're really, *really* bad at getting away with murder." He tossed the towel over his shoulder. "What do you think?"

Kat shrugged. "I have no idea. They had no obvious motive. And it's not like she died at her parents' house. It was at work. The stairs were wet. It doesn't seem like there's much more to go on. But . . ."

Emrah raised an eyebrow. "But?"

"I don't know," Kat sighed. "What else would explain their behavior?"

Emrah leaned back against the counter. "Perhaps—" He thumped his head against the cupboard. "Ow. Perhaps they couldn't handle the grief of losing their only child, so they kidnapped a baby. Now, people will wonder where this baby came from, so they must hide away from the relatives as they relive the glory days of being parents—as kidnappers." He smiled and looked at Kat.

"I think you cracked this case wide open."

He smiled and grabbed his mug. "What's your theory?" He drank the last remnants of his coffee.

Kat pressed her lips together. "They have gone into so much denial they no longer remember ever having a daughter. They don't remember anyone that's ever been in their lives."

Emrah laughed, then grimaced. "That's . . . Has there been a wellness check on the parents?"

"Héloïse saw the lights on in the house, and she knows they're inside. They just won't answer the door."

"You know, she could use her powers. Slip through the door and then force a conversation," Emrah said.

"Yeah, and then someone reports her for using her abilities."

Emrah rinsed out his mug in the sink. "Oh, I'm sure the FBI would understand."

Kat rolled her eyes. Yeah, because the FBI was so understanding. "They're not known for being nice. And it wouldn't be them. It'd be ERA."

"Same difference. It's all government alphabet soup."

"True." Kat stared at the ceiling. As much as she wanted to help Héloïse, there might not be a case to solve. Was she taking advantage of a desperate widow? "There's a chance this was all an accident and we're not going to find anything."

"Yeah, but we'll find what we can."

"It felt weird taking her money," Kat said. "I'm worried we might let her down."

"Think of it this way," Emrah said. "You're not being paid to find her killer. You're being paid to find out why Mr. and Mrs. Line are ignoring everyone. Or to at least try until Tuesday. And if she wants to keep paying us to keep looking, well, that's her prerogative."

"That's a more approachable perspective," Kat said. She wouldn't be able to use her magic until midnight. At least then she'd know if it was an accident or not. "We'll start on the parents until we have a clear lead."

"Refusing a funeral. It's not . . . money troubles, is it?" Emrah asked. "Maybe it's too expensive to bury her?"

"I doubt it." Kat reached behind her and fiddled with the cabinet doors. "Héloïse had a lovely engagement ring. I don't think a stenographer's salary bought it. Serena might've had a trust."

"If the parents are loaded, could that play a part?" Emrah asked, adjusting his glasses.

"I wouldn't eliminate that possibility." Héloïse didn't have much money. And if Serena came from wealth, it was one more disparity stacked against them. "Maybe they're embarrassed."

Emrah stared at her. "Embarrassed that their daughter died?"

"Maybe people shamed them." Kat swung her legs on the counter, her flats dangling off her toes. "Serena died at work. Maybe people said their daughter shouldn't have had a job. Or shouldn't have been marrying an Exalter. Or an immigrant. Or a woman. Just because Pennsylvania legalized it doesn't mean their friends and neighbors agreed with it."

Emrah rested his elbows behind him on the counter. "You think the parents secretly despised all those things?"

Kat stared at the wood grain on the cabinet doors. "No, not necessarily, but . . . they're dealing with grief. And then, they get backhanded condolences from friends and neighbors. It might explain their strange behavior. They're ashamed of what happened."

"That's . . . plausible," Emrah said as he scrunched his face, "but messed up."

Kat gripped the edge of the cabinet. The whole situation was messed up. Héloïse had lost everything because of the war. Her family. Her home. Her whole way of living. Then she'd had a moment of hope that life might be okay. She had fallen in love. She had fallen in love with a woman brave enough to love her back. A woman with a father-in-law that approved of their marriage. Perhaps her in-laws could've been a surrogate family. Héloïse could have regained a sense of normalcy. A stable and happy life lay ahead. But it was all taken away. And it turned out her in-laws didn't want her around. She was still an outcast, even to them.

"You alright?" Emrah asked.

"Huh?" Kat looked at him and unclenched her jaw.

"You look a little hostile."

"I . . . no." She shook her head and took a breath. "Just a sad case. That's all."

"Never had a grieving spouse?"

"No, I have. This one's just . . ." There was no point getting into it. Kat and Emrah didn't share personal information. They weren't friends. Kat swallowed and stared at the clock. Besides, she didn't have time. "I need to head out," she said and slid off the counter. "Can you stop by the county records and order background checks?"

"We're doing a full investigation?" Emrah asked. He pulled a notepad out of his pocket.

"We were paid." Kat fixed her shoe back on her foot. "Get them for Héloïse Keeler, Serena Line, and the parents. Any family for them."

Emrah wrote down the list. "Got it."

"Actually, stop by city hall first. See if you can find who Serena's colleagues were and order their files too."

"I'll pick them up before I come in tomorrow," he said, then looked up at her and smiled. "Anything else?"

"No, get out of here."

Emrah nodded, and Kat went upstairs to get ready for dinner.

# CHAPTER 3

# THE FAMILY

It was still bright when Kat walked to the Mabel Diner. Cars filled the streets and people leaving work or going to dinner crowded the sidewalks. Thursday evenings weren't usually this busy, but the weather was getting warmer. Despite it being the first day of June, the heat was manageable.

Most of Kat's family would be at dinner, except for two of her cousins that were out of town. Kat's family arranged a dinner every year to celebrate her late grandmother's birthday. She would've turned seventy-one today had she still been alive. She'd passed away when Kat was twelve, when they still lived in San Francisco.

Kat didn't have siblings, but she'd grown up with her cousins in California. They'd all been raised together before they were separated. Kat hadn't been sure she would see them again until her mother received correspondence that her uncles had gotten out and gone to Philadelphia. They had been hired at the paint factories and had saved enough money to bring over their wives and children. Nothing was left for them in San Francisco. So Kat, her mother, and her aunt joined the rest of the family.

They arrived in Philly the day before Kat's twentieth birthday. It was the middle of January and the coldest winter she had ever felt. And it was wonderful. Even after four and a half years of living in Philly, Kat was still grateful for the cold winters and cooler summers.

As she approached the restaurant, the smell of fries wafted in the air. Kat yanked open the heavy door, releasing the boisterous ambience. The diner bustled with chattering people and clattering dishes, the ruckus of the restaurant drowning out the jazz music that played overhead. Black and white checkered tiles contrasted against the bright red booths. In the back, a dozen of Kat's family members sat at a long table. They were the only Asian people in the diner. They had pushed the table next to the adjacent corner booth so the "kids" could sit with them.

Kat walked over, weaving between the crowded tables and hustling waitresses. Her uncle Tsukuru noticed her first and smiled. He stood to greet her, and everyone else turned to her. "Hey, you made it," he said, hugging her.

"Hello, everyone." Kat gave an assembly line of hugs around the table while exchanging pleasantries. She walked over to her cousins' booth. "How are you all?" Four of them sat in the booth, including Maiki. "You!"

"Me," Maiki said with a smirk.

"What are you—how did you—" Maiki climbed over her brother and leapt onto Kat.

Kat wrapped her arms around her cousin and held her tightly. Kat was the oldest grandchild and Maiki the second oldest, only ten months younger. They shared similar features. Straight black hair and brown, monolid eyes. The biggest differences were that Maiki was a couple inches shorter than Kat, and Maiki had bangs.

They'd been inseparable as children. When they were small, they'd shared a chair at the dinner table. They would eat fresh strawberries together until their hands were stained bright red. Then they'd smear the juice on each other's faces, laughing like it was blood. They waded in the water together, wondering if they'd find magic rocks. So many late nights they stayed up talking for hours on end. But it hadn't been like that in a while.

It was supposed to go back to normal when they'd gotten to Philly. But Maiki left before they could catch up. When they'd first arrived, everyone worked tirelessly to support the family. Kat spent months as a janitor in the hospitals. Her shifts took up half the day, and she would spend the other half trying to sleep. Or washing the smell of bleach off her. Then three years ago, Maiki bought a one-way train ticket to Washington, DC. They wrote letters to keep in touch, but sometimes the months slipped away.

Kat held Maiki tightly until they started teetering. Her cousin's bangs had grown longer. They swept against her eyebrows. Her hair was cut to her shoulders, and she wore her gold plum blossom locket. "You didn't tell me you were in town!" Kat said.

"Yeah, that's how surprises work," Maiki said.

Kat held on to Maiki's arms and smiled. "It's been so long! How's DC?"

Maiki shrugged, pulling her arms back. "You know, busy. Always in a rush. Everyone's mad about something or someone these days."

"Oh, yeah," Kat said, smoothing out her shirt. "Yeah, I can't imagine how hectic it is. How's your job?"

Maiki's eyes drifted to the side. "Eh, government work. Always got a meeting or a trial or another meeting." She tucked her hair behind her ears. "Sorry, it's confidential. I can't talk about that."

"Oh, right, yeah," Kat said. Over the last three years, Maiki had worked her way up to a secretary for the Supreme Court. Her branch was created after the Munich Treaty and the resulting changes to US magic legislation. The court cases she worked on pertained to Exalters and other illegal uses of magic. Kat didn't know much else. Their letters had become less frequent recently. The last time they wrote, Maiki had wished Kat a happy birthday, but Kat had never responded. She'd gotten caught up dealing with Emrah's lies, a murder investigation, and fixing a broken pipe that had burst after a freeze.

Maiki shoved her brother into the wall to make room for herself and Kat in the booth. The only cousin who wasn't with them was their youngest cousin, Reita. Reita was Maiki and Tamotsu's sister. She was almost sixteen and had gone back to San Francisco for the summer. Reita's mother was a housecleaner for a music professor, and he had offered to get Reita vocal lessons that would help her get into a renowned music school.

Family dinner was the same as usual. Playfully taunting each other. Switching plates when someone wasn't looking and waiting for them to realize. Telling funny stories. Sharing what new events everyone had going on. Kat's younger cousin Yoyo was still in high school. Tamotsu had a steady and might bring her around for a less formal dinner sometime. Their other cousin Skip was still waiting for decision letters on his medical school applications. Kat preferred when the attention was on her cousins. She didn't know how to explain to her relatives why she was a private detective. But she was supporting herself and able to help her family when times were hard. And she was happy. That was what mattered to them anyway. At least for now, it mattered more than finding a husband.

THE SKY WAS orange by the time the dinner finished. All eleven of them sat together a little longer to reminisce. Kat's cousins fiddled with the napkins, twisting them into snakes and pretending to bite each other's hands. Maiki had stayed unusually quiet for the whole meal. Kat tried to get a conversation going, but she was met with polite one-word answers. Perhaps Maiki was tired from traveling. Or perhaps the years apart had done more damage than they could recover from.

Kat's stomach twisted when her aunt finally mentioned heading out before it got too dark. Her mom and uncles bickered about who would get the bill and raced to the counter to pay first.

The others slid out of the booths and got up from their chairs. Maiki stood up. Kat hopped out of the booth and leaned against her.

"Will you be around for the weekend?" Kat asked.

"Yeah," Maiki said as she fixed her dress.

"Alright, kids." Their other aunt came over and hugged them both tightly. "Maiki, it was wonderful seeing you. I hope you come visit more often."

"I'll try to arrange that," Maiki said with a smile.

The others started coming back around to exchange hugs. Kat kept glancing back at Maiki, but Maiki wasn't looking at her. She was busy saying goodbye to the others.

Kat snagged Maiki's elbow. "Hey, when the others leave, you want to get milkshakes?"

Maiki looked surprised. "Sure."

It took another three minutes of goodbyes before they went to the counter and got chocolate milkshakes.

Kat sat on the stool with her feet tucked up under her. Maiki slouched forward with her elbow on the counter. She propped her head up with one hand, swirling her long spoon around the tall glass to mix the whipped cream inside. "I thought you'd get a strawberry milkshake," Maiki said.

Kat shrugged and ate a spoonful of her chocolate shake. "It's not the same," she said.

Maiki glanced at her softly. "Is it because of your dad?"

"Nope." Kat shook her head. "I just meant that the berries aren't as fresh here."

"Oh, yeah, I guess that makes sense," Maiki said. "Sorry."

"Don't be." Kat took another bite.

"Do you want to talk about it?"

"Not really."

"I don't think you ever talked—"

"I said not really."

"Okay." Maiki nodded and went back to churning her milkshake.

An ache spread in Kat's chest. This wasn't how it was supposed to be. They were supposed to be talking. Just not about that. But they still had plenty to talk about.

"I'm sorry," Kat said.

"For what?" Maiki asked.

"I don't know," Kat mumbled. "Are you okay?"

"Oh, yeah, I'm great," Maiki said. She sat up and looked at Kat. "You?"

Kat set the glass on the counter. "Not really." Maiki tilted her head, and Kat took a breath. "What happened between us?"

"What do you mean?" Maiki asked.

"Come on. You know it's not the same between us," Kat said. "I get that things changed, but you were the one person I could always talk to. Now it's like pulling teeth trying to get a conversation going."

Genuine remorse lingered in Maiki's eyes, and she stared at the table. "I'm sorry," she whispered.

"I don't want an apology. I just want to know what's going on." Kat leaned forward, trying to meet Maiki's eyes. "Am I still someone that gets to know what's going on in your life?"

"I missed you a lot," Maiki said. "I don't know what to do

with myself anymore." She picked up her spoon, dribbling ice cream back into the glass and watching it fall. The chocolate ice cream splattered against the sides. A shadow of a grin formed on her lips. "Do you remember when we were kids and used to make mud pies?"

"Yeah," Kat said with a smile. "We'd take the yuck berries from the containers and mash them into the bucket of mud."

"You found that really good stick, and it was perfect for stirring. And we were so scared we'd lose the stick, or my brother would find it and break it in half."

"Yeah, where did we keep it? Was it under the porch?"

Maiki laughed. "I think so. He found it anyway, and we both screamed and chased him to get it back."

"Then my mom found our bucket and thought it was so adorable we were trying to make compost." Kat laughed. "She had no idea we were playing some weird make-believe."

"I think she'd be concerned if she knew we were cooking dinner for our pretend children because our pretend husbands died in the mines and the mud pies were all we could afford," Maiki said. Kat laughed and ate another spoonful of her milkshake. "We were strange when we were little."

"It was fun. We were having fun."

"Yeah," Maiki said. She stared off at the kitchen and sighed. "I had so much fun doing that. Everything was perfect back then." Her smile faded. "Seems like a lifetime ago." She went back to stirring her melting shake. "Now I'm a secretary." Her spoon stabbed into the glass as she churned the milkshake, which melted further into a liquid.

"Is that a bad thing?" Kat asked.

"No, but that's not the point." A sharpness cut into Maiki's voice.

"Did you want a different career?"

"I wanted my life!" Maiki smacked her spoon into her glass. Kat hunched down and lowered her head. "Doesn't it bother you?" Maiki huffed.

Kat's heart pounded in her chest. "What?" she whispered.

"Any of it!" Maiki snapped. Kat's eyes darted around the diner. No one had been paying attention to them, but Maiki was getting louder. "We were interned, and nobody talks about it. We aren't home, and we pretend like we are!"

Kat grabbed Maiki's wrist. "This is our home," she whispered.

Maiki yanked her hand free. "No, it's not," she said at a lower volume.

"It's our home now."

"You're telling me you're happy here?" Maiki narrowed her eyes at Kat. "You like it here?"

"Yes!"

Maiki scowled and turned away. "And that's exactly my point," she said. "We lost everything. But everybody's forgotten." She drained her milkshake until the straw slurped at the bottom.

Kat held her breath to keep silent. Her heart pounded faster as the feeling of cement filled her mouth. Parted lips and a weighted tongue. She couldn't say anything. This paralysis consumed her every time it resurfaced. So, she swallowed her feelings, and the cement vanished. "What's the point in talking about it?" Kat said. "It won't change anything."

Maiki set her glass down. "My mom used to say if anyone should be angry, it's Katsumi. She has the most to be angry about." Maiki looked at Kat. "Yet you seem to care the least."

Kat's eyes prickled, but she took a deep breath. She wasn't going to let it upset her any more than it already did. "So you're mad at me?"

"No." Maiki held her head in her hands. "You think it's like pulling teeth to talk to me now? You should've seen yourself when you got to this city. I assumed you were putting on a brave face for the family. I figured you'd be honest with me when we were alone. But you didn't talk to me at all."

Kat blinked and stared at her. "What? We talked. What do you mean?"

"No, we didn't," Maiki said. "You were always working or exhausted."

"We were all exhausted," Kat said. "We needed the money. We had no savings."

"But you never stopped working," Maiki said. "Even when we got the money."

"You left before we got to that point." Kat's voice wavered.

"No, I didn't." Maiki stared at her with bloodshot eyes, tears pooling.

"It was supposed to get better, but you left," Kat said.

"It was *never* getting better, so I had to leave." Maiki blinked, and the tears fell down her cheek.

Kat slumped back in the stool. That sinking feeling pulled her down again. "Do you still feel that's the case?" she asked.

"I don't want it to be." Maiki wiped her cheeks with her napkin. Her mascara smudged under her eyes.

Kat nodded. Her face burned as tears threatened to form, but she forced the feeling away. There was no point in crying. "Then let's fix it." Her voice came out steady. "How long are you in town?"

Maiki stared at the counter. "A few days."

Kat took a breath, and her face cooled. "Maybe we can get lunch?"

"When? Tomorrow?" Maiki asked, flicking her eyes in Kat's direction.

"I have work—" Maiki rolled her eyes. "But I'll make time! I'll make it work."

"Forget—"

"No, no." Kat grabbed on to Maiki's arm. "I'll make it work. I promise. We'll have lunch tomorrow."

Maiki looked down at Kat's hand and nodded. "Where'd you want to go?"

"Maybe my house? I have a client that might stop by, so I

need to be there if he does. But I can buy lunch, and we can hang out while I'm waiting. It'll be just us. We can talk." Maiki took her arm back and pulled out her purse as Kat asked, "Does that work?"

"I'd like that," Maiki said. "I get to see your house finally."

Kat stifled a laugh. "It's not much to look at."

"But it's your place. And I want to see it." Maiki took a breath and put on a smile. "Does this mean I can meet your assistant too?"

Kat laughed nervously. "Uh, if he's there?"

"What's his name? Emmet?"

"Emrah."

"Interesting," Maiki said. She took a breath and eased her posture. "So, you're a boss and everything. Does he help you snoop for footprints?"

Kat tilted her head. "Is that what you think I do?"

Maiki shrugged. "I have no idea. Whenever you wrote to me, it was about solving a kidnapping or catching a cheating husband, so I pictured you with your magnifying glass checking for footprints and clues."

Kat laughed to herself. "I don't think I ever found footprints on a case."

"Wow, some detective you are," Maiki said. "You don't even check for footprints?"

"It doesn't come up often. My job is usually paperwork."

"That's not what it sounds like in your letters."

"Yeah, because I'm not going to bother writing about all the tedious office tasks that make up ninety percent of my day. I'm not telling you about . . . the time I filled out so many forms my pen ran out of ink. I only write about the exciting stuff ."

Maiki grabbed Kat's arm and looked concerned. "Well, now hold on," she said. "What happened to your pen? Did you get more ink? You have me on the edge of my seat."

Kat laughed and tapped Maiki's foot under the counter. "I got a new pen."

"Oh, thank goodness. Now I can sleep at night."

Kat finished her milkshake, and they left the diner. The dim light from the red sun faded quickly. The streetlamps provided more light outside. Kat hugged Maiki goodbye, and they went their separate ways.

Maybe the tension between them would get better. They could find something else to talk about. Kat didn't need to dwell on the past any more than she already had. For four years, she had wondered why this happened. For four years, she had fixated on every alternative outcome. If they had fled San Francisco sooner. If her family hadn't been separated. If her father hadn't left. All it did was make her crazy. And she was tired of being crazy.

The desert had taken up too much of her life already. There was no point in letting it take up more. There was no point in going crazy again.

# CHAPTER 4
# THE DETECTIVE

The sun had nearly disappeared by the time Kat made it back to the house. It was cool and dark, but the quiet ended when she walked through the front door and the floorboards crackled. She locked up and closed the blinds. There were still a few hours until she could use her magic. She had to keep herself occupied until midnight so she wouldn't obsess.

She ironed her clothes while she listened to the radio. She had grown a large wardrobe since coming to Philadelphia. Dozens of silk shirts hung in an array of colors, many of them blue or teal. She had a lot of pants too. The dresses and skirts got pushed to the back due to infrequent wear.

Kat had spent most of her life wearing dresses and skirts. Growing up, she'd been told to stop climbing trees or running around or sitting with her feet up in the chairs. Her skirt would ride up, and she'd be exposed indecently. The obvious solution was to change her wardrobe instead of her behavior. Pants were more forgiving when sitting with your knees up. And it wasn't like she had grown out of running around or climbing in obscure places. That was part of her job.

Despite infrequent wear, she kept all her dresses. Partly

because she sometimes needed a dress to fit in. But also, because she couldn't bear to get rid of her clothes again. Even if she didn't wear them often, they were still her clothes.

Every article of clothing she had brought from California was stored safely in the back of her closet. She couldn't wear most of it anymore. She no longer had the body of a sixteen-year-old. The only pieces she could still fit into were a few of her grandmother's dresses she had salvaged.

Kat changed into her pajamas and washed off her makeup. Two more hours until midnight. She sat in bed and read her Radclyffe Hall book to pass the time.

She had to force herself not to obsess over the time. Reading, gardening, or laundry were acceptable time passers. Kat couldn't waste her whole evening waiting for it to be midnight. Even now that it was for her job, it didn't put her in the best headspace.

In the concentration camp, magic had been her only comfort. It had given her some semblance of power. But then it had festered into an addiction, only worsening her anxiety. Not that magic was the sole culprit behind her terrible mental state in the camp. But it was one of the few things she'd had control of in Manzanar.

She couldn't control where they were sent. Her family was shoved on a horse stall train car and taken to the godforsaken desert. There was a reason nobody had built a town where the camps were. Because nobody wanted to live there.

The summers were unbearably hot. The barracks had been constructed hastily out of wood and black tar paper. Four cots were crammed into the room for her, her parents, and her aunt. No running water, yet it was considered a living space. It was hardly livable. The black tar paper absorbed the heat from the sun, creating an oven. White corpses of insects littered the floor. Even creatures that naturally inhabited the desert died inside the barracks.

Kat spent the days outside in the gardens so she wouldn't

suffocate like the insects. But the sun soaked into her black hair and seared her scalp. She often wore her hair up to cool off her neck, but it came at the price of getting burnt. Her skin always prickled with heat and became excessively oily. Her hands were always grimy. Her lips were always chapped. Her eyes burned the entire time. If it wasn't from the brightness of the sun, it was from the wind.

The wind always carried dust, scratching her entire body because her skirts and shorts exposed her legs. Thousands of grains of sand stabbed her calves like tiny needles, resembling the prickly pain of limbs falling asleep. Except sharper. The dust coated her body, inside and out, leaving a sticky, salty film in her mouth and throat. It clogged her ears. It burrowed under her eyelids, causing her eyes to ceaselessly water. No amount of tears or rubbing or rinsing would alleviate the burning torment. It was always fucking windy. So it was always fucking dusty.

The dust embedded in her clothes and shoes and the beds and the barracks. Outside, everyone's hair and eyebrows turned white from it. During meals, her teeth would crunch on gritty sand. The water didn't always run clear. Every now and then, a murky haze would spout from the shower pipes.

The only thing worse than the dust was the lack of privacy. The showers were in a giant room with soggy floors. Pipes lined the wall, with punctured holes for water to spit down. No knobs to turn it on or off. No knobs to change the temperature. And no stalls or curtains either.

Kat refused to strip completely naked in front of strangers. Instead, she showered in her undergarments, which still left too much exposed. She refused to wash for as long as possible, going almost two weeks before she couldn't stand the putrid reek of her own odor. She waited until nearly the end of curfew, when the fewest people showered. She scrubbed herself quickly with the harsh soap provided, shivering under the water. It was the one place she was allowed to cry.

The showers weren't the only violation of privacy. The toilets were just as vile. No doors or stalls. Just a few rows of long planks of wood with half a dozen holes carved out to defecate over pans. The pans weren't rinsed daily, so the smells would stagger. Her barrack's assigned latrine was shared among a few hundred other people, and there was never a time they were completely empty. Kat minimized how often she'd need to use the bathroom, holding her pee for hours and limiting her water intake. Though the summers made dehydration dangerous.

The desert made people go crazy. Perhaps it was the unbearable heat. Or the continuous dust storms. Or perhaps it was the fence.

There was no other town for dozens of miles. Nowhere to run to. Nowhere to escape. Yet they still built the barbed-wire fences around the camp. They still built the machine-gun watchtowers. They still shot anyone who tried to run.

Kat hadn't been at the camp long. Maybe a couple months. She was in the garden with her aunt Hideko, kneeling in the slimming shadow of the barrack as the sun shifted overhead. The heels of her feet pressed against the tar paper as she savored every second of shade. Screams erupted ahead.

"Don't shoot! Please, don't shoot!"

Her aunt grabbed her arm and hauled her back to their barrack. A man had jumped onto the fence, climbing toward the barbed wire. Someone tried grabbing his legs to yank him back. Others fell to their knees in front of the soldiers, pleading with them to spare him. The machine guns tore his body apart until he fell off the fence.

It wasn't an escape attempt. Not in broad daylight. Something inside him had snapped. His wife and five children were still missing. They'd been taken elsewhere, and he needed to find them. Not that jumping the fence would have solved it— but in his mind, he had to try. He was unwell. However, the soldiers called him crazy. They said he was dangerous. He was a threat. They had no choice.

No displays of hysteria were tolerated. And if anyone couldn't control themselves, they hid in the hospital. An inconsolable mother watched her toddler die of tuberculosis and wouldn't stop screaming. A man who didn't speak English tried to run toward the fence. A teenager had a breakdown in the showers and kept striking at the pipes. Their neighbors brought them to the hospitals before the soldiers found them. Before the soldiers intervened.

The hospitals were run by imprisoned doctors. They trained others who could help. And the doctors needed all the help they could get. They had enough children dying from measles, patients suffocating from asthma attacks brought on by the dust, outbreaks of food poisoning from the mess hall. The doctors couldn't watch more people get shot. So they sedated the crazy people—for their protection. So they wouldn't scare the soldiers. So they wouldn't be shot.

Kat wasn't allowed to be crazy. Nothing was allowed to be wrong with her. In fact, she should be grateful.

She had it better than others. Young couples were forced to marry quickly for better chances of going to the same camp. But nothing was guaranteed. Families were split. Children were separated from their parents. Others were taken from their country. Peruvians and Bolivians and Colombians with Japanese ancestry were taken and imprisoned too. Many spoke no English and understood even less of what was happening, what they did wrong.

Kat was supposed to be grateful for how lucky she was. She was still together with some of her family. And she'd gotten to keep at least some of her belongings.

One suitcase. That was all they'd been allowed to pack. What didn't fit had to go. Including all of Kat's late grandmother's belongings. Kat had sobbed when they'd given away her grandmother's clothes. Dresses and shawls and shoes she had wanted to hold on to. Clothing she had hoped one day to grow into and wear herself. She had wanted to keep it all, but it hadn't fit in the suitcase. Kat couldn't even fit all of her own clothes.

Clothes weren't all that was lost. Family heirlooms had been taken too. Kat's great-grandfather had brought a painting of Mount Asama with him to America. The edges had yellowed, but the colors were still vivid, the sky a delicate gradient of pinks and blues. A road weaved through a small village, the mountain in the distance remained a bold blue.

Maiki's father had been devastated when it was sold. That was the first time Kat had seen her uncle Tsukuru cry. Before, he had always joked around and laughed. He would pick up her and her cousins and throw them onto the couches when they were younger. He would play games with them. When someone fell and got hurt, he would joke around until they were so busy giggling that they stopped crying. He would draw with them, coloring on paper and then folding it into animals. He was the fun uncle. He never cried until the painting was gone.

Books were too heavy to bring. None of the furniture could be moved. Their kitchenware was too bulky. Kat's mother lost her favorite cast-iron pan. Her father lost his camera. He had saved everything to buy that camera, and then it was gone in an instant. They lost all their radios. They lost anything that looked like a relic. They lost the house—the house they had all grown up in. The house her great-grandfather had built. And they lost the flower fields. They lost the strawberry fields. Crops they had spent generations tending to. They sold everything at a fraction of the cost.

They piled their belongings outside the house to sell or give away. It grew into a mountain range, and in places, it was taller than Kat. She couldn't breathe at the sight of it. Her mother told her not to look through it because it would only hurt her to see how much they were losing. But Kat needed to know. She snuck outside at night and sifted through the piles. She rummaged through chests full of blankets and pillows, boxes of kitchenware and plates and the silver, dressers with drawers full to the brim with more clothes. Kat pulled out a few of her grandmother's dresses she couldn't lose. She found a way to keep what really mattered.

In her grandmother's nightstand, the drawer was full of miscellaneous hair pieces, a hairbrush, clips, ribbons, and silk fans. And the old compact mirror with a peony etched in its center. The dull bronze had lost its sheen. Scratches were scattered across the surface. Kat used to play with this compact mirror when she was younger. She didn't know why her grandmother had kept it, because it was useless. The insides were a foggy white. The material had an iridescent quality despite its lack of a proper reflection. But her grandmother had said it was special. Peonies told secrets. Peonies were good fortune to those brave enough to pursue it. Kat didn't understand what that meant, but she took it as a sign. She took the compact and kept it in her pocket. She didn't realize it was a relic until a year later, when she was in the camp.

The barrack's lack of insulation made sleep impossible. If it was summer, it was too hot, but if it was winter, it was too cold. Kat's family didn't own any winter clothes, and the temperature drops chilled her whole body. Her fingers and toes and nose were numb throughout the weeks around her birthday. Regardless of the temperature, it was never quiet.

Sound carried through the barracks. Kat could hear everything through the walls. All the voices and thumping and the sand raining on the wood. Often, she fiddled with the compact while she tried to drift off. She would open and close the lid, the rhythmic fiddling grounding her and the sound comforting. On one particularly noisy, restless night, she saw it happen.

The white stones inside the compact illuminated with a pearlescent glow. Kat shoved it under the blanket and held her breath. The bright light disturbed her aunt, but Kat kept the compact under the covers until her aunt quieted down. When she peeked back, the light was gone. It took her a few nights to realize it glowed at midnight.

After several months, Kat figured out what her grandmother meant. Peonies tell secrets. If she asked a question within the minute after midnight, the compact would reveal the truth. It never appeared directly, though. Instead, a flower emerged in the light of the stones. Each flower had a meaning, and Kat kept track of her nightly questions and the flowers that appeared in answer. Eventually, she cracked the code. The compact had predicted the future, unveiled the past, and exposed secrets about her family and strangers. It was never wrong.

Her family didn't know she had kept the compact. They couldn't know it was a relic. Otherwise, they would've protected it better—or gotten rid of it so as not to incriminate themselves. They certainly wouldn't have let Kat have it. But she deserved it. She was the one to rescue it from the junk pile. Her grandmother would've wanted her to have it. Kat's mother was the oldest child, and Kat was the oldest grandchild, so it would've been hers anyway. Why else would her grandmother have told her about peonies? It was hers. It was her right to keep it.

Over the months and years, her fascination with the magic had grown into nausea. She couldn't tell anyone she had it. The last thing she needed was for the guards to confiscate it. Or shoot her or her family. The paranoia ate at her. Whenever she didn't know what a new flower meant, she assumed the worst. She obsessed over it. All she wanted was for the days to pass. For midnight to come so she could ask another question.

Some questions terrified her. Would they ever get out? Would she ever see the rest of her family again? Would her father come back? Would the war ever end? Would America win? The unknown scared her, but some truths she was more terrified of knowing. If this was the end of the world, she didn't want to know.

Over the weeks and months, Kat's paranoia morphed into delirium. Her heart rate wouldn't slow down. Her tears would fall on their own, and her weeping became louder and more frequent. She couldn't be crazy. They'd kill her or put her to sleep. She couldn't leave her mother. Not after her father left. Kat couldn't control what happened in the camps, but she could control how she used her magic. She gave herself three conditions, which she still followed.

First, she couldn't tell anyone she had it. Not her mother, not her cousins, not Emrah. Second, any question she asked had to be about something she could control. No pondering about death or the fate of the world. And third, she could only ask questions for others. She couldn't puzzle over her own fate or curiosities anymore. Instead, she used the compact to solve other people's problems.

Being a private detective had restored Kat's sanity. She could focus on something else, anything else. Not what was lost. Not what happened to her family. Not her feelings. She could do good for others, and they would see she wasn't a threat. She could help people—people no one else was willing to help. People like Héloïse.

A few minutes before midnight, Kat set her book on her nightstand and reached into the drawer. Inside were hair accessories she never wore, expired makeup, and an abundance of jewelry, all disorganized. Diversions. The drawer had a hidden latch at the back that released the false bottom. Underneath, she kept her journal and the compact.

The first thing to know about Héloïse's case was if

anything was worth discovering. If Serena Line had died in a tragic accident, they could focus their investigation on the parents' strange behavior.

Kat opened the compact and ran her fingers against the metal. She traced the etching of the peony and stared at the clock on her wall. The second hand closed in on midnight, and Kat's eyes darted to the stones. The shimmers began.

Like ringlets of water droplets, the white light emerged from the center of the stones and rippled outward. The light twinkled in anticipation. "How did Serena Line die?" Kat asked.

Streaks of light rotated and flickered as the compact contemplated. The white light shifted into a vibrant orange. Detailed lines scattered over the surface as the flower took shape. Marigold.

Kat's stomach twisted. Marigolds weren't good. She didn't get them often, but they were never good. She flipped through the pages of the journal and found the marigold. This flower had shown up when the riots happened. And when Kat had worked a domestic assault case. And when a person had ended up in jail for premeditated battery. Always violence. With intention to harm.

Marigolds meant murder.

# CHAPTER 5

# THE UNCLE

Kat's hair was mostly dried from her morning shower, and any volume left in it had collapsed. Her hair was pin straight, falling just below her collarbone. If she spent more time using curlers and products, it would hold beautifully, but she didn't bother unless she was going somewhere specific. The makeup she'd put on was enough effort for a casual day.

An aroma of butter and garlic greeted her as she entered the kitchen. Kat wasn't much of a cook. She knew enough to feed herself, but if she wanted to enjoy a good meal, she went to a restaurant. Emrah used the kitchen far more than she did, and he made *good* use of it.

Kat used to make okayu for breakfast. When they had just met, Emrah watched her cook it a few times before he asked if he could try something. He prepared the rice differently, adding butter and raw crushed garlic to the pot. In a separate pan, he seared onions, peppers, celery, and more garlic in a bath of butter until it was golden and crispy. And he dropped the eggs into bubbling paprika oil. The whites foamed up fluffy and delicate. He drained the rice and poured Kat's shoyu over it but also covered it in oregano. He smothered the rice with the vegetables and then gently placed the eggs on top.

Kat melted when she took the first bite. It didn't taste like her childhood, but it was delicious. Emrah's effortless ability to cook mesmerized her. No measuring the seasoning. Just dumping varying amounts into his hands and then tossing them into the pans. Even when he made food from scratch, he poured flour onto the counter straight from the bag and added water until it "felt right." No measurements. No hesitation. Yet made perfect each time.

She picked up her bowl and sat on the countertop near Emrah. The dish was still hot, and the golden yolk bobbled when she moved. Emrah passed her the tea he had already made. Hot black tea, soaked for six minutes, then two spoons of cocoa powder, a drizzle of honey, and a splash of cream. Her favorite abomination. She kept green tea on stash for whenever her mother or relatives visited. They would be appalled to see what she normally drank. But Emrah didn't judge her. At least not out loud. He'd watched her make it a few times, then started having it ready for her in the morning.

They finished eating, and Emrah took the bowls to wash. Kat looked over at the stack of background checks piled on the table. "Did you grab the paper?" she asked.

Emrah glanced back while the water filled the sink. "Uh, my arms were full this morning. I forgot."

"That's alright." Kat grabbed the stacks of background checks and set them on the coffee table in the lobby.

She went to the porch and retrieved the paper at the base of her steps. The front page covered the arrest of a couple teenage gang members for Alchemy and weapons dealings. Another headline demanded peace against the Red Scare. Kat's eyes glazed over the word "Communist," and she stopped reading.

The crisp morning air chilled her damp hair as the sun was still warming up the day. Cars bustled along the road, and the sidewalks were crowded. Everyone was busy getting to work. But someone was watching her.

Across the street, a Caucasian man in a beige suit stared her down. There wasn't a bus stop on the corner, and nothing else was in his line of sight. An unsettling feeling grew in Kat's chest. He was undoubtedly watching her.

A bus chugged down the street, blocking her view. She hopped back onto the porch and peered from behind one of the pillars. By the time the bus pulled away, the man was gone.

Kat stared at the newspaper headlines. Communist spies in America. While she had nothing of value for the Soviets, it wouldn't be the first time her own government suspected her of being a traitor. But the war was over.

She took the newspaper inside and tossed it onto the coffee table. The unsettling feeling lingered. Kat glanced out the window at the empty street corner. Her heart beating faster, she flopped on the couch, pushed the thoughts out of her head, and grabbed Serena's files.

Most of the files were small print with legal jargon. But Kat had learned how to spot the important information. Serena Ann Line. Unmarried. Born 1926 in Philadelphia, Pennsylvania. Parents Cynthia and Gerald Line. Deceased May 23rd, 1950. Cause of death: Broken neck due to an accident at work.

The police report stated she slipped down wet stairs and broke her neck. Wet stairs. Either the stairs were conveniently wet already, or the killer had purposely spilled water so she would fall. Or they had spilled the water afterward as a diversion.

The rest of Serena's file pertained to her education. She had graduated high school from Grandview Academy in 1944. She had completed her court reporter's associate's degree two years later. She also had the NCRA Registered Professional Reporter certification. Her only employment history was working at city hall as the stenographer for over a year. No criminal records.

Kat grabbed Héloïse's folder. It was much thinner than Serena's. Héloïse Keeler. Unmarried. Born 1927 in Lille, France. Previously Héloïse Keyser. She immigrated to the US alone in 1946. She changed her surname to Keeler when she became a US citizen. Registered as a civilian Exalter, classified as a Material Phaser. No listed employment history, though she could have done work under the table. No criminal record. She'd never had an incident with her powers, or at least she hadn't been caught.

Considering the police had dropped the investigation, Serena's killer hadn't drawn any suspicion. They knew how to make it look like an accident without someone questioning it. Which likely eliminated Serena's parents as suspects. If they were smart enough to trick the police, they would also be smart enough to keep up the act.

However, perhaps the parents' isolation suggested a different type of guilt. They might not have murdered Serena, but maybe they knew something about her death. Still, why not go to the police if they had a suspicion? Unless the threat wasn't gone yet.

Perhaps the parents had their own enemies, and Serena was collateral damage. Or perhaps the killer needed to get Serena out of the picture, as she was an only child to parents with a large estate. With her dead, who was their next of kin? Kat sifted through the stack of files, looking for the parents. She grabbed Serena's father first, Gerald Line.

Emrah finished the dishes and joined Kat in the sitting area. He had more coffee with him. "Find the list of all the murder suspects that would want Serena dead?" he asked.

"You know, I think county records forgot to include that," Kat said as she flipped through the papers.

"They never make it easy for us." Emrah sat in the chair

across from her. "What do you have so far?" He took another sip of his coffee and picked up one of the folders.

Kat flipped to the front of the file. "Gerald Line. The victim's father," she said. "Like Serena, her father also graduated from Grandview Academy. A year later, he married Cynthia Line in 1926."

Emrah nodded along. "That's—wait, twenty-six?" He tilted his head. "When was Serena born?"

Kat glanced back at the birth certificate. "Six and a half months later."

"Grandview, huh? That's a fancy private school." Emrah smirked as Kat nodded. After reading through enough records, it wasn't difficult to spot a rushed wedding. So many firstborns of upper-class families were born "prematurely" seven or eight months after the parents' wedding. Kat didn't judge them. It wasn't like her own parents had been married when she was born.

"Where's the victim's mother?" Emrah asked, digging through the different folders. Kat passed Cynthia Line's folder to him, and he took it.

Kat skimmed through Gerald's documents until she found a copy of his last will and testament. All his assets were shared with his wife, Cynthia Line. In the event of both of their passing, his daughter Serena Line would be the sole beneficiary of their estate, including his real estate business, multiple properties, and several brokerage accounts. No alternative beneficiaries for asset distribution were listed. Serena's death had created a hole in the will that could've been the killer's motive.

"The victim's mother—are her parents still alive?" Kat asked as she searched through the pile of folders. "Does she have any siblings?"

Emrah looked back and adjusted his glasses. "Uh, both of the mother's parents are deceased. But she has a younger sister." He looked up at Kat. "What are you thinking?"

Kat found another file, which contained only a couple documents. "I'm following a theory," she said.

Emrah grinned and leaned back in his chair. "Murder suspects already? Lay it on me."

"Don't get your hopes up," Kat said. Without proof, this was a conspiracy theory at best. Kat needed tangible evidence, or at least reasonable suspicion, before she could call this case a murder investigation. "There is potentially a shortcoming in the Lines' will that could be a motive for a family member to exploit. With Serena deceased and unmarried, if her parents were to die before drafting a new will, any siblings of her parents would be defaulted as next of kin by the state." Kat passed the last will and testament to Emrah. "Gerald inherited the entire family fortune after his mother passed away."

Emrah narrowed his eyes while reading the documents. "Yeah, so?"

"Gerald has an older brother, Peter Line."

Emrah scrunched his face. "Huh, he does," he muttered. "Here, their parents' will on file was modified in 1924; it states Gerald is the sole beneficiary. They disinherited Peter." He flipped over to the next page, and his eyes widened. "And Peter tried to contest the will. They went to court, but he didn't get a dime. The will must've been airtight."

"Or they had good lawyers," Kat said as she read through Peter's file. He was three years older than Gerald. No criminal records. Not much of a record at all.

"What do we have on Peter Line?" Emrah asked.

"He also graduated from Grandview Academy in 1922. A few months later, his residency changed to Brooklyn, New York," Kat said. "And that's it."

Emrah scanned through the probate court documents again. "Any criminal record? Birth certificates for children out of wedlock?"

"There's nothing on him," Kat said.

"Did he go to college?"

Kat shook the folder in front of Emrah. "Do you see an invisible document? There's nothing else in here."

"Alright, alright." Emrah laughed, setting the files down. "Why would they have disowned Peter?"

Kat shrugged. "Could be for any number of reasons. Just because we don't have records doesn't mean he didn't do something wrong that they buried. Or perhaps personality differences. But it was big enough for them to cut him out of their life."

Emrah gazed off into the distance. "What if the uncle killed Serena?"

Kat raised an eyebrow. "Yeah?"

"Work with me," Emrah said, holding out his hands. "Peter screws up somehow. Doesn't matter. Point is, he's a disgrace. They disown him. So, he leaves town angry. Meanwhile, Gerald stays close to home, marries, and has a child. Takes over the family business. Probably convinces dear old Mother that Serena was conceived on the honeymoon and born very early so he can stay in good graces."

"Or perhaps she knew but didn't hold it against him since she'd already lost contact with her other son," Kat said.

"Yes, but she could've been spiteful and donated everything to charity if she wanted to deprive him. We don't know. Either way, Mother passes. And Gerald gets everything. The life Peter was supposed to have. Peter's furious."

"Furious enough to kill his niece that he's never met?" Kat asked.

"People have done worse for less," Emrah said. "Say Peter figures his parents are dead—he might as well get to know his brother. They catch up, and it turns out Gerald and Cynthia didn't wait until marriage. Uh oh, Gerald's a disgrace too. But if they both messed up, Peter should be entitled to the inheritance after all? In a blind fit of rage, he kills Serena. With her out of the picture, all he has to do is take out Gerald and his wife—then boom, Peter finally gets his parents' fortune that was rightfully his."

Emrah sat back with a proud grin. Kat couldn't help but match his smile. "I'll go call the sheriff," she said. "We got our answers."

"You opened this can of worms," Emrah said. "I'm just following your theory."

"Yeah, but you're shoehorning in a narrative full of assumptions. We don't know what caused Peter to be disowned. And we don't know that *if* Serena was conceived out of wedlock, it would've jeopardized Gerald's inheritance."

Emrah shrugged. "Educated guesses."

"No, assumptions. And those don't hold up in court."

"So you don't think Peter would've had any motive at all?"

"I'm not saying that," Kat said. "I'm not eliminating Peter as a suspect. However, I'm also not getting ahead of myself on a lead that has very little ground. We need more proof before we can come to any conclusions."

"You're no fun when we actually have a job to do." Emrah laughed, then picked up the mother's file and resumed reading. "You know, if it turns out to be true, you'll have to take me more seriously."

Kat shook her head and searched through the rest of Gerald's file. He had no criminal record. Outside of his inheritance, there were no other motive indicators. Background checks served their purpose, but they hardly solved these types of cases by themselves. Surveillance and interviews, legwork, were more beneficial.

Perhaps looking for a motive in the background checks wasn't the best use of time. Instead, they should be searching for suspects with opportunity. Serena had died at work, after all. Kat grabbed the stack of files on Serena's coworkers.

All of them were other stenographers, lawyers, and secretaries. None of them had any criminal records, nor any financial discrepancies. She would have to interview the coworkers to get better insight. And visit the scene of the crime.

"We don't know this was actually a murder, right?" Emrah asked. He had a few folders spread open in his lap.

"No, it's circumstantial," Kat said. "All we know is that Serena's parents are behaving strangely about their daughter's passing, and we are trying to figure out why." Emrah furrowed his brows together as he held two different documents side by side. "Have another theory?"

"Yeah, but it's more grounded this time," he said, holding out a few files. "Charlotte Walker. She's Serena's maternal aunt who's hosting the memorial. Cynthia Line's younger sister."

Kat leaned over and glanced at the file. Charlotte would be another eligible suspect for the next-of-kin murder theory. "Héloïse mentioned the aunt was close to Serena."

"Maybe the family doesn't grieve," Emrah said.

"What do you mean?"

"Look, Charlotte's a widow." He pointed at one of the documents. "She was married to this guy, Edmund Clark. But Clark was drafted and KIA in 1944. Then in 1946, she married another man. Alvin Walker. A year later, she had a son with Walker." Emrah adjusted his glasses and looked at Kat. "She moved on rather quickly after her first husband passed. What if this family doesn't talk about grief? They just move on?"

Kat narrowed her eyes. It wasn't the craziest theory he'd come up with. "Two years is a short grieving period. But she might've had to move on."

"It had to have been less than two years. Walker was a veteran. He didn't come home until after the war."

"Yeah, that's a bit accelerated but not unheard of," Kat said.

"I'm just saying, what if Serena's mom saw how her sister moved on so quickly and felt she had to do the same?"

Under normal circumstances, it would be plausible. "If that's the case, we'd still need more of an explanation for our client's sake. At least rule out other possibilities."

"I figured," Emrah said.

"Don't sound too disappointed." Kat smiled softly. "I assume your levelheaded theories mean the family didn't give you any leads."

"They're pretty bland." Emrah sighed and slouched against the chair. "Well, I still think Uncle Peter has a bone to pick with Gerald. And Charlotte has some skeletons in the closet."

"Because she remarried?"

"Well, no." He winced in disgust. "I should rephrase—her late husband had some skeletons. Charlotte is young. She's thirty-five. She married her first husband, Clark, in 1934 when she was nineteen."

"Cynthia and Gerald were both nineteen when they married—"

"Yeah, they *both* were," Emrah said. "Charlotte was nineteen. Clark was twenty-seven."

Kat grimaced. "That's . . . odd, but unfortunately, not uncommon."

"You'd marry a man that's thirty-two?" Emrah asked. Kat's face soured. "Exactly. What's worse is he might've known her as a kid. Clark went to school with Serena's parents."

"What?" Kat grabbed Clark's file and skimmed through. "He graduated from Grandview Academy the same year as them."

"Private school class sizes can be small," Emrah said. "Don't know how well he knew them, but either way, it's bizarre."

Clark didn't have education records beyond high school, and no employment records until the military. In his early twenties, he'd had a couple arrests for public intoxication during Prohibition but hadn't served time since he'd paid bail. "Tell me Walker's a better husband than this guy was," Kat muttered.

"I'd say so," Emrah said. "He's only a year older than her. He works at the Corn Exchange Bank. He moved in with her since she kept the house after Clark died."

"They had a house?" Kat muttered.

"Yeah."

"Does Charlotte work?"

Emrah flipped through her documents. "No, she never had a job."

"Then where did their money come from?"

"What do you mean?"

"Clark didn't go to college or have a job. He doesn't have any financial records that indicate he's a beneficiary of a trust either. Yet he bought a house and supported his wife—and his drinking problem. He paid the fines to get out of jail multiple times. But with what money?"

Emrah looked back. "I don't think Charlotte got any money from him after he passed. Only from the government, since he was killed in action."

Kat rubbed her face. "But what was he doing? Where was he getting the money?"

Emrah shifted in his chair. "Considering he knew a bootlegger, he probably operated paperless. Paid under the table for whatever jobs he was doing."

"Yeah, I guess," Kat said. Clark was the only one with a criminal record. But Prohibition arrests and tax evasion didn't mean he was a killer. And even if it did, Clark had died six years ago in Cherbourg, France. "You think Charlotte knew what he was up to?"

Emrah tilted his head to the side. "He could've kept a lot hidden from her. Could've lied the whole time." His eyes glistened with intrigue. "Or maybe she knew."

Kat rolled her eyes in Emrah's direction. "Now what?"

"Perhaps Charlotte knew what her late husband was up to. She didn't care as it paid the bills and kept a roof over her head. Maybe they had a nice lifestyle too. But then Clark is taken away, and she loses her way of living. And the government compensation is a slap to the face. She figures her only chance is to marry the first schmuck she can get her hands on. However, it's not enough. Walker's honest employment doesn't fund luxury the way crime does. But, dear old sister married wisely. Hit the jackpot with her real estate husband. So, what does Charlotte do? Takes care of her niece so she can go after her sister and brother-in-law for the money she so badly misses."

Kat leaned on her head and stared at him. "What happened to your theories being more grounded?"

"I got bored," Emrah said, leaning back. "Or, you know, maybe Charlotte was kept in the dark by Clark and would be disgusted to know the truth."

"He's been dead for a while," Kat said. "Charlotte would've found out by now. Something would've been uncovered when she went through his affairs. Unless he buried it really well."

"Maybe he did, maybe he didn't. But if she found out, maybe getting remarried wasn't as hard," Emrah said. "Her grief became anger when she found out who her late husband really was. So, she pretends it never happened at all. Same way Cynthia and Gerald are pretending now."

"I wouldn't call this the same situation," Kat said.

"Close enough," Emrah said.

"Horseshoes and hand grenades."

"I would call this a hand grenade of a marriage."

Kat rubbed her temples as she tried to keep the family members straight in her head. "Where did Walker serve?"

"Uh, somewhere in France." Emrah glanced around the table, but Kat picked up Walker's military documents. He was an infantryman. Received a Purple Heart after the invasion of

Normandy. "Lots of French involvement in this case," Emrah muttered.

"Huh, they were both in the 314th Infantry Regiment," Kat said.

"What? Who?"

"Walker and Clark." Kat grabbed Clark's service records and compared them to Walker's. "No, they were in the same platoon," she gasped.

Emrah looked at her. "What does that mean?"

Kat laughed. "Em, they were in the same platoon when they served."

He stared at her blankly. "I've never been to war. What does that mean?"

"They probably knew each other," Kat said. "Especially considering Walker ended up marrying Charlotte?"

"Oh," Emrah muttered. His eyes widened, magnified through his glasses. "Oh!"

The similarities couldn't be a coincidence. "Wow, perhaps Charlotte—"

"Walker killed Clark!" Emrah cried out.

Kat rolled her head in his direction. "What?"

Emrah had a wild grin on his face. "He and his war buddy know each other. They're talking, griping about missing home. Clark's got a wife waiting for him. Walker doesn't have anybody. Maybe he sees a photo of Charlotte and he's thinking, 'What's a gal like her doing with a guy like him?' He wishes that was his wife. Then he realizes that *could* be his wife. He's got to take care of this dude. And what better cover-up for murder than the war?"

Emrah stared at Kat with an amused smirk, and she laughed. "Amazing. But unfortunately, we're not here to investigate Clark's cause of death."

Emrah slouched back in his chair. "Serena has such interesting relatives. Such compelling lives." He stared up at the ceiling. "What if Walker was a Telepath?"

"Wrong part of France," Kat said. "They stayed north, so he wouldn't have gotten infected. He isn't registered as an Exalter. And I highly doubt the banks would let a Telepath work there."

"Yeah, probably not." Emrah stared up at the ceiling, deflated.

It was nearly seven o'clock. They could waste the whole morning reading background checks, but the day was starting. "I'm sticking you on surveillance at the parents' house."

"Me?" Emrah sat up in his chair.

"Yeah," Kat said. "I want to interview the coworkers and see where Serena died. Go to the source. Then I'm coming back. Jerry might stop by, and I need to be here."

Emrah laughed. "Petak je. I'll happily do surveillance if it means I'm off Jerry duty."

Kat smiled to herself. "You're lucky that my cousin's having lunch with me today. Otherwise, I'd have you stick around."

"Well, tell your cousin thanks."

"Will do." Kat stood up and collected the files. "Do light surveillance for now. Don't get caught."

"It's not in my nature."

"Yeah, but just be careful," Kat said. "Get lunch and we can meet up for dinner."

Emrah nodded and grabbed his mug. "Usual place?"

"Yep."

"I can do that." He finished his coffee and stood up. "I'll catch you later then."

Kat watched him head out. Nobody else was following him, and nobody was watching her. At least, not for now.

# CHAPTER 6
## THE WITNESS

City hall was a massive fortress. It was one of the largest and most breathtaking buildings Kat had seen. Intricate white marble towered over the skyline and sparkled in the morning sun. It was still early, but Pennsylvania Boulevard was bustling with crowds. It was already busy at city hall.

Throngs of people flowed in and out of the courtyard. The stairwells were jammed, with Kat slowly inching along the steps through the cluster of people. While she couldn't admire the mosaic of tiles hidden by the crowd, she could see the twinkling designs on the ceiling above.

Serena'd had several coworkers, and Kat didn't have time to question them all. Serena's boss would be the best place to start. Luther Erikson. Nothing was suspicious in his file. Clean records, stable finances, and a spick-and-span work history. Kat navigated her way to his office's wing, slowly trudging through the crowd.

A Black woman sat at a desk outside the office suite. Her dark hair rested above her shoulders in deep, rolled curls. She was a young lady in a green dress with large glasses similar to

Emrah's. The woman stood when she saw Kat approaching. "Good morning, how can I help you?"

"Hi," Kat said with a warm smile. "May I speak to Mr. Erikson?"

"And what would this be regarding?"

"I understand he was Serena Line's boss?"

"Oh." The woman faltered, and her eyes widened. "Um, yes, he was. Who are you?"

"My name's Miss Okazaki. I'm a private investigator. I appreciate any cooperation you can offer," Kat said. The woman trembled and stared down at her desk, fiddling with her glasses. "If this is a bad time, could I schedule a meeting?"

The woman gave Kat a pressed smile. "Um, one moment," she said. She scurried over to the office door with the name Luther Erikson etched into the glass and rattled her knuckles on it before entering. Faint voices murmured from inside the room.

The rest of the wing was quiet. People sat in the cubicles further down. A few popped their heads up and glanced at Kat. She didn't make eye contact with anyone, just stared at the desk cluttered with papers. Buried under a stack of folders, a name plaque poked out. Kat lifted the papers. Dorthea Morgan. One of the secretaries in the background checks. Young woman still in school for her court reporter's associate's degree. No criminal background.

Dorthea stepped back out of the room, and a middle-aged gentleman came through the door. He was Caucasian, with thinning hair and a bushy mustache. He wore a button-up shirt with the tie slacked and the sleeves scrunched up.

"Miss?" he said, his voice nasally but somber. "If you make it brief, I have time for you."

Kat followed him over to the office. It was cramped with all the filing cabinets and bookshelves lining the walls. One chair sat across from his desk. He had the window open, a smoking cigarette tray resting on the ledge. Wisps of smoke trailed off the burning edge and out the window. Kat sat down across from him.

"This is about Serena?" Mr. Erikson had a thick city accent. "Poor kid. Can't believe this happened."

"I'm sorry for your loss," Kat said.

He sat back in his chair and sighed. "Yeah, me too. So, what's this all about? Police already came by."

"I'm not with the police. I'm a private investigator looking into Serena Line's death."

Mr. Erikson scrunched his face. "Wasn't it an accident?"

Kat nodded. "Yes, but my client wishes to be thorough." Kat pulled out her pen and a small notebook. "Do you mind telling me about the day of the accident?" She flipped to a blank page.

The man's brows became heavy as he stared at the wall. "Serena was one of our court reporters. She had a morning hearing that day, but no one saw her come back afterward. She must've fallen when the court got out." He shook his head and sighed. "She liked taking the side stairs. Less foot traffic. Dora found her later. Poor thing almost had a heart attack herself."

Kat jotted down his words on her notepad. "Do you know how long it was before she was found?"

He shook his head and shrugged. "Hard to say. I don't know when the court got out. Dora found her just before lunch, say around quarter after eleven. Called for help, but it was too late."

No one saw her fall. No one knew the exact time it happened. A large window of opportunity. "I hate to ask this, but did Miss Line have any problems with her coworkers?"

Mr. Erikson twisted his face in surprise. "Heavens no," he said. "Everyone liked her. She was great at her job and got along with everyone. She's going to be hard to replace." He stared at Kat with wide eyes. "Are you saying this wasn't an accident?"

"Not necessarily."

He stared off at the wall, grabbed his cigarette, and took a puff. Kat leaned back as the smoke trailed around his desk. "I can't imagine anyone would do something malicious like that. Everyone's been down since it happened."

Kat glanced over her notes. "You said Dora found her?"

"Yeah, my secretary out there. Poor thing's been trembling ever since."

"Is there anything else you can think of that might be important to know?" Kat asked.

Mr. Erikson sighed. "Nothing comes to mind. I thought this was all just an accident."

"I'm being thorough," Kat said. He seemed like he was telling the truth. "Would I be able to talk to Dora? Or perhaps see the stairwell where Serena fell?"

He grimaced. "Don't know if you can get much out of Dora, but you can try. She can show you the stairwell, but don't think she'll go in there with you. She's been avoiding it ever since."

Kat nodded. "Thank you for your time."

Mr. Erikson led her out of the office. "Hey, Dora." She popped her head up from her desk. "Would you be able to show Miss, uh—" He glanced at Kat, then back at Dora. "Show her where it happened."

Dora's eyes widened, and her expression fell. "I—Yes, Mr. Erikson." She stood up and smoothed out her dress.

Kat walked over to her. She didn't want to traumatize the poor woman, but she needed answers. "I'm terribly sorry about what happened," Kat said softly.

"Oh, it's . . . it's not been easy," Dora said, trembling. "But we're managing. Right this way."

Dora's heels clicked on the tiles, and Kat followed. "Did you know Serena well?"

"She helped me a lot," Dora murmured, adjusting her

glasses. "If any of the secretaries fell behind, Serena always gave us a hand. Mr. Erikson never knew about that."

"She sounds like a great colleague."

"She was, yeah," Dora muttered. "She was my friend. We'd get lunch together sometimes."

Dora navigated them through the building. People crowded the hallways, shoulders bumping, causing a commotion as they bickered around. Stacks of papers teetered in arms, and a couple briefcases clipped Kat's legs.

Dora pulled into a side hallway that was less congested and much quieter. The hallways were less spectacular than the main floor, with generic tiles and a plain ceiling. Dora gestured to a side door further down. "This is where it happened."

Kat pushed the door open and peered down. The stairwell was empty and musty. A lot dingier than the rest of the building. "I know this must be hard for you," Kat said, "but can you describe how you found Serena?"

Dora fiddled with her glasses and took a breath. She took a half-step forward and peered over Kat's shoulder. "Around the corner on the next landing. She was on the ground. The stairs were slick. Must've been how she . . ."

Kat went into the stairwell. The air was stuffy, with a dull, bitter smell. There weren't any windows, and it was several degrees warmer inside. "And no one else was in here?" Kat asked. Her voice echoed in the stairwell.

Dora shook her head. "No, nobody. I don't know how long it would've been before she was found if I hadn't come this way."

"Gotcha." Kat's voice echoed again, but she wasn't speaking loudly. If Serena screamed when she fell, the sound would've carried. Someone must've heard it if she'd had the chance to scream. Kat held the railing as she went down the stairs. Dirt had accumulated, and a gritty texture rubbed beneath her shoes. Salt crud was smeared on the stairs. "You said the stairs were wet?"

Dora peered her head through the doorway. Her complexion had paled further, and she looked on the verge of fainting. "Yeah, the tiles get slick after they mop."

"There's winter salt on the stairs," Kat said. "I don't think it's been mopped in months."

"It . . ." Dora furrowed her eyebrows. "Maybe it rained that day. I don't know. I remember the floor was wet. I almost slipped myself."

Nothing else was peculiar about the stairwell. Kat's shoes gritted on the floor as she went back up. "Did you notice anyone acting strange the day Serena fell?" she asked. Her voice reverberated against the walls.

"What do you mean?" Dora looked at her with wide eyes.

Kat softened her expression. "Anyone absent that day or acting paranoid?"

"Not that I can think of." Dora stared at Kat, concerned. "Why do you ask?"

"My job is to be thorough, that's all," Kat said, and then she smiled. "Thank you for your help. I think you answered all my questions."

Dora nodded and shuffled back. Her heels clicked on the marble floor while they walked down the empty corridor. "I can't imagine anyone that would want to hurt Serena," she said, staring down at the floor. "She was everyone's friend. Who would want to hurt her?"

"I wouldn't dwell on it too much," Kat said. "It's looking like an unfortunate accident. I'll be out of your hair in a jiff." They turned back into the crowded main hall. A big, burly gentleman bumped into Kat, and she stumbled forward. He let out a grumbled apology as he passed through the crowd. Dora disappeared from Kat's sight.

Whoever killed Serena had known her schedule. They'd known she used an empty stairwell. They'd had the opportunity and an escape route, seeing how easy it was to disappear into the crowded hallways. The labyrinth of stairwells and different corridors filled with a sea of people made it impossible to keep track of anyone. Any of Serena's coworkers would've been able to get away with it. But had any of them had a reason to kill her?

Kat managed to squeeze her way out of the flow of foot traffic to head downstairs. If she went back to her office now, she'd get there with plenty of time before Maiki or Jerry would show up. She'd even have enough time to pick up lunch for herself and Maiki.

Kat walked down the brick sidewalks along the storefront. The streets were still full of others walking about. Cars were honking, and a few sirens wailed in the distance. The ambience of the city whistled along while she looked over her notes.

Perhaps one of the coworkers had killed Serena. They'd planned it out and followed through, pushing her down the stairs . . . If Serena had been pushed down the stairs, wouldn't she have screamed? Even Kat's speaking voice had echoed in the stairwell. A scream would've carried through the whole building. Someone would've noticed. Someone would've checked it out and found her much sooner. And if they'd intended to kill her, a push wouldn't necessarily do the job. Serena could've survived the fall, and then the killer would've had to finish it. There would've been a fight. A commotion. And that would've been heard.

Serena's official cause of death was a broken neck. Could the killer have snapped her neck and then dropped her body down the stairs? She wouldn't have had time to scream. There were no signs of strangulation. Otherwise, her case would've been investigated further. The killer must've broken her neck quickly. They knew how to kill. None of the coworkers had given Kat that impression. Barely any of them had served in the military, and none had criminal offenses. If it wasn't a coworker, then who?

Kat made it about halfway home. Different bakeries and

delis lined the sidewalk, polished glass windows showcasing their food. The displays of sandwiches made her hungry. Perhaps she could grab lunch to share with Maiki.

Sunlight sparkled in the window before Kat, the glass defining her reflection like a mirror. She could see everyone behind her. People ambled down the sidewalk. Mothers with strollers and groceries, children racing along and rushing into candy shops. An elderly gentleman rested on a bench to smoke. Across the street, a man in a suit lingered by a newspaper stand.

The unsettled feeling prickled in Kat's chest. The man wasn't watching her, and he wasn't the man from that morning. But something familiar stirred about him. His hair was cut short like the other man, but it was darker, and his suit was grey instead of beige. Despite the difference, there was something familiar about him. Both men looked bland. Nondescript. Adhering to a certain regulation of appearance.

Kat scooted down the sidewalk, glancing at the window reflections. The man didn't follow her. He didn't even look at her. His newspaper was the only thing he paid attention to.

She popped into the deli and got into the small line. The commotion inside the restaurant overwhelmed the distant sirens outside. After several minutes, Kat ordered a couple sandwiches to go. She left the shop, carrying a brown paper bag. The man turned over his paper in the same spot. Kat walked back home and tried to shake the feeling. Her heart raced in her chest, but she forced herself to take slow breaths. Nothing was happening. There wasn't a war. Nobody was being taken anywhere.

Kat hurried along the sidewalk, realizing the sirens were growing louder. She glanced around and saw an ambulance rushing past her on the street. It slowed as it darted around the corner she was heading toward.

Kat turned down a block but stopped at the commotion ahead. A horde of people were gathered on the sidewalks and streets. The road was closed off, blue and red lights flashing. Police officers moved the crowds off the street to let the ambulance through. The siren kept wailing.

Kat approached, standing on her tiptoes and peeking between the heads of others. A few police officers were ushering the crowd to get back.

"What's going on?" asked a woman beside her.

"They're closing the road down," a different man said.

"An Exalter went crazy."

Kat held her bag near her chest as she ducked between a few people. A wooden barricade blocked off the sidewalk. Up ahead, broken glass and crumbled bricks littered the cobblestone. The front entrance to one of the stores had been ripped apart. The windows were shattered and one wall reduced to a pile of bricks. From underneath the pile, legs stuck out.

"Everyone get back!" one of the police officers barked. "Go about your day. Mind your business. Nothing to see here."

Kat took a step back. Outside the store, a few distressed people gave statements to the other officers. One woman was crying. Another man kept aggressively pointing and shouting. Medics rushed out of the ambulance and attended to an older woman sitting on a bench, her head bleeding.

"Go home." The officer moved down the line and ushered more people away. "Move along."

"What happened?" asked someone from the crowd.

"There's been an accident. Just move along."

Another ambulance rolled onto the scene. None of the paramedics or officers were going near the buried body. They must already know the person was dead.

Another police officer marched over and started yelling at the crowd. Kat disappeared before he made it near her.

Ever since the war ended, there'd been occasional Exalter outbursts. Material Phasers had caused damage to a few buildings, sometimes hurting people nearby. Telepaths had allegedly been responsible for causing outbreaks of hysteria or spontaneous strokes to those in range. Kat hadn't seen such events happen, but the newspaper provided vivid details.

Kat walked a few extra blocks before she continued on her way home. She passed another stretch of stores with windows displaying different pairs of summer heels. The glass caught the reflection of the people on the sidewalk, and the man from the newspaper stand popped into view again.

He was still across the street, strolling with a newspaper tucked under his arm. He stared ahead, not looking in Kat's direction at all. Her stomach twisted, and she gripped her bag. Maybe it was a coincidence. Maybe he'd also been rerouted by the Exalter accident.

Kat kept walking, watching him through the windows' reflections. What would happen if she stared at him? What would he do? Disappear like the last guy? Or would he chase her? Neither option comforted her.

Kat veered left and walked faster around the block. If he was just going about his day, she'd look crazy confronting him. But if he was following her, he'd have to try harder than that.

She picked up her pace, nearly jogging while she clutched the sandwich bag in her arms. She weaved around the people on the sidewalk until she made it to the end of the block, where she turned left again.

A group of women popped out from around the corner, and Kat bumped into them. "Sorry, I'm sorry," she sputtered, cutting through their formation. They awkwardly laughed as she stumbled along. She raced down the rest of the sidewalk, drawing looks from the passersby. Her eyes were getting hot, but she refused to cry. There was nothing wrong. Nobody was after her.

She turned left again and slipped into a women's boutique. She scurried behind a few clothing racks to conceal herself while she caught her breath. Nobody in their right mind would go around the same block in a circle. Unless they were, coincidentally, *very* lost on the same block—or they were following her. She held on to the bag and sifted through the clothes in front of her while she eyed the front window. The man didn't show up.

"Can I help you, miss?" One of the saleswomen approached Kat with a cheery smile that calmed her.

"Oh, I'm just browsing," Kat panted. Her cheeks were flushed, and her forehead probably glistened with sweat. Kat quickly shuffled through the hangers of clothes.

"Let me know if you need anything." The woman moved along.

Kat picked through the hangers, pretending to look interested in some dresses. Her breathing slowed, but her heart continued to pound in her chest. She was being ridiculous. If that had been a federal agent, they would've confronted her. They didn't play mind games. They used any force they deemed necessary. Whatever it took to neutralize a threat, even when there was no threat. If they wanted to get her, they would've taken her already. They wouldn't be wasting their time following her.

Kat glanced out the window. The man appeared. Her heart stopped, and her knees sank to the floor. She melted behind the clothing racks and peered through the gaps between the fabric. He stood outside the store, winded and looking around. She held her breath as if he'd hear her if she made a sound.

He faced the store window. Kat shoved the blouses in front of her. There was only one entrance. Maybe she could crawl through the clothing racks and get past him. If needed, she could chuck the sandwiches to slow him down. She squatted on her toes, listening for the door to open, ready to launch. But it was silent. Kat peered through the clothes. He was gone. She slowly stood up. There was no sight of him.

It wasn't a trick, right? To go out of view and lure her outside? But what kind of trap would they be planning?

Kidnap her in public in broad daylight? No, they wouldn't call it kidnapping. It'd be relocating. But what if it wasn't the government? That thought almost comforted her.

Kat waited another moment, then quickly left the store. There was no sign of the man in the grey suit. She bolted across the street and sprinted home.

# THE COUSIN

Kat alternated between running and power walking the rest of the way home. The paper bag had crumpled and tattered, but the food was still intact. She kept glancing behind her, but she couldn't see the man. Then again, they already knew where she lived. But she still didn't want them chasing her.

The sun got hotter, soaking into her hair, and the heat seared her scalp. By the time she made it back, her face was hot, and she was sweating.

Maiki stood outside the house. She wore a periwinkle dress with a matching headband that tucked her hair out of her face. Her gold pendant glimmered in the sunlight. The bright pastels of her outfit contrasted against the dark, dull wood of the house. "I was wondering if I was in the wrong place," Maiki said.

Kat raced up the steps and unlocked the door. "No, no, this is it," she said, out of breath. Her hands shook as she fumbled with her keys.

"Are you alright?" Maiki asked.

"Oh, yeah, yeah, I'm fine." Kat unlocked the door and rushed inside. The floorboards squeaked when they entered, and she set the bag on the coffee table. She glanced out the window but didn't see anybody charging down the sidewalk. Her heart pounded in her ears as she slowly caught her breath.

Kat glanced back at Maiki, who looked at her with anticipation. "What?" Kat asked.

"Are you sure you're alright?" Maiki gave her an uneasy look.

"Oh, yeah," Kat said, forcing a smile. Maiki didn't look convinced. "Just didn't want to be late for my client. But he's not here yet." She took another deep breath to steady her voice.

Maiki nodded, then glanced around the house. Whenever someone came to visit, the necessary repairs became more obvious. Kat had grown used to how the place looked. The water-stained ceiling reminded her of the Sistine Chapel, and the squeaky floorboards were her security system. But her contentment morphed into humility when her family came by. She still had so many repairs to make. New coats of paint and varnish. Perhaps replacing the front door with something sturdy that had better locks. "It's not much to look at, but you have to start somewhere, right?" Kat said, coming closer to Maiki.

Maiki looked back with a grin. "It's so big. And your ceilings are so tall."

Kat relaxed seeing her smile. "Yeah, it's nice having space for my things. I'm trying to make it look like a business. I ordered a front desk and that should be here by next week."

"Why don't you show me around?" Maiki said.

"It's not the most exciting tour you'll be on," Kat said, but she held out her arms and led Maiki past the kitchen and down the hallway. "This is my office." Kat pushed the door open, and it bounced off the doorstop.

Her desk was organized. Her plants lined the windows, basking in the sun. She smiled at the floor-to-ceiling shelves she had worked hard to fill with books. A few filing cabinets were sandwiched between the shelves and the small closet, where she kept extra office supplies. The wood of the door matched the wood of the bookshelves. Her office was much cozier than the foyer.

Maiki stepped inside. "You have a whole office?" She grinned as she admired the room. "I think this room is bigger than the bedrooms in our first apartment."

"Oh, it definitely is bigger," Kat said. "That first apartment was a hole in the wall."

"And you have so many books," Maiki said, scanning the shelves.

"It's a growing collection." The shelves were hard to organize since Kat had books on a plethora of different topics. Law books, medical books, psychology books, finance books, wildlife books. She had books on proper etiquette for dining and drinking, different dialects and linguistic practices, and the customs of different religions. There were beginner's guides for all sorts of hobbies, including baseball, golf, tennis, boating, camping, fishing, fashion, billiards, and bridge. There were pamphlets about salesmen with scripts for religious solicitation or door-to-door services. Kat had acquired her personal library bit by bit over the years and used the knowledge for her cases. Sometimes it helped her to better understand a client's situation, and other times it helped her pretend to be someone else.

Maiki finished looking, and Kat took her back out to the hallway. "That's Emrah's office, but he's out."

"Emrah's got his own office too?" Maiki asked, glancing through the doorway.

Emrah's room had more filing cabinets for archives. Stacks of papers and open files were scattered all over his desk and on top of different filing cabinets. But it was his own system. While his office was smaller than Kat's, it had a bigger closet, which he used to store his clothes. Sometimes surveillance required outfit changes to blend in better. Attending a cocktail party called for different attire than occupying a park bench. Keeping his clothes at the office made it easier for him.

Next to Emrah's office was the darkroom, which had eaten through most of what was left of Kat's bank account after purchasing the building. The enlarger, the developing tank, and a stock supply of chemicals had depleted a decent chunk of her funds. All what was needed to make it a functional darkroom. She'd had the windows covered up and installed the proper lights. She'd built chemical bath stations and put up a heavy curtain over the door.

"That's pretty much it," she said as they left the darkroom.

"What about upstairs?" Maiki asked.

"Huh?"

"There's stairs." Maiki pointed to the end of the hall, where the staircase led to Kat's residence.

"It's . . . under construction," Kat said. The upstairs didn't matter, since she never had visitors there. It was in shambles since she'd prioritized fixing the downstairs. Patches of mold covered the bathroom. Paint peeled off the walls in fistfuls.

"Where do you live then?"

"Um, upstairs." Maiki grabbed Kat's wrist and headed up the stairs. "Oh no," Kat muttered. "Watch your step. Some of the floorboards are loose."

Maiki glanced around at the top of the stairs. "It's not that bad."

"Are we looking at the same thing?"

"You made it sound much worse." Maiki peered out the window with a smile. "You actually have a garden!"

"I tried. Flowers don't grow as nicely here."

Maiki leaned in and bonked her forehead on the glass. "It's more than we've had since we got here." She tilted her head. "This is your room?" The floor creaked as she hopped over to the door.

Kat's room wasn't messy, but it wasn't organized either.

She'd left the ironing board out. Her pajamas were crumpled in a pile on her floor, and her bed wasn't made. Kat flung her blanket over the bed and kicked her pajamas to the side. "I didn't think you'd be up here."

"You have so many things," Maiki said. She gazed at the nightstand cluttered with jewelry, knickknacks, and different jars while she fiddled with her gold necklace. "Do you have Grandma's jewelry here?"

"I don't have any."

Maiki's head shot back at Kat. "What? You—you didn't get anything?"

Kat stared at Maiki's necklace. It was eighteen karat gold. The delicate chain held a circular pendant with an engraving of a twisting tree branch with a plum blossom. The flower petals were set with mother-of-pearl, and the branches were made of dark bone. It had come in a set with gold stud earrings.

Their parents had sold the jewelry with the least amount of sentimental value and divided what they kept amongst themselves. Kat had been disappointed when Maiki got Grandmother's necklace and earring set. But Kat's mother had gotten Grandmother's engagement ring and wedding band and told Kat to let Maiki have the set. "It's okay," Kat said.

"I can't believe they didn't give you anything, but Reita whined her way into taking my earrings," Maiki said.

"You could buy replicas—"

"But I want *my* earrings. They were part of *my* set."

"Yeah, buy the replicas and swap them out when your sister's back in town."

Maiki narrowed her eyes. "Sneaky, but tempting. I can't believe you didn't get anything."

"I'm okay. I have some of her clothes."

"What?" Maiki asked. Her face softened. "You have her clothes?" Kat pointed to her closet, and Maiki peered inside.

"You have so many clothes!" Maiki laughed when she stepped in. "My God, it's huge in here!" She shuffled through the clothes. "How many shirts do you need, woman?"

Kat hopped behind Maiki with a smile. "I like . . . options."

"You have a dozen of the same exact blue shirt."

"What? No," Kat said. "They're all different!"

"What are you talking about? It's all blue!"

"No!" Kat reached over Maiki and grabbed the sleeves. "This one is more of a sky blue, and this is a jewel-tone blue."

"What about these?" Maiki pulled up two shirts that were arguably the same color.

Kat scrunched her nose and muttered, "One has a shirt pocket. The other doesn't."

Maiki laughed and put the hangers back. She moved to the back of the closet. "Is this . . ." She pulled out one of their grandmother's dresses. "Oh my God, it is." The dress was tan with ivory patterns across the fabric. It had short sleeves, wooden buttons on the front, and pockets in the skirt. "You do have her clothes!"

"I saved a few things," Kat said.

"I thought we got rid of everything." Maiki stared at it in awe. "I didn't know we kept her clothes."

"I rummaged for it one night. That's the only reason I have it."

Maiki ran her fingers across the wooden buttons. "Glad you saved something."

Kat couldn't fit into that dress well. She could put it on, but her arms were restricted, and it was snug at the waist. Even if she could comfortably wear it, she wouldn't. It wouldn't be practical to wear a dress to work, and it was far too precious to wear on the job. She couldn't risk it getting dirty or damaged. "Why don't you keep it?" she said.

Maiki stared at her. "What?"

"You should keep her dress. It'd fit you better."

Maiki's eyes widened. "Are you sure?"

"I have other clothes of hers I wear," Kat said. She also had the compact, and that was more than enough.

Maiki stared at the dress and then smiled. "Thank you." She folded it carefully and tucked it under her arms, then went back into Kat's room and approached her bookshelf. "More books up here?"

"You'd be amazed at what you can find in secondhand stores," Kat said. "Besides, I need something to pass the time when I'm on surveillance."

Maiki scanned some of the titles. "You have some of those science-fiction books?"

"Some of them. Mostly romance stuff." Maiki glanced at Kat with narrow eyes. "What?"

"You didn't strike me as the type that was interested in that." Maiki stood up and glanced at Kat's nightstand. "Is that what you're currently reading?"

Kat stared at *The Well of Loneliness*. "Yeah, it's . . ." Maiki picked it up and flipped through the pages. She stopped at Kat's bookmark and read the page. What part had Kat left off at? It wasn't incriminating, was it? Kat peered over to check what page Maiki was on, but she couldn't see. "So—um, do you, do you read?" Kat asked, her cheeks growing hot.

"Um, not really," Maiki said. She closed the book and set it back on the nightstand. "I never have time."

"You don't have time after work?"

"Well, I work long days." Maiki sighed and tucked her hair behind her ears. "I want to crash when I get to my apartment. And I'm still exhausted by the time I need to wake up." She put on a smile. "Besides, I spend most of my day reading reports and legislation and previous trial cases. I don't exactly want to read more."

"That's . . . intense? But you like it at least?"

Maiki let out a resentful laugh.

"You don't like it?"

"Sure, yeah." Maiki smiled at Kat. "I am starving. You got a secret passageway to show me, or can we get lunch?"

"If there are tunnels in the walls, I don't know about them," Kat said. "I got sandwiches downstairs."

They went downstairs and sat on the couch with their feet propped on the table while eating. Kat glanced out the window occasionally, but she didn't see anybody. No Jerry and no stalkers.

"How long are you actually in town?" Kat asked. "Do I get to see you again before you go back?"

Maiki stared across the room while she chewed. Kat took another bite of her sandwich and waited. "We can hang out again."

"Okay, but when do you go back?"

Maiki flopped her head on the back of the couch and stared at the ceiling. "I'm not going back," she mumbled.

Kat stopped chewing. "What?" Without moving her head, Maiki brought her sandwich up to her mouth and took another bite. "What do you mean?" Maiki idly chewed. "What about your job? You don't have to go back?" Maiki rolled her head from side to side on the back of the couch. "No?"

"I quit." Maiki turned to Kat. "Your eyes will fall out of your head if you keep staring like that."

Kat took a breath. "You quit?"

"Yep."

"Why?"

"It was soul sucking."

"But I thought you loved it?"

"No." Maiki sat up. "I was tired of cleaning floors in Philly. That was the most I would've done if I'd stayed in this city," she said, her voice softer and raw.

Kat rubbed her temple. "It was a starter job," she said. "We all had starter jobs when we first got here."

"But you were going somewhere with your life," Maiki said. "You got a job at the flower shop after six months."

"I had been trying to get that job for months—"

"Then you got a job with the Claytons."

Kat deflated. "I got lucky meeting them."

"But Jack still offered you a job," Maiki said. Kat tensed at hearing her old boss's name. "I was here for a year and a half, and I didn't make anything of myself. I didn't belong in this city."

"Do you feel like you belong in DC?"

Maiki plucked a tomato out of her sandwich and dropped it in her mouth. "I figured if the government hired me, that means they don't see us as the bad guys anymore."

Kat's stomach twisted at the desolate gleam on Maiki's face. "Is that not the case?" she asked.

"They found new people to consider the bad guys," Maiki said. "The Exalters. None of them asked for what happened to them. Many of them served our country and became collateral. Others immigrated because they had no home to return to. The Exalters get arrested for something they can't control. The system that took us away still exists—it just found a new target to focus on. And I can't work for the system. I can't hurt people the same way we were hurt."

"They're only arrested for using their powers because that can hurt people," Kat said. Maiki bitterly laughed, and Kat grimaced. "That's not the case?"

"They can't always control their powers," Maiki said. "Even if they don't intend to use them, if they have an accident, they're arrested."

"Is there no way for them to control it?"

"That's the thing." Maiki sat up and sighed. "They can only learn control if they practice harnessing their powers. They need to use their powers to have fewer accidents. But it's illegal to practice, so their powers stay unstable. Which eventually gets them arrested. They can't win. And nobody has a problem with that because Exalters *could* be dangerous. Hypothetical danger is treated the same as actually committing the crime."

Hypothetical danger. Kat's family had been taken because they looked like the enemy. Detained without due process, all to prevent hypothetical danger. "Is there anything else that can stabilize their powers?" Kat asked.

"If there is, I've never heard of it." Maiki stared vacantly at the ceiling. "I've attended so many trials where the Supreme Court had no sympathy and made the wrong verdict. And if they ever did make the right verdict, they fought tooth and nail for it."

"Was there a case in particular?" Kat whispered. Maiki's eyes glazed over, and her jaw tightened. "Or you can't talk about it?"

Maiki sighed. "Most of it's classified. But the cases . . ." She gritted her teeth. "The Justices will never do what's right. And nobody else wants to stop them. All they see is damaged property or organ entanglement, and everybody agrees prison is the only way."

Kat slowly tilted her head. "Organ entanglement?"

"Yeah." Maiki grimaced. "Intestines are very long and very particular about their placement. It's, um—have you ever tried to untangle a bunch of delicate necklaces? And if you pull too hard, a chain snaps—" Kat put her sandwich on the coffee table and clutched her head. "Sorry, sorry, not a lunch conversation," Maiki said. Kat stared at the wood grain on the table. "The Exalters are not dangerous, though. None of this is their fault. They are victims of the government's failings."

Kat slumped back. Despair gnawed at her stomach, and the heavy weight pulled her down. "I don't blame you for leaving. I would've left too."

"Yeah, but at least I saved up enough money to go back home," Maiki mumbled.

Perhaps one silver lining. "So, you're staying in Philly now?" Kat asked.

Maiki pushed her hair out of her face. "You seem so content with this city. How did you get over it?" She looked back at Kat. "I understand the younger ones. They don't remember home. But you remember. Don't you miss it?"

Kat stared at her, surprised, and stuttered, "Of—Of course, I miss it. But this is our life now."

"What if it wasn't? Don't you wish we never left?"

Kat's head buzzed as the tightness came back to her chest. "But we did leave," she whispered. "And we're here now."

"What if you could go back?" Maiki crouched on her knees and leaned toward Kat. "What if you could get your real life back?"

"What is my real life?" Kat asked.

"The lives we were robbed of having! The people we were supposed to be. I want it back." Maiki took Kat's arms and squeezed them in hers. "I'm going home. To San Francisco."

Kat closed her eyes and fought to keep her breathing steady. "You can't go back."

"Yes, I can. Reita's there right now."

"For the summer, but she's not staying there!" Kat stared at Maiki. "Right?"

Maiki shrugged. "Maybe she will if I'm there. And you?"

"What?"

"What if you came with me?" Maiki took Kat's hand. "We can fix it. We can be close again. But we can't do that here. We don't belong here."

Kat stared at their hands. Maiki's fingers were smaller than her own. "This is our home now," Kat whispered.

"How?" Maiki said. "This isn't our city. It's not our ocean. The flowers aren't the same. The food is all different. We don't belong here." Her eyes watered as she stared at Kat. "We don't talk like them. We don't look like them. What makes this home?"

There wasn't an answer to that question. Kat didn't have much attachment to her house. It was falling apart, an embarrassment. It wasn't like she had friends. She had cut off contact with her old colleagues. And her clients were clients, not friends. There was Emrah. She cared about him a lot and wished they were friends, but they weren't. This was a job for him. He only cared about his paycheck.

Maybe Maiki was right. There wasn't any reason to care about this city. Other than her family. But even still, Kat couldn't go back.

"Our family is here," she said. "And I've built my career here."

"You can't be a detective in San Francisco?"

Kat shook her head. "My clients are here. And my license is for the state of Pennsylvania. I'd be starting over."

"That's the point. We'd start over and get to be the people we were meant to be."

"You can't do that here?" Kat asked. She squeezed Maiki's hands.

Maiki tried smiling, but heartbreak filled her eyes. "I need to go home."

No silver lining after all. Maybe it wasn't going to get better between them. "You're really going?"

"Next week," Maiki said. "I was hoping it'd be enough time for you to pack and come with me."

"I can't."

"Could you at least think about it?"

What more was there to think about? There was no point in going back when their home was gone. The house wasn't theirs anymore. The fields weren't theirs anymore. The flowers hadn't known their hands for eight seasons. Their neighbors had been taken too, and there was no guarantee they'd come back. They weren't in school anymore, so they had no classmates. San Francisco had carried on without them. The city had forgotten about them. So, they needed to forget about it too. "Time won't change my mind."

"Well, if you do change your mind, let me know before next Thursday."

Kat's heart sank into her stomach. It didn't have to be this way again. But sometimes, life didn't go the way it was supposed to. "If you're in town until then, I'd like to spend time with you," Kat whispered.

"We can hang out until then," Maiki said. She tried again to smile, but sadness lingered in her eyes. "More opportunities to convince you to come with."

"Yeah, sure," Kat said with a forced smile of her own.

"It's the weekend. Are you free?"

Kat pressed her lips together. "I have to work."

Maiki looked disappointed, and Kat felt worse. "On the weekend? Still?"

"I have a case, and I need to do some interviews and surveillance."

"Don't you have an assistant for that?"

"Yeah, but he's doing a lot already," Kat said. She stared out the window. It had been an hour, and Jerry hadn't shown. She'd prefer if he came today, but this gave her an opportunity to see Maiki again. "My client probably won't be here today, so I'll have to meet with him Monday. I could see you then? In the morning?"

"Yeah, I guess." Maiki picked up the last of her sandwich. Kat wasn't hungry anymore, but she ate the rest of her sandwich anyway.

# CHAPTER 8

# THE FATHER

Maiki left shortly after lunch. Kat periodically checked outside her windows, but nobody was watching her. She didn't know if that was better or worse. She spent the rest of the afternoon working on her suspects list.

After creating a timeline around Serena's death, she sorted through any potential suspects that fit with motive, opportunity, or means. The only clear motive could be the money. And all of Serena's coworkers had the opportunity. The means weren't as clear. Unfortunately, no one had previous murder charges or certificates of neck snapping in their files. The killer could be anyone able to overpower Serena quickly and quietly.

There weren't many military records. Only two of Serena's coworkers had served. Donald Haines, currently a city hall chaplain who had served as a Navy chaplain on the USS McFarland. While it was unlikely a chaplain would commit murder, it wasn't impossible. However, Navy chaplains were noncombative, so his military service wouldn't have trained him to kill.

Then there was Serena's other coworker, Vincent Giudice,

one of the prosecutors at city hall. He had served as an army engineer in the 332nd Engineer General Service Regiment, and he would've had combat training. He potentially had the means and the opportunity, but no clear motive. Along with his work at city hall, he also consulted at a private law firm. His finances were more than stable. But Kat couldn't assume money was the only motive at play. She kept her list open.

Outside of Serena's coworkers, the only other service records were her uncles. Edmund Clark had been KIA years ago. And Alvin Walker had an alibi. Kat had called the Corn Exchange Bank where Walker worked, and his manager had confirmed Walker was present the whole day. So he wouldn't have been able to do it. No other connections to Serena had military experience.

Kat went through her old newspaper stack and found last week's copy. It had the old weather report, confirming her suspicions, so she brought it to DeLacey's.

It was early in the evening on a Friday night. The bar wasn't too crowded yet, but the dark wood walls and dim lights made it easy to blend in with the background. Emrah had introduced Kat to the place a couple months ago. The pubs she used to go to were part of the Claytons' turf, and she avoided her old colleagues like the plague. But DeLacey's was in a different part of town with no familiar faces. Since it was within walking distance, it had quickly become their regular place.

Kat hopped onto her usual stool at the counter and tucked the newspaper in her lap. A moment later, Ray slid to the counter in front of her. "What are we having tonight, Kitty Kat?" he asked. He wore his black bartender uniform, and his slicked-back dark hair contrasted with his pale skin. A few strands fell in front of his face. He had an infectious, lopsided grin.

Kat smiled. "Surprise me."

"Sure thing, baby doll," he said. "You and your buddy want dinner?"

"Yeah, he should be here eventually."

"Then I'll get you started." He headed off to the liquor shelves and started mixing a concoction.

Clusters of customers scattered sparsely around the bar, but the patio area with outdoor seating was still empty. A group of older gentlemen gathered at a table behind Kat, eating and drinking beer. The empty stage would have a performer on it later in the evening. For now, the radio on the counter filled the air with jazz music.

Ray returned with a glass containing a bright blood-orange liquid that practically illuminated the ice. "It's Friday. I figured I would kick off the night strong," he said.

Kat picked up the drink and admired its color. "What's it called?" She took a sip. It singed her tongue with a citrus flavor, cherry carbonation, and vodka.

"Neon God. Too strong?"

Kat shook her head. "I'll drink it slowly. Let the ice do its job."

Ray smiled. "Let me know if you need to top it off." He tapped the counter and glided over to the other customers at the bar.

Kat swirled the liquid in the glass. It was one of the better ones he'd made for her. He was homing in on her preferences.

"Drinking alone?"

Kat jolted as Emrah sat next to her. "Not anymore," she said.

"What'd you get this time?" he asked. She set the glass down, and he took a small sip, nodding. "Not bad. But I'd need something stronger if I'd just gotten back from meeting with Jerry." He slid the glass back to her.

"Funny story," Kat said, and she took another sip. "Good news and bad news."

Emrah stared at the ceiling. "Lord, if it's about Jerry, wouldn't it be bad news and worse news?"

"Bad news, he didn't show."

Emrah rolled his eyes back. "And let me guess, I need to see him on Monday?"

"No, good news is I'll still be doing that." He raised an eyebrow at her. "Apparently, my cousin is in town longer than I thought, so I'm seeing her again before she leaves."

Emrah smiled in disbelief. "Don't get me wrong, I'm extremely grateful for your cousin. But Monday is the last day of investigation for the client."

Kat scrunched her nose. "I know. I'm not thrilled about the timing, but I need to see her."

"What's the urgency?"

Kat stared at the ice floating in her drink. "She's leaving, and if I don't try fixing our relationship, there might not be a relationship at all."

"Leaving?" Emrah tilted his head back at her. "Going back to DC?"

Kat shook her head. "No, San Francisco. I don't know if I'll see her again after this."

"San Francisco?" he muttered to himself, staring off. "Where you're from, right?"

Kat blinked. "Have I told you that before?"

He shook his head. "You don't have an East Coast accent. Your words are smooth together. So, you had to be from somewhere else."

"Practicing your deductive reasoning on me?" Kat asked.

"Need to refine my skills somehow," he said. Ray passed by and set a chokanche down in front of Emrah. "Thanks."

The glass was small with a wide, flat bottom and a narrow

neck. DeLacey's was one of the few places in the city where Emrah could find this drink. The bar always kept a bottle in stock.

The first and only time Kat had ever tried a sip, basically she'd died. It had burned her tongue and gums and throat and nose and eyes and ears. A warmth had spread inside her esophagus and hit the bottom of her stomach instantaneously. It would've been a comforting, fuzzy feeling had she not hacked her sinuses so clear she could smell new colors. While she was fighting for her life, Emrah had sat on his stool. He'd watched her gag and slap the counter before he'd taken the glass from her and smirked. He'd sipped it like water, held it in his mouth for a moment like wine, and swallowed it, unfazed. Kat had tears in her eyes before she recovered.

"Want another sip?" Emrah grinned.

"I'm good," Kat said. "My diaphragm still hurts from the last time."

"A little one, for your health."

"You know, it turns out I already have a drink," Kat said. She picked up her glass, and the ice gently clinked inside. "Cheers."

Emrah raised his glass. "Nazdravlje," he said, then took a sip with a straight face. Kat sipped her drink. The ice had started to dilute it, making it more tolerable.

Kat set her glass down. "How was surveillance?" she asked.

Emrah adjusted his glasses. "Their property's bigger than I expected. They have a couple entrances. I might've missed something."

"What happened?"

Emrah shook his head. "Gerald left for work in the morning. Cynthia said goodbye to him at the front. I stayed at the house since I assumed he was going to work." Kat scrunched her nose. "Should I have followed him instead?"

"Did you catch Cynthia doing anything?"

Emrah shifted his jaw to the side. "Not really," he muttered. "Didn't see her leave the house. I only left for lunch. I was gone maybe twenty or thirty minutes? But she must've slipped out while I was gone, because I saw her return to the house in the midafternoon. She was carrying grocery bags, but I don't know what she did." He leaned on his head and rubbed his face in his palm.

"She also could've gone out through one of the side doors where you couldn't see," Kat said. "Don't beat yourself up. It's bigger than we anticipated."

"Maybe I should've gone after Gerald. Taken a taxi and followed him."

"You can only be in so many places at once," Kat said. Perhaps she should join in on surveillance. Then they'd be able to split up and cover more entrances. "What did they look like?"

Emrah sipped on his drink. "Both of them dressed nicely. Cynthia wore a dress, dark brown hair. Gerald's blond, and he wore a suit."

Kat pursed her lips to the side. "What type of suit?"

"Huh? Like a brown one? A light brown suit."

"But what style?"

Emrah scrunched his eyebrows. "He had a jacket? And a tie?" Kat leaned on the counter. "If you want me to pull the name of the designer, I couldn't tell you. It looked nice."

"I'll take your word for it," Kat said. Gerald was a businessman. He likely wore the type of suit that makes a statement, grabs attention. Not like the people trying to inconspicuously watch her. "Did you notice anything strange?"

"A pigeon carrying a hoagie roll bigger than his body."

Kat rolled her eyes in Emrah's direction. "Did you see anybody watching you?"

He inhaled deeply and sighed dramatically, like he was contemplating. "Besides the pigeon staring me down? No."

Kat nodded. Emrah was usually aware of people watching him. Maybe whoever had followed her this morning hadn't gotten to him yet.

"I think somebody was tailing me," Kat said. She picked up her drink and slowly sipped it.

Emrah raised an eyebrow. "What happened?"

Kat set her glass down as the ice cubes bobbed. "Someone was following me after city hall," she said. "I ran around the block and ducked into a store. He passed by looking around." Emrah's face twisted into concern. "And someone was watching the office this morning."

"What'd he look like?"

"Average man. He was wearing a grey suit." Kat fiddled with her drink, and the ice tinked against the glass. "I'm worried it's the police," she whispered.

"Police? Why? You haven't done anything."

Kat shook her head. "I just have this feeling."

Emrah tapped on the counter. "Because of the case? Or something—"

"I don't know." Kat rubbed her face. She didn't have enough evidence to reveal this was a murder investigation. But she was starting to build reasonable suspicion. "Maybe it's the case," she muttered.

Emrah stared at the counter, thoughts churning in his eyes. "What happened at city hall?" he asked.

Kat sat up and took a breath. "I interviewed Serena's boss and a coworker. Nothing unusual. She had a hearing the morning she died. She usually took the side stairs. There's less foot traffic, so she could get around quicker. I don't blame her for it—the main stairs get congested."

"So, she knew her way around the building," Emrah said.

"The reports said the stairs were wet when she fell," Kat said. "She must've slipped and broken her neck. But I saw the stairs, and trust me, they haven't been mopped in a long time." Kat pulled the newspaper from her lap. "This is from last week. The day she died, it was sunny. No rain."

Emrah turned the paper and read over the column. "So, how'd the stairs get wet?"

Kat shrugged. "No one seemed to have an answer for that. Also, the stairwell was echoey. My voice carried at a conversational volume. It would have alerted the whole building if Serena screamed during a fall."

"But no one heard anything?" Emrah asked. "You said it was off to the side. Maybe it was too far away?"

Kat shook her head. "They still would've heard her if she screamed. It would've echoed."

"What do you think happened?" Emrah asked.

"There are too many anomalies, but nothing tangible yet."

"Besides your stalker," Emrah said. "Maybe the client's on to something and Serena was murdered." Kat raised her eyebrows at him. "Maybe someone waited for Serena," he continued. "They knew her route, so they ambushed her in the stairwell. Broke her neck before she had a chance to scream. Left her body and poured water on the stairs as a coverup."

"That possibility crossed my mind," Kat said. "But finding a suspect hasn't been easy."

"Serena doesn't have a lot of enemies?"

"No, and we don't know what the hypothetical connection would be," Kat said. "Coworkers, family, friends, acquaintances. Anybody. And it might not be someone directly connected to her. Perhaps someone who knew her relatives. Or a complete stranger, like a stalker."

"Any of the coworkers seem shifty?" Emrah asked.

"Not that I could tell, but I didn't have time to interview everyone."

Emrah sipped from his glass and sighed. "Well, I'll round up every person that set foot in city hall that day and interrogate them for you."

"Thanks."

Emrah stared at the counter, spinning the glass stem of his chokanche between his fingers. "You think the parents know something?"

Kat shrugged. "It's possible." The waitress approached them with their food.

"But if they knew who killed—" Kat tapped Emrah's leg. "Hi," he said when the waitress set the plates down.

"Thank you," Kat said.

Emrah kept his head down for a beat until they were alone. "If," he said in a lower voice, "they knew something, why not go to the police?"

"I don't know. But we can't make assumptions," Kat said. She picked up her burger and took a bite.

"I just can't figure out why they'd act this way. It doesn't make any sense."

"We can do more surveillance tomorrow," Kat said.

"We or me?" Emrah asked.

"I can join you and help cover some of the house before the memorial lunch," Kat said. "If they split up again, we can split up. And if nothing comes of it, hopefully we learn something from the extended family."

"Nothing like interrogating the mourning." Emrah took a bite of his burger.

Kat tapped the back of the compact. Her fingers traced against the etching of the peony. One minute until midnight. A dozen questions swirled in her mind. Who was following her? Did it have to do with the case? Was she in danger? As tempting as it was, she refused to break her own rules. She couldn't ask the compact questions about herself.

But even regarding the case, she had too many questions. Who had killed Serena? Or why had Serena died? She could only ask one. What was more important?

There were too many potential suspects. Too many leads to follow. If she asked who had killed Serena, the compact wouldn't give her a name. She'd have to decipher the flower's meaning. If she couldn't understand it, it'd be a waste.

On the other hand, the answer to why Serena was murdered would be easier to decipher. Disappointment, jealousy, anger. Kat was confident she'd understand what the compact meant. But would the motive be a strong enough lead without a suspect? And what if the compact showed her a marigold again? The system wasn't perfect.

Ten seconds. The memorial was tomorrow. Serena's family would be there. Plenty of suspects. Maybe if she knew the motive, she could land on a culprit. But would the killer even be at the memorial? If she knew who to look for, it would narrow the search. The light shimmered in her hands.

"Who is responsible for Serena Line's death?" The words fell out of her mouth. The light shifted into a salmon color. No going back now. She could ask about the motive tomorrow. The petals formed as the flower took shape. Gladiolus. The compact went dark.

Gladiolus? Kat flipped through her journal. She'd seen them before but couldn't remember the meaning. Daffodil . . . Iris . . . Gladiolus: paternity or fatherhood.

Kat wrote down her question in the journal to keep her log updated. If Gerald Line had killed Serena, he would have the common sense to act innocent. He wouldn't be avoiding the family and refusing to hold a funeral. The gladiolus likely didn't mean that her father killed her. But the killer had a paternal connection to Serena. Perhaps one of Gerald's business associates. Or maybe his own brother.

Kat put the compact and journal back in her drawer.

Emrah should've followed Gerald. They could try again tomorrow.

The next morning, Kat was downstairs before Emrah arrived. She flipped through her suspects list and focused on anyone that could have connections with Serena's father. Serena's coworkers could temporarily be dismissed. Her maternal relatives, while less likely, weren't off the hook yet. Gerald could have a strong connection to one of his in-laws, and the compact could only reveal one flower at a time. Kat didn't have the list of Gerald's employees, and she couldn't request it without sounding like she'd had a fever dream. She'd need a plausible lead before she could jump down that rabbit hole. And the only strong paternal connection she already knew about was Peter Line, Serena's uncle.

Emrah arrived and made breakfast in the kitchen. Kat brought her notebook and joined him. The newspaper rested on the table. An article about the Exalter mishap covered the front page. Two dead and five injured after a Material Phaser had ripped through a building. Veteran Hank Simmons had been taken into federal custody as the investigation continued.

A photograph of the damaged street corner was displayed in the center of the paper. In the background, the crowd of people gathered behind the barricades. Kat examined the photo, but she couldn't distinguish any of the faces on the grainy newspaper print. Even if her stalker was in the picture, she couldn't identify him.

The aroma of cooked vegetables made her mouth water. She was hungrier than she realized. Emrah set her bowl of okayu on the table. "Thank you," she said and started eating.

The hot yolk scalded the roof of her mouth, and she subtly exhaled the steam without spitting out her food.

Emrah glanced back at her. "In a rush?"

Kat covered her mouth while the food cooled to a manageable temperature. "I need to follow some leads before I join you on surveillance," she said.

Emrah poured the rest of the food in the pan into his bowl. "What leads?"

Kat blew on another forkful of eggy rice, and the steam billowed. "We don't have a lot of information on Peter Line. I'll make a few calls to see where he's been."

Emrah leaned against the counter. "Maybe his New York file will reveal he's got a long history of murdering nieces."

"You know, it just might," Kat said. She took another bite. Despite her mouth already blistering, it tasted wonderful.

Kat finished the rest of her breakfast and chugged her tea. "I'll meet you outside their house," she said. "Hopefully it's early enough that they don't split up."

"If they do, who'd you rather me stay on?" Emrah asked while swirling his coffee.

Kat grabbed the newspaper off the table and tucked it under her arm. "Maybe follow Gerald today." Emrah nodded. It was times like these she wished she could be in two places at once. Or that she had another assistant.

Kat didn't have a phone in her office yet. It was on the list of many renovations and purchases she still needed to make. It wasn't as high of a priority as it should be, however, because it would be a large, regularly occurring expense that would stress her out during slow business periods. She couldn't justify paying for a phone that wouldn't always see much use. Not when she could use the public ones.

This early on a Saturday morning, the streets weren't too busy. Not as many cars or people on the sidewalks compared to the day before. The sun lingered behind the buildings' silhouettes. Most of the stores weren't open yet but would be soon. Public records in New York would be open shortly.

The morning was quiet. Kat walked along the cobblestone sidewalks. A few loose bricks wobbled under her feet, and mourning doves scattered when she approached. A couple bakeries were open, people lining up outside to get their coffee and breakfast.

Kat found an empty phone booth and tucked herself inside. There was a shelf of massive phone books stored, including for New York. She read through her notes in her journal. Peter Line had moved to Brooklyn in 1922, shortly after he graduated. And while he didn't have the most unique name, she had his birth date to confirm with records.

Kat found the number for Brooklyn Public Records and connected with the operator. She gave her billing address, and they patched her through. It took several tries to confirm with the clerk she had the right Peter Line. He kept putting her on hold to search for a new file. The minutes were racking up, and she didn't want to bankrupt Héloïse with a phone bill for a lead that might not pan out.

"Alright, ma'am," the clerk said after another long hold.

Kat lifted her forehead off the glass of the phone booth. "Still here," she said. She'd been staring at her watch as the minutes slipped by.

He cleared his throat away from the receiver. "I have a Peter Line, born on October eleventh, 1904."

"Yes!" Kat called out, straightening and clutching the phone. "Yes, that's him, I believe."

"You said you were from Pittsburgh?"

"Philly," Kat said. "Philadelphia, Pennsylvania."

"Ah," he said while taking a deep breath. "That'd take about two weeks to mail it over to you."

Kat grimaced, and her grip tightened on the phone. "That's a bit too long. Is there any way you can read some of it over?"

"Ma'am, we'd be here all day. This is a large file." He sounded slightly annoyed.

"Alright, alright, could you maybe read over the—"

"Please hold," he said. "What!" he shouted away from the receiver, his voice muffled. Kat bounced on her toes. The file might have something she needed. But two weeks was far too long to keep the investigation open. And it would be ridiculous to wait that long for what might be a false lead. "You still there?"

"Yes, hi," Kat said. "Can you read over just part of his file?"

The clerk grumbled over the line. "I need to get back—"

"Can you tell me his employer?" Kat said. "Please, his current employer and his marital status?" She could only hear static over the phone. "Hello?"

"Fine," he said.

"Thank you," Kat said. "Thank you so much." She took out her pen and flipped to a new page in her journal."

"Your Peter Line is married to a Thelma Line," the clerk said, "previously Thelma Jackson."

Kat cradled the phone between her shoulder and her ear while she wrote the name down. "Thank you. What year?"

He muttered under his breath. "1922 at the courthouse."

1922? Right after he had graduated and moved there. "Thank you. Where does Peter Line work now?"

"Looks like he's at the Freedom Fairness Law Firm. Your boy's some civil rights lawyer."

Kat scribbled everything down. "Thank you. I really appreciate it."

"Yeah, have a good day." The call disconnected. Kat

winced at her watch. Seventeen minutes for a long-distance out-of-state call. Hopefully it paid off. Kat hung up the phone and went to the Lines' residence on Addison Street.

Surveillance didn't always pay off, but it was critical. If they waited long enough, they'd find something eventually. The problem involved the amount of waiting needed in the first place. After three hours outside the Lines' house, there was nothing to report. Kat sat on a bench a few houses down from the Lines'. She held up her magazine even though she'd read through it all an hour ago. Not exactly ideal reading material, but it was new enough to kill the time. Different homemaking articles, advice columns about how to please your husband, and ads to make your husband's coffee better.

As the morning crept by, the sun got hotter. Thankfully, the tree overhead provided adequate shade so her scalp didn't burn. The wind, which she usually hated, was cooperating for a change. The cool breeze felt nice.

Midday approached, and the streets got busier. Women walked down the sidewalks with babies in strollers. Clusters of children ran around the block. Cars shuffled by on the road. Everyone was too wrapped up in their own lives to notice Kat or Emrah loitering for hours.

The Lines kept their blinds closed, and no one left the house. Kat caught small glimpses of movement through the windows, but not enough to see what they were doing. Enough to know someone was home.

The memorial lunch was at noon. It was best to arrive fashionably late and blend in with the grieving. But they'd have to leave soon. At least at the memorial, Kat could get insight into the parents from the relatives. It would be more productive than waiting for nothing here.

Kat folded the newspaper under her arms and crossed the street. Emrah sat on a bench across the road diagonal to the house. He glanced at Kat above his paper but kept reading. Kat turned around the block and waited at the crosswalk. She stayed far enough away from the curb that cars wouldn't stop to let her cross. A few minutes later, Emrah appeared.

"See anything interesting?" he asked.

"Not what I hoped for," Kat said.

"What were you hoping for? A confession?"

"I wouldn't—" The wind blew her hair into her mouth, and she swiped it down. "I wouldn't complain if we got one," Kat said. "And I didn't notice anyone watching us."

"I didn't either. Maybe they lost interest in you?"

"Maybe." Kat glanced back around the street. "They haven't left their house at all. They would've left by now if they were going to the memorial."

"They probably won't go," Emrah said.

"We can see what the relatives know."

"If the Lines have cut off everyone, maybe the family doesn't know anything," he said. A group of people walked past them, and Emrah stepped closer to Kat. The lunch crowd was coming in. The buses would be packed on the way to the memorial.

"We'll cross that bridge when we get to it," Kat said. Emrah raised his eyebrows. The wind blew her hair into her eyes, and she turned her head to the side. "Any insight could help us get the big picture later," she said as she pulled her hair out of her mouth and eyes. She glanced back at him. Emrah's eyes bugged out of his head, and he clenched his jaw. "Even if they didn't ki—"

"Care!" Emrah sputtered. "Of course they care!" His voice pitched up.

"What?" Kat whispered.

"Your sister just had a baby!" He snatched her forearm and pulled her toward him. "They probably want family time, sweetheart."

Sweetheart. Their code word. "You're right," Kat said. Emrah's eyes flicked past her head. She tried glancing behind, but he squeezed her wrist, and she went still. Was someone watching them? "I guess I don't know what I'm looking for." The wind blew her hair again. She withheld the urge to rip it out of her skull.

"Let me help you." Emrah swept his fingers through her hair and gathered it out of her face. His hands rested on her jaw, and he tilted her head. A middle-aged gentleman stood behind her at the crosswalk. He wore a beige suit and carried a briefcase. His face was clean-shaven and pale, but his complexion matched his blond hair. He wasn't watching them, was he? She hadn't noticed him before.

One of the cars slowed, and the gentleman crossed the street. Emrah leaned into Kat's ear. "That's Gerald."

He was across the street. He was right behind her, and he was getting away. Kat grabbed Emrah's arm. He was right there. He'd left the house. He was right there. "Follow him," she whispered.

"The memorial—"

"Follow him." She pushed Emrah toward the crosswalk. "Find me later."

Emrah jogged across the street. He tipped his head down, shifting his posture and gait to blend in with the crowd. Even though Kat could still spot Gerald ahead, she lost sight of Emrah. Emrah knew how to disappear.

# CHAPTER 9
# THE MOURNERS

Kat made it to her house and quickly changed into her funeral clothes. She had already done her makeup, but the wind had tangled her hair. She combed through it before throwing on her black dress and pantyhose. Her black flats pinched her toes, but she only needed to wear them for a few hours. She didn't have a black purse, but the dark purple would suffice. It was big enough to hold a sympathy card with generic condolences and an incomprehensible signature.

She took the bus down to Charlotte's home. It wasn't as lavish as Gerald and Cynthia's house but still lovely. Their neighborhood didn't have any apartments, and the houses in rows were all two stories with a garage. The rose bushes around Charlotte's porch desperately needed watering in this summer heat. Several cars spilled out of their driveway, filling the entire street surrounding the house.

Kat arrived half an hour late. Most of the guests had already arrived, so no one noticed her entrance. A somber lull filled the rooms. The guests stood in clusters and whispered amongst themselves. Everyone in the room was Caucasian. Many people were blond but not everyone. Several people were smoking, but the open windows didn't let the smell linger in the air. Everyone wore black and spoke in hushed murmurs. A handful of the guests wore jeweled necklaces or expensive watches.

The inside of the house was nice. Various arrangements of roses and carnations and lilies were scattered on every surface and cluttered in piles along the walls. The beautiful hardwood floors matched the wood on the furniture sets. Large artwork and various photographs hung on the walls, different landscape paintings of the countryside. A gilded-framed medal hung on the wall, displaying a Purple Heart.

Lace tablecloths draped to the floor over a long table that held an abundant display of tea sandwiches and appetizers. Framed pictures of the family lined the back of the table, portraits of Serena and photographs of her with her family. Color photos mixed with black-and-white ones.

Serena was a beautiful young lady. She had long, dark hair and a tanned complexion. Her smile was big and bright, her eyebrows dark and full. All the pictures had been taken recently or within the last few years. In the oldest, Serena looked like she was in her late teens. None were from her childhood.

The pictures were from different family events. Christmas photos around a fireplace, a summer barbeque at a park, and an older photo at a wedding. Serena looked younger, wearing an elegant gown and holding a bouquet of white roses and lavender. Next to her stood a newlywed couple, the bride draped in white ruffles with blonde hair shining through her veil. She held an even more elaborate bouquet of lilies and green foliage. The groom was taller and had brunette hair. He wore a white tuxedo with a boutonniere matching the bride's lily bouquet.

There were pictures of Serena with Héloïse, who was almost unrecognizable. She looked full of life, smiling, hope in her eyes. She still looked thin, but she looked happy.

There were also photos of her with her relatives. It was easy to spot her in the group photos. Her dark hair stood out amongst her blond relatives. Only one family picture showed Serena with her parents. It was a black-and-white graduation photo from a few years ago. Serena looked younger in her mortarboard, and her hair was a few inches shorter. She stood between her parents, holding her diploma. Gerald smiled stoically beside a brunette woman, presumably Cynthia. Cynthia was paler than Serena but looked just like her daughter. Dark brunette hair, thick dark eyebrows, bright smiles with big teeth, and heart-shaped faces.

Gerald and Cynthia weren't in any other pictures. Serena's aunt probably didn't want to display them since they'd disrespected their daughter. They probably only included the one photo because it was from Serena's graduation.

A flock of middle-aged women clustered by Kat, reloading their plates with deviled eggs and tea sandwiches while whispering to each other. Kat took a step closer to the women and grabbed the water pitcher. She slowly poured herself a glass while watching them in her peripheral vision.

"I'm still waiting for them to show their faces," one of the older ladies scoffed. She had on a pearl necklace with matching earrings.

"I doubt they will," a middle-aged woman said, stacking a heap of deviled eggs on her plate. "They have a lot to answer for."

"At least Lottie's taking care of it," a different older lady said. She wasn't wearing black but dark navy.

"But she shouldn't have to. Cynthia should've stepped up. Or at least helped Lottie."

"I can't believe them."

"Can we really be surprised?" the woman in the pearl necklace muttered. "I swear, Cynthia threw a temper tantrum when Lottie married Eddie. She didn't even go to their wedding."

"But she didn't like Eddie. This is her own daughter—"

"Are you here by yourself?" A brunette gentleman approached Kat. He wore a black suit and a smile that seemed tired but friendly.

Kat froze, staring at him for a moment before she softened her gaze. "Hi, yes," she said. He seemed familiar. Possibly the groom from the wedding photo.

He glanced at the spread of food on the table. "My wife made these deviled eggs. They are quite special."

"I'll have to try them then," Kat said. She set the pitcher down and held out her hand. "Kathryn."

The gentlemen smiled and shook her hand. "I'm Alvin, Serena's uncle."

Alvin Walker. Charlotte's second husband. "My condolences to you and your family," Kat said.

"Thank you." He nodded solemnly. "How did you know her?"

"She was a friend from work."

"Ah, I see." Alvin stared at Kat and tilted his head. "Did—did Héloïse invite you?"

Kat maintained a polite smile. "There was a memo left for Serena's office about today. One of the secretaries informed me. Dora?"

He nodded. "Ah, Dora. Serena talked about her a lot. I'm surprised I haven't seen her around here then."

Maybe Serena's coworkers hadn't actually been invited. "She's been under a lot of stress ever since. She might stop by later."

"Understood," he said. "You said your name was Kathryn?"

"Yeah."

He stared at her like he was trying to recognize her. How much had Serena talked about her coworkers? "I'm sorry, my memory is a bit scattered. Were you one of the other court reporters?"

How well did he know Serena's coworkers? "Custodial, actually," Kat said. Alvin looked even more surprised. "Serena and I would talk on our breaks. She spoke highly of you."

"She did?" he asked, raising his eyebrows.

"Of course." Kat couldn't read his expression anymore. Had he actually been close to Serena? How badly was this falling apart? "You take care of her aunt."

His eyes softened. "That's reassuring," he said. "It hasn't been easy for Lottie the last few years. I try my best to be there for her."

"Well, Serena certainly thought you were good." Kat glanced around the room, and her eyes caught the medal on the wall. "I noticed the Purple Heart. Thank you for your service."

"Oh." Alvin glanced back at it. "Thank you . . ." His voice trailed off.

"Were you in the infantry?"

"Yeah." He narrowed his eyes curiously. "Did you know someone that served?"

This wasn't the conversation she wanted to have, but it was the easiest way to get answers. "My father was also in the infantry," she said. "He was in the 442nd."

Alvin nodded, and his shoulders eased. "That makes sense. I was in the 314th myself."

Kat's heart rate increased against her will. She maintained her composure. "Oh, you were in France? Or am I mistaken?"

"France, yeah. I was injured in Normandy. Thankfully, it wasn't life threatening. Was your father in France?"

"Um, no. Germany." Kat gripped the strap of her purse.

"Oh, did he . . . with Munich?"

Kat's face grew hot. "Oh, no, no—he was gone before that." Her throat dried, her tongue heavy. Cement filled her mouth and suffocated her words. Alvin's expression dropped, and her stomach twisted. She hated that look people gave her. "Yeah, they uh, he got out before then," Kat corrected. She cleared her throat. "He was in Italy when Munich happened."

Alvin's eyes softened. "Lucky," he said. "I heard what happened from Héloïse. I'm glad I wasn't any further south."

"Yeah." Her throat was still dry, and the nausea lingered. If she could get Alvin to talk about the family, then the conversation might be worth it. "My dad knew some people that didn't make it out of Germany. He lost a lot of friends."

That sadness returned to Alvin's face as he nodded along. "Yeah, even before Munich, we lost enough good men," he said. "In a way, it's how I met my wife."

*Perfect.* "Oh, how do you mean?" Kat asked.

"Well, I'm sure Serena's mentioned that my wife's been married before," he said, and Kat nodded. "I knew Lottie's late husband. We served together." Alvin cleared his throat and kept his voice steady. "Eddie found this gold locket. He wanted to give it to his wife after the war, but . . . he didn't make it out of France. I took the locket from him so I could give it to his wife for him. But something just made sense when I met her."

So, Alvin had fully known Lottie's late husband. Considering he'd taken the locket, he must've been with Edmund when he died. "That's very sweet. I believe Serena mentioned she went to your wedding."

Alvin nodded and smiled fondly. "She was Lottie's maid of honor."

"Oh, I recall her telling me now," Kat said. "She told me how excited she was about her bouquet."

"She helped Lottie pick everything out. The two of them were close." Sadness crept back into his voice. "This all has been devastating for my wife."

"I can't imagine how hard this has been for the whole family," Kat said. "Are you close to Serena's parents?"

Alvin maintained a polite smile, but his eyes filled with disdain. "I can't say that I am." He sighed and glanced at his wristwatch. "Well, I'd better make my rounds. It's been nice chatting."

Kat nodded and took a step back. "Yes, I'm glad to have met you."

He gave her a grim smile. "Same to you," he said. "Hope your father's doing well."

She pressed her lips together and stepped out of his way. Alvin strolled over to the group of chatting older women.

Kat meandered further down the table. She didn't draw attention from two Caucasian women whispering in the corner. The women were younger, perhaps Kat's age. Maybe friends of Serena. One of them was holding a glass with a champagne-colored beverage. The other rummaged through her bag while an unlit cigarette dangled from her lips.

Kat dug into her purse and pulled out a lighter. She didn't smoke, but she carried around a pack of cigarettes and a fancy brass lighter. It made for a useful conversation gateway at times. "Need a light?" she asked.

The woman with the dangling cigarette glanced at her, then smiled. She wore a well-fitted black dress with black heels. Her curled red hair matched her lipstick. "Don't mind if I do," she said in a raspy voice.

"Anytime," Kat said, lighting the woman's cigarette.

"How did you know Serena?" the other woman asked. She held her champagne flute up in her left hand, showing off a massive diamond ring.

"We were friends from work," Kat said. "And you?"

"High school," the engaged woman said. "We used to be close, but Serena went to a different college."

"One where you actually get your degree," the cigarette woman said as she blew a puff of smoke to the side.

Kat turned her head away from the smell but smiled. "Well, she was very smart."

"Serena was always trying to be smart," the engaged

woman said. "Always excelled in school, even when she didn't have to try so hard."

"And that's a bad thing?" Kat asked.

The woman narrowed her eyes and smiled. "I think if she had embraced a more feminine role, it would've been . . . better for her health."

"Hattie, please, you've never cared about the workforce," the cigarette woman said.

"Because what's the point?" Hattie said, then took a sip of her beverage. Oh, one of those housewives.

"Perhaps for independence," Kat said in a calm voice. "Or self-fulfillment?"

Hattie laughed. "Of course *you* would say so."

"What's that mean?" Kat asked.

"You have a job." Hattie shrugged. "No ring, so you're not married, right? So, you have to provide for yourself." Kat kept a neutral expression. Hattie's tone wasn't derogatory but pragmatic. Somehow that made it worse. "Wouldn't it be easier if you had a husband to worry for you about things like money and career?"

"Not necessarily," Kat said. "I like my job."

"What, as a stenographer?" Hattie swirled her drink in the glass and smiled. "We're never going to be important." Her blue eyes bore into Kat like icicles. "None of us are. A woman will always be a secretary to the boss or a court reporter for the judge and lawyers. Even if Serena could live her full life, she'd work twice as hard for half the career any man would have. So, it'd be easier if she let her husband take care of it."

"Serena didn't want a husband," the cigarette woman said. "She never fancied boys."

"I know," Hattie said. "But if she married a man, he would've been the breadwinner."

"She loved Héloïse."

"Love isn't everything."

Kat gritted her teeth but kept a smile. She wasn't here to

win an argument. "But it's not like Serena needed the money," she said.

"It's true. Her father was loaded," the cigarette woman said.

"Which makes it even more ridiculous," Hattie said. "She was playing a man's game. She was never going to win. If she had taken the traditional route, she never would've been on those stairs."

"Oh, stop it," the cigarette woman said as she took a drag, the smell of smoke accumulating around her.

"It's true, Darla," Hattie said with a shrug.

"I'm sure her family found a silver lining," Darla said. The words came out with a puff of smoke. "Serena didn't mind working, so she would've taken over the family business someday."

Kat raised an eyebrow. Was that the motive? Not just the trust, but that Serena would've inherited the business? Could one of Gerald's male colleagues have felt entitled and killed Serena to inherit the real estate business? "Was that the long-term plan?" Kat asked.

Darla shrugged. "No clue."

"But it doesn't really matter now, does it?" Hattie sighed.

Darla rolled her eyes. "Don't be like that," she scolded, then leaned over to the side table and smashed out her cigarette. "I need to use the washroom. Get me one of those drinks." She went into the hallway.

Hattie raised her eyebrows at Kat. "Well, you heard her," she said and walked past Kat.

After she was out of Hattie's line of sight, Kat dropped her smile and wandered into the hallway, where several family pictures hung on the wall. Alvin and Lottie's wedding photos. Lottie looked radiant in her stunning gown with bright golden locks.

The hallway led to the dining room, which was just as crowded as the living room. Older relatives sat in the chairs while eating. Younger people stood in clusters, holding their plates while talking. Kat weaved through the crowd, catching snippets of conversation, mostly about the absence of Serena's parents. How strange it was. What this could mean. Others seemed genuinely heartbroken about Serena while some whispered with sickening grins. Though they piped down when Kat got closer to them, their confusion about her presence silencing them. She pretended not to notice.

There was another door in the corner of the dining room. It was shut, and a group of ladies leaned against it while they ate their tea sandwiches. Kat squeezed through the crowd by them. They all stopped talking when she approached. "Hi, is this another bathroom?"

A woman with eyebrows plucked way too thin stared at her in surprise—or maybe not surprise, but her eyebrows made it seem like that. "No, this leads upstairs."

"Oh, thanks," Kat said. They stared at her, and she couldn't decipher what their facial expressions were trying to convey. She disappeared around a different group of people so they couldn't stare at her anymore.

Enough people had already noticed Kat. Double glances and lingering glares from across the room. She was an outsider, and it made her skin crawl.

Kat couldn't snoop around with so many people nearby. Especially since she stood out. Emrah could get away with it easier. He was sneakier but also Caucasian and blond. He could probably convince a few of the relatives he was a part of the family. Hell, he could probably convince some of the older ones that he'd met them before and act hurt that they'd forgotten him. Why had she told him to skip the memorial? Tailing Gerald had better pay off.

Without talking to more people, there wasn't much more Kat could learn. Even if she could dig around without getting caught, there likely wasn't anything worth finding downstairs. Considering how gossipy the family was, Lottie and Alvin probably kept their personal belongings upstairs. She needed a way up.

To the side of the room, a group of men stood around the fireplace, leaning against the bricks and smoking cigars. A haze lingered around them despite the open windows. A middle-aged woman brought out a tray of food to them, and they picked at it without looking at her. Her blonde hair was falling out of her bun. She wore an all-black outfit, except for the gold locket that dangled around her neck. Was that Lottie? She looked older than in the wedding portrait. Maybe not older, but definitely more depressed.

Once the tray had been cleared off, the woman hustled back to the kitchen, which connected to the dining room through a small doorway. Inside, two girls arranged more appetizers on platters. Perhaps Lottie could be Kat's ticket upstairs.

Kat circled the living room until she found a couple of half-empty platters of deviled eggs. She consolidated the food onto a single tray. She took a bite of an egg, which was so delightful it caught her off guard. Delicate yet creamy, with a rich, tangy mustard at the end. She ate another egg, then took the empty tray with her to the kitchen.

Lottie refilled the pitchers with whatever drink was in Hattie's glass earlier. Next to her, the two girls were preparing another platter of tea sandwiches at the table. The older girl was cutting the sandwiches into careful triangles while the younger one neatly arranged them on the tray. A timer buzzed, and Lottie ran over to the stove to tend to a boiling pot of water.

The girls stared at Kat when she entered the kitchen. Kat smiled at them, but they kept looking at her strangely. Kat went over to Lottie, who scooped out another batch of hard-boiled eggs. "Hi, Mrs. Walker?"

The woman looked up at Kat, bewildered. "Yes?" She brushed the fallen strands of hair out of her face. "Is everything alright?" Her makeup concealed the redness of her face, but it couldn't hide how puffy her eyes were.

"Yeah, someone knocked over one of the empty trays. I wanted to make sure it didn't get put back with the rest."

"Oh, thank you, dear. That's"—she blew a strand of hair out of her face—"thoughtful. Could you set it down there?" She pointed to the counter next to the sink where dishes were already piled up.

"Absolutely." Kat set it down. "Do you need help with anything?"

"Oh, I've got everything under control," Lottie said.

"I truly don't mind. You put all the effort into arranging this. Perhaps I can wash the dishes?"

Lottie stared at the pile in the sink and contemplated. "If you insist, then I suppose that's fine."

Kat smiled at her and grabbed the sponge. Dozens of sticky cups were stacked together, some of them not completely empty. Piles of plates with crumbs or abandoned cucumbers left behind. Most of the dishes were tiny and easy to wash. A few bigger pots and trays were piled further down the counter.

"Auntie Lottie, we finished the bread," one of the girls said.

"Already?" Lottie asked and glanced back at them. "Why don't you pass the food around to the guests, girls?"

The girls took the trays out of the kitchen. Kat dried off another plate while Lottie rummaged through the cabinets. "I swear, we had more food," she said, shoving a few cans to the side. "I went shopping this morning."

The counter was cluttered with different condiments. Behind the jars of mayonnaise, relish, mustard, and ketchup was an untouched loaf of bread. Kat set the last plate down and pointed at the counter. "Is this what you're looking for?"

Lottie glanced back, and her eyes widened. "Yes! Thank

you." She grabbed it and took a breath. "Thank you for your help."

"Oh, it's the least I could do," Kat said.

Lottie smiled at her and shook her head. "I'm terribly sorry. I'm having a hard time recalling you. You knew Serena?"

"I was her friend from work." Kat dried her hands off with the hanging towel.

"Oh, you must be Dora?"

"Actually, I'm Kathryn."

Lottie laughed. "Oh, right, Kathryn!" There was still no recollection in her eyes. "Oh, yes, Serena mentioned you before. She liked you a lot." Lottie's voice faltered, and she tucked her hair behind her ears.

At least she was playing along. "I always saw her as a friend," Kat said. "I'm glad she felt the same way." Kat reached into her purse and pulled out the card. "I wanted to give my condolences."

Lottie's lips parted as she stared at the card. She hesitantly took the envelope and turned it over in her hands. "Oh, I . . . Thank you. That's very thoughtful."

"It's the least I could do," Kat said. "Serena was a wonderful friend, and everyone at work is going to miss her a lot."

Lottie opened the card and read it. While it wasn't personal, it had a seemingly thoughtful message written inside. Lottie's cheeks flushed. "This is, um, this is very sweet." Her voice broke, her eyes turning red.

"Thank you for arranging the memorial."

Lottie let out a laugh of relief and wiped away her tears. "I'm glad it's not a complete disaster. It was a bit last minute that I was the one to do it." She cleared her throat.

Kat nodded and kept her voice gentle. "I was surprised her parents didn't arrange something. Serena always spoke fondly of them."

"Her parents have abandoned us on the matter," Lottie muttered. "Though it's rather typical."

Kat did her best to feign shock. "Oh, were they not as close as I thought?"

Lottie shook her head and waved Kat off. "No, it's . . . My sister has been in and out of my life on more than one occasion. When she can't get her way, she shuts everyone out."

"I'm so sorry. I didn't know," Kat said. "I always thought they were nice folks, the way Serena talked about them. But this seems to be a pattern?"

Lottie bitterly chuckled to herself. "Cynthia cut off all her old friends from high school when she married Gerald." Lottie's voice had a resentful edge to it, like she'd been wanting to rant for a while.

"Wait, what?" Kat leaned in closer.

"It would be one thing if she'd grown apart from her friends, but no—it happened overnight. She stopped talking to everyone when she was engaged. None of them were invited to the wedding. Her husband's friends and family, sure. But only her closest family."

Kat matched Lottie's tone. "Was he forcing her to cut them off?"

Lottie shrugged. "I couldn't think of Gerald doing such a thing. I suspected she wanted to impress her rich in-laws. Didn't think her other friends were worthy enough to make a good impression."

"What? Are you serious?"

"And . . ." Lottie gritted her teeth. "I'm not sure how much Serena has told you about me and my husband?"

"She mentioned that you were a widow before you met Alvin."

"Yes, my first husband. God rest his soul, but . . ." She grimaced, a sliver of contempt lingering in her eyes. "He may not have been the best husband."

"Oh, I'm so sorry."

Lottie put her hand on Kat's arm. "It's alright, dear," she said. "I was young and in love. But love and marriage are very different." Lottie shook her head. "He was . . . a drunk and a slob. I always had to clean up after him. I . . . I swear, he didn't care if he lived in a pigsty. Always spilling and hoarding garbage. He didn't care when ants invaded our house since it meant he didn't have to clean."

"Oh, that's awful."

Lottie shrugged. "At least he never beat me. Even when he was drunk. But . . . so disgusting." She shuddered, and Kat grimaced. "I suppose Cynthia saw what I couldn't. But instead of being there for me, she cut me out of her life."

"Really? But she's your sister." Kat managed to sound surprised enough.

"I tried reaching out, but she wouldn't accept it," Lottie said. "She didn't visit me for years until his funeral, where I finally got an apology. I was too optimistic it would never happen again. And now, with Serena?"

If it weren't for the compact, Kat would be convinced Serena's parents had shitty coping skills and there was no more to it. "I can't believe it. And her husband's the same?"

Lottie leaned back and shrugged. "They know how to agree with each other." She rubbed at her face and took a breath, fanning herself.

Tiny footsteps stomped into the kitchen. "Auntie Lottie, we finished," the older girl said.

Lottie looked at them. "I have more bread. Wash your hands, and you can make more." She smiled at Kat. "I need to get back to cooking."

"Oh, yes, of course."

"Thanks for your help. And thanks for listening, I guess. I feel like I'm going crazy."

Kat gave her a soft smile. "You're not crazy. I promise."

Lottie took a breath and fixed her hair. "Thank you."

Kat stepped out of the kitchen and meandered down the

hallway. After a moment, she popped back into the kitchen. "Hi, again." Lottie smiled at her. "I hate to ask this of you, but there's a line for the bathroom. By any chance, is there another one I could use? A bit of an emergency?"

"Oh, yeah, yeah, we have one upstairs." Lottie dried off her hands.

"You're a lifesaver." Kat smiled.

Lottie led her through the dining room, past the cluster of women loitering against the wall. She took out a key and unlocked the door, opening it for Kat. The stairwell was dark, but daylight streamed at the top of the floor.

"Just shut the door behind you and it'll lock."

"Thanks so much." Kat went up the steps, and the door locked behind her. No one would follow her. Kat glanced at her watch. 1:17. She had maybe ten minutes, give or take, before someone would notice how long she'd been.

She peered around the hallway and found a nursery with a bookcase showcasing different hand-painted model airplanes on the top shelf. The lower shelves held different books. A pile of stuffed animals sat on the toy box.

Kat crept into the master bedroom. It had been upheaved, with boxes scattered everywhere. They were piled around the bed, where different photo albums lay spread out. Probably from trying to find pictures of Serena to put on display.

Kat grabbed one of the closer piles and flipped through. Several photos were missing from the album. A majority of the ones left behind were of Gerald and Cynthia, or duplicates of the ones already downstairs. But all the pictures of Serena showed her as a teenager or young adult. None of them were from her childhood. If Cynthia had cut Lottie out while she was married to Edmund, maybe Lottie didn't have any pictures from that time.

There were several pictures of Lottie next to Cynthia. Even though they had very contrasting hair, the resemblance in their features was prominent. Big smiles and bright eyes.

Kat grabbed a different album and flipped through. Several older black-and-white pictures were of Lottie with a little blonde girl that looked almost identical to her. Pictures of them at different houses, posing with other relatives. There was a graduation photo of Lottie in her cap and gown with the younger girl. Grandview Academy, Class of 1925.

Kat stared at the photo. 1925? That couldn't be Lottie. She still would've been a kid. Kat flipped a few pages later. There were wedding photos. Lottie's white wedding dress, washed out in the photos, with her frilly veil covering her head. Her cheeks were slightly puffy. In the next photo, standing next to the bride, was a very young Gerald.

That wasn't Lottie. It was Cynthia. She had graduated in 1925. Lottie was the younger girl. Kat skimmed through the wedding photos. One showed the bride and groom cutting the cake together. Cynthia wasn't wearing her veil anymore, revealing her intricately braided dark brown hair. Cynthia had dyed her hair for the wedding.

Assuming the photographs were in chronological order, Cynthia had remained brunette after the wedding. Kat stared at the different pictures of family gatherings, holidays, and social events. Her hair never showed its blonde roots.

Kat flipped back to the graduation photo. With blonde hair, Cynthia and Lottie looked identical. Lottie was a kid with pigtail braids, a foot shorter than Cynthia. She was a child. A kid. Giddily wrapping her arms around her sister's waist. Edmund had been in the same class as Cynthia. Yet he'd married Lottie. Seeing the pictures made it look worse than just their birth dates on a document. Especially now that Kat knew the marriage hadn't been good.

A few older albums had been left in a box to the side, the fabric on the covers worn out and stained with age. One was white and had silver bells under an arch of pastel ivy.

Kat grabbed the white album. Engraved on the front was the date: May 26th, 1934. The first photo was an enlarged portrait of the bride and groom. Lottie wore a white dress, plain but nice. It was much simpler than the dress she wore when she married Alvin. She stood with her first husband, Edmund Clark. A small smile adorned his otherwise stoic expression. His dark curls were unkempt despite it being his wedding day, and his dark hair matched his dark eyes.

The rest of the wedding photos were group pictures of Lottie and Edmund with various relatives. The blond relatives looked like Lottie while those with tan complexions and darker hair resembled Edmund. Cynthia or Gerald weren't in any of the pictures.

Gerald was blond. Cynthia dyed her hair, but she was naturally blonde. Kat skimmed through a different album until she found a portrait of Serena from her sixteenth birthday. Next to the enlarged picture of Edmund, the similarities popped even more. The dark eyes. The thicker brows. The ridge of her nose. Serena didn't have his smile, jawline, or cheekbones. With those, she took after Cynthia. But her tan complexion. And dark hair. Her wavy hair was long, past her shoulders. The weight pulled down her curls. If cut short, it was possible it'd be naturally curly.

What if Edmund was her father? He looked too similar to her. Serena looked like her mom, but nothing like Gerald. And her dark hair had to come from someone. If it was Edmund, that would explain why Cynthia had boycotted the wedding. And Cynthia, as radiant as she'd looked on her wedding day, had puffy cheeks in the photos. Like she'd gained some weight from pregnancy.

The gladiolus from the compact implied the murderer had a paternal connection to Serena. Under different circumstances, Edmund would have become a new lead. However, Edmund was long dead. And the compact wasn't an exact science. Gladiolus didn't necessarily mean biological father but any paternal connection, such as Gerald or his brother. Based on the evidence, Peter was still the strongest lead.

Kat crawled around, peeking into different boxes of photo albums. One box contained a stack of yearbooks from Grandview Academy. Kat slid it over and dug through. The top ones were from the early '30s when Lottie was in high school. However, there were Edmund's yearbooks from the early '20s at the bottom of the box. Kat grabbed the 1925 yearbook and opened the cover. Inside, signatures littered the pages.

*"Thanks for always bringing the booze. ~Larry"*

*"Will always remember Carl's parties with you. ~JT"*

*"Best year ever. ~Bobby"*

*"Spring break was unforgettable. Love you. ~CC"*

*"Best senior prank! ~Phillip"*

*"Find me if you're still in town. ~Louisa"*

Several other similar messages from other girls. Edmund hadn't lacked options. There were other messages about wild nights together and how great senior year had been. None of the signatures were from Gerald or Cynthia.

Kat flipped to the senior class photos. She found Edmund Clark, who arguably looked like a handsome young man. Strong jawline, swept-back dark curly hair, and an alluring smug grin. He looked a lot more presentable than in his wedding photo. There was an undeniable charm to him that explained the flirting.

Further down, Kat found Gerald Line, much younger and more refined looking in a clean-cut suit and reserved smile. Kind eyes, though. Cynthia wasn't pictured with the L last names, so Kat started at the front and went through the list. There was a Cynthia Cooper accompanied by the portrait of a young blonde woman with a big, bright smile.

Cynthia Cooper. Could she be CC? It would solidify the theory that she and Edmund had been an item. Perhaps Edmund *was* Serena's biological father. Which was where Serena inherited her dark hair from and why Cynthia dyed hers—and cut off contact with her old life? If it was true, how well had Cynthia hid the truth? Lottie didn't seem to know. Did Gerald?

In the junior yearbook, CC wrote about how hot he looked playing football and called him a stud. Kat rolled her eyes and grabbed the sophomore yearbook, in which CC only wrote about how great it was to sit with him in English class. In the freshman yearbook, CC didn't write anything, but their freshman year was 1922, which was the year Peter Line graduated.

His photo was among the senior portraits. He looked much like Gerald, with fair hair and similar eyes. He had a brighter smile though. Kat flipped a few pages back to the J surnames and found a Thelma Jackson. The accompanying photo was of a young Black woman, her dark, tight curls spiraling around her face. That had to be the same Thelma Jackson Peter had ended up marrying. Was this why he'd been cut from the will? His parents discriminating against his relationship?

Peter currently worked as a civil rights lawyer. He might've understood some of the legal aspects when he'd tried to contest the will. But what if he'd never gotten over it and found a different loophole? His brother's will made Serena the sole beneficiary of the estate. However, if she died, Peter would potentially default as next of kin. It was the most established motive so far. However, the means and opportunity were still missing.

Kat glanced at her watch. 1:31. Her heart jumped to her throat. Someone was bound to notice how long she'd been up here if she didn't leave soon. She took out the portrait of Serena and the enlarged wedding photo of Edmund with Lottie and put them in her purse. She could give the pictures to Héloïse to return later, but right now she needed the evidence.

Kat copied the messages from the yearbook into her journal, then put everything back the way she'd found it. Or as close as she could remember.

Nobody looked at her when she slipped back downstairs, and she made her way toward the front door.

A few more people had come in, and the rooms were warmer. A family with four small children bounced around as they made their way greeting others. Kat ducked out of there, catching a glimpse of Héloïse.

Héloïse sat on the sofa alone. She wore all black and gripped her cane. Her hair was braided out of her face. Her cheeks were so thin, her eyes swollen red. Even surrounded by a room full of people, she was still an outsider to them. Héloïse looked up, her eyes widening when she saw Kat. Kat nodded to her, and Héloïse gave her a small smile.

Kat grabbed another deviled egg and slipped out of the house.

# CHAPTER 10
## THE WATCHERS

Emrah wasn't at the office when Kat got back.

She had taken the bus to get out of the heat, but the sun had still soaked into her black funeral clothes and made her sweat. She changed into light capri pants and a loose button-up blouse, grabbed her surveillance bag, and headed out again.

The afternoon was more crowded, children running in the streets and more pedestrians about. Long lines snaked out of ice cream shops and curled around the block. Kat walked in the shadows of the buildings to stay out of the blistering sun. She stopped at a phone booth.

Kat flipped through the New York phone book, searching for the number for Peter's law firm. She connected with the operator, and the call transferred through. After a couple rings, a bubbly voice with a Brooklyn accent greeted her.

"Hi," Kat said and cleared her throat. "I'm calling for Peter Line. Is this the right number?"

"Yes, ma'am. However, Mr. Line has been out of office for the month, but he will be back next week. Can I leave a message for him?"

Kat raised her eyebrows. "Sorry, you said he's been gone all month?"

"Yes, it was out of the blue." The secretary sighed. "He's never taken this long of a vacation before. His calendar's backed up, so it may be a while before he can fit in an appointment for you."

If Peter had been out of office for a month, he'd had the opportunity to commit the murder. Kat gripped the phone. "I understand. Do you know when he might be back so I could call him?"

"Uh, let me check, toots." The secretary rustled the background. "Yeah, June 5th—he said he'd be back Monday. You can call him then, or you can leave a message with me."

If she called back Monday, she could at least check that he'd returned. "I'll try calling later. Thank you." Kat hung up. Peter'd had motive and opportunity. She needed to find Emrah. Depending on where he'd followed Gerald, he could be anywhere. The Lines' residence was the best starting place.

The late afternoon had turned into early evening by the time she made it there. The neighborhood bustled with people. Couples strolled together, women walked home with grocery bags, children ran around in the street. Whenever a car drove by, the children scattered to the curb until it passed. Across the street, Emrah sat on a bench reading a newspaper.

Gerald must've come home. Or Emrah had lost sight of him and figured to return to the house. Kat leisurely made her way toward him.

A car cruised down the street, and the children cleared away as it drove past. The sleek black polish glistened in the sun, the reflection off the tinted windows blinding Kat. The children ran back into the street with their soccer ball as the car pulled up to the curb and parked.

The car doors opened, and four Caucasian gentlemen got out. All grey suits. Kat's heart rate skyrocketed. They marched down the sidewalk toward her. They all had generic short haircuts and clean-shaven faces. However, their suit jackets didn't sit right. The right side of each jacket bulged over their hips.

The familiarity churned in Kat's stomach. She kept her head forward as her insides climbed into her throat. They couldn't be here for her. She'd just gotten here. They couldn't have known where she was. And she hadn't done anything wrong. She rummaged through her purse to look busy. They couldn't arrest her. Their shoes scuffled along the brick sidewalk. They couldn't take her. Even if they tried, she could run this time.

Kat slowed her strides and moved over to the curb. If they wanted to get her, they'd have to try harder. Her fingers wrapped around a regular compact mirror in her purse, and she dug it out. Holding her breath, she opened the compact and lifted the mirror up as if to check her eyes, but she angled the reflection over her shoulder. The men had stopped outside one of the houses, one of them knocking on the front door. They were at the Lines' house?

Kat glanced across the street and locked eyes with Emrah. He kept his head tilted down at the newspaper, but he was watching. If something happened to Kat, at least he'd know.

The front door opened. Kat couldn't see who it was, but the men went inside. Kat tossed the mirror into her purse and kept walking calmly in their direction. Further down, she caught a glance of Cynthia at the door. Three of the men went inside, but one lingered on the porch. Kat averted her gaze and stared at the sky, feigning fascination.

The last gentleman stared at Kat as she walked past. If they were going to take her, it would've happened already. Kat put on a smile despite wanting to vomit. "Good evening, sir," she said with a city accent. "Beautiful day we're having."

"Quite so," he said in a monotone voice, his eyes fixated on her.

She continued down the sidewalk without letting her

nerves show. She didn't glance at the holster under his jacket. She didn't look in Emrah's direction. She kept her head forward and her shoulders relaxed, and she walked at an uncomfortably leisurely pace. He didn't follow her, but her heart still pounded in her throat. It didn't slow down until she turned the corner and got out of his line of sight.

Kat leaned against the side of the building and took a deeper breath. They couldn't arrest her. She hadn't done anything wrong. Crashing a memorial was tacky but not illegal. She took another breath, and her eyes watered with relief. What the hell was she upset about? The war was over.

These men were federal agents, and so were the ones from yesterday. They had to be. Their haircuts, their nondescript suits, the way they concealed their guns. But they weren't here for Kat. They weren't questioning her. Not like the FBI agents that had interrogated her family.

Her father had worked on the Nisei strawberry fields where the owners had been accused of using magic on the crops. And her aunt Hideko had sold a suspicious amount of jewelry to a pawnshop. The FBI had accused her father and aunt of possessing magic and committing treason. But her aunt had only sold the jewelry because they were only allowed one suitcase. They were trying to get any value out of it while they could. The jewelry wasn't magic. Neither were the strawberries. The farmers tended to the fields, using volcanic and marine-rich soils to fertilize the crops. The volcanic ash contained minerals that made the fruit sweeter. It was minerals, not magic. But the FBI needed to be thorough.

Japan, surrounded by Pacific volcanoes, had a surplus of volcanic ash. On its own, the ash was as useful as dirt. But when processed, it created magic. Part of Japan's alliance with Germany had included supplying the Nazis with processed ash, which was how Germany had created their own Exalters.

Despite being Nisei—second generation—the US government had assumed Kat's family was not American enough. If they were not relocated away from the coast, if they were not detained, if they were not stripped of all communication or potentially magic items, they would aid Japan. No amount of pleading or demonstrations of loyalty could convince the government until the war was over.

When Kat's father and aunt were questioned by the FBI, those agents were not as subtle about concealing their weapons. They flaunted their guns, waving them around and pointing them at her family during interrogation. They wouldn't let them go. Kat and her mother couldn't leave either. But her mother's two brothers and their wives and children were forced to relocate without them. The rest of her family were taken to Heart Mountain. By the time the FBI released her father and aunt, they were sent to Manzanar.

Kat's breathing eased, and her heart returned to a steady beat. The wind cooperated and gently cooled her face. Emrah silently appeared in her peripheral view.

"You alright?" He looked worried.

Kat stood upright. "Yeah, why?"

"You look flushed." Emrah gestured at her cheeks.

"Huh? I'm fine." She took his arm and guided him down the sidewalk toward DeLacey's. "That's what the man looked like yesterday."

"Figured. It must be for the case then."

At least it wasn't the government suspecting Kat of Communism or treason again. "Did you see something?" she asked.

"The one outside lit a cigarette," Emrah said. "That's about it."

Why would federal agents show up to the Lines' house? If not to arrest them, then to question them? Did this have to do with Serena's murder or some other coincidental investigation? "What happened this morning with Gerald?" Kat asked.

"Yeah . . ." Emrah pushed his glasses up his face. "Funny thing about that."

"Did you lose him?"

"No, I caught up. Went to a bank." Emrah softened his voice as a few people passed them on the sidewalk.

"A bank?" Kat walked closer to Emrah so she could hear him.

"Yeah, well, at first, I thought we went to some Ritz-Carlton. They had people holding the doors open. I somehow looked underdressed."

"Because they had a doorman?" Kat asked.

"What? No, the whole bank. The architecture, the marble tiles, the freaking chandelier. It was way too fancy for a bank."

Kat swayed her head from side to side. "Well, we knew the Lines were well-off."

Emrah shook his head. "No, this is not *well-off*," he said. "This isn't like the Carvalho case. The Carvalhos were well-off. This . . . this is old-money rich. Like never-get-enlisted rich. Like own-the-railroads rich . . ." He sighed. "Anyways."

"Anyways," Kat said, "you were underdressed for a bank?"

"Yeah, Gerald took a long time with the bankers. He must've made a large cash withdrawal, and that's what the briefcase was for. Or he had something in a safety deposit box that he was carrying out."

They waited for a car to pass before crossing the street. "You didn't happen to see what he got, did you?" Kat asked.

"No, I wasn't able to follow him to the back. And I was busy being a fool with the poor teller."

"What'd you do this time?"

"Well, Gerald was taking forever. I needed to stall," Emrah said. "I pretended I had an account with the bank, and they didn't look convinced. But I said I needed a withdrawal. And they couldn't find my nonexistent account, so I had to keep insisting until Gerald left."

Kat laughed. "How many times—"

"Six," Emrah grumbled, rubbing his face. "I accused them of spelling my name wrong. Probably looked like a dumbass."

"Probably?"

"Shhh."

"How'd that end for you?" Kat asked.

"I . . . had a moment of clarity and realized I was at the wrong bank. They looked so irritated. So never send me back there."

"Oh, by the way, I need you to go back to the bank tomorrow morning." Emrah whipped his head at Kat, and she smirked. "Kidding."

"Oh, you think you're so funny."

"I'm hilarious," she said. "So, you followed Gerald after?"

"Yeah, he headed back to the house. Didn't stop anywhere else."

What had he taken out from the bank? The Lines didn't leave their house for much, but Gerald had made this trip. And the same day, the agents showed up at the house? "The timing can't be a coincidence," Kat muttered.

"What if they put a hit out on Serena?" Emrah asked. "And this is the payment for finishing the job? And those men are some mobsters."

"I don't think they're mobsters," Kat said. "They might be federal agents."

"How do you know?" Emrah asked.

"I . . . have this feeling. The way they looked. And their suit jackets didn't sit right. They were carrying guns."

"Mobsters can have guns."

"But they were also too well kept."

"Oh, and so you think mobsters look like slobs?"

"That's—" Kat stared at Emrah, and he laughed. Was he joking or speaking from experience? "Should I ask?"

Emrah smirked to himself and then straightened his face. "You think they're federal agents?"

"Yeah, they looked bland. Regulated. Like they weren't supposed to be noticeable. I've seen it before, and I have a feeling."

"You've seen it before?" Emrah looked at her. "Should I ask?" Kat kept her eyes ahead of her. "If it's the feds, they're not taking payments . . . unless they've gone rogue."

"I don't know," Kat said. "Could they be arresting the Lines?"

"A bit underwhelming for an arrest," Emrah said. "What happened at the memorial?"

Kat debriefed Emrah about her findings on the way to DeLacey's. She told him about Cynthia's previous behavior, how Alvin knew Edmund, and about Peter Line's relationship with Thelma Jackson. The bar had drawn a larger crowd that night. Someone played the piano onstage, and a few folks danced around. Between the music and boisterous chatter, nobody could overhear their conversation.

After they'd ordered drinks, Kat took the stolen pictures out of her purse. "This is what Serena looked like," she said.

Emrah examined the photo. "She looks like Cynthia," he said. "But Cynthia's a natural blonde?"

"Most of the family is," Kat said.

Emrah raised an eyebrow at her. "Anyone ask how you were related to Serena?"

"I said I was her coworker."

Emrah rolled his eyes. "Oh, take the easy way out, I see."

"Well, I didn't exactly have much of a choice."

"Really?" Emrah rested his chin on his hand and stared at Kat. "You didn't have a choice when Serena's distant long-lost third cousin twice removed was the clear option?"

Kat threw her hands into the air. "You're right, I'm an amateur at this gig."

Emrah held the photo of Serena up to Kat's face. "I totally see the resemblance. Sisters right there."

She pushed Emrah's wrist away. "Speaking of resemblances." Kat slapped the wedding photo on the counter.

"And what do we have here?" He picked it up while adjusting his glasses.

"This is from Lottie's first wedding," Kat said. She held Serena's photo next to Edmund's. "And that's Edmund Clark. See the resemblance?" A grin spread across Emrah's face. "Edmund went to high school with Cynthia, who refused to go to his wedding."

"You think Cynthia and Edmund were an item?"

Kat pulled out her journal where she'd copied down the messages. "I found some of his yearbooks in storage." Emrah raised an eyebrow. "What?"

"You dig through their whole house?"

"They had albums out to set up pictures for the memorial. There wasn't much digging required," Kat said. "Cynthia's maiden name was Cooper. And this 'CC' wrote some affectionate messages in his yearbook. I think this is sufficient evidence to suggest they were an item. Especially considering that Cynthia's naturally blonde. She's been dyeing her hair to cover the truth?"

Emrah read the notes in the journal again. "Unforgettable spring break, huh?" He smirked. "You think that's when Serena was conceived?"

Kat gave him a look. "Mathematically, she would've had to give birth to a toddler then."

"Oh, yeah, forgot about that part," he muttered.

"They had to have been together just a couple months before Cynthia's wedding with Gerald," Kat said. "Either she'd just broken up with him before getting engaged or she went behind Gerald's back."

"She definitely cheated."

"I wouldn't say definitely, but it's possible," Kat said.

"Come on." Emrah leaned his back against the counter. "Their dating window is too short for there to be no overlap."

"The messages in the yearbook imply Cynthia and Edmund were dating. If any cheating happened, it likely happened to Edmund. But that is still an assumption we can't prove."

Emrah's eyes flicked back and forth. "Alright, so she's two-timing Edmund—"

"That's not what I —"

Emrah held up a hand. "She's sleeping with both of them, then finds out she's with child. It's fifty-fifty whose baby it is. But if you're having a baby, you pick the better husband, right?" Emrah glanced back at Kat with a grin. "So she picks the man with the family fortune and dumps Edmund. She even goes as far as to dye her hair for her in-laws *just* in case the baby is Edmund's. Sure enough, it is. So Cynthia's a brunette to keep up the lie."

"That's—"

"And!" Emrah leaned closer to Kat. "Gerald knows his parents cut off Peter for, in their eyes, a disgraceful relationship. He can't let them know he knocked up a girl out of wedlock. So, shotgun wedding. Now, Edmund was in love with the blonde dame who left him for some reason. But CC is now Mrs. Line and a brunette. So Edmund marries the younger carbon copy who kept her golden locks. Cynthia's too far into the lie. Too much money's at stake. So what does she do? Cuts off contact with her own sister so her ex never finds out." Kat opened her mouth, but Emrah held his hands up. "Before you object, please humor me a little."

Kat leaned her elbow on the counter. "Fine," she said. "What does your theory have to do with our case?"

Emrah furrowed his eyebrows. "You're no fun," he muttered.

"No, I'm humoring you," she said. "Gerald doesn't know any of this?"

"Not until recently," he says. "Either he forgot his wife's naturally a blonde or really doesn't understand how genetics work. Eventually, he finds out. He's livid at all the deception and lies. So in the heat of passion, he kills Serena."

"Heat of passion is killing in the moment," Kat said. "Ambushing Serena at work with no witnesses, then having the foresight to bring water to spill down the stairs? That's premeditated."

"Okay, so maybe it was premeditated?"

"Then why kill his daughter?" Kat asked. Emrah shifted his jaw, contemplating. "Why not his wife who lied?"

"I'm working on it," Emrah muttered.

Kat leaned closer to him. "I don't think Gerald did it."

Emrah glanced at her. "You think it's Peter Line."

"Out of all the suspects, he's the only one with a clear motive and a window of opportunity."

"And the federal mobsters are waiting for Peter Line to show up? Unless they are mobsters working for Peter."

"I don't know. Maybe?"

Emrah grinned at her. "You agreeing with my mobsters theory?"

"More like the former one," Kat said. If the agents knew Peter committed the murder, they would've arrested him already. Perhaps they didn't know who the threat was. Ray came over with two drinks. "Incoming."

"Alright, the usual for you," Ray said, handing Emrah his chokanche. Emrah gave him a nod. "Today's concoction for you, a car crash." Ray handed Kat a martini glass filled with a pale pink liquor, wedges of grapefruit, and a leafy garnish on the side. Was it sage?

"Thanks, Ray," she said and took a sip of whatever he'd decided to make for her. The grapefruit was pungently tart. The gin enhanced the juice, but the earthy flavor of the sage complimented it in a surprising way. "I like this one."

"Right on," Ray said. "Dinner will be out soon. Kitchen's backed up." He tapped the counter and moved on to the next group.

"Maybe they don't know if it's Peter," Kat said as she slid the drink across the counter.

"What do you mean?" Emrah asked, picking up her drink to sniff it. He furrowed his eyebrows. "That's . . . interesting."

"It tastes better than it smells," Kat said. Emrah took a sip and looked surprised. "Why else wouldn't they have arrested him, or any suspect, yet? Maybe the Lines are being black-mailed, hence the bank trip. But they don't know who's doing the blackmailing." Emrah scrunched his face. "What do you think?"

"I think that you're a liar." He handed back her drink. "That tastes exactly like it smells."

"You don't like it?" she asked.

"It's not bad, but I wouldn't call it fantastic."

"Drink your rubbing alcohol."

"Gladly." Emrah took a sip of his drink and set it down. "If Peter was trying to blackmail them, he wouldn't have killed the collateral before he got the money."

"Unless Serena was the warning. To show them he's serious and could do it again."

Emrah swayed his head from side to side. "Possible," he said. "If they don't know, do we send in a tip?"

"That's assuming half of these theories are correct," Kat said. If the agents didn't know Peter was a plausible suspect, perhaps it'd be worth warning them. The Lines could still be in danger. Though, if Kat turned out to be wrong or—God forbid—they were mobsters, that wouldn't end well.

"What're you thinking?" Emrah asked. "Should we do more surveillance after dinner?"

As tempting as it was, it wouldn't be worth it for now. Anonymity was an advantage they couldn't get back once they lost it. And with it getting dark, Emrah wouldn't be able to see much anyway, so there'd be no point. "We can go in the morning. Hope it's not too late by then," she said, then rubbed her hand against her temple and took another sip of her drink.

They finished dinner, and Kat paid their tabs. Emrah walked her back to the house and then went home. She spent the remainder of her evening lounging on the couch as she read over the case files. The probate court reports from when Peter had contested the will, the timeline of Cynthia and Gerald's youth, from high school graduation to their marriage certificate to Serena's birth certificate. The words on the documents grew blurry as her eyes burned from strain. It was only ten o'clock. Too late to continue working but too early to go to sleep. Kat tidied up her office and locked up her case files before getting ready for bed.

She showered, changed, and paced around her room. The radio played an evening talk show, but Kat's mind didn't retain the discussion. The floorboards squeaked under her bare feet as she paced. There were too many gaps in her theory. The evidence wasn't as tangible as she'd prefer. While Peter Line had a motive, Kat couldn't confirm it was the *real* motive behind Serena's death. Not like the compact could. And as much as she wanted to know what Gerald had gotten at the bank or why those agents had been at the house, there was a small possibility it had nothing to do with Serena's case. She couldn't risk wasting a night. She was running out of time for Héloïse. The motive was too crucial.

Kat sat on her bed and picked up her book for a third time. She knew what her question would be. No point in dwelling anymore. Her eyes skimmed across the page, but none of the words made it through to her head. What if those agents were mobsters? What if it wasn't one of Emrah's absurd theories but that he knew what mobsters looked like? Gerald came from old money. Was real estate just a front? Was the mob how he'd gotten so rich? Had Serena known about it?

Was that why she'd wanted to work, for an honest living and clean money?

Assuming any of this was plausible, did Héloïse know about the mob affiliation? Had she known what she was marrying into? Had she been spared from a life of crime? Either way, she still needed closure. Though closure wouldn't bring Serena back.

Would Héloïse be able to move on? She was young with her whole life ahead of her. Perhaps someday, she could find peace and meet someone else. Lottie had married again and loved again. Granted, Lottie hadn't exactly gotten it right the first time. What if Serena was *the one* for Héloïse?

Kat's heart pounded in her chest. She closed the book and set it back on the nightstand. She couldn't keep rereading the same page a dozen times without recalling any of it. A dull ache spread inside her, and she couldn't focus on anything else. What if there was only one person she was meant to love in life? And once they were lost, they were gone for good.

There was more to life than romance. Career, family, hobbies, friends. It wouldn't be a meaningless life. But it would be lonelier without someone to share it with. Someone to sit with at breakfast and lie with at night. Someone to tell about every small thing that happened in her day. And to hear every detail about their day in return. To know someone so intimately they were a part of herself. Why was life so cruel as to rob anyone of companionship? Why wasn't it fair? Hadn't enough tragedy happened in the world? Why was love too much to ask for?

The night dragged on. Kat stared at the clock in agony. She needed to go to sleep. She needed to turn off her mind. It was the only solution to stop the thoughts. She took out the compact and her journal. The bronze felt cold in her hands, and she traced the etchings of the peony. She ran her finger along the embossed metal like she'd done since she was a kid. But this time, she didn't feel grounded.

The temptation to ask something else burned inside of her. She could ask anything she wanted, and it would tell her. She'd have to decipher it, but the answer would be there. She shook her head. She had made her rules for a reason.

Midnight approached. The metal grew warm in her sweating hands. Kat stared at the pale opal stones. She slowed her breathing, but her heart kept racing. The shimmers began. Twinkling white light illuminated her hands.

"What was the killer's motive for murdering Serena Line?" Kat asked.

The light remained white while it twisted into shape. It revealed a flower with a grotesque, chunky center and gangly white petals. Edelweiss.

Kat had seen it enough as a detective. Especially when she'd worked for the Claytons. She didn't need her notes. Edelweiss meant coercion or manipulation. When threats were made about exploitation. When there was blackmail.

# CHAPTER II

# THE AGENT

Kat rushed outside when Emrah showed up. She was ready to leave with breakfast to go. The coffee and bagels she'd picked up would have to suffice for him. There was no more time to waste.

They approached the Lines' neighborhood. The morning air was cooler and the streets quieter, with few people outside at this time of day.

"Wait here," Emrah said as he turned the corner. In the event the same feds were still outside the house, they would recognize Kat, but Emrah hadn't been made yet.

Kat waited at the corner, out of sight of the Lines' street view. She pulled out a cigarette and lit it. The rancid smell of smoke wafted toward her. She let it burn between her fingers, watching the trails of smoke disperse in the air. She hated the smell and what it reminded her of. But it was the easiest way to look unsuspecting while loitering outside without a bus stop nearby.

The cigarette had nearly burned down to the end by the time Emrah came around the other side of the block. "Coast clear?" Kat asked, and she put it out.

"Think they're still outside the house," Emrah said.

"Really?" she asked. Had they been there all night?

"I think it's them. They're spread out. Possibly four around the house. Like they're conducting surveillance."

"They might be if they're waiting for the suspect. Possibly a blackmail exchange."

Emrah adjusted his glasses. "If it was Peter, wouldn't they know by now?" he asked.

"When you're that rich, anybody could be a suspect," Kat said. "And if Gerald hasn't spoken to Peter in years, decades even, he may not think of him. Or he may not want to think his own brother would do something like this."

"Not all families are innocent," Emrah said. "What do we do? Surveillance with them?"

"I'm worried it'd be a waste of time." Kat peeked around the corner, but they were too far away to see the Lines' house inconspicuously. "Maybe I should intervene."

"Why?"

Kat's heart started beating faster, but she kept her voice steady. "We're cutting it down to the wire. If we know something, we should help."

"And if they're mobsters?"

"I would almost prefer that," Kat muttered. She leaned her head against the brick wall and kept her breathing steady. Emrah didn't need to know how on edge she was. She glanced up at him. The sunlight reflected off his glasses. "They haven't noticed you, so you're my backup if this goes south."

"Sorry, I left my sniper rifle at home," he said. Kat swatted at his arm. "What backup are you expecting?"

"If I'm wrong, we still need to find the truth for Héloïse. Keep watching what they do. And don't get caught."

"And if they kill you?"

Kat's throat went dry. They'd been stalking her for days. If they wanted to kill her, it would've happened already. "I'll take my chances."

"There's got to be another way." Emrah glanced down the

street they'd come down. "I saw a bookstore not too far from here."

"You need some reading material?" she asked.

"What if we buy a whole set of encyclopedias? Then we go around pretending to be salesmen and knock on their door. We go in. Scope the place out without drawing suspicion."

"Salesmen don't work on Sundays."

"Well—"

"And that's assuming they'd even let us inside."

"Fine, fine . . . Just be careful," he grumbled. "I'd like to still have a boss by the end of the day."

"I'll do my best," Kat said. "Take a lap around the block. Hopefully I can distract them so they don't recognize you passing by again." Emrah patted her shoulder, and they split up.

Kat leisurely strolled down the sidewalk toward the Lines' house. The agents weren't directly outside. Instead, the generic suits were scattered down the sidewalks on different benches. Not so close to the Lines' house to be obvious, but close enough to keep an eye on it.

A row of cars had parked along the curb. One of the parked cars was similar to the car from yesterday with the sleek black polish. The driver still sat inside. A few feet away, a man in a grey suit sat on a bench reading a newspaper. Kat kept walking toward the Lines' house, avoiding direct eye contact with them.

There was no point in lying. She couldn't think of any cover that would increase her chances of talking to the Lines. The best way inside would be to tell the truth and say she had information about their daughter's murder.

Footsteps approached her. She kept her head down. Long shadows from the morning sun stretched down the sidewalk and crept up behind her. By the outline of short hair and square shoulders, it looked like one of the agents. They couldn't arrest her. She hadn't broken any laws. She hadn't done anything yet. Kat started walking faster, but the shadow kept up its pace.

One of the agents ahead got up from the bench and walked toward her. He was also Caucasian and in a grey suit. Kat clenched her fists at her sides. Nothing was going to happen. There wasn't a war. She had a right to public spaces. They couldn't take her away.

Her stomach churned as she approached the Lines' front steps. Did they think she was the blackmailer? But they'd been watching her all this time. They had to be smarter than that.

Their shadows crept closer behind her, their shoes scraping against the cobblestone. Her heart pounded in her ears, and the edges of her vision darkened. Kat stared at the front door. They'd kill her.

Kat veered off the sidewalk toward the street, but the agent grabbed her arm. "Miss." The man behind her spoke in a low but firm voice. Kat pulled at her arm, but he tightened his grasp. "Miss." Kat tilted her head at him. He had greying brown hair.

"What?" she whispered. She couldn't breathe.

The other man approached her. He had a scar on the side of his forehead. "Can you come with us?"

Kat looked at him, but her eyes wouldn't focus. "Who are you?" she asked.

"Don't make a scene," he said. The older man reached into his jacket pocket and revealed a bronze badge. Before Kat could read the embossed lettering, he put it away. "You need to come with us."

The man with the scarred forehead grabbed her under her other arm, and they dragged her along. Her skin went numb as their fingers dug into her arm. "What's happening?" She wedged her shoes against the uneven cobblestones and pulled against their grip. "I didn't do anything."

"You need to cooperate, Miss." They yanked her forward, and her toes scraped against the sidewalk. The men hauled her toward the black car on the side of the street. The engine was running.

Kat's heart rate skyrocketed. She jolted away. It was happening again. They tightened their grip and pulled her. "Where are you taking me?" Kat raised her voice as they dragged her to the curb.

"Quiet," the older man snapped. He opened the door while the other held her in place. "Get in the car."

"Tell me where I'm going," Kat said.

"We're federal agents," the scarred one muttered in her ear. The clammy warmth of his voice prickled the skin on her neck.

Kat leaned away from him. "That means nothing to me."

"For your safety, get in the car," the older man said.

Kat's stomach twisted. Safety was a lie. It was what the FBI had told them in California. It was all a lie. She threw her weight backward. The older man grabbed her. They hoisted her off the ground, her feet scraping off the curb. She shrieked as they threw her into the car.

She fell on the seats. The door slammed behind her. Still screaming, she reached for the door handle, but the driver took off. She rolled to the floor as the car sped away, then climbed up to the seat and glanced out the back window. Emrah wasn't coming.

An older Caucasian man sat in the back with her. He had a large mouth with a heavy jaw. His grey hair matched the color of his suit. Not looking at Kat, he focused on lighting the cigarette between his teeth.

The driver sped down the street. Kat jolted from the bumps in the road. She held on to the door for balance and stared out the window, contemplating how fast they were traveling. Her fingers inched toward the handle.

"Miss Okazaki," the man said, pronouncing the vowels too harshly. Worse than Jerry. He lit his cigarette and took a long puff. "My people noticed you lurking around the Lines' house the last few days." Spirals of smoke spilled from his lips.

How'd he know her name already? Not that this was her most pressing concern at the moment. "Where are you taking me?" Kat asked. She was still out of breath.

"You don't live in this neighborhood."

"That's irrelevant. Where are you taking me?" The man laughed and reached into his jacket pocket. "Am I under arrest?"

"No—"

"Then I'm free to go."

"No," he said, sharper, the cigarette dangling from his lips.

Kat brushed her hair out of her face. "So, you are detaining me?" She kept her voice steady.

"My name is Agent Terrance Baker." He pulled out a badge like the one the other agent had, holding it long enough for Kat to read it this time.

"You work for ERA?" she asked. He nodded and put his badge away. ERA was the Federal Bureau of Exalters, Relics, and Alchemy. Their task force had multiplied when the war ended, and the magic regulations changed. If ERA was involved, they were investigating illegal magic usage. Was this about Héloïse? "Where are you taking me, Agent Baker?"

"We're going to your residence, Miss Okazaki."

Kat eased back in the seat but kept her eyes on Baker. Was he lying? Perhaps, to prevent her from jumping out of the car. She'd realize eventually if they weren't going to her house. She could jump out of the car later. "Have I done something wrong?" she asked.

"I know you're a private investigator. But for your own safety, you need to stay off this case."

"My safety?" Kat scoffed. Baker let out another drag. "Why is ERA investigating?" He didn't look at her. Was Peter Line still a plausible suspect? Or was ERA involved because of Héloïse? Then why would they be at the Lines' house? Was this about Serena's murder? Had magic killed Serena? Or was it the blackmail? Maybe the briefcase hadn't been full of money, but some relic from a safety deposit box.

The driver continued down the road. They were headed in the correct direction of her house. So far. "You're a smart girl, Miss Okazaki." The cigarette embers glowed as Baker inhaled deeply. "What do you know about this case?" Smoke wafted from his mouth, and Kat scrunched her nose.

"Well, if ERA's here, then illegal magic must be involved," Kat said.

"What else?" he asked. Kat stared at him blankly and shrugged. "Don't be so shy. You've been digging around for a couple days. Surely, you know something." His words got sharper, the smoke from his breath billowing in her face.

Kat turned her head away and grimaced at the rancid smell. She could never escape it when she'd worked with the Claytons. They all smoked obsessively. It hadn't bothered her as much back then. Hell, she'd even liked it. She'd had to like it considering how often she'd been tasting it. But she couldn't stand the smell anymore. It made her sick.

Kat stared out the window. They were closer to her neighborhood. Maybe she would make it to her house. "My client suspected Serena Line's death may have been malicious. And after investigating, I suspect her uncle might've had something to do with it."

Baker chewed on his cigarette, holding the tension in his jaw. "And how have you come to that conclusion?" His voice was firm.

"He had motive and opportunity," Kat said, looking back at him. His gaze pierced through her, making her skin crawl.

"What motive?" He scanned her face, analyzing her. Her cheeks prickled, but she stared back at him.

"The—the will. Peter Line never got his inheritance," she said. Baker narrowed his eyes and almost chuckled. "I— what?"

"You know more. What is it?"

Kat blinked. What did he want her to say? That Serena wasn't Gerald's biological daughter? He blew smoke toward her, and she shrank back. What did he want her to admit? That she was using magic?

"Don't play dumb. You pulled some files from county records. Why?"

"It's part of my job," Kat said. The smoke burned her nostrils. "They're public records. Anyone can access them, and I have a registered investigation license."

"You pulled more than Serena and Peter Line. Why?" he said, raising his voice.

"The Transparency Act protects my rights to know about the people I work with." Straining her voice, Kat spoke firmly despite the fact she was shaking. "I run background checks on anyone that could be involved in a case so I know what I'm getting into."

"Why did you pull the whole family tree?"

"Standard practice. I need to see the whole picture," Kat said. Baker glared at her, dissatisfied. "Why is ERA involved?"

"You're not going to work me," Baker scoffed. "For your safety, you need to drop the case."

Every time he said the word "safety," she got more irritated. "I haven't committed any crimes. I have a right to do my job."

"Not if you're interfering with a federal investigation."

"What do I tell my client?" she asked.

"Tell 'em you hit a dead end."

Kat rolled her eyes. "That's not good enough."

Baker almost looked amused. "Then think of something clever." The driver pulled over to the curb in front of her house. "Get out. Go home. Stay home. Forget about this case." He glared at Kat. "Get out."

Kat's fingers curled on the handle, and the door opened. She needed more answers. She couldn't wait until midnight.

Not when this agent was right there. She scooted to the edge of the seat but turned back to Baker. "You know I have no stake in this, right?"

"What?" he grumbled.

"I was just doing my job. Someone else paid me to investigate."

Baker squinted at her. "I know. And I'm telling you to stop."

"My client wants closure. If I don't give them a good reason for dropping their case, they'll hire someone else to investigate. And you'll have another person digging around where you don't want them." Baker shifted his jaw. "Do you want that?" Kat asked.

His expression hardened. If he weren't so irritated, he'd look impressed. "You don't quit, do you?" he grumbled. "Your client wants closure, huh? What would give them that?"

"The truth."

He stared at her, but she stared right back. "Tell Ms. Keeler the police have an ongoing investigation underway. If she wants justice for Serena, it's best to stay out of it. And if she does, she'll get the life insurance payout she needs when all's said and done." His expression shifted back to stern. "Are we done now?"

Kat nodded. "Thank you." She stepped out of the car.

"Miss Okazaki," he said, and Kat leaned down to look at him. "I don't want to see you anywhere near the Lines' house again, understood?"

Kat exaggerated a sweet smile. "Understood."

"Good. I have eyes everywhere." He yanked the door shut. The car pulled out into the street and drove off, blending into traffic before it eventually disappeared around a corner. Kat went back to the house, which was quiet until she stepped on the creaking floorboards. Emrah wasn't there.

# CHAPTER 12
# THE MIDDLEMAN

Kat raced into her office and took out her journal. She ripped out several blank pages and shredded them into smaller pieces. With too many questions, she needed to work nonlinearly. She frantically scribbled down different theories and arranged them on her desk.

Peter Line was still her prime suspect. However, ERA was a new lead. With Héloïse being an Exalter, she had to be brought back into the equation. Kat paced around her desk, scooting her papers around. Her heart pounded in her chest, still racing with adrenaline from the car ride.

She ripped out another piece of paper and wrote down "blackmail." The pencil tip snapped under her hand. She threw it to the side and snatched a pen. The bank withdrawal could have been money. But it also could have been a relic. Kat's heavy breaths scattered the papers on her desk.

She grabbed the scraps and realigned them into sloppy rows. Her fingers trembled. She couldn't catch her breath, and her heart still pounded. Maybe she needed to sit down.

She fell in her chair, her legs on fire. Leaning back, she took a deep breath, but it hurt to inhale. A sharp pain stabbed her in her ribs, and she cried out. Her pulse pounded behind her eyes. The water stains on the ceiling danced around, racing in lines like the lights of a passing train.

Kat tilted her head toward the window, but the sunlight blinded her. Her ears were ringing. There wasn't enough oxygen. She inhaled faster, drying out her throat. Her fingers tingled. Her nerves prickled up her arms and down her spine. She took a deeper breath and held her stomach, her arms numb. Tears fell from her face.

Since when had she been crying? Nothing had happened. She wiped her face. Her skin itched from her shirt, the silk fabric now like sandpaper. She unbuttoned the collar, breathing deeper. Like a tie constricting around her throat, something blocked her airway. Her vision blurred as the pain in her ribs spread to her chest, stabbing her under the bra.

Kat reached back, trying to unhook her bra, but tilting her head sent shooting stars across her vision. She jolted forward. Her knees hit the ground, and her chair slid away. She melted onto the carpet, hyperventilating. Her fingers slipped under the wire and pulled the tension from her ribcage. Tears streamed down her face. The stabbing continued. She was having a heart attack.

Kat curled up against her desk, the shirt scraping against her skin. She whimpered. The shirt needed to come off. It scratched her. It was contaminated. The putrid scent of cigarettes wafted around her. It reeked of smoke. Her fingers fumbled with the buttons, spasming violently. She couldn't feel her fingers. She couldn't see through the tears. She wasn't supposed to cry. Not in her office. Nothing was wrong. They couldn't see her cry.

She gripped the edge of her desk and hauled herself to her feet. They couldn't find her. She sprinted out of her office. Her shoulder collided into the doorframe, but her feet kept going. Up the stairs. Into her room. To her bathroom.

She yanked her shirt over her head, hair flying into her

face. Out of her pants. Out of her undergarments. Into the shower.

She spun the knob. Water burst from the faucet and splattered down her back. Kat spun the metal knob all the way. She had a knob. Her shower had a knob. Had she locked the door?

Water dripped off her body as she bolted to the door. Her finger pressed over the already locked handle. Locked. It was locked. Nobody was coming in. Her wet feet skidded over the slippery tiles, and she hobbled back into the shower. The water scalded her. She yelled, her arm whipping into the shelf and knocking over her soaps. The bottles fell and clattered in the tub. Her fingers latched around the shower knob but didn't turn it. She held still. The boiling temperature was sanitizing.

She gripped the knob, staring at it in her hand. The shower had knobs. She was home. Nobody was taking her. Nothing was wrong. She was home. Hot tears fell from her face and down the drain with the rest of the water. She took a deep breath, and the steam soothed her throat.

Kat picked up her bottles and soaps. Her sweet-pea scented soap. Her soap. She had bought it from the store. It was gentle on her skin. She had picked out the scent because it calmed her. It was hers. She lathered it all over her arms and her neck. Her heart rate slowed.

Kat rinsed off. Her vibrating skin glowed tomato red in the foggy mirror. But she was clean. No smell of smoke on her. The man's grip washed off and down the drain.

Kat took a slow, steady breath, savoring the sweetness of the steamy air. She couldn't feel her heart anymore when she grabbed her watch off the floor. If they were dropping Emrah off too, he would be downstairs by now.

She quickly got dressed in fresh clothes and dried as much water from her hair as she could with a towel. The downstairs was empty. Were they taking Emrah to his home? Or was he in trouble? Unless they hadn't noticed him somehow? Did ERA only know about her? But how *did* they know about her? They'd already been outside her house before she started the investigation. At that point, she had only ordered the background checks.

The background checks.

Agent Baker knew that Kat had run background checks on Serena's family at county records. Emrah used Kat's license whenever he submitted orders for background checks. ERA must've flagged anyone requesting those files. They would've known her name before she'd even shown up to the Lines'. They would've gotten her address from her PI license and sent someone to watch her house. Maybe they hadn't noticed Emrah.

Kat went back to her office. She reorganized her scraps of paper and continued brainstorming. It wasn't yet dark out. She couldn't worry about Emrah until she had proof he was in danger. She had to assume he hadn't gotten caught and was finishing the surveillance. In the meantime, she brainstormed.

She pushed her list of suspects off to the side while she focused on ERA's involvement. ERA oversaw Exalters, Relics, and Alchemy. Those were the three branches of magic. If Kat could pinpoint the class of magic, it would narrow down her search.

There were only four types of Exalters. Héloïse was the only registered Exalter in Serena's family. And based on Baker's reaction, they likely weren't investigating her. Gerald didn't have service records. Peter would've been in his thirties when the draft started, so he might've been exempt. Alvin was the only living member that had served, but he was in the wrong part of France at the time of the Munich Incident. The only other military personnel were Serena's two coworkers, who hadn't been stationed in the fallout regions either. Unless ERA was after Héloïse, it likely wasn't an Exalter.

Relics were harder to come by since they needed to be

forged with lava from the Pacific Ocean volcanoes. Because of the complications, new relics weren't created often. The ones around were old, usually family heirlooms. Like Kat's compact. Sometimes, people didn't realize what they were, and they ended up in estate sales or pawn shops. If a relic was involved in the case, it could be what Gerald had taken out of a safety deposit box. If it was a family heirloom, Peter could be demanding it from him. Or if word had gotten around about Gerald's relic, anyone could be hunting for it.

The only other option was Alchemy. While relics needed to be forged close to the volcanoes they were sourced from, Alchemy had a wider window of opportunity. Volcanic ash could be collected, transported to other regions, and then used to create potions. The West Coast had natural access to ash from the volcanoes in the region. Smugglers often transported shipments across the country to the East Coast where demand was high. After the war, the government had cracked down on magic regulations, but the old bootleggers had just switched from smuggling booze to ash.

The front door exploded open. "Kat!" Emrah shouted from the lobby.

"Emrah!" she called out. The front door slammed, and the floorboards crackled as he sprinted through the lobby. Kat rushed from her desk, but Emrah flew through her doorway. "You're back!"

He leaned against the doorframe, hyperventilating. "Yeah, yeah," he panted, his face beet red and glistening. "You, what happened?"

"Did you run all the way here—"

"Are you okay?" He gripped the edge of the doorframe and leaned forward.

"I'm fine! I'm fine." Emrah nodded, then groaned as he took a deeper breath. "Jeez, why don't you sit down?" Kat grabbed his arm and planted him in the chair across from her desk.

Emrah leaned on his legs and kept breathing hard. "What happened?"

"They knew who I was. I didn't even make it to the front door before they brought me back here."

"Who's they?" he asked. "Mob? FBI?"

"ERA."

Emrah scrunched his face. "Magic cops?" he wheezed. Kat nodded. He leaned back in the chair and pushed his glasses up his face. "They for Héloïse?"

"I don't think so," Kat said. "Did you run to find me, or were you chased?"

"They didn't notice me," he said. "After they took you, an hour or two later, some lady went over to one of the agents."

"Lady? Was it Lottie?"

Emrah shook his head. "No, she'd black hair."

Kat glanced over her list of suspects. "What did she look like? Was she Caucasian?"

"Uh, maybe? I don't know?" he said. "Didn't want to stare too hard. She looked tan."

"What was she wearing?"

Emrah shook his head, looking down. "Can't remember. Brown? She was wearing something dark brown."

"Dress? Pants?"

"Pants," he said. "Definitely pants and a light jacket. A knit jacket."

"Cardigan?"

He flicked his eyes at Kat. "I don't know what it's called," he said, and Kat huffed. "She went over to one of the agents on the bench. She was talking to him, and he shooed her away. Then she left. Some messenger. Maybe another agent of theirs."

"And that's it? That's all—"

"No, somebody else showed up later," he said. "Some guy, and he actually went inside the Lines' house. He definitely wasn't an agent."

"How do you know?"

"He was too grungy. I could tell from across the street. Hair was longer and messy. He had a beard, and he didn't seem all there. Shuffling gait, looking over his shoulder."

Kat sat on top of her desk and faced Emrah. "Do you think he's who they were waiting for?"

"Pretty sure. He left after a few minutes with that briefcase Gerald took to the bank."

Kat leaned forward. "Did you see where he went?"

Emrah sat upright in the chair. He had mostly caught his breath, but his face still had some glow to it. "Not only that, I followed him."

Kat's eyes widened. "The feds didn't notice you?"

"Well, they didn't give me a ride home. And I would've appreciated it. I had to take a bus back. Then ran the rest of the way."

"Where did he go?"

"Went down to some office on 18th. It looked closed. He went in, dropped off the briefcase, and left. But the feds that were following him, they stuck around the building. Lit some smokes and stayed back."

"They stopped following the guy?" Kat asked. They were more interested in where the briefcase was taken than who had taken it. Emrah had just found the delivery man.

"Yeah, I got the address," Emrah said. "But I kept following the courier. He went to a rundown apartment building and up to the third floor, but I didn't catch which unit." Emrah pulled out a folded slip of paper from his pocket and passed it to Kat. "I waited two hours in the diner across the street. But he didn't come back down."

Kat unfolded the paper. It had the addresses for the office and the apartment. "This is good—you did really good."

"Would've stayed longer, but I figured I should see if you were alive."

"Glad to know you have my back."

"Hard to have a job if you're in jail," he said. "What happened in the car? They waterboard you?"

"What?"

He gestured at Kat's hair. "Your hair's wet."

She blinked at him. "I took a shower," she whispered. Emrah scrunched his face at her. "They were smoking in the car. It was . . . They told me to drop the case. They don't want us interfering with their work."

Emrah nodded and leaned back. "What do we tell our client?"

Kat leaned back on her desk and glanced at the scraps of paper she'd spread around. "We promised her four days of investigation. We still have tomorrow."

Emrah crossed his arms. "We keep investigating? That's not going to get us arrested?"

"Well, they said they didn't want to see *me* near the *house* again." Kat glanced up at Emrah, who raised an eyebrow. "They didn't say anything about *you* going by the house. Besides, I've got two new addresses to check out." She waved the slip of paper between her fingers.

"I'll give you that I haven't been caught yet. I can continue on your behalf. But they know what you look like, and they won't appreciate you bending their words."

"I'll just have to be sneakier."

"Kat, how do I say this delicately?" Emrah muttered, rubbing his face. "You're not exactly nondescript. You stand out in this city."

She pressed her lips together. "I'm aware," she said. He narrowed his eyes. "Look, if you want off this case—"

"I didn't say that."

"Well, what do you want?" Kat asked.

"I don't want you getting arrested." Emrah grabbed onto the chair's armrests. "We can continue the investigation, but if you go to jail, I'm a bit in a bind with getting my paycheck."

Kat glanced at her notes. Finding out why ERA was

involved would give them their next lead. "What kind of office was it? Where the courier dropped off the briefcase."

Emrah shrugged. "It didn't have any signs. Looked empty. Maybe a front for a fake business."

"I want to know what was in that briefcase," Kat said. She grabbed her pen.

"Likely illegal stuff. Money, relics, incriminating documents."

Kat added "incriminating documents" to the pile. "If he dropped it off, they're waiting to see who picks it up. The person that picks it up is who they're after." Kat stared at the list of names.

"You think whoever picks up that briefcase is the one who killed Serena?"

The compact had said she'd been killed for coercion or manipulation. Likely blackmail. "It must be. What else could it be?"

Emrah rolled his head back on the wall and thought. "I got nothing."

Kat looked at the clock. The workday was wrapping up soon. "You did good today. I'll let you go home early."

He raised an eyebrow. "Really?"

"Yeah, *you* didn't get noticed. I call that doing good. We can investigate those addresses tomorrow."

"We?" Emrah sat up in the chair. "You're going out there too?"

"I can't stay at the office on our last day," Kat said. "If we can figure out everything tomorrow, we'll wrap it up in time for Héloïse." Emrah stared at Kat with a glint in his eyes. "Have a little faith in me."

"Oh, I have faith in you, but I have no faith in the agents."

Kat scanned over the papers. "I need to help Héloïse."

"I understand that." Emrah took a breath. "You have the most integrity of any person I've worked for." He leaned on the desk across from her. "I'd do anything you asked of me. Let me take care of this for you."

She looked at him. His glasses magnified his stare. "If this is some speech to get a raise—"

"Kat," he whispered. The vivid blue in his eyes pierced into hers.

She turned away and stared at the calendar. She had one more day. Héloïse would come by on Tuesday and . . . Tomorrow was Monday. "Shit," she muttered.

"What?"

"Jerry's coming tomorrow," Kat mumbled, rubbing her temples.

"You need to get the candidates from him." Emrah sounded too pleased with himself.

"You just wanted to get out of Jerry duty, isn't it?"

Emrah shook his head. "That's not what this is about."

"Once he leaves, I can help you finish surveillance."

"I'm serious," Emrah said. "Let me take care of this for you."

Kat wasn't going to convince him. It was better to seek forgiveness than ask permission. "Fine," she mumbled. "I'll work on the paperwork after Jerry comes by. Just be thorough while you're out there."

Emrah nodded but looked at her skeptically. "You . . . really?"

"Yeah." She looked at the two addresses again. "You can't be in two places at once. Do surveillance on the office building. It's more important."

"The whole day?" he asked.

"Yeah. If the feds aren't wasting their time with the courier, then it's not worth our time."

He nodded. "You're sure?"

"Of course," she said. "Get out of here. Enjoy your night."

Emrah left, and Kat threw together a sad hodgepodge

dinner. She looked over a map of where the courier's apartment building was. She'd have to switch buses to get there. If Jerry came earlier, she could sneak out and find something useful. Emrah said the courier lived on the third floor. She'd have to start by figuring out which unit and then go from there.

Kat paced around her bedroom, waiting for midnight. She'd brought the two photographs upstairs with her and held them side by side. Serena had to be Edmund's daughter. Did that connect to the case at all, or was it just some dark secret the family happened to carry? If Peter Line was still a suspect, would he know? Supposedly, he would be back in New York tomorrow. A quick phone call could verify if that was the case. But if it wasn't Peter, there weren't any other prominent suspects. ERA would be their only lead.

She set the photographs on her vanity. There were too many loose strings and not enough hard evidence. She sat on the edge of her bed and picked up the compact, tapping her nails against the bronze metal. Héloïse was coming on Tuesday. She had two questions left. Tonight and Monday night. And that was it. Unless she continued the investigation afterward.

Kat lay back on her bed, her hair sprawled out against the sheets. She held the compact to her chest, and that dull ache crept back into her. Kat would give anything to have what Héloïse had lost.

She hadn't realized how much it still hurt until she'd taken this case. How much it hurt pretending that the only reason she wasn't married was because she was too focused on work. How much it hurt to have to focus on work so intensely to stop her mind from dwelling on the pain she buried. The pain was easy to hide. Until Héloïse had walked through her door.

Solving the case wouldn't bring Serena back. It wouldn't give Héloïse a happy marriage. But Kat could at least offer closure. And in times of tragedy, that was the most anyone could ask for. Oftentimes it was more than what most people got. At least Héloïse would get closure. Kat would make sure of it.

She knew her question.

When midnight came, the compact radiated white light. Kat held it in her hands. "Will the ERA agents working on this case give Héloïse Keeler closure?"

The light remained partially white, but purple emerged at the edges. Morning glory. Kat closed her eyes and sighed. The infamous morning glories. They always came when she was let down. They had appeared when she'd asked if her family would be reunited. If they would get to go back to San Francisco. When she'd asked if she'd had a real career with the Claytons. The flowers had also appeared the day she met Emrah, and it turned out he'd been lying to her then.

Morning glories meant preparing for disappointment. She couldn't give up on Héloïse.

# CHAPTER 13

# THE VISITOR

Kat finished up her breakfast while Emrah washed the dishes. Her lazy dinner hadn't held her down, so she was hungrier than usual. Emrah had put on nice clothes in neutral colors. Nothing that would draw unnecessary attention to him. If the agents were waiting outside the office building, they'd be on alert for anyone in the area. The last thing Kat needed was the feds assuming Emrah was their target.

"You sure you'll be fine here?" Emrah asked. He dried off his hands and rolled down his sleeves.

"Yeah." Kat took another bite of her okayu. She had the paperwork for case summaries in front of her. "I've got plenty of work to finish while I wait for Jerry."

"What time do you want me back?" Emrah asked.

"I'd say end of day." As long as he was gone while she investigated the courier, it didn't matter. "Don't get caught."

"It's not in my nature." He left, and Kat finished her breakfast while he headed down the street.

After setting her bowl in the sink, she raced to her upstairs bathroom, pulled out her makeup and hair products, and got to work.

It took a few attempts to get her hair in place. It was too straight and resisted being curled. But the pins secured it how she needed. If she weren't trying to be subtle, she would've left rollers in her hair overnight. But Emrah might've noticed her departure from routine. She didn't need him to lecture her again.

She added more makeup than usual. Foundation and rouge that made her glow. Dewy eyes, lashes coated in mascara, and sophisticated red lipstick like the department-store girls. Maybe Emrah wouldn't have noticed Kat's hair curled, but he would've questioned her makeup. His vision wasn't that bad.

She changed out of her slacks and put on a navy skirt. The fabric was rich in color and flowed with her movements. Her blouse matched the color of the skirt perfectly. When she tucked her shirt in, the silhouette looked like a dress. She put on a faux pearl necklace with a matching set of pearl earrings.

All she needed were shoes. She dug around the closet looking for a pair that matched, eventually grabbing her navy heels to take with her.

The closet door moved by itself behind her, bouncing against the doorframe even though she hadn't touched it. It only did that when the front door opened.

She glanced at her watch. 8:57. Jerry never came in the morning. Had Emrah forgotten something? If he was back, then Kat was screwed. She had no way to convince him she'd decided to play dress up because she was bored.

Kat tip-toed out of her room and listened over the banister. The downstairs floorboards were squeaking. Emrah wouldn't be making noise. Was it Jerry? Or a different client?

Kat held her heels in her hands as she crept down the stairs and peered down the hall. Maiki stood in the doorway. Crap. Maiki. They were supposed to hang out.

Kat walked down the hallway, and the floorboards

creaked. Maiki turned around and saw her. "Whoa," Maiki said with a smile.

"Hi," Kat said. She held her heels behind her back. "You're here early?"

Maiki raised an eyebrow at her. "You told me to come by in the morning? Is this not morning?"

Kat laughed. "Oh, yeah, that's right. Yeah, we're . . ."

Maiki deflated. "You forgot, didn't you?"

"No! No, I didn't forget."

"Why are you all dolled up?" Maiki said. "Are you going somewhere?" Kat opened her mouth, but the words didn't come through. "Are you okay?"

"Look, you caught me in a box. I'm . . . trying to . . ." Maiki shifted back. "This has been a really busy week."

Maiki's shoulders sank, and she nodded. "I understand," she said. "You have a job to do."

"No, it's not like that," Kat said. "This week *has* been really busy. It's normally not like this."

"You're always busy though," Maiki whispered. Dejection lingered in her eyes.

"I swear, I'm trying—"

"It's okay." Maiki smiled. A pained and defeated smile. It hurt more than if she had just yelled at Kat. "I don't want to fight now. Just thought it would be different than before. Ever since we got here, you've always been working."

"If you came a different week, it wouldn't be like this," Kat said.

Maiki laughed. "When we were at the hospital, you always stayed late because you wanted the extra money."

"But that *was* when we needed the money—"

"Yeah, but then at the flower shop, it was Mother's Day. And then graduation season. Then wedding season. Always busy."

Kat huffed at her, gripping her heels in her hand. "That job was demanding in the warm seasons."

"But even at the Claytons', you always stayed there late," Maiki said. "You worked weekends and were never home for family dinner."

Kat pressed her lips together. Not all of the late nights at the Claytons' were because of work. However, telling her family she had to catch up on paperwork was much easier than explaining what she actually did on all those late nights. "Please don't go," Kat said. "I miss you. I miss you a lot, and I want to see you while I can."

"Are you sure?" Maiki's eyes watered, but she rolled her eyes and laughed to herself. "I get that your job is important to you, and I don't want—"

"Someone's been murdered."

Maiki froze and stared wide-eyed. "What?"

Kat took Maiki's hand and led her to sit down in the kitchen. "If I tell you, please keep it to yourself, okay?" Maiki nodded and wiped her eyes. "I'm serious—you can't know about this."

"I won't. I promise," Maiki whispered.

"My client's wife died last week," Kat said. "The police declared it an accident, but she was murdered, and there's been a coverup."

"Are you serious?" Maiki said. "You're actually working a murder case?"

"Yes, and if we don't keep digging, the killer's going to get away. Emrah's chasing a lead, but I need to look into something too."

Maiki slid back in the chair. "What do you need to find out?"

"There's some . . . delivery that happened. Blackmail or maybe a payment. Emrah is on the drop site, but I need to find the guy that took the payment."

"This is . . . this is your job? This sounds like you should go to the police."

"What, the police that declared it was an accident?" Kat

leaned back against the counter and fidgeted with her shoes, clicking the heels together in her hands. "I don't know if I'll get anything out of it. But I have to try. It's more than anyone else has done for my client."

"So . . ." Maiki gestured at Kat's outfit. "This getup is part of your investigation?"

Kat stared at her skirt and laughed. "Yeah, I had this plan . . . Maybe a dumb plan." Kat stared at the clock. 9:02. The minutes were slipping away, and she couldn't risk missing Jerry. As much as she wanted to help Héloïse, the bills still needed to be paid. "But it won't work."

"We can meet up later," Maiki said. "I'm sorry I held you up. I didn't know."

Kat shook her head. "It's not that. I had this other client . . . I'm supposed to wait for him. I have no idea when he's showing up though."

"Do you have a meeting with him?" Maiki asked.

"He's dropping off some candidates, and I need their application files so I can run background checks on them."

"Is that all?" Maiki asked.

"Yeah, I need the folder he has, but I have no idea when he's coming." Maybe if Jerry came at noon, she could leave right after and make it to the courier's address. But what if the courier wasn't home by then? What good would that do her? She didn't even know what he looked like, just Emrah's description of longer hair and a beard. But that description could fit anyone. And if the courier had cut his hair and shaved after the drop-off, she'd be screwed.

"Kat?"

"Huh? What?" She looked back at Maiki.

"Is it something your assistant can do for you?"

"Well, yeah," Kat said. "I usually have Emrah do it, but I needed him out."

Maiki fixed her hair back. "So, it doesn't have to be you?

Could it be me?" Kat stared at her, and Maiki shrugged. "What if . . . I got the folder for you?" she asked.

"Are . . ." Kat *could* be in two places at once. "Do you really mean that?" she asked.

"Yeah, you seem pretty stressed. If I stay here, then you can go look for footprints and find the guy." Maiki smiled. Kat grabbed her hand and yanked her into a hug. Maiki burst out laughing. "Easy, easy."

"Thank you." Kat gave her a tight squeeze. "I promise I will make this up to you as soon as I can."

"Does this mean you're coming to San Francisco?"

"Don't push it."

"Fine, fine," Maiki said, and she let go. "I'm just getting this folder, right?"

"Yeah, Jerry Morris. He's a bit of a chatter and . . . opinionated at times. But tell him you're a temp assistant."

Maiki shrugged. "If that's all it is, then I can do it."

"Thank you so much." Kat slipped her heels on.

Maiki tilted her head at the heels. "Are you trying to seduce the guy?"

"Ew." Kat laughed.

"I've never seen you this fancy. Do you even know how to walk in those shoes?" Kat spun around, heels clicking on the floorboards. "I guess so," Maiki said.

"There's tea in the cupboards, so help yourself. I'll see you later today."

Kat grabbed one of her larger bags and double-checked that she'd packed everything she needed. Especially her bottle of perfume. Then she headed out.

# CHAPTER 14

# THE COURIER

It was an overcast Monday, and the bus was crowded. Kat changed buses a few times and eventually made it to the other side of town where the address was. It wasn't anything like the Lines' neighborhood. The buildings were older and run-down, grungy bricks covered in moss. And the people in the streets weren't dressed as formally, making Kat stand out more than she wanted.

Emrah had said the guy had gone to the third floor. Knocking on all the doors was her best bet. Even if the courier hadn't changed his appearance, a man with longer hair and a beard wasn't exactly a unique description. There was also a chance he wouldn't answer the door. Or that he would have someone else answer the door. But this was the best she could do.

The lobby of the building smelled old and musty. Even with a dark carpet, stains and dirt were obviously encrusted in the fibers. Paint was peeling off the walls, and the corners had gouges in them. It reminded her of the first apartment she'd lived in when they'd moved to Philly.

The building had no elevator, and the stairwell was cramped and dingy. Grime and dust coated the windows, blocking out the sunlight. A distinct smell of fungus lingered inside.

The third floor only had six units. Kat retrieved the yellow perfume bottle from her bag, then set the bag on the floor behind her. It was large and cuboid, containing a change of clothes and her notebook. Hopefully the scent of the grungy carpet wouldn't transfer to it.

Kat fixed her hair to make sure it was still secure and posed the bottle in her hand before she knocked on the first apartment door. Someone scuffled inside, and the door opened a moment later. A middle-aged Caucasian woman with bags under her eyes stared at Kat. Her brown dress fit her loosely, and frizzy strands of hair framed her face. From what Kat could see, the apartment was otherwise empty. "Can I help you?" the woman asked in a raspy, city accent.

Kat smiled brightly. "Hi, my name is Kathryn, and I'm from Gimbels Department Store," she said in a bubbly voice and a city accent. "We have a new line of luxury perfume in stock, and you can be the first to try it!"

Kat held up the bottle as the woman's face twisted in confusion. "Not today," the woman said.

"It could be a lovely surprise for your husband."

The woman gave an unamused smile. "I don't have a husband. And I'm not interested." She shut the door and locked it.

One down, five to go.

Kat knocked on the next door, but nobody answered. Unit two could potentially be the courier, if he was out somewhere. Kat went to unit three and knocked. A moment passed before an elderly Black gentleman with grey hair opened the door. "What's this about?"

"Hi, my name is Kathryn and—"

"I don't know any Kathryn," the man grumbled. His glasses slid down his nose, and he glared at her.

"I'm with Gimbels Department Store," Kat said.

A younger Black man came to the door. "Dad, she's a saleswoman," he said. Kat smiled. Probably not them either, since she was looking for a Caucasian guy. "Sorry, we're not interested," the son said. "Have a good day." He pulled the older gentleman back into the apartment and shut the door. Likely not units one or three.

Kat knocked on unit four. A Hispanic woman around her age peeked through the door. Her black hair was pulled back in a braid. She wore a simple blue dress with an apron tied to her waist. The colors made her look radiant. She glared at Kat, but Kat pretended she didn't notice. "Hi, my name is Kathryn, and I'm—"

"I already heard your spiel," the woman said with a hint of a Southern accent. "You know, people around here aren't interested in luxury perfume. Why is your company sending you out here?" The sweetness of her voice mellowed out the harshness of her tone.

Kat maintained a smile. "We want to reach new customers at the convenience of their homes."

The woman crossed her arms. She wasn't wearing a wedding ring. Probably not this unit either. But Kat was running out of doors. "Do you have some business cards?" the woman asked.

"You know, unfortunately, I don't at the moment. However, I could come back another time and give you one."

"You don't need to. I'm not interested." She shut the door. Kat nodded to herself and went to the next unit.

She knocked on the door, and a Caucasian man opened it. He had longer greasy hair and an overgrown beard. Was this the courier? He looked about Emrah's height, maybe shorter. His heavy, dark eyes stared at Kat. Something twisted in her stomach looking at his eyes. "What do you want?" His voice was gruff and cold.

A faint buzzing sound came from inside the apartment. Was that some electric shaver? "Hi," Kat said. She stared at his eyes, then cleared her throat. "My name is Kathryn, and I'm from Gimbels Department Store. Perhaps you'd be interested in our new perfume."

The man slammed the door, and Kat stood in the hall. That had to be him, right? Kat walked across the hall and knocked on the last unit to check anyway. But no one answered. Unit five had to be the courier.

Kat put the perfume back in her bag and left the building. The fresh air smelled sweet. She crossed the street and went to the cafe.

The place was still clattering from the morning rush, several waitresses hopping around to different tables with platters of food. The scents of bacon grease and pungent coffee filled the air. A counter wrapped around the kitchen area, and a few individuals were sitting there by themselves. A small empty table sat right by the front windows. It had a clear view of the apartment building's entrance. Kat could watch for the courier in case he left the building.

She slipped into the women's bathroom and changed in one of the stalls. Her toes wiggled free as she slipped off her heels. She put on capri pants and a grey blouse. Neutral colors. She wiped off her red lipstick and the bright rouge on her cheeks. She couldn't get all the makeup off, but she got enough that she looked different.

Taking her hair down, she scrunched it until the curls lost their shape. She could be a different Asian woman walking around, not the same department-store girl from the morning.

Kat packed up her bag and left the bathroom. She picked up one of the morning papers at the front and took a seat at the table by the window. After tucking her notebook under the newspaper, she wrote down descriptions of the different tenants on the third floor. The courier was probably the man from unit five, but extra information was never a bad thing.

Something was off about the man from unit five. Something hadn't felt right when she'd seen him. Something about him had felt . . . strange? No, familiar? She closed her eyes and pictured his face again. Dark brown hair, a few grey strands. Broader shoulders but average height. His eyebrows were heavy and unkempt, but most men never defined their brow shape. Who did he look like? Maybe her intuition knew he was a bad guy.

Kat ordered a small omelet and coffee. Well, she thought she ordered coffee, but it turned out the waitress gave her motor oil. At least the omelet was digestible. Nothing like Emrah's eggs, but decent enough. She dumped packets of sugar into the coffee and a heap of creamer. But she had to keep ordering refills so she would have a reason to stay at her table.

The morning passed by, and it was almost noon. No sign of the courier leaving the building. Perhaps he wouldn't leave at all. The buzzing she'd heard . . . If it was an electric razor, then maybe he was changing his appearance already. Despite the crowded streets, only a few people came out of the apartment building, and none of them were him. Even if he had shaved his whole face and head, she saw no one else that fit his build.

The waitress came by to take Kat's plate. "More coffee, miss?" she asked.

"Um, sure," Kat said, glancing at her watch. "Do you happen to have a phone I could use?"

The waitress gestured behind her. "Yeah, it's down by the bathrooms—but the other side."

"Thank you." Kat grabbed her purse and took out her journal while she headed over. She found the number for Peter Line's office written in her notes. If he'd come back, he would be at work by now.

The operator connected her through, and a secretary answered. "Hi, is this Peter Line's office?"

"Yes, it is. Would you like me to transfer you?"

"I—yes, thank you," Kat said. He was in?

"One moment." The call transferred over and started ringing. Peter was already back in New York?

"Hello, this is Line here," a male voice answered. Was it actually him? "Hello?"

"Hi," Kat croaked. He actually answered. "My name is Miss Okazaki. I'm a private investigator, and I was wondering if I could ask you a couple questions."

He cleared his throat. "Alright, I can spare a few minutes. What's this about?"

"Um, your brother, Gerald Line." Kat brushed her hair away from her ear and adjusted the phone. "When was the last time you saw him?"

"Oh, it's been a while," he sighed. His voice was steady and relaxed. "It's been a few years since he and his family visited."

"He—he visited you?" Kat asked. "You're still in touch?"

"Yes, he's my brother." Peter's voice was lighthearted. "What's this about?"

Kat started taking notes in her journal. "I have records that show you tried to contest your parents' will. Is that correct?"

"Yeah," he said, trailing off.

"Would you be able to tell me about what happened?"

He sighed into the receiver. "Look, my folks weren't the most progressive lot. They didn't approve of my wife being African American. Or my career ambitions. I contested the will but didn't get a dime. My brother felt bad because he didn't agree with how they divided it all. So after the lawyers gave him everything, he gave me more than my fair share. It was his idea, and I am very grateful for what he did."

Kat's pen halted in the notebook. Either he was lying, or her main suspect had just lost all motive. "He divided the estate himself?"

"He kept the business, a few of their big properties, and . . . he must've kept some of their accounts, but I ended up with a lot of the money and the rest of the properties. More than I would've gotten had they never disowned me."

Kat shifted her jaw to the side. Those types of financial records wouldn't be as public, so she didn't have an easy way to prove he was telling her the truth. "Thank you so much. One more question if you have time?" It was quiet on the other end. "Um, you were out of office for a while. Your secretary said it was out of character?"

Peter sighed on the other end. "Yes, I don't usually take time off, but it was my thirtieth anniversary."

"Oh," Kat whispered. Thirty years ago would've been 1920, which would've made them sophomores in high school. Not necessarily marriage, but possibly a dating anniversary? "I see. And you hadn't done that before?"

"I spent my whole life working to help others," he said. "I've done a lot of good, I'd like to think. But the years go by faster than you realize." His voice was gentle but assured. A nagging feeling pulled in her chest. "If you don't make time for your family, you go your whole life without them. And I'm not getting any younger. So I took the month off to be with my wife." He let out a gentle laugh. "I apologize if that put a damper on your job."

Kat shook her head before remembering he couldn't see her. "No, no, it's okay." Her voice cracked against her will. "That's really sweet." She cleared her throat and closed her journal. "That's all, thank you." She hung up before he could say anything else.

She stared at the black and white tiles on the floor. Heat prickled her cheeks. There was no reason to be upset just because one suspect hadn't panned out. She trudged back to her table and sipped her coffee. The abhorrent taste snapped her out of her haze, and she quickly dumped cream and sugar in it.

Business in the restaurant died down for a while, but more customers flooded in around lunchtime. No one paid attention to Kat besides the waitress occasionally refilling her coffee. Kat focused on the building. Hopefully the courier hadn't decided to slip past her during the few minutes she'd been on the phone. Perhaps he wouldn't be going anywhere today, and Kat was waiting for nothing. If that ended up being the case, at least she hadn't abandoned Jerry for a busted surveillance. Maiki had been a lifesaver today. Kat needed to make it up to her as soon as the case was over. In the few days she had before Maiki left again. Time was running out, and anxiety swelled in her throat.

"Another refill?" the waitress asked.

Kat smiled at her. "Yes, please." She watched in horror as the woman poured coffee too close to the top of the mug. There was no room for extra cream. "Thanks," she said, trying to hide her pain.

The waitress left, and Kat stared at her cup. How much more could she drink before she'd need her stomach pumped? She took a large gulp, forcing the bitterness down. At least she had room to fix it now. She dumped another couple sugar packets in and finished off the last of the creamer at the table. She took another sip. Still rancid, but better. Maybe she could order something for lunch to absorb the toxicity of the coffee.

Footsteps approached from behind her, and she guarded her coffee to prevent another refill. "Well, what do we have here?" Kat closed her eyes hearing the Slavic accent.

She tilted her head up at Emrah and tried to smile. He stared at her, baffled. "Hi," she muttered.

Emrah took a seat across from her and rested his arms on

the table. "You have a funny way of staying at the office," he said.

"You have a funny way of watching the drop site."

He stared at her but then glanced down, his expression shifting from irritated to confused. "You drinking chocolate milk in a mug?"

"What?" Kat stared at her cup. "No, that's coffee."

"Why's it pale?" he asked in disgust. "What'd you do?"

"I didn't do shit," Kat whispered.

Emrah gestured to the mountain of emptied creamer containers on the side of the table. "Clearly."

"Alright, wise guy." She slid the mug closer to him. "Have a go at it."

He picked it up and smelled it but winced. He took a sip, and his eyes bulged out. "Oh, God, you definitely did something."

Kat took the mug from him. "Yeah, it's called sparing my stomach lining."

Emrah grabbed a napkin and wiped inside his mouth. "My teeth have diabetes."

"What are you doing?" Kat asked.

"Saving my enamel," he murmured. The napkin stuck on his tongue.

"No, what are you doing here?" Kat asked.

Emrah crumpled up the napkin and tossed it with the empty creamers. "I could ask you the same thing." He stared at her face. "You didn't look like that this morning."

"What?"

"Mascara?" He leaned closer and squinted at her. "You put on more makeup after I left. What'd you do?"

Apparently he was more observant than she'd anticipated. "Don't worry about it," she said.

"I'm going to worry about it. The whole point of you staying at the office was so I had less to worry about. And what about Jerry?"

"What about Jerry?"

Emrah shifted his jaw. "Look, I don't blame you for ditching him, but it's not like you."

"He's taken care of," Kat said. "I needed to see what the courier was up to."

"You don't know what he looks like, so how exactly were you planning to do surveillance?" Emrah narrowed his eyes and scowled. "What'd you do?"

"What? I didn't do anything!"

"You made a face—that face." He pointed at her. "Oh my God, you know what he looks like?" Emrah hissed and dropped his hands on the table. His whispering became sharper as he glared at her. "Is that what the makeup's for?"

Kat pressed her lips together. Sometimes she hated how good Emrah was at the job. "I was . . . seeing if . . . the residents of the third floor were interested in the new Miss Dior fragrance." Emrah's jaw slacked, and he laughed in disbelief. "No one suspected anything. I'm pretty sure he's in unit five. And he's still there."

Emrah rubbed his face in his hands, then adjusted his glasses. "I can't believe you," he groaned.

"What are you doing here anyway? What happened to the drop site?"

Emrah leaned back in the chair and huffed. "More feds showed up. They started paying attention to me after a while. Granted, they stared down everyone in the area."

"I was afraid that would happen." Kat sighed. "I take it nothing interesting happened while you were there." Emrah stared at the table, shifting his jaw to the side. "Did something happen?"

He sat up, refusing to meet her eyes. "Someone showed up and went into the building. A few minutes later, he came out with the briefcase from yesterday."

Kat's eyes widened. "Did you follow—"

"I lost him." Emrah furrowed his brows.

Kat drummed her fingers against her mug. "Did you see what he looked like?"

"I couldn't see his face. He kept his head down and had some hat that matched his suit. No tie though. And he was wearing boots."

That didn't seem like the regulated appearance of a federal agent. Kat glanced out the window at the apartment building. "You don't think it was the guy from yesterday?"

Emrah shook his head. "No, definitely a different guy."

"Did any of the agents go after him?"

"Don't think so. It was strange. I mean, he took the courier's briefcase, but everyone stayed put."

The agents hadn't followed the courier yesterday. "They're waiting for something else at the site," Kat said. "And you couldn't follow the guy? Did something happen?"

"I tried. I saw where he was headed but went the opposite direction so nobody would think I was with him. But I couldn't catch up to wherever he went. Maybe I should've just followed—"

"It wasn't worth the risk," Kat said. Emrah glanced up at her. "You made the right call."

Emrah eased his shoulders. "Figured the agents would notice if I went back to the drop site. So I came to the next best place to survey. And lo and behold, you beat me to it."

The waitress came back to the table. "Hi, some coffee for your friend?"

Emrah shook his head subtly, but Kat smiled at the waitress. "He'd love some coffee. And you think we can see the lunch menus?"

"Sure thing. I'll bring those right over," the waitress said.

Kat smiled at Emrah. "You sicken me," he said.

"You're welcome."

Emrah rolled his eyes. "I'm assuming you haven't bumped into any of the feds yourself?"

"If I had, I'm pretty sure I wouldn't be sitting here."

"What's the plan?" Emrah asked. "Follow him if he comes out?"

Kat swayed her head from side to side. "He might lead us to whoever he works for. Or if he leaves, we can see if there's anything inside his place."

"If the feds didn't find him worthy of their time, what makes you think he'll be any use to us?"

Kat swirled her mug around and watched the vortex of liquid spiral. "It's the only lead we have at this point. What else do we do?"

Emrah stared at the table and shrugged. "What about Peter Line?"

"I called his office. It's probably a bust," Kat muttered.

"Alright, sir." The waitress came back and set down a mug of bubbling tar for Emrah. "That was freshly brewed, so it's very hot."

"Oh, thanks," he said, his eyes magnified in horror behind his glasses.

"And here are your menus. I'll be back in a jiff."

Emrah lifted the coffee to examine it. "The hell is this?" he pouted. He smelled it and gagged. "They burnt it . . . How'd they burn a liquid?"

"I don't think it's liquid anymore. It's a new state of matter," Kat said as she skimmed over the lunch menu. Emrah grabbed a sugar packet. "I thought your teeth had diabetes."

"I like sugar in my coffee, but you had coffee in your sugar." He stirred it up, took a sip, and shuddered. "This is a disgrace."

"Their breakfast was surprisingly not bad," Kat said.

Emrah held his head as he read the menu. "I'm concerned about all these items. Clam chowder?" His face contorted in horror. "That could kill a man."

"Perhaps, but the grilled cheese seems safe."

Emrah rubbed his temple and groaned. "Yeah, I'll get that

too then," he said. "If something's wrong with it, we'll have the same symptoms." He brushed his hair back. "How long have you been here?"

Kat glanced at her watch. "A few hours. He hasn't left the building yet. He had longer dark hair and was a larger guy?"

Emrah shrugged. "Longer hair, yes. He wasn't exactly tall but had wide shoulders."

"Yeah, I think that was him," Kat said. "Something about him was familiar."

"What do you mean?" Emrah took another sip of his coffee and winced.

"I don't know. I feel like I've seen him before."

"He from the memorial?"

Most of Serena's relatives were blond, and they'd all looked refined there. Posh, stuffy, and overdressed. Nobody with a wildly long beard. "No, I would've remembered that," Kat said. "Something was unsettling about him. Maybe he looked like someone I've seen."

The waitress came back, and they both smiled at her. "Hi, how's that coffee for you?" she asked.

"Oh, it's fantastic," Emrah said.

They both ordered the grilled cheese, and the sandwiches came surprisingly decent. The bread was toasted golden with evenly melted cheese.

"This is . . . good," Emrah said, taking another bite. "Maybe not good, but compared to the sludge?"

Kat nodded along while chewing. She was halfway through her sandwich. "It's enjoyable."

"You notice anything else in the courier's apartment?" Emrah took another bite.

"Not really. He only stuck his head through the crack. I couldn't see inside."

Emrah covered his mouth while he chewed. "No murder board on the walls?"

"Unfortunately, he didn't leave it in line of sight to the

door." Kat glanced out the window. The sidewalks were crowded, the street congested with a few cars that obscured the view of the apartment building.

"They never make it easy for us," Emrah said. "One of these days, maybe we'll get lucky."

"Maybe." Kat took another bite.

"What's the easiest case you've ever had?"

A few more people came into the cafe, and Kat watched them file in. "Employee background checks."

Emrah rolled his eyes. "That doesn't count. I mean this kind of case."

"I—" He was here. He was inside. Kat wrapped her feet around Emrah's legs under the table.

Emrah jolted and stared at her. "Um, Kat?" The courier was in the cafe. He was wearing the same clothes as earlier. It was him. "Kat?"

"Don't move," she whispered, holding her head down near her plate. Her feet gripped Emrah's ankles. "He's here, sweetheart."

Emrah tensed. "Behind me?" he mouthed.

"At the front." The courier picked through the pile of newspapers and lingered by their only exit.

"Will he recognize you?" Emrah asked.

Kat had changed her appearance, but not by much. "Maybe," she said. Emrah stood up in front of her, blocking her from the courier's view. Kat grabbed her wallet and pulled out more than enough cash to cover the whole tab, plus a considerate tip.

Emrah stepped to the side. The courier took a seat at the counter, his back to them. If he was ordering lunch, he would be here for a while.

Kat folded the last of her grilled cheese into her mouth and snatched her purse. Emrah grabbed the other half of his sandwich, and they fled the cafe. Kat's cheeks bulged like a chipmunk's as she scooted down the sidewalk.

Emrah stood next to her. "How classy," he said. Kat covered her mouth with her hand while she chewed vigorously. Emrah took another bite of his sandwich and laughed to himself. "What're the odds that unit five is empty?"

Kat swallowed half her mouthful. Enough to talk. "That's what I was thinking," she muttered. They waited for a car to pass before crossing the street. Two steps into the building and she already missed the smell of fresh air. The musty and dingy fumes were suffocating.

They took the stairs up to the third floor, where Emrah finished the last of his sandwich. "Wait here," he whispered. He crept into the hallway and knocked on the door to unit five. A moment passed. No answer. No sound.

Kat peered into the hallway. Emrah knelt on the floor, fiddling with silver tools in the lock. Kat stood behind him, covering what he was doing. He wiggled deeper into the keyhole and turned the pick. The lock clicked. Emrah stood and cracked the door open. The faint buzzing sound returned.

Emrah whipped backward and gagged. He smacked the side of his head into the doorframe, and the whack of his skull echoed. "Ah, jebem ti," he hissed as he clutched his head and stumbled into the wall.

"Shut up," Kat snarled. She grabbed his arms to stop his flailing. He hissed out in pain and held his breath to keep quiet. A shuffle came from one of the other units. Kat shoved Emrah into the apartment and then followed after him. The buzzing grew louder. She quietly closed the door behind them.

The smell of death hit her like a punch to the gut. Her stomach lurched, and she hunched over, covering her mouth. The bitter coffee mixed with her stomach acid burned the back of her throat. The apartment reeked of rotting food and dead animals. Tears poured down her cheeks, and her mascara smeared into her eyes. Black splotches soaked in her vision. She blinked, but it didn't help. She couldn't see clearly. Like her eyeballs were dissolving.

Trash lined the walls of the apartment. Clusters of empty beer cans and whiskey bottles littered every table surface. Moldy, disintegrating cardboard boxes wilted on the ground, barely containing the pile of unrinsed empty bean cans. Several cans spilled out of the box and gathered on the floor. Gunk was plastered on the floors, and it stuck to the bottoms of their shoes when they tried to step forward. A chicken-pox pattern of mold speckled the walls and climbed onto the ceiling. The buzzing roared in her ears.

It wasn't Kat's mascara that was clouding her vision. Swarms of black clusters floated around the room. The buzzing that deafened her wasn't from anything motorized. The apartment was infested with hordes of flies.

# CHAPTER 15

# THE TENANT

"What the hell?" Kat coughed. Her eyes wouldn't stop watering, and the air agitated her lungs.

Emrah held his mouth as he retched. Kat reached over to grab his shoulder, but her flats stuck to the floor. The sticky substance coating the tiles stole a shoe from her, and Kat's nails dug into Emrah's shoulder as she hobbled back to it.

Emrah gritted his teeth and groaned while he gripped his head. Kat put her shoe back on and swatted at the flies near them. "He's jebena svinja," he muttered. Tears splattered on his glasses lenses. "Who the fuck lives like this?"

"We don't have much time," Kat said. Her stomach gurgled, and her mouth filled with saliva. Oh God. She covered her mouth and shut her eyes as she fought to keep her stomach contents down.

"We're not fucking leaving?" Emrah hissed, his body shaking and his breaths shallow.

Kat held on to Emrah's arm while she collected herself. "He'll be back in maybe half an hour," she mumbled. "An hour if we're lucky."

"An hour?" Emrah coughed out. "We'll suffocate before

then." He swatted at more flies and frantically wiped his hands on his pants.

"Then we better hurry." Kat pulled her shoes off the floor. She walked on her toes to minimize contact with the sticky tiles. Empty glass bottles rolled to the side as she walked through the garbage. Her eyes burned, and her lungs itched. She coughed into her arm to minimize the sound.

Emrah followed her, his arms flailing erratically as he swatted at flies. "What're we looking for?"

"Anything about who he is."

"A svinja," Emrah grumbled.

"I meant who he works for," Kat said, taking another step deeper into the trenches of garbage. "What was he doing at the Lines'? How's he connected?" A couch was buried under a massive pile of clothes. Kat hopped over it and rummaged through. The fabric was greasy and reeked of body odor. She breathed through her mouth to minimize the putrid smell, but it came at the risk of inhaling flies. She swatted them away while she dug through the clothes, which were all larger men's shirts, industrial clothes, and jumpsuits.

A thump came from behind her, and Emrah let out a guttural retching sound.

"Don't kill yourself," Kat said. Emrah muttered something in an unintelligible whine. "What?" Looking back at him, she blinked a few times, but her eyes kept burning. Emrah knelt next to an overflowing box of jars and bottles. His face was bright red, and the veins in his neck bulged. "Are you alright?"

He looked at her with desperate eyes and asked, "You wouldn't happen to have gloves in that bag of yours?"

"No, but I'll carry some after this."

He groaned and huffed, "I'm billing you for a new shirt."

"Deal." Gagging, Emrah rolled his sleeve down to cover his hand. He reached into the garbage and pulled out a soggy letter. "Is that mail?" Kat asked.

Emrah nodded. "Looks like—oh, God." Brown liquid

dripped off the letter and onto him. He flapped his hand around to get the droplets off. "We've a Frank Smith." He threw the letter down, and it made a wet splat against the trash pile. "Name ring a bell?"

Frank Smith? Wow, what an incredibly easy name to run a background check on that totally wouldn't come up with dozens of other people. "No one I can think of," Kat said. "When you're done with that bin, could you check the ones by the window?"

"Window?" Emrah looked ahead. Over what used to be a coffee table, there were a couple small windows. "Oxygen."

"I think it faces the restaurant. We can keep tabs on his status."

"Can also breathe again." Emrah turned his head and coughed into his shoulder.

Kat set the heap of clothes back. Behind her was a pile of rotting corned beef cans. She leapt over it but hit the edge of a few cans. The pile shifted, and roaches scattered.

Kat let out a guttural groan, her skin crawling. She jumped away as the roaches skittered around her feet. Flies tapped her face, and she vigorously shook her head to get them off. The crawling feeling lingered on her legs and arms and neck. Hot tears spilled down her cheeks when she couldn't shake the feeling off. "I'm bathing in bleach when we get home," she whimpered.

Emrah stared at the ceiling, collecting his breath. His cheeks glistened with tears that dribbled off his chin. "If we're sick after this, it's not from the coffee." Emrah trudged over to the grungy window and yanked it open. A breeze of fresh air wafted into the apartment. Kat wanted to go to the window, but she needed to check the rest of the apartment.

The archway led to the kitchen, and she jumped over another rotting pile of cans. She didn't make the mistake of bumping it again. Thank God she'd changed out of her skirt. If only she hadn't worn capris.

In the kitchen, the buzzing droned on in her ears. Dead fly carcasses covered the floor. Garbage overflowed against all corners of the room. The trash piles did a good job disguising how much mold covered the walls. All the cabinets were dingy, and the stove was crusted in a pool of grease. The greasy splatter on the wall near the stove resembled blood, as if someone had been shot in the head. Roaches skittered on the countertops.

Dozens of flies were having a bash over the rotting and burnt pots on the stove. Was the courier still eating all this food out of that pot? The amount of garbage in here had to be from years of disgusting living. How could anyone live like this? Kat wasn't expecting him to be homemaker of the year, but he could've had some sanitation.

She swatted through the flies and ducked her head under the cloud to take a step forward. Something crunched under her shoe. Her jaw trembled as she remembered the white insects covering the barrack floors. How her bare feet had stepped on their sharp carcasses, embedding them in her skin. Kat shook the visual out of her head as saliva pooled in her mouth. She pressed her palm against her lips, but bile fought its way up her throat. It burned her tongue.

Kat grabbed onto the wall. Her nails sank into the plaster, and mold scraped under her nails. She leaned over a garbage pile. Maggots squirmed out of some slab of grey meat that reeked of sour cream. She closed her eyes and parted her lips. Vomit drained out of her mouth and splattered into the abyss of garbage.

Her stomach lurched again, and her body shuddered. Granules of coffee grinds gritted on her teeth. The acid burned her esophagus and sinuses. Tears streamed down her cheeks as she spit up. Nearly black bile pooled in the can.

Her nose dripped down her lips. She tried sniffling, but the putrid odor stung her nostrils. She wiped it with her sleeve and darted out of the kitchen into the room at the end.

The bedroom had less of a rotting food smell and more of a fungal foot stench. Somehow the foot stench was better. There weren't as many flies in the bedroom. Not that Kat normally considered seven flies in a room a small amount.

A single cot lay on the floor. No bed frame. No sheets. The mattress and pillow were stained yellow, like someone had smeared popcorn butter into them. Piles of clothing were stacked in broken laundry baskets, no telling what was clean or dirty. Nothing folded or ironed. Like wrinkled clothes were this guy's biggest concern.

Kat picked up a wool blanket and shook it around. Nothing. She pinched the pillow with two fingers and scooted it to the side. Nothing. She looked at the clothing piles and rummaged through any pockets. Shirt pockets. Pants pockets. Jacket pockets. Nothing in any of the pockets. All these clothes and all these pockets, but nothing. Why have pockets if you don't leave anything in them for other people to find? What was the point at all?

The rest of the room had little to search through. Bare walls, except for the mold, and an empty closet beside the clothes on the floor she'd already checked. Nothing on hangers. No possessions. No personal items. Kat had dropped all expectations of finding a vacuum or mop, but she'd figured there'd be something else. No storage bins of old memories, no photographs, no books.

The only place left was under the mattress on the floor. Her stomach lurched again. Her abdomen was already sore, and burning acid lingered at the back of her throat. Saliva filled her mouth again. "No, don't," she whispered as she clutched her stomach and chest. "Please, don't." She closed her eyes and leaned against the wall. She burped, but nothing came up. Just a bitter taste, but at least no more vomit. She blinked away more tears.

Something crawled on her neck, and she cried as she slapped herself. She sniffled as the tears streamed down her face, then took a breath and bent over the mattress. *Please no rats reproducing tenfold. Please no flies having a christening for their maggot babies.* She lifted the mattress. Thankfully, no critters were unleashed. The carpet underneath was a lighter color than the rest of the house. Something was tucked further back. A journal? She grabbed it and set the mattress down. The cover was leather bound and heavy-duty. She flipped through the pages. A calendar. Finally, something she could work with.

The pages were organized by weeks, and the courier had filled out sporadic days. But Kat couldn't make sense of the code. *"1600 21"* written on one day. *"0200 Sterling"* written for another. And every other week, the word *"Refill"* scrawled on one day. Was it a ledger? People who owed money? Or delivery addresses for his job?

Kat flipped to the current week. Nothing was listed for today, but there was a listing for the previous day. *"1200 Addison."* Addison? That was the Lines' street name. 1200—was that a time? The agents had escorted her away before then. They hadn't wanted her around for the courier's appointment. It was times and street names?

There wasn't anything for today or tomorrow. But Wednesday, June 7th had something written. *"0000 18 Final Refill."* What was the final refill?

Kat tucked her face into her shirt before she reentered the kitchen. She dodged the swarm of flies and made her way back to Emrah. He was by the open window, sifting through the bins of empty bottles. The glass surfaces clicked against each other. He looked disturbingly pale. "He's still at the diner," Emrah said, his voice slow and raw.

A breeze of clean air wafted through the window, and it relieved Kat's agitated lungs. "Anything insightful on your end?" she asked, her vocal cords burning. The taste of stomach acid lingered in the back of her mouth.

"I'm no doctor, but Frank's an alcoholic. Surprised he's

not dead. This is all liquor. Whiskey and beer. And these strange ones." He held up a pile of small glass vials.

"What are those?" Kat asked. Something buzzed in her ear, and she ducked down. Emrah swatted at the flies. He grabbed the window ledge to steady himself as he blinked and lurched forward. "Are you alright?" Kat asked.

He held his breath for a minute and closed his eyes. "Don't know," he muttered, then handed her the vials while he held his stomach.

Kat turned the vials over. All of them were identical. Thin glass tubes, each the length of her finger. No label, but black ink scrawled on the side. The handwriting didn't match the journal. It was too sloppy. All the vials had the same writing: *"Sparrow e darlc."* But they had different dates written underneath.

"What's e darlc?" Kat asked.

"No idea." Emrah pressed his face into the screen and took a slow breath. "And all the dates are different. About two weeks apart." He tilted his head back and stared at Kat's hands. "What'd you got there?" She held up the journal. "Diary?

"Calendar." She swatted at the flies around her mouth.

"Damn, is it seriously too much to find a confession these days?"

Kat handed back the vials. "Can you read me some of the dates?" she asked, flipping through the pages.

Emrah picked up one of the vials. "May 12th."

Kat flipped a few pages back. "May 12th . . . it only says refill."

"What about March 31st?"

Kat flipped to that week. "Refill too. It looks like every other Friday, he gets a refill."

Emrah skimmed through the different vials. "That seems right. Does it say what these are?"

"Nothing. No dates or times. Just refill," Kat said. Emrah rolled the vials in his hands. "What are you thinking? Drugs?"

"Or Alchemy," he said.

"Why Alchemy?"

"If it was drugs, wouldn't it be more often?" he asked. "When's his next refill?"

"There's one on Wednesday. But it says 0000 18 Final Refill," Kat said. "I think 0000 means midnight."

"Maybe, but what does final mean?"

"Maybe he won't get more after this?" Kat flipped ahead, but the pages were blank. She skimmed ahead for the next few months, but nothing was written down at all. Maybe he didn't need more after Wednesday. "Usually when there's a time, underneath it's a street?"

Emrah scrunched his face. "Wait, 18th," he muttered. "That's the address where he dropped off the briefcase."

"So, he's meeting back there?"

"That's got to be it. And he's getting some refill?"

"I guess?"

Emrah used the back of his wrist to push his glasses up his face. "What else is in there? Anything from this week?"

"Just for yesterday. There's 1200 Addison."

"Addison is where the Lines are," Emrah said. Kat skimmed a couple pages back. "He came around noon for the briefcase." The rest of Emrah's words were drowned out while Kat stared at the pages. On Tuesday, May 23rd, there was a log. *"1015 Pennsylvania."*

"What's with the face?" he asked. Kat looked up at Emrah. "What? What's it say?"

"Didn't Serena die on the 23rd?"

"Yeah?"

Kat held out the calendar for him. "City hall is on Pennsylvania Boulevard. She died after her morning hearing got out."

Emrah's eyes widened, and he looked up at Kat. "Frank killed Serena?"

How was Frank connected to all of this? Somehow through her father—but if he was just a courier, who did he work for? And if he was the one that killed Serena, why wasn't ERA after him? Were these vials what had been in Gerald's briefcase? No, the refill dates were different. Someone else was refilling the vials.

"Time to go," Emrah said, peering out the window. "Frank's leaving the diner." Kat leaned over Emrah and helped him shut the window. The stagnant air and smell of death accumulated instantly. She stared outside. After a gap in traffic, Frank crossed the street.

Emrah grabbed the stack of bottles he'd taken out and tossed them back in the bins. When he grabbed another whiskey bottle, a roach skittered across his fingers. He flailed, and the glass shattered.

Kat grabbed his shoulder as he whipped his hand into the wall. The bug chirped and bounced off of him. Kat held Emrah's shoulders as he hyperventilated and clawed at his skin. "Shhh, gently. Gently," she said.

He groaned and shrugged her off. "It's fine. I'm fine," he muttered. He yanked his sleeve over his hands and grabbed a few more bottles. He placed them down softly, and the glass clinked quietly.

Kat dug out her journal and copied down the information from the calendar. The next appointment date and time. The dates of the refills. The courier's meeting with the Lines and when he killed Serena. Something buzzed against her lip, and she spit out and thrashed her head.

They were running out of time. Frank would catch them in the stairwell. They'd have to run up to the fourth floor and wait for him to leave before they could make their exit without him noticing.

"Should I keep one?" Emrah asked.

Kat looked up and brushed her hair out of her face. Emrah had a vial in his hand. "Maybe he won't notice," she said. She put her journal away and hopped back over to the kitchen.

Kat held her breath as her stomach lurched again. Flies collided into her face, but their guts would splatter all over her if she smacked them. More tears streamed down her cheeks. She shook her head to get the flies off until she was dizzy in the bedroom.

She shoved the journal under the mattress and put the clothes back where she'd found them. Or as close to how she remembered. Would Frank notice this wasn't how he'd left his belongings? She couldn't do anything about it either way.

Another glass shattered in the other room. Something else must've attacked Emrah. Kat took a breath and approached the kitchen. Her knees locked. She couldn't keep going through this room. But it was the last time, and then she could get out. She braced herself, ducked her head down, and then raced back through the kitchen.

Emrah reached out, his sticky hands catching hers as she jumped over the piles of cans, and he hauled her to the front door. Rustling came from the hallway. Kat squeezed Emrah's hands in a death grip. He froze.

"Someone," she breathed. Emrah leaned toward the door and stared through the peephole. He clenched his jaw. "Frank?" She pulled Emrah away from the door.

Emrah squeezed her hands back and stayed put. "Someone else," he whispered. "Old guy."

"Run?"

"Wait," he said. Kat held her breath and gripped his hands. A fly zipped into her ear, and she squeaked. "Shhh."

Kat shook her head and pressed her forehead against Emrah's sleeve. They could hide. They had plenty of garbage to cover themselves with. Probably contract tetanus or gangrene. But they could hide and sneak out later if Frank was already in the hallway. Another fly buzzed by, and she shuddered.

"Dad, get back inside," a voice called from the hall. The neighbors.

"I heard something," the older gentleman called out. Emrah's grip tightened. Kat's fingers went numb. Her nails dug into his hands, and her eyes burned as she stared at the door handle. If the courier caught them snooping, they might all spook. Then the next meeting could fall through. She stared at the brass knob. They couldn't get caught. She stared at the lock. Frank couldn't know they were in there. The lock.

"He's leaving," Emrah whispered and cracked open the door. Footsteps echoed in the stairwell.

"The lock," Kat whispered.

Emrah closed his eyes. A look of despair washed over him. He swung the door open and shoved her in the hall.

The dingy hallway was a relief of air. The door shut silently, and the lock faintly clicked. Emrah wasn't with her.

The shuffling footsteps trudged onto the third floor behind her. Heat pricked the back of Kat's neck. "Can I help you?" It was Frank's gruff voice from before. Kat took out one of her pearl earrings and slowly turned around. He narrowed his eyes at her. "You? What are you . . ."

Kat clutched the earring in her hand. "Oh, I'm so sorry, sir," she said in a chipper voice. She sniffled, her cheeks still damp. Her eyes were probably bloodshot from the poisonous air. "I lost an earring while making my rounds. You haven't noticed anything, have you?" Her voice burned from the stomach acid that had coated her throat.

He stared her up and down. "You look different from before."

Kat wiped her cheeks with the back of her hand. Black mascara smeared on her skin. "Oh, I seem to have cried off all my makeup. These earrings were my grandmother's, you see. They're very important to me." *Step one, don't get caught. Step two, buy Emrah enough time to hide.*

"Weren't you . . . wearing a dress?"

"This is my work uniform at Gimbels Department Store." She held up her bag, which was the same as before, and pulled out the bottle of perfume. "Perhaps you have changed your mind—"

"Forget it," Frank said, tucking his newspaper under his arm to pull out his keys. He shuffled to the door and unlocked it. When he opened the door, there was no sign of Emrah. Maybe he'd had enough time to hide. The buzzing sound returned, and it made her skin crawl. "What's your problem?" Frank asked. He glared back at her.

Kat blinked. "Oh, nothing, I'm just—I'm just trying to find my earring." Kat knelt on the ground and crawled around. But Frank didn't go inside. He stood in the doorway and watched her. What if he sat on the couch and Emrah couldn't get out? Could he go out the window? Three floors . . . maybe he could survive the jump? The odds were better than him surviving in that hellhole of an apartment. Frank was still glaring at her, refusing to budge from the doorway. "Are you sure you haven't seen it?" she asked. "It looks exactly like this one." She gestured to the earring in her other ear.

"Nope." Frank leaned against the doorway. Between his legs, Kat saw Emrah dart behind him.

"Uh!" Kat said. What the hell was Emrah doing? He needed to hide. Why was he prancing behind Frank? "You, um, you sure you didn't see it? Maybe in the stairwell?" Her heart was racing.

"Lady, it's not here," Frank said, his tone sharper.

Kat crawled to the other side of the hallway. Emrah was tall but lanky. Not built like Frank. Not as strong. Even if Frank wasn't some hitman, Emrah didn't stand a chance. "I need to be thorough," she said. He needed to get away from the door. "This set is a family heirloom."

Frank took a step toward her. "Perhaps check a different floor."

"I appreciate your help," Kat said. "Are you sure you're not interested in our new fragrance?"

"Still not interested." He took another step closer.

Kat crawled down the hallway, patting the ground. "But perhaps you could get it for a special lady. It's the perfect gift for birthdays and anniversaries."

"I said I'm not interested."

"It's the fragrance of the summer. She'd love it."

Frank stormed over to her, and Kat teetered backward. "Are you even looking for an earring? What are you doing here?"

Kat's heart jumped to her throat. Frank towered over her. His dark eyes drilled holes in hers. "I'm so sorry, sir." Maybe he'd kill her, but he was at least away from the door. "I'm only trying to meet my quota. I work on commission." She forced her eyes to stay on his. Not Emrah. Not on Emrah as he emerged from the doorway.

"And how's that going for you?" Frank sneered.

Emrah darted into the hallway. Kat gasped loudly and flailed her arms in the other direction. "Oh heavens! There it is!" she exclaimed. She scurried to the side of Frank's foot and pretended to pick something up. She revealed the pearl earring in her hand. His face softened. "Oh, thank you so much for your help. I can't believe you found it!" Emrah vanished into the stairwell.

Frank stared at Kat, dumbfounded. "Oh, okay," he grumbled, glaring at her. Maybe he wasn't convinced. But it didn't matter. Emrah was safe.

"Well, I won't take up any more of your time." Kat stood up and tried to smile at him.

"You said you worked for Gimbels?" he asked.

"Um, yes."

He looked her up and down. "Why is Gimbels sending girls out here?"

Kat stared at him, but the door behind her opened. The Hispanic woman from earlier smiled at her. "Oh, you're still here! Kathryn, was it?" she asked.

Kat stared at her and then remembered to smile back. "Hi, yes?"

"You know, I'm glad I caught you," she said, her Southern accent a soothing melody. She opened the door further. "I was wondering if it wasn't too late. I'd like to buy some of your perfume."

"Really?" Kat said. Frank looked at her in surprise. "Wonderful, yes."

The woman held the door open. "Why don't you come in?" Kat squeezed past Frank. His body odor reeked. Frank shuffled backward and went into his unit. He shut the door.

Kat followed the woman into her apartment. No garbage. She could see the floor. There weren't flies or roaches. The tiles didn't stick to her shoes. Nothing was piled on the couch or coffee table. Her kitchen looked cozy. The air was sweet and sterile.

The woman shut the door and locked it behind Kat. "Make yourself comfortable." She gestured to the couch. "I'll make us some coffee."

Kat's stomach flipped. "No coffee. Perhaps some water?"

The woman smiled at her. "Of course." She went back to the kitchen and rummaged through things on the counter.

Kat quickly sniffed her shirt and her sleeves. A bitter odor lingered. The smell was much stronger on her hands. God, she needed to wash her hands.

Kat sat on the edge of the couch to minimize contact. The couch fabric was soft and smelled clean. Nothing sticky. Nothing crawling on her. A nice place to catch her breath and then get out. She could just name a price and get this over with. The day didn't need to be any longer.

"What are you doing here?" The sweet Southern accent had turned harsh. Kat glanced up. The woman was pointing something at her. Something metal. Gun. It was a gun. Kat jumped off the couch. "Don't move!" The woman kept the gun aimed at Kat.

Kat froze and held her hands out. She stared at the woman, heart pounding in her throat. If she were going to kill her, she would've done it already, right? "You don't really want to buy the perfume, do you?" Kat asked.

The woman cracked a grin and held her aim. "And you don't really want to sell it, do you?"

# CHAPTER 16

# THE SOLDIER

Kat was maybe twenty feet from the door. She would need to run around the coffee table, then unlock the door. She wouldn't make it out before the woman grabbed her. Or shot her. But if she were going to kill her, she would've done it already. People pointed guns at others all the time. It didn't mean they always wanted them dead. She wasn't going to die.

"Listen," Kat said softly. "I didn't see anything. I don't know what's going on. You can keep the perfume for free, and I won't tell my boss—"

"Cut the crap."

"What are you talking about?" Kat did her best not to show fear despite how terrified she was.

"You're really committed to the saleswoman bit," the woman said. "You know, I was wondering if it was a coincidence you showed up today. Then you bring a buddy to break into Smith's apartment. That can't be a coincidence."

"Coincidence for what?" Kat asked.

The woman fished something out of her apron. She held up a badge. Kat's stomach twisted. "My boss told you to drop the case, Miss Okazaki."

"Oh," Kat muttered. Her terror morphed into dismay. The ERA agents hadn't tailed Clark after the drop-off because they already had an agent stationed outside his residence. The woman's apartment looked lived in. The furniture had left impressions on the carpet. Dust had collected along some shelves. "How long has Agent Baker had you out here?" Kat asked, dropping the fake accent. "Weeks? Months?"

The woman narrowed her eyes. "You were told what would happen if you didn't mind your business." Keeping the gun aimed at Kat, she reached into her apron again, then tossed a pair of cuffs on the carpet in front of Kat.

Kat stared at the metal cuffs. Her heart pounded in her ears. This wasn't happening. Not today. "Who are you?" she asked.

"My name is Agent Esqueda. I work for ERA, and you're under arrest for interfering with our investigation."

Esqueda looked like she was in her mid-twenties. She was stationed alone to keep an eye on Frank, who wasn't even the real target but the middleman. Esqueda had been sent to babysit. Maybe this was her first time on a bigger case. Maybe she finally felt important at work and needed to prove herself. "I can give you information."

Esqueda laughed. "I doubt you have anything we don't already know. Put on the cuffs."

"I know who killed Serena Line," Kat said.

Esqueda contorted her face in bewildered amusement. "Why was my boss worried about you?" She laughed.

Kat narrowed her eyes. "Excuse me?"

"He told me to watch out for you yesterday, but you clearly don't know anything."

Kat stared at her. Yesterday, huh? What were the chances Esqueda was the messenger Emrah had seen before Frank Smith showed up? The messenger they'd shooed away. Black hair, tan skin. If she was babysitting Smith, she could've warned the other agents he was coming. What were the odds they didn't treat her as one of them? Or that she felt the need to prove herself? Typically, it wouldn't be acceptable to make such assumptions. But sometimes the circumstances called for it. "I can help you."

Esqueda rolled her eyes. "I doubt it. Serena's death was nothing more than an accident."

"I already know the truth," Kat said. "There's no point in lying." Esqueda stared at her. "You . . . do know she was murdered, right?"

"She broke her neck at work," Esqueda said.

This had to be some kind of tactic to cover up their case. There was no way ERA didn't realize Serena had been murdered. Right? But they hadn't arrested anyone yet. They weren't arresting Frank, even though he'd probably done it. If they didn't know, what were they even doing here? "So, if it's not for the murder, then why is ERA investigating?" Kat said. "For some other magic-related crime a week after Serena's death?" Esqueda's eyes narrowed. Did it even have to do with Serena's death? If Emrah were here, he could probably read Esqueda's expressions better than Kat.

"Alright, say she was murdered. Then who killed her?" Esqueda asked.

"Frank Smith."

Esqueda's expression hardened. "What do you know about him?"

"I can tell you—if you help me," Kat said. The gun was still aimed at her face. "Maybe start by putting that down."

"Not a chance," Esqueda said. "Why don't you just tell me what you know about him, and I can forget I ever saw you."

Kat stared at her. If she had faith ERA would do the job right, she'd let it all go. Hell, she probably wouldn't have bothered chasing the courier to begin with. But the compact had shown her morning glories. ERA would disappoint Héloïse. Not that Kat would confess to an ERA agent that she used magic with questionable legality. "I promised my client I would find the truth."

"Ms. Keeler?" Esqueda grinned. "It's cute you're trying to keep confidentiality, but we already know she hired you." She stepped closer to Kat. "If you really want to help her, stay out of our way."

Kat held her gaze. "You didn't even know Serena was murdered. How am I supposed to believe that?"

"We're federal agents. It's our job."

"Well, forgive me, but the government doesn't have the best track record in my experience." Kat's voice went flat, and Esqueda's eyes softened as she swallowed. "Do you know what it's like to never get closure?" Kat asked. "It's bad enough when you don't understand why something happened. But what's worse is never knowing what happened at all." She walked closer to Esqueda. "Let me help my client, and I'll help you."

"You really think you're helping anyone?" Esqueda asked, her voice wavering. "Say I believe you. What makes you think Smith's guilty of murder?"

"Well, you saw me snooping in his apartment," Kat said. "I found a calendar. The morning Serena died, he logged her time and location—"

"Wait, calendar?" Esqueda lowered the gun but kept it aimed at Kat's legs. At least it wasn't pointed at her head anymore.

"Yeah," Kat said, "like an appointment book."

"You found it?" Esqueda's eyes were wide as she took a step closer. "It was actually in there? Did you take it?"

Kat stared at her. "I put it back."

"But you saw it? Did you see anything else written? Another meeting?" Kat smiled, although her heart was racing so fast she was getting lightheaded. "You did see it?" Esqueda asked. "When was it?"

"What are you investigating?" Kat asked.

Esqueda huffed. "I can't tell you that."

"Then I guess I don't remember what the calendar said."

Esqueda tilted her head back in what looked like an attempt to suppress her irritation. "How about I don't arrest you and you tell me?"

"Or . . ." Kat softened her gaze. "How about you tell me what you're investigating. And you also don't arrest me."

Esqueda shook her head. "I can't do that. It's classified."

"Fine, then . . . what kind of magic put this in your jurisdiction?" Kat asked. Esqueda shifted her jaw to the side. "Alchemy?" Kat asked.

Esqueda gritted her teeth together. "Exalter."

"What?" Exalters? But the vials . . . Were they unrelated? This wasn't about Alchemy—or relics? Not some magical artifact from a safety deposit box? Exalters? Was this about Héloïse? "Why haven't you made an arrest yet?"

"We can't," Esqueda grumbled, brushing her hair out of her face. "We don't . . . know who he is exactly. Which is why I need the time."

*He?* "And this is the Exalter?" Kat asked. Esqueda nodded. Then it couldn't be Héloïse. Some other Exalter had broken the law, and ERA was after him? And the Lines were connected to him? "What do Gerald and Cynthia Line have to do with any of this?" Kat asked.

"Look, you said Frank Smith killed her?" Almost pouting, Esqueda failed to not look desperate. "Smith is already done for. The only reason we haven't made the arrest is so we can take down someone bigger. Your precious client will get her closure, alright?"

Kat tilted her head. Was Esqueda just saying that to placate her? "If you didn't know Smith killed Serena, why would you arrest him?"

"For aiding and abetting our bigger target."

"The Exalter?" Kat asked, and Esqueda nodded. "Then what about the Lines? How are they involved?"

Esqueda rolled her eyes. "I've told you more than enough already."

"That's my last question. And then I'll tell you the time."

Esqueda huffed. "If my boss finds out I told you, I'll be lucky if I'm stuck at a desk for the rest of my career."

"I don't snitch on my sources," Kat said. Esqueda didn't look convinced. "When did they start putting you in the field? Recently?" Esqueda stared at her. "And you're stuck on babysitting duty?"

"Someone needs to keep tabs on Smith." The edge returned to Esqueda's voice.

"What, did you draw the short stick?" Kat asked. "Or do they not even let you pick sticks? They just tell you where to go?"

"Yeah, because that's how a job works," Esqueda said. "Your boss tells you what to do, so you do it."

"Like babysitting the accomplice?"

"It's not babysitting—"

"Or fixing someone's report?" Kat said. Esqueda's lips parted. "Because oh, you're just so much better at these secretary things. You're just a natural." Esqueda clenched her jaw. As much as Kat disliked Hattie from the memorial, she'd had a point. "We have to work twice as hard as our male colleagues for half the career. But if you tell them the meeting time, maybe they'll take you more seriously, right?"

Esqueda's eyes softened, like she wanted to believe Kat. "The Lines . . . agreed to cooperate with our investigation if we didn't press charges."

"Press charges for what?" Kat asked.

"They're our lead to get to the Exalter." Esqueda stared at her. "I can't tell you more than that."

The Lines knew some other Exalter? And they were turning him in for their own protection?

"I've held up my end of the deal," Esqueda said. "What time is the meeting?"

"It's midnight after Tuesday. Wednesday morning, technically."

"And the location?"

"Where Frank Smith dropped off the briefcase." Relief washed over Esqueda's face, and she grinned. "Am I free to leave now?" Kat asked.

Esqueda walked back toward the door, keeping her eyes on Kat. "Are you going to make me regret this?"

"No, no," Kat said, "unless you make me regret this." Esqueda rolled her eyes and unlocked the door.

Kat left, and the door shut behind her. She bolted into the stairwell, colliding into Emrah. Her head smacked into his collarbone, and they teetered over the banister. Kat braced herself as they stumbled backward.

Emrah caught the railing as Kat gripped the front of his shirt. Their scuffling echoed, but the stairwell went silent when they froze. Kat's nose burned from the putrid odor of his clothes. It smelled of rotten bile and fermented mouse shit.

"You trying to end up like Serena?" Emrah whispered in her ear. Kat smacked his shoulder. Emrah's hands were sticky against her shirt. He'd dug around in those garbage bins, and he smelled far worse than her. Now the smell was on her too. The day needed to be done. She grabbed his arm and led him downstairs.

Kat opened the door and stepped out onto the sidewalk. Fresh air had never been more sacred.

"Where were you?" Emrah hissed next to her.

"I got held up," she said. The afternoon sun shone on her face. The warmth felt nice for a change. She headed down the sidewalk.

"No shit." Emrah followed Kat. "I thought he dragged you back into his unit."

"One of the neighbors is an agent," Kat said. "She saw us go in."

"What?" Emrah glanced over his shoulder.

"Don't worry," Kat said. "We came to an understanding of sorts."

Kat filled him in on the way back to the office. The sunshine quickly got old as they started to sweat in the summer heat. Emrah's clothes were grimy, and they both reeked of that dumpster apartment. There was no way they could make it on public transportation without getting fined for a health violation. But they could walk back and talk without being overheard.

The sun had shifted closer to golden hour when they made it back to the office. "So the Lines were avoiding the family because they had to deal with the feds?" Emrah asked.

"I can only assume," Kat said. "However, assumptions aren't good enough."

Emrah shrugged. "Yeah, but it sounds like our job is done. Smith killed Serena, and Esqueda said he'd be arrested. Serena gets justice and Héloïse gets answers."

"But we don't have the answers," Kat huffed, fishing her keys out of her bag. ERA was going to fail Héloïse somehow. Why else would there be morning glories? Even if ERA arrested Smith, it wouldn't be for Serena's murder. And there was still no clear motive for whoever had wanted Serena dead.

"Well, we're out of time," Emrah said. "Héloïse is coming tomorrow, and ERA probably won't be so nice next time we're caught."

Kat jammed her keys in the door, but it was already unlocked. She opened the door, and the floorboards squeaked. Maiki popped into view. "I was wondering if you were coming back at all," she said.

Kat stared at her and stepped inside. "I am so sorry. We weren't supposed to be gone all day. I got held up."

"Hi," Emrah said as he followed inside. "Who's this?"

Kat glanced back at him. "Um, Emrah, this is my cousin Maiki."

Maiki smiled at him. "So, you're the famous Emrah, huh?" She swayed side to side.

"I . . . didn't know I was famous," he said and looked at Kat with raised brows. "What'd you tell her?"

"All good things, don't worry," Kat said. She didn't need her family questioning her hiring choices. None of them knew about how she and Emrah had met. Kat looked back at Maiki. "Um, did you get it?"

"I left it on your desk," Maiki said, then winced and leaned away from them. "Good thing you had me stick around. He didn't show until almost three o'clock." She casually took a step back from them.

"Who? Jerry?" Emrah asked. He whipped his head in Kat's direction, but she refused to look at him. "You said you took care of him before you left?"

Kat pressed her lips together. "I said he was taken care of, but I never said *I* was the one taking care of him."

Emrah squinted at her. "Devious," he muttered. "Thought you said she was your favorite cousin."

"She is," Kat said.

"I am?" Maiki asked.

"What?" Kat looked at her. "Yeah, obviously." Maiki smiled.

"Oh, is it obvious?" Emrah said. "Your favorite cousin, and yet you stick Jerry on her?"

Kat rolled her head in his direction. "Look, she offered!"

"It's true. I did offer," Maiki said. "You know, Jerry was such a sweet guy."

Kat and Emrah snapped their heads to her. "Huh?" Emrah said.

"Oh, he was really pleasant. I chatted his ear off for over half an hour."

"Jerry?" Emrah asked. "Jerry Morris? Tall guy? Big face? Enough hair oil to cook an egg?"

Maiki looked at Kat. "Um, yeah, I guess?"

Emrah shrugged and shuddered. "Pleasant is not a word I'd use to describe him."

"What? No, he was so funny!" Maiki said. "He was telling me the story about the interviewers." Maiki started laughing. "He hired John Thompson, but he meant to hire Thomas Johnson. The previous investigator he hired mixed up the folders. And Jerry hired a finance analyst to be an operations manager, he . . . he . . ." Maiki laughed to herself while Emrah and Kat stared at her, bewildered.

"I don't know what you're referencing," Kat said.

"Oh, come on, you have to know!" Maiki said. "'Where are my division layouts? You've just given me spreadsheets!'" she said in a gruff voice with a city accent like Jerry's. Kat smirked but shook her head. "That debacle was why he switched to you. He needed someone new to do better background checks."

Kat blinked a few times. "Huh, I never heard that story."

"Oh, you've got to ask him. It was funnier the way he told it." Maiki waved her hands and took a breath. "Anyway, I got the list, and it's on your desk."

"I can get started on that if you'd like," Emrah said. Kat stared at him but hesitated. His shirt was stained in some . . . liquid. And he was still glistening with sweat from the walk back. "I'll wash myself first," he said.

"Thank you."

"I'll crawl into your utility sink if that's fine." He walked backward, toward the downstairs bathroom where her washing machines were.

"Em, do you want to just go home and shower?"

"This is fine for now. Trust me, I'll shower when I get home. I'll use industrial bleach."

"Really, you've done enough today," Kat said.

"You still have paperwork for Héloïse," he argued. "I can get started on the new checks."

He was trying to get overtime again. Not that she cared. She could bill Jerry's company for it since he'd be working on their checks. But she'd put Emrah through enough trauma for one day. "Are you sure?" she asked.

"You want to read Jerry's handwriting?"

Emrah had a knack for deciphering Jerry's chicken scratch. Jerry must've been a doctor in another life, judging by how awful his penmanship was. "You're welcome to go home for the day. But if you want to get the paperwork started, then I'll buy us dinner after."

"Deal," he said and clicked his tongue. Kat clicked back at him, and Emrah went into the bathroom.

"You're still working then?" Maiki asked.

Kat looked at her. "No, I'm spending time with you," she said. "And thank you so much for your help. You don't know how much it means to me that you did that," Kat said. "Jerry wasn't a problem for you?"

"Oh, please. After all the psychopaths I've dealt with in DC—trust me, he was a breeze."

Kat smiled at Maiki, but her own stench was getting to her. Her sweat had plastered her clothes to her skin. "I promise I want to keep talking," Kat said, "but I really, *really* need to shower."

"That's fine." Maiki laughed and leaned closer to her. "No offense, but you both stink," she whispered.

Kat laughed under her breath. "We were in a dumpster, basically."

"Dumpster?"

"I can tell you about it later, but I need to wash myself

before my skin falls off. Then we can talk and maybe get dinner too?"

Maiki nodded. "Yeah, go ahead. I'll bother Emrah if he's done before you're back."

"Yeah . . ." That thought didn't sit well with Kat. With Maiki's intimate knowledge of her life and Emrah's ability to psychoanalyze . . . They could figure out too much about her. More than Kat preferred. "I'll be quick." She went down the hall.

Water ran from the utility sink in her bathroom. Kat knocked on the door. After a stumble and a thud, Emrah opened it. "I'll clean it up! I swear!" he said. His glasses were off, and his hair was dripping. The water made his hair darker. He'd taken off his dress shirt, and the front of his white t-shirt was soaked.

"I wasn't going to ask," Kat said.

Emrah squinted at her, trying to focus his eyes without his glasses. "What is it?" Water dripped down his chin, and he wiped it off.

"Do you still have the vial? I can put it in a bag so we don't have to touch it again."

He laughed and then took it out of his pants pocket. "Yeah, yeah, good idea."

Kat took it from him. "Don't flood my house."

"Don't worry about it." He shut the door, and Kat raced upstairs. She found a small, clear bag to stick the vial inside and set it on her vanity.

She stripped in her bathroom and put the contaminated clothing in a separate laundry bag. Then she scrubbed herself down in the shower. The steaming water boiled her skin, but the sanitary sensation made her finally feel clean.

Four times she shampooed her hair. She scraped every inch of her skin with her nails until she'd exposed a new layer of epidermis. And then she scrubbed it all out from under her nails. Her bar of soap shrank to half its size. Her skin was pruned and bright red with claw marks everywhere by the time she was done.

She dried off and twisted her hair in a towel hat before getting dressed. Forty-five minutes had passed, but it was fine. She was clean, and she smelled of sweet peas and roses. Her skin was smooth and silky. The steam had soothed her sore esophagus. Emrah and Maiki's voices traveled through the floorboards as she dressed in her closet. Great, they were already scheming behind her back.

Kat left the towel twisted in her hair while she rummaged through her vanity. The photographs of Lottie's wedding and Serena rested where she'd left them last night. She probably should bring them downstairs so she could give them back to Héloïse tomorrow.

Kat picked up the bag with the vial in it. The outside glass stuck to the bag, and she was glad her skin wasn't making contact. The vial was totally empty. Maybe its contents had left an odor, but she wasn't about to sniff it.

No manufacturing labels appeared on the vial. The only detail was the *"Sparrow e darlc 04/28"* sloppily scrawled on the glass. The handwriting almost reminded her of Jerry's. He had a terrible habit of making his r's and c's indistinguishable. And all his letters were spread far apart. It was nearly impossible to tell when one word ended and the next began.

Kat stared at the lettering. *Sparrow e darlc* didn't make sense. But the "l" and the "c" were nearly touching. Almost like a "k" instead. *e dark?* Well, "dark" was actually a word. Was it *Sparrow e dark* instead? That made more sense. What did it mean, though? Did it matter what any of it meant? Was the vial even connected to the case? Or was this some other part of Smith's life?

Kat glanced at the photograph of Serena, staring at her face. Her dark wavy hair. Her heavy eyebrows. Her dark eyes. A chill went down her spine.

"Holy shit." She stumbled backward and covered her

mouth. There was no way. She grabbed Lottie's old wedding photo and stared at Edmund Clark. Fifteen years could change the way a person looked. Especially if he'd gone to war. Gained some weight. Gained some muscle mass. Grown out his hair and beard. Maybe even started to grey. But his eyes wouldn't change.

His dark eyes and heavy brows. Frank Smith was actually Edmund Clark? Clark had faked his death? He was alive? He was alive this whole time? Alive and a *suspect* this whole damn time? The gladiolus.

Clark was Serena's biological father. The compact had been dead-on for once. Clark had killed his own daughter. But why? What had he stood to gain?

Kat's head spun, and she stumbled into the edge of the vanity. The heavy wood shook the wall. She slowed her breathing. So, Clark faked his death after the war. He set up a fake name and never went home so he could start over? But why come back to his old life? Why kill Serena and work with the Lines? Did Lottie know he was alive? Did she know but not want to go back to her old life? She'd hated how disgusting he was. An alcoholic and a slob. Considering the state of his apartment, "slob" was an understatement. Lottie had remarried someone better . . . Alvin. But Alvin had seen Clark die. That was how he'd gotten the locket for Lottie. Unless he was in on it too? How big was this secret? And why did Serena have to die?

Kat clutched the vial in her hand. She stared at the lettering. *Sparrow e dark.* The letters smashed together in the middle. It wasn't *dark.* It wasn't a "d." The letters were touching. It was a "c" and an "l" instead. *"Sparrow e clark."*

# CHAPTER 17

# THE SECRETARY

"Emrah!" Kat sprinted down the stairs in bare feet, clutching the vial and the photos. Her collapsed towel hat had fallen to the floor. "Em!"

"What!" He flew into the hallway. She ran into him. "You alright?" He grabbed her shoulders to steady her. "What's wrong?" he asked, his eyes bugging out in alarm.

"Clark!" Kat shook the vial in his face. "Clark's alive!"

"What're you—" Emrah snatched the vial from her. "What?"

"Edmund Clark faked his death," she said, out of breath. "E Clark!" He adjusted his glasses and stared at the lettering. "E Clark—that's what the middle says."

"Frank Smith's . . ." Emrah's jaw fell.

"It's him." Kat held up the wedding photograph with a mad grin. "That's him! That's the courier."

Emrah stared at the photograph, and his eyes sparked with shock. "How's he alive? I thought Alvin said he saw him die—"

"He must've faked his death. But that's why he looked familiar."

Emrah pinched the bridge of his nose while he stared at

the photo. His hair was still damp and dark. He'd changed his whole outfit to one of the backups he stored in his office.

The floorboards in the hallway creaked. Maiki peered around from behind Emrah. "Is everything alright?"

Kat stared at her. "The . . . murderer possibly faked his death during the war," she said. Maiki's eyes widened.

"Not to mention he was the victim's uncle," Emrah muttered, "who's also her biological father. The family tree's a daisy chain."

"What?" Maiki looked at Kat. "Is he serious?"

"It's a bit strange right now."

Maiki laughed. "I thought you said most of your job was boring paperwork."

"This is a really, *really* big exception."

"So, ERA doesn't know it's a murder investigation," Emrah said. "But they're going to arrest Clark anyway. Because he went AWOL?"

"No, she said he was some accomplice to the Exalter," Kat said.

"What Exalter?" Maiki asked.

"I don't know," Kat said. "I ran into an ERA agent before we got back. I asked about their investigation. They're trying to catch an Exalter, but she didn't elaborate."

"You think it's someone from his past?" Emrah spun the vial between his fingers to examine it.

"But there weren't Exalters before the war," Kat said. Well, the Soviets had supposedly created Shapeshifters after their revolution. But Exalters hadn't become prevalent in the US until after Munich.

"What is that?" Maiki snapped, pointing at Emrah's hand.

"This? Some vial." Emrah held it up for Maiki, and her jaw dropped. "Why?"

Her eyes darted to Kat. "What's the matter?" Kat asked.

Maiki took a step back, and the floorboards creaked under her heel. "Where did you find that?"

"It was in Clark's apartment," Kat said.

"The fake dead guy?" Maiki's voice cracked.

"You know what this is?" Emrah asked. He held it in front of her, and Maiki went pale. Was this something that had come up at her old job? Either that, or Kat's cousin was in some deep trouble and going to California on the run.

Maiki opened her mouth, but she hesitated. "Do you?" Kat asked.

"That guy, Clark. Where did he serve?" Maiki asked. She cleared her throat. "Where was he?"

"It was, what, France?" Emrah said.

"Normandy?" Maiki asked.

Kat narrowed her eyes on Maiki, who paled and looked sick. "What do you know?" Kat asked. Unease crept into her stomach.

Maiki stared at the vial. "I'm not sure," she muttered. "I never saw them in person, but I heard about them. The tiny glass containers. Some of them were labeled Sparrow."

"Where did you hear about them?" Emrah asked.

"My coworkers. They heard the testimonies," she said. "I think your Clark guy died."

"He faked his death," Kat said. "We just saw him today. I spoke to him."

"It had to be him, right?" Emrah asked. "What if . . ." His eyes widened. "An evil twin—"

"Clark died in Normandy," Maiki said. She pointed to the vial. "He was brought back by a Necromancer."

"What?" Kat whispered.

"There was this trial," Maiki said in a low voice. "I heard about it. There's a Necromancer going around and bringing people back . . . for a price."

Necromancers had functioned as specialized US medics on D-Day. Their powers had saved the lives of hundreds of men. It had been a turning point for the Allies, and the Necromancers had continued with the rest of the troops during the liberation of France. Alvin could've seen Edmund die—and then, later, a Necromancer could've resurrected him.

Emrah grabbed Kat's wrist. "The Exalter," he said, squeezing her arm. "That's the connection to Clark. That's who ERA's after." Kat's eyes widened. "Clark's the connection to a Necromancer for the Lines. The Lines—they're trying to bring Serena back!"

Kat pulled away from him. "Emrah—"

"Do *not* tell me I've gone off the rails. I'm right," he said with a maniacal grin. "Héloïse said the Lines were fine at first, but then they started acting weird—when they realized they knew a guy who knew a guy that could bring Serena back." He choked out a gasp. "That's why they didn't have a funeral! They're not letting her stay dead." Emrah glanced at Maiki. "You said this Necromancer will do it for a price?" he asked. Maiki nodded. "Gerald went to the bank for the payment." He started laughing, almost cackling. "I'm on fire. You cannot stop me. Don't give me the 'we need evidence' crap."

"We *do* need evidence!" Kat said.

"No!" He groaned and threw his head back. "You're going to stand there and tell me I'm wrong?"

"Did you not, half a minute ago, suggest an evil twin?" Kat said.

Emrah snapped his head in her direction. "I'm a different man now. Wiser. Clairvoyant."

Kat rolled her eyes but smiled. If she hadn't thought his logic made sense, she would have cut him off sooner. "If, for some reason, you aren't entirely delusional, why was Serena murdered in the first place?" Emrah almost pouted trying to conjure a rebuttal. Kat pursed her lips to the side. He was rubbing off on her. "Perhaps . . . Clark knew how wealthy the Lines were. Perhaps he knew they would've paid any price to bring her back." Emrah smirked. "ERA didn't know Serena was murdered. Maybe the Lines didn't either. If Clark is working for the Necromancer and he killed Serena, then he's creating a false demand for the business."

"I'm loving this side of you," Emrah said.

Kat shook her head. "This is all speculation—"

"No, no speculation!" Emrah pointed a finger at her. "I want conspiracy-theory Kat back."

Kat swatted his hand away. "If this is true, then hiring the Necromancer is the crime ERA's been investigating," she said.

Emrah narrowed his eyes. "You'd think bringing someone back from the dead wouldn't be illegal."

"You'd think," Maiki muttered. They both looked at her, but Maiki kept her gaze on the floor. "ERA's not going to let them bring her back," she said.

"What?" Emrah asked.

Maiki shrugged, then glanced up at them. "If she's resurrected before they can arrest him, that's one thing. But they're probably planning to leave her dead."

Kat leaned toward Maiki. The unsettled feeling returned. "What else do you know?" she asked.

Maiki clenched her jaw. "The trial I mentioned," she said with a grimace, "was for the person brought back."

"What do you mean?" Emrah asked.

Maiki scowled. "The guy resurrected. He was some rich college kid. He drowned over spring break in an accident. His family wanted him back, and they got in contact with the Necromancer. And he . . . brought the kid back."

The sinking tightened inside Kat's chest. "And it's a crime for Exalters to use their powers. So he was alive unlawfully."

"No . . . that has to be an exception," Emrah said. "Taking money for it, yeah—it's one hell of a business model. And the IRS probably didn't get their cut. But he saved the guy's life. And they were going to arrest the family for saving him?"

Maiki laughed bitterly. "The trial was to determine if the student should be allowed to stay alive."

Emrah stared at her. "What was the plan? Kill him?"

"I have no clue," Maiki said. "It was ruled that persons resurrected, even unlawfully, were not at fault and not to be executed. But it was a vote of six to three, and that didn't sit right with me."

"That's why you left?" Kat asked. She leaned back against the wall, her shoulders deflated.

"I was already on the fence about leaving," Maiki said. "I'm glad they came to the right verdict. But the fact that they had to question it . . . The Supreme Court Justices serve for life. Their agendas aren't going away anytime soon, and I'm not working for their system."

"What was the justification?" Emrah asked.

"Their argument was that the life force had to have come from somewhere, and the source had been questionably obtained."

"What do you mean?" Kat asked.

"I don't know exactly how Necromancy works," Maiki said, "but the life force always comes from a different living person. To bring someone back, you have to use the life force of someone of 'equal value,' whatever that means." She gestured to the vial again. "Whoever this Necromancer is, he modified his powers. He makes elixirs, and whoever drinks them comes back to life."

"You said the vials say Sparrow?" Emrah asked. He turned the glass over in his hand. "What's that mean?"

Maiki shrugged. "I don't know. But all the vials had some label. Most say Sparrow. Others say something else. Something . . . Pan sear?"

"Pan sear?" Kat asked.

Maiki shook her head. "No, it wasn't that. I can't remember."

"And they haven't been able to catch this guy?" Kat asked.

"It's not like he's performing a ritual anymore," Maiki

said. "He doesn't have to be present when the person is resurrected if they drink the elixir."

"Isn't there some record of all the medics that had the power?" Emrah asked.

"Yeah, but it's not a short list," Maiki said. "Especially when many of them are MIA. Or were reported KIA but, considering what they're dealing with, that's not a permanent status anymore."

"How badly does ERA want this guy?" Kat said. "I mean, a rogue Necromancer? If word got out . . ."

"Quickly and quietly," Maiki said.

"If they're that desperate, maybe they'd make an exception for the Lines?" Kat asked. "Why would the Lines be cooperating if they couldn't get Serena back in the end?"

"To avoid prison?" Maiki said. "Or ERA lied to them."

"But at the trial, they said the guy should live," Emrah said.

"He'd already been brought back," Maiki said. "They won't kill someone already resurrected, but that doesn't mean they're going to allow more to happen."

Kat rubbed her face in her hands as anger boiled in her chest. "I see why you left," she grumbled, then leaned her head against the wall and stared at the water stains on the ceiling. This might've been what the morning glories had meant. As much as Kat wished Maiki was wrong, there was no point in having faith. When had the government been known for their kindness?

"What're you thinking?" Emrah asked.

"I don't know," Kat muttered. "I need to process this. I'm also hungry."

"You want me to pick something up?" he asked, his voice more grounded now.

Kat leaned against the wall and rubbed her temples. "How far along did you get on the checks?"

"Only started."

"I can grab something then," Kat said.

"Would you like some company?" Maiki asked.

Kat smiled despite the dread building inside her. "I'd like that."

Kat went back upstairs and found her shoes. Her hair was still damp, but it could dry on the way to the deli.

The streets were crowded, clusters of cars bustling on the road while people filled the sidewalks. "Sorry your case isn't working out the way you hoped," Maiki said. She walked in stride with Kat, their feet matching pace.

"I had no idea what direction it was going to take, but this wasn't it," Kat said. "I don't know what I'm going to tell my client."

"You could tell her the truth."

The hot sun soaked into Kat's black hair as the water evaporated, and the wind blew strands of hair in her face. "I don't know what the truth is," she said. "While I'm willing to believe it, I can't present theories as evidence."

"Maybe you can omit the wild theory part."

"That's not great either," Kat said. Ideally, if this were real, then Serena would come back, and everything would be perfect. "Do you really think they're not going to save her?"

Maiki shrugged. "I mean, there's always a chance. But after what they did to us?"

"But Serena's a rich White woman. Maybe it'll be different for her?" It wasn't supposed to come out as a question, but Kat's voice faltered.

"I don't think that's enough to save her," Maiki said, her cheeks flushed. Then her voice turned sharp. "I've been around politicians long enough. They don't care when their legislation kills someone. Because when you make the laws, it's not murder. It's policy."

Kat clenched her jaw. Maiki was right, and she hated it. ERA wasn't going to do what was right. Just what the law demanded. And laws weren't about right and wrong. They were about control. "If ERA isn't going to do it, maybe I could," Kat muttered.

"How?" Maiki said.

If Kat hadn't given Esqueda the meeting time, it could've been possible for her to sneak in. Sneaking past a couple agents would've been hard but maybe not impossible. Now, ERA knew when to expect the Necromancer. The place would be crawling with agents ready to make an arrest. Kat couldn't make it within a hundred feet of the front doors without getting caught.

"I don't know," she sighed. A pit of guilt gnawed in her stomach.

"You're never going to feel like you've done enough. You know that, right?" Maiki said. "You are always working. You have a great career because of it. I used to be jealous of you, but I've seen the price you pay."

"What are you talking about?" Kat asked.

Maiki looked at her. "You're never satisfied," she said. "You've never done enough. You have to keep pushing. You have to keep saving money. You have to keep climbing this ladder. But what's at the top of the ladder?" Maiki's voice broke, and she stared at Kat.

"I don't . . . I don't know," Kat whispered.

"You don't even know what you're chasing?" Maiki asked.

Kat's face heated. "Well, what about you?"

"What about me? I quit my job. I'm the exact opposite of you."

"Not that," Kat said. "What do you think you'll find in California?" Maiki looked away from her and huffed. "Our home is gone. There's nothing back there."

"There's nothing for me here—" Maiki's voice broke off. "I haven't felt whole since we left California. Maybe I can find myself again, or maybe I can't. But at least I won't be around everyone."

Kat stopped walking. A sickness crept into her throat. "What do you mean?"

Maiki turned back to her and sighed. "I don't know how everyone else moved on. But I'm tired of being the only one that's still angry." She sniffled. "A part of me wants to get over it like everybody else. But another part of me needs my anger. And that part of me resents you all for losing yours." Kat's eyes stung, her cheeks burning. "But I hate that I'm resenting my own family." Maiki looked at her, tears spilling from her eyes, waiting for Kat to say something. And when she didn't, Maiki's shoulders sank. "I know California's not the same. I'm not expecting it to be. But at least if I'm there, I can stop pretending everything is perfect—"

"I hated this city when we first came here."

Maiki did a double take. "What?"

Kat stared at the cement sidewalks. Cigarette butts clustered at the curb, and dried bird poop was scattered across the grungy bricks. "I hated the smell," Kat said. "I hated how loud it was and the way everything looked. The buildings were so crammed together." Maiki blinked and quickly wiped her eyes. "I didn't mind the cold though. That was a nice change of pace."

Maiki took a step toward her. "You hated Philadelphia?"

"Yeah." Kat stared at the rooftops where the golden rays of sun glistened through the skyline. "I couldn't understand why the hell we came here of all places."

"But you never said anything," Maiki whispered.

Kat took a slow breath. "What was the point? We were already here. I had to get used to it, so why complain?" Kat's chest tightened as her heart pounded. "I don't like talking about these things. But I don't want you to think you're alone." She stared at Maiki's bloodshot eyes. "I never moved on like you thought I did."

The wind blew Maiki's bangs out of place, and she brushed them back. "Really?" Maiki whispered.

"I just buried it." Kat's eyes stung. She wanted to fling herself into traffic, but that wasn't an option. "It hurts pretending none of it happened. But I would rather live with the pain of denial than the pain of acceptance."

"Why would you want that?"

Kat bitterly laughed, her eyes prickling. Her face burned, and the heat trickled down her neck, strangling her. "I miss my dad so much," she whispered. "I wish every day that he came back." Her voice cracked. "Actually, I wish he never enlisted in the first place." Tears fell, and Kat smacked her cheek to wipe them off. "I spend every waking second thinking about work so I don't suffocate from how furious I am." More tears fell, and Kat swatted at her cheeks. Her voice trembled. "I miss how easy it was to talk to you before all this."

Maiki collided into her and hugged her tightly. Kat went limp in her arms. She rested her chin on Maiki's shoulder and exhaled. Tears fell into Maiki's hair.

People gawked at the two of them in passing. Kat shut her eyes to block out their stares. "I'm sorry I said those things," Maiki said.

Kat shook her head and hugged her cousin back. "I don't blame you. How would you have known? It's not like I told you." She sniffled and took a breath. "It's fine. I'm fine."

Maiki let go of her and tried smiling. "Do you still hate the city?"

Kat shook her head. "No, no, I don't," she said. "I've gotten used to the food and the stores. The ocean isn't the same, but I like it enough. And our family's here." Kat wiped her cheeks with her hand and dried her face. "I'm sorry I don't tell you things."

"Well, maybe you can start." Maiki tried to smile but kept crying.

"I'll make the next couple of days worth your time."

Maiki looked at the ground and wiped her eyes. "I hope so." She nudged Kat's arm. "Your assistant's going to wither away if we don't get dinner."

"I'm going to wither away if we don't get dinner," Kat laughed. She pressed her eyes into her sleeve. Thank God she hadn't put her makeup back on. She led Maiki back to the deli.

"He's a funny guy," Maiki said. "Emrah."

Kat let out a nervous laugh. "What'd he say while I was upstairs?"

"Nothing much." Maiki fixed her hair. "Just that he likes working for you, and he's glad he got the job. He spoke very highly of you."

Kat smiled to herself. "Huh, glad I don't make him miserable." Especially after what he'd gone through today. When this case was over, he would get some time off.

"He cares about you a lot," Maiki said.

"Well, I pay his salary."

"Yeah, but you guys are friends. You made it seem like that wasn't the case."

"We're not friends," Kat said. "I'm his boss. He only cares about the money."

"But you also spend a lot of time together. You're getting him dinner now?"

"That's the least I can do for him, considering he might have tetanus."

"He also mentioned that he does some errands for you." Maiki grinned. "He cooks for you?"

The more Kat thought about it, the more she wished Emrah was her friend. She enjoyed his company and cared about him a lot. Yeah, she'd like to know more about his life, provided it wasn't entirely illegal. She missed having friends.

She craved companionship. Emrah was her closest outlet. No, he was her only outlet.

Her family were close, but not in a friendship way. Her mother was her mother. And they didn't always see eye to eye. They could enjoy each other's company, but if her mother knew more about her life, Kat would risk being a disappointment. And her mother had already suffered enough. Her other relatives had their own children to worry about. As for Kat's other cousins, they were much younger than her. She was more of a role model to them, not exactly a friend. Maiki was the exception. She was the sister Kat had never had. Her first friend in life. But that had fizzled out after they were separated. There used to be the Claytons, but that had gone to hell. Emrah really was Kat's only friend. And he wasn't even a real friend.

"He's my assistant," Kat said. "I pay him to help me."

"Yeah, with your cases," Maiki said. "But everything else? Unless you pay him *really* well . . ."

It wasn't the way Maiki was implying. Kat hoped to God it wasn't. Being friends was one thing. That was something she'd be more than happy to reciprocate. But a relationship? She couldn't mix business with pleasure again. Not after what had happened last time. Even if they weren't coworkers, Emrah was a man. He was great, but she couldn't love him that way even if she tried.

"I just pay him *really* well."

The rest of the evening was spent in better spirits. Kat and Maiki brought dinner back to the office, and the three of them ate together. Maiki and Emrah got along rather well. Better than she'd hoped. Maiki had made plans with her brother for tomorrow, but she was free Wednesday and could see Kat one more time before she left.

It was dark by the time they headed out. Emrah left late in the night, and Maiki went home soon after. Their company had made the evening pass quickly. Kat was grateful for the distraction. She needed to use her compact, and she would've gone insane if she'd had hours to dwell on it.

Originally, she'd planned on asking the compact if Emrah was right about the case. If there was a Necromancer involved or if Serena could come back. The longer she thought about it, the more sense it made. They were out of time and couldn't get more proof. Jumping to conclusions was the only option she had left. And it wasn't like she was making far jumps. The pieces all fell into place. The story wrote itself. And perhaps Serena didn't have to stay dead. Unless that was what the morning glories meant.

Kat could ask the compact if ERA would let Serena come back. But the answer would be tricky to interpret. ERA perhaps wouldn't purposefully let Serena come back, but might it happen unintentionally? And what if the answer was no? What if ERA would prevent her from coming back entirely? Then what?

Then there was the alternative question. If Kat intervened, could she save Serena? Or if she tried, would she fail and get arrested? She wasn't enthusiastic about going to jail, but she could perhaps cope if her incarceration was for a good cause this time.

Of course, there was also the chance ERA would let Serena come back anyway. Then there'd be no reason for Kat to intervene. She'd get arrested for nothing. The ideal question would identify the best scenario for Serena to come back *and* for Kat to not get in trouble.

Kat hadn't even gotten to the morals of the situation. Someone else would need to die for Serena to live. Was it someone the Lines knew? How did it work? All those vials of

Clark's were refills. Would Serena need refills for the rest of her life? Or did *final refill* mean she wouldn't need more? And where would the life force come from? What if it came from a person that was already dead? Wouldn't that at least make it acceptable? One question per night wasn't enough.

Midnight approached. Kat held the compact in her hands. She traced the embossed etchings of the peony petals against her fingertips. The metal was warm under her clammy skin. What was she supposed to do? She leaned against her headboard. If she were in Héloïse's shoes, she'd do anything to get her wife back. But Kat was a selfish person. Then again, after everything Héloïse had been through, she deserved to be selfish too.

The shimmers lit up the room, and Kat lurched forward. She clutched the compact in her hand as the light twirled. "Would I make a positive difference for Serena Line if I got involved tomorrow?" The pristine white light shifted to a warm glow. The flower revealed itself. Begonia.

Kat looked through her journal. Begonias had come up when she was in the camps. When she'd asked if going to Philly was a good idea. When she'd worked for Jack Clayton. A few other cases too. Sometimes the outcomes were good, sometimes bad.

The meaning of begonias wasn't perfectly clear. Overall, it seemed more positive in the long run. The bad incidents had come from impulsive behaviors or poor planning. Kat had determined that begonias meant to proceed with caution for success. The risk was worth the reward, even if the reward wasn't guaranteed. It wasn't the best interpretation, but it was what she had.

# CHAPTER 18
# THE EXALTER

Kat pressed her face into her desk. She hadn't slept well last night. She'd kept trying to conjure a plan, but every outcome had ended with her getting arrested. Or killed.

She had a half-written summary for Héloïse's closing report. Her stomach churned, her abdomen still sore from vomiting the day before. Emrah had made breakfast, but it was a struggle to get through. The tea he'd made her sat cold and untouched on her desk.

Emrah knocked on her office door. "Yeah?" Kat sat up, but one of the papers stuck to her forehead. Emrah smirked, and she yanked the paper off. "Yeah?"

"I'm going to go request the background check orders for Jerry," he said. "You need me to do anything before I go? Or while I'm out?" Kat rubbed her eyes. "You want me to stop by the local incinerator and burn our clothes from Clark's apartment?"

"But then the toxicities on the clothes would pollute the air and cause a health violation for the city."

"Smart thinking." He leaned against the doorway. "You almost done?"

"Yeah," Kat muttered and stared at the closing report. She had most of it done. Statements of what expenses they'd incurred and the payments needed. Documents stating they were not liable for what might come from this information and that anything Héloïse did with it was her responsibility. The usual legal forms to protect the business. The only thing left to finish was the summary of what Kat had uncovered.

"What's on your mind?" Emrah asked.

Kat looked at him, twirling her pen in her hand. "What if we could get her back?" Emrah raised an eyebrow. "Serena. What if you're right and she doesn't have to stay dead?"

Emrah laughed. "Well, we could ask for one hell of a commission from Serena's parents."

"If the vials have already been made, we'd just need to get one for Serena. And we know where the meeting is." Kat glanced at the city map on the corner of her desk. "What if they're already inside the building? If we get there early, there wouldn't be as many agents." God, if only she had lied to Esqueda about the time. Sure, lying to a federal agent who had her home address would've bitten her in the ass later. But at least sneaking inside would've been a breeze. "Maybe one of the side buildings is connected," Kat mumbled.

"You're not serious, are you?" Emrah asked.

"I'm just saying, there has to be a way."

"Kat." She leaned over the map. Perhaps she could cause a diversion further down the block? And Emrah could sneak in during the chaos. "Kat."

"What?" She looked at him.

"This is beyond our control," he said, his voice flat.

She narrowed her eyes and flopped against her chair. "We could do something," she said. "We could save her."

"At the price of someone else dying?" he asked.

"But what if they were already dead?"

Emrah furrowed his brows. "You don't know that."

"But what if they were?" Kat rolled her eyes as he

clenched his jaw. "Oh, what's gotten into you?" Kat asked. "You love coming up with crazy theories. You've suggested far more crude things before."

"This isn't . . ." Emrah gave her a grim look and adjusted his glasses. "When I suggest something crazy, it's a joke. But I don't think you're joking right now."

Kat groaned and spun around in her chair. She stared out the window at the ivy creeping against the glass. "You're acting like I'm asking you to kill someone," she said. "You wouldn't do that." The chair continued rotating until she faced Emrah again. His blue eyes pierced into hers from across the room. An unsettling chill went down her spine, and she nervously laughed. "You wouldn't . . . You haven't—"

"Don't ask me that," he said. His voice came out sharper than usual.

Kat swallowed. "If . . . If they're already dead," she said, "then it doesn't really matter, does it? Then it'd be a waste not to save Serena." She tapped her pen against the desk.

"Whether they're dead or not is beside the point," Emrah said. "We can't go to the drop site without getting caught or killed. We have no way in, and we definitely have no way out."

"But what if we did?"

"But we don't!" he said. "I'm not going to humor this because if I say something facetiously, I'm worried you'll be desperate enough to try it. Why do you care so much?"

Kat looked away from him. "What if she was your wife?" she asked, then cleared her throat. "What if it was someone you cared about? Would you do it then?" Kat dropped the pen, and it rolled across her papers. "Serena had her whole life ahead of her. It's not fair." There was a way it could all work out, but Kat wasn't smart enough to come up with a plan. Emrah could probably figure something out, but he refused. Now Serena would stay dead. Héloïse would stay a widow. Kat put her head into her hands.

Emrah rested his head against the wall and sighed. "I

would." He swayed his head from side to side. "If it was someone important to me, I'd do it." He had a pained expression. "But just because it's what I'd do doesn't mean it's a good idea."

Kat slouched in her chair. "We just need a vial," she whispered. "You saw someone pick up the payment at the site. What if they had the vials, and they dropped them off too? We just need to get one for Serena."

"And then what?" Emrah asked. "We don't know where her body is."

"We'll cross that bridge when we get there."

Emrah stepped into her office. "What's your big plan?" Kat looked up at him, and he laughed. "The place is crawling with agents," he said. "If you want to take them all out for me, I'll gladly lockpick the door for you."

"Perfect, we don't need a Plan B." Kat rubbed her face in her palms.

"Yeah, well, until you figure out how to get past all the agents, we're dead on arrival." Emrah softened his tone of voice and took a breath. "Is there something I can get you?"

Kat looked at him with a smile. "Invisibility?"

"Ah, wouldn't you know it? I used to know a guy for that, but I lost sight of him."

"Do you actually—"

"No," he laughed. "I don't think there's any Alchemist that can do that."

"Bummer." Kat slouched back in her chair. "You're right. This is . . . I can't do anything," she muttered, then cleared her throat and tried swallowing the despair. "You can head out."

Emrah adjusted his glasses and looked at her. "You did the best you could. Don't hold it against yourself." He clicked his tongue twice. Kat stared at the desk and clicked back at him. "I'll pick up lunch on the way back," he said as he left her office. Kat didn't say anything. She doubted she'd have an appetite by the time he got back.

When he shut the front door, the house became quiet. Too quiet. Kat picked up her tea. It had gone cold, but she chugged it all. She held the empty mug in her hands, staring at the chipped maroon ceramic. It was old, secondhand, one of the first mugs she'd gotten in Philly.

They'd had to buy all new dishware. Plates, silverware, cups. More than just dishware. Towels, bed sheets, blankets. They hadn't had furniture either. Kat had spent the first five months sleeping on the hard floor of the apartment. It was where she'd eaten her meals too. They'd had no savings. Any money after rent had gone to buy cookware, winter coats, boots, and clothes for her growing cousins. Everything was secondhand since they'd also had to get food on the table.

Kat's first paycheck from the Claytons was the most money she'd had since getting to Philly. She'd given most of it to her mother to buy a used sewing machine. Though Kat had kept a part of her paycheck to indulge herself with a small reward.

She had bought herself a beautiful silk blouse from the women's boutique. Not the secondhand store, though she did tell her mother it was a miracle thrift. Kat had wanted something nice for once. Something only she had ever owned. Like how it had been in San Francisco.

Kat set her mug down. She meandered out of her office and across the hall to her darkroom. Her camera rested on her shelf in the corner. Kat picked it up, fiddling with the little, silver buttons. It wasn't like her father's camera. Hers was a newer model and smaller. She could also develop the pictures faster with crisper quality. Her father had never gotten to develop pictures. The camera was confiscated too soon after he'd bought it. Whatever film had been inside was gone.

Kat slid against the wall and sank down to the floor,

cradling her camera. What did trading a life of "equal value" even mean? And how bad could it be? Sure, nobody was happy when it was *their* life lost, but who wouldn't take any life to save their own? For Serena to live, someone else had to die. There was nothing wrong with that. Trading a life for another life happened all the time. And a one-to-one trade was a far better deal than what the government had done. According to them, the lives of four Nisei had been of equal value to the life of one Texan.

Despite being born on American soil, the Nisei had been classified as enemy aliens and stripped of their freedoms—until the US needed more bodies to fight the war. The Nisei had been drafted out of the concentration camps and turned into cannon fodder.

When Kat got out of the camps, she had scavenged for every public report, scoured for every document released. She'd dug through archived newspapers, found statements from veterans, read political books at the library about the structure of the US military. Anything that could explain what had happened.

The Lost Battalion had been cut off behind enemy lines with the Nazis closing in and supplies running out. Between the mountains, the forest, and the fog, it was impossible to locate them, impossible even for aircrafts to drop supply crates. After two failed rescue attempts, the generals deemed it a suicide mission. So they sent in the 442nd, the segregated second-generation Japanese American unit.

The 442nd fought an uphill battle in brutal terrain for days. After the fifth day, they breached the German defenses and recused the Lost Battalion, saving two hundred eleven Texan soldiers. A victory only achieved after the 442nd suffered over eight hundred casualties, including Kat's father.

A faint tapping on the front door snapped Kat out of her thoughts. She jumped to her feet and wiped her eyes while she put her camera away. The floorboards sputtered when she stepped into the hallway. Héloïse stood outside on the porch.

Kat hopped over and opened the door for her. "Good afternoon," she said.

Héloïse stepped inside with her cane. She looked worriedly at Kat. "Is this time good?"

Kat smiled as best she could with her heart pounding in her chest. "Now is good. Please, right this way."

Kat led Héloïse to the office in small, manageable strides. Héloïse hobbled next to her with the cane. She still wore dark, baggy clothing. Kat helped her into the chair across from the desk.

"Were you able to find anything?" Héloïse asked.

Kat bit her lip as she took her seat. She pulled out the folder and stared at it. Her handwriting was scrawled and scratched out. It wasn't acceptable to include that in the report. "Yes," she said softly. Héloïse looked at her with hope in her eyes, and Kat sat up. "I apologize, I don't have everything in order. I was still uncovering new information even last night."

Héloïse leaned forward, almost out of her chair. "And?"

"You were right about her parents acting strange," Kat said softly. Héloïse's eyes widened. Kat picked up a few of the notes tucked into her journal. "The Federal Bureau of Exalters, Relics, and Alchemy have an ongoing investigation pertaining to circumstances that involve Serena's passing. Gerald and Cynthia Line are cooperating witnesses."

Héloïse furrowed her brows. "What does all that mean?" she asked. "Witnesses? Witnesses of what?"

"ERA is arresting a wanted Exalter." Kat grimaced, her chest tightening as Héloïse shifted uneasily in the chair. "Now, I don't have all the evidence to confirm this, but I have reason to believe they're looking for a Necromancer."

"Necromancer?" Héloïse tilted her head, her face contorted in confusion.

Kat pressed her lips together as Héloïse stared blankly. "An Exalter that can resurrect the dead." Slowly the confusion washed away, and Héloïse's eyes went wild. "But they—"

"Porteur de vie?" Héloïse shot out of the chair. "Je jure, I know them! I saw! I saw them stop the death à l'hôpital." A smile twisted on Héloïse's face, and Kat's ribs constricted around her lungs. "They will save Serena?" Héloïse asked.

"No," Kat said. Her voice didn't sound like her own.

"No?" Héloïse gripped her cane, and her smile faltered. "What do you mean?"

Kat's eyes watered. "If this is true, ERA likely intends to arrest the Necromancer before he can bring her back."

"What?" Héloïse choked out a cry, as if Kat had stabbed her in the heart. She fell back in her seat, staring off. "She will not be back?" The light dwindled out of her eyes.

"I know this is a lot to process," Kat said. "I don't have evidence for this either, but I am fairly certain her death was not an accident. The Necromancer that would have saved her was also responsible for her death in the first place. I have reason to believe Serena's late uncle Edmund Clark was involved too."

Héloïse shook her head. "Eddie? No, but he . . . Eddie is alive now?"

"It is likely, yes. That would explain how Serena's parents were in contact with the Necromancer. I believe he was after your in-laws' money since they'd likely pay any price to get Serena back. They didn't hold a funeral because they thought she would be back. ERA will catch him. Serena's killer will be arrested." The words came out of Kat's mouth even though she couldn't breathe.

Tears streamed down Héloïse's cheeks. "Eddie is alive, but Serena will not live?"

"I'm afraid not," Kat whispered. Heat spiked down her neck. "But your in-laws were not avoiding you. They've been held up by this investigation. You were right that they were hiding something."

Héloïse dropped her head and cried out. Kat closed her eyes, listening to the high-pitched whimpers. "I'm sorry. Sorry," Héloïse sniffled.

"You have nothing to be sorry about." Kat turned her head to wipe her eyes.

Héloïse grabbed a tissue off the desk and blotted her own eyes. "I was so consumed with grief that I thought . . . She was the only family I had, and I miss her so much." Héloïse crumpled the tissue in her hand and gripped her cane. "Have you ever been in love?" Kat's throat went dry as a fire of dread ignited in her chest. Héloïse looked at her and winced. "I'm sorry, I should not ask—"

"Once," Kat said. The back of her throat burned, but she kept her composure. Héloïse tilted her head. "But . . . we're not together now."

Héloïse took a breath as more tears trickled down her face. "How did you move on?"

The heat flared into Kat's face, her cheeks and neck prickling. "I didn't," she whispered. She had never talked about this to anyone. She'd tried before, but her mouth always filled with cement and the words got stuck. She forgot how to breathe at the thought of talking about it with anyone she knew. But with a stranger, the idea didn't suffocate her as much. The words came with grace. "She married a man." Héloïse's expression softened. "She was the love of my life, but she wanted . . . a normal life. I couldn't give her that. And her father would never sign the marriage papers anyway."

"And your father wouldn't either?" Héloïse asked.

Kat smiled bitterly and gritted her teeth. "My dad died in combat," she said. Hot tears spilled down her cheeks, and she wiped them away. "I'd like to think he would've signed it. If he were alive. But that's not the case. And she knew that too."

Héloïse looked at her softly. Kat laughed under her breath

and grabbed a tissue to wipe her face. "What's her name?" Héloïse asked.

Kat crumpled the tissue in her fist. "Penny Clayton." She missed how the name felt on her lips. It had been a long time since she'd said it out loud. "I don't think I'll ever move on from her." Kat glanced at Héloïse, whose eyes were bloodshot and watering.

"I fear I will never move on either," Héloïse said. "I don't know what to do."

Kat passed the tissues closer to Héloïse. "Time doesn't make it better, but it makes it more manageable."

"I suppose." Héloïse took another tissue and blew her nose into it. Kat stared at the diamond ring on Héloïse's finger. The beautiful gemstone twinkled even in the terrible office lighting. Her knuckles gripped her cane tightly. Her flesh had turned bright white, almost sparkling as brilliantly as her diamond. She gripped her cane. The cane she needed to steady herself. No . . . She needed the cane to steady her atoms.

"You're a Material Phaser," Kat whispered.

Héloïse tensed. "I—Yes, is something wrong?" She stared at her hands.

Kat tilted her head and slowly stood from her chair. "No, no, nothing's wrong." Maybe they didn't need to be invisible. "Can you go through walls?"

Héloïse's eyes widened. "I try my best not to. I don't want to."

"But could you?" Kat asked. "Or does it hurt?"

"No, it's—it's against the law."

"But say it wasn't. Or say you knew you wouldn't be caught. Could you do it?"

Héloïse stared at Kat and furrowed her brows. "What is this about?" Her tone had sharpened in offense.

Maybe this was what the compact had meant by proceeding with caution. "Listen to me very carefully," Kat said. She walked around the desk and stood in front of

Héloïse. "I may have an idea for how to save Serena, but I need your help."

Héloïse shook her head. "What can I do? I'm not that kind of Exalter."

"But you can go through walls, right?"

"I—" Héloïse trailed off and stared at her.

Kat tapped on the surface of her desk. "There's a drawer under this side. I want you to reach through the wood and take something out of it."

"What?" Héloïse sputtered. Her hands were shaking. "I can't! It's illegal."

"I know, I know, but if we can get into the building, we might be able to save her." Kat kept her voice calm and took Héloïse's shoulders. "I promise I'm not trying to incriminate you. Do you trust me?" Héloïse's blue eyes peered into Kat's, and she nodded. Kat scooted Héloïse closer to the desk.

Héloïse stared at it and swallowed. "I've never done this on purpose," she said. "I only wanted it to stop." She took a few deep breaths, then reached over the desk. Kat took a step to the side and watched. Héloïse's pallid skin illuminated the dark wood. Her five fingers went out of focus. Six fingers. Seven fingers. The outline of her hand blurred and grew transparent.

Kat blinked several times. It was like her eyes had lost focus just like that. But the rest of Héloïse's arm was in focus. Her hand dipped into the surface of the desk like it was submerging in a liquid. Héloïse gasped. "Are you alright?" Kat asked. Héloïse nodded. "You're doing good. Can you take something out?"

Héloïse grimaced and shifted her arm further down. Her wrist disappeared, then her forearm. She retracted her hand. The white silhouette of her flesh emerged from the wood, clutching a dark smudge underneath. Her hand returned to focus, slowly revealing the silhouette of a stapler. Héloïse looked just as surprised as Kat. The metal crunched, and shards flung through the air.

A sharp pain struck Kat. She screamed, clutching her leg, and stumbled backward into the bookcase. Her spine rammed into the shelf. Books plummeted onto her head.

"What!" Héloïse dropped the stapler, and it clattered on the desk. Blood soaked through Kat's light pants where shards of staples were embedded, seeping further down her thigh. "Mon Dieu!"

Kat clenched her teeth together to stop her yelling. The fabric was stapled to her skin. "It's fine, it's fine!" she groaned as she yanked the fabric of her pants up, ripping staples out of her skin. A chunk of staples remained. "Shit." Her back slammed into the wall as she hoisted her leg up.

"Qu'est-ce que j'ai fais?" Héloïse staggered away, hugging her cane to her chest.

"It's fine," Kat hissed. She burrowed her fingers through the rips in the fabric and pried the staples out. Blood squirted onto her fingers, and the skinny metal fragments stabbed under her fingernails. Tears fell from her eyes. The hooks of the staples had caught under her skin.

"I'm sorry. I am really sorry." Héloïse covered her mouth. "This was terrible. I never should have done this. Please. Please, I am sorry."

Kat closed her eyes and gritted her teeth while she ripped the staples out. Even after they were out of her skin, it was agony. She took a breath and stared at the ceiling. "It's my fault. It's fine," Kat said. She limped forward, tossing the bloody staples in the trash, then grabbed a tissue to wipe her fingers with. The remains of her spare stapler lay on her chest, warped into ambiguous scrap metal. A few other fragments littered the floor around her desk. "Maybe we shouldn't have started with a stapler."

"I am so sorry," Héloïse whimpered. Her face was bright red.

"It's not your fault, understand?" Kat said. She grabbed a wad of tissues and compressed it against her thigh. "Just a small cut. Not bad." Despite being small, the staples had pierced her deeper than she'd thought possible. "Perhaps we try that again."

Héloïse gaped at her. "I nearly killed you!"

"That's a stretch," Kat said. She checked her leg and found the bleeding was slowing. "Is your hand alright?"

Héloïse looked at her hand. She still had five fingers where they were supposed to be. Nothing was embedded that didn't belong. "Yes, but—"

"Please. If you try it again, it could work," Kat said. Héloïse shook her head. "Then we can bring back Serena."

Héloïse pouted but lowered her hand on the desk. "No more staplers, yes?"

"Shouldn't be," Kat said. Héloïse pressed her hand against the desk. "Actually, wait!" Héloïse yanked her hand away. Kat flung open the drawer and removed her pair of scissors. "Proceed." Héloïse stared at her nervously, then leaned on the desk. Her fingers vibrated into a blurry silhouette. Her hand disappeared through the wood, and she pulled something out.

Kat braced herself as Héloïse's hand came back into focus. In her palm was a perfectly intact eraser. "See? You can do it!" Kat said. Héloïse almost smiled, but then she stared back at Kat's bloody leg. "Don't worry about that. Let's try again."

Kat and Héloïse practiced grabbing different items from the desk drawer. There was a near mishap as a pencil catapulted through the air, but Kat ducked faster that time. Héloïse picked out all the pencils, erasers, and paper clips, then put them back. Eventually, she picked up the warped stapler and tried twisting it back the correct way. Kat made sure to empty out the rest of the staples inside before letting her try. While it wasn't functional, the metal at least resembled the shape of a stapler.

After a while, Héloïse graduated from desk to window. Her arm passed through the clear glass and moved seamlessly like water. She grabbed a leaf off the creeping ivy on the side of the building and pulled it through. The leaf dissolved immediately, turning Héloïse's fingers green. "What?" Héloïse muttered, staring in disbelief.

Kat bit her lip. Had the leaf juices just smeared on her skin, or had her hand absorbed the plant cells? Héloïse turned her hand back into a blur, shaking it until the green color vanished. No photosynthesis powers for that hand. "Try another leaf," Kat said.

Héloïse put her hand back through the glass. "What if I kill it too?"

"We can keep practicing," Kat said. If Héloïse couldn't touch organic matter, then the plan might not work. She thought of what Maiki had mentioned the other day, organ entanglement. Not an activity she wanted to participate in.

Héloïse grabbed another leaf and pulled it through. It didn't dissolve, but it came back slightly asymmetrical. "I am getting better," Héloïse said.

Perhaps not organ entanglement but organ reconfiguration. Not on her bucket list either. "Grab another?" The third leaf Héloïse grabbed came back intact. Héloïse smiled at Kat, and Kat smiled back. "I want to try something." Kat grabbed her potted philodendron off her windowsill and opened the closet door where she kept space for storage. "Here." Kat handed the plant to Héloïse. "If you could go in there, I'll close the door and see if you can walk out."

"All of me?" Héloïse asked. "With this?" She held up the philodendron.

"I would prefer that."

Héloïse tilted her head to the side and stroked a green leaf with her fingertip.

"Only if you want," Kat added.

Héloïse nodded tentatively. "I could try," she said as she walked into the closet. Kat shut the door and took a step back. The wooden door stayed still. A blurry silhouette emerged. Héloïse's pale face and light hair contrasted with her dark clothing. In the center was a fuzzy green haze. It was all transparent. Even through the silhouette, the wood grain was visible until her body came back into focus. Her outline became sharp and her features distinguishable. Héloïse smiled.

She looked the same. "How do you feel?" Kat asked. She checked over the stems of her plant, turning over the leaves.

Héloïse patted her face. "I feel fine," she said. Her voice quivered in delighted surprise. "Is the plant alright?"

Kat looked up at her and smiled. "Plant's alive." Perhaps this could work.

Héloïse repeated it a few more times, walking in and out through the closed door. Even after she'd walked through the wooden door a dozen times, Kat was impressed each time.

"I want to try one more thing." Kat closed the door to her office.

"Out of your office?" Héloïse asked. "With the wood and glass?"

Kat took the plant from Héloïse and set it on the desk. "Yeah, but bring me through with you." Héloïse's smile dropped, and Kat laughed. "It'll be okay."

"I don't want to hurt you," Héloïse said. Her body tensed as she stared at Kat's leg.

"Think of me as another plant," Kat said.

Héloïse looked back at her. "But you are more big than a plant." Héloïse's eyes widened. "And I killed the first leaf."

Kat smiled at her. Ideally, they'd practice more before

taking this leap. Perhaps graduate to bugs first to test organs. But there wasn't enough time and, technically, plants did have organs. Maybe not brains or hearts, but close enough, right? "I'll be okay," Kat said. She held out her non-bloody hand, and Héloïse stared at it. "I promise, it'll be okay." Well, she hoped it would be okay. But Héloïse didn't need to know about her hesitancy.

Héloïse took Kat's hand and approached the door. "And you're sure about this?" she asked.

"Positive." Kat's heart rate skyrocketed.

Héloïse nodded, and her body started blurring to a transparent silhouette. The flickering spread down her arm and toward Kat's hand, which tingled and dissolved into a blur. It would be funny if Kat screamed. But the poor woman had been through enough already.

The tingling spread up her arm. As if her whole limb had gone numb and fallen asleep. It prickled with pins and needles, spreading to her shoulder and neck. Her breath hitched as the sensation spread to her face. She shut her eyes. The needles on her face stung more, but then they traveled down her body to her legs and feet.

Héloïse pulled Kat along as she stepped forward. Kat peeked her eyes open. Her vision was distorted, like she was looking through a fishbowl. The disorientation made her dizzy.

Héloïse disappeared through the other side of the door, and Kat approached the wood. It didn't feel like wood when she pressed against it. It was like a wall of water. Like liquid pouring over her head—and through her head. Could she get a splinter through her organs? Her stomach lurched at the thought. She emerged on the other side and took a breath.

Héloïse let go of her, and the tingling stopped. Kat stared at her hands. Her sight was restored. Five fingers on each hand. She patted herself down, and everything felt right. Nothing twisted or out of place. No sharp splinters in her intestines. No intestines dangling out like jump ropes. She touched her hair, which came down past her collar. Had it always been this length? Yeah, it was fine. She stared down at her legs. Two legs. Two feet. She laughed with relief.

"I told you it would work," Kat said. Héloïse somberly stared down the hall. Emrah stood in the foyer. "Oh, you're back."

Even from across the house, she could see how stern he looked. "What's going on here?" he asked, setting their bag with lunch down on the coffee table and walking toward them.

Héloïse moved behind Kat. "I figured out how to get inside," Kat said.

Emrah's eyes bugged out of his head as he approached her. "You're not serious."

"This is a big misunderstanding," Héloïse stuttered. She gripped her skirt and twisted the fabric. "I . . . I—"

"It's okay." Kat put a hand on Héloïse's shoulder. "He won't tell."

"I didn't see anything," Emrah said, and he adjusted his glasses. "My vision is just terrible." He smiled at Héloïse. "You mind waiting a second? I need to speak with my boss."

Héloïse stared at him, then at Kat. "I'll be back in a minute," Kat said, opening her office door. Héloïse stepped through and shut it. Emrah took off his glasses and rubbed his eyes. He trudged across the hall to his office. "It'll work," she said as she followed him.

"Kat, you don't know that," he said, clutching his glasses in his hand.

"That's how we get in." She shut his office door and looked at him. "We won't be seen if we go in through the side walls."

Emrah squinted at her. "What're you doing?"

"We can save Serena." Kat tripped over a stack of papers on the floor, but she nudged them to the side. "We can do it."

"She put you up to this?" Emrah pointed his glasses at her. "She paying you more?"

"It was my idea—"

"Oh, svakom loncu poklopac!" He leaned against the filing cabinets and put his glasses back on. "You're a lid to every pot." His voice sharpened on every syllable. "You did more than enough. Why can't you leave it alone?"

"I'm not forcing you to come," Kat said. "This doesn't concern you."

Emrah laughed. His eyes locked on hers, and he cackled in an unsettling manner. Kat stepped back. "I've a *big* concern with this," he snarled. "Makes it a little hard for me to do my job if you're in prison. Or dead."

Kat clenched her jaw and shook her head. "That won't happen."

"You sure about that?" He gestured to her bloody thigh. Kat turned her body to hide her leg. "Take it that's from Héloïse?" he said. "Imagine what ERA will do. Or, oh, I don't know, the fucking Necromancer."

Kat scowled at him. "It was an accident," she said. "It's not going to happen again."

"How? How do you know that?" Kat opened her mouth, but the words didn't come. Emrah stared at her, waiting. She couldn't tell him about the compact, and any other explanation would sound deranged. "Permission to speak freely?" he asked in a lower voice.

"Permission granted," Kat whispered.

"You've gone insane." He stomped closer to her and stared her down. Kat straightened her posture so he wouldn't tower over her so much. "It's terrible what happened to Serena. It's a real tragedy." His voice was gravelly. "But you don't know her. Stop caring so much."

Kat clenched her jaw. "Em, I need to do this."

He shook his head, and his glasses slid down his face. "That's the thing. You really don't!"

"No one helped me when I needed it." Kat's voice broke, but she tried to ignore it. "I never got a second chance. And I never will." His eyes softened at her. "It doesn't have to be the same way for her."

"You can't save them all," Emrah said. "I don't know what you've been through, and I'm sorry for whatever it was. But doing this won't get back whatever you lost."

The unsettling feeling crept back into Kat's stomach. Heat pricked her face. "I know that," she muttered.

"Do you?" Emrah whispered, pain lingering in his eyes. He sighed. "You can spend your life planting a thousand trees, but it won't replace the one that was cut down."

Kat glared at him. "So you expect me to let it keep happening to others? I can't stand around when I could fix it."

Emrah tilted his head at her and raised his voice. "You feel guilty because you can't fix a problem you didn't cause?"

"Yes!" Kat leaned toward him on her toes. "I'm trying to be a good person!"

"You are a good person!"

"But they don't know that!" she yelled in his face. "I need to save her!"

He slammed her shoulders into the filing cabinets. It knocked the air out of her, and she took in a raspy breath. "You can't help anyone else if you're dead," he hissed. He hovered over her face, and Kat caught her breath. The handles of the drawers stabbed into her spine. "If you die, nobody's getting saved. Not Serena. Not Héloïse. Not any other client that would've come to you over the years. Nobody."

Kat's heartbeat pounded in her throat. As much as anger burned in Emrah's eyes, there was also fear. There was no point in trying to convince him. Not unless she was going to admit more about herself than she wanted to. "Why don't you take the rest of the day off?" She tried pushing him off. "Come back tomorrow—"

"And then what?" he asked. His fingers pressed into her shoulders. "Let you get hurt?"

"Em—"

"What's your plan, huh?" He shoved her back and crossed his arms. "Go ahead. What's your big plan? Did you finally come up with one?"

Kat rubbed her arms where his nails had dug into her. "To look for one of those vials?"

He narrowed his eyes on her. "You asking me or telling me?"

"I don't know!" Kat threw her hands in the air. "I just need one! I'll work out what's next from there."

He shook his head. "And if it's not there?"

"Then I'll find out where they are! We can search the place and find out who's behind this so we can get one," she said.

Emrah slumped his head back and bonked into the filing cabinet. Kat brushed her hair out of her face, breathing hard. She had the rest of the day to figure out a plan. It wasn't like she was crazy. The compact had said it could work. If her plan was certain death, Kat would've seen a different flower. Begonias meant saving Serena was possible.

"You're doing this no matter what, aren't you?" Emrah asked, his voice now much drier and calm.

Kat stared at him. His voice might be softer, but his gaze was still harsh. "If Héloïse wants to, yes."

"Someone ever shot at you before?"

Not directly. The FBI had pointed their guns at Kat's family when they'd been taken. And the soldiers had aimed at them while they'd entered the camps. She'd seen others get shot. During the riots or escape attempts. It had also happened while she'd worked at the Claytons'. And Esqueda had pointed a gun at her the other day. But that was different from being shot at.

"No."

"You don't know how you're going to react," Emrah said. "It's easy to assume what you can do until you're standing in the middle of flying bullets."

Kat shifted her jaw to the side. "I take it you have experience?"

He didn't look at her, but he nodded. "If you go, I go."

"You don't have to come with me."

"You're not thinking this through. I'm not letting you die that easily."

Maybe Emrah was the extra precaution Kat needed. But she couldn't let him get hurt. Granted, he was thinking the same thing about her. "Fine," she said, "but for the record, you volunteered."

He smiled insincerely at her. "Don't worry. I won't ask for a raise."

# CHAPTER 19

# THE INTRUDERS

The sky had shifted to a dim orange by the time the three of them approached 18th Street. Emrah had taken them an indirect path to get there. He'd periodically glanced over his shoulder, but no one seemed to have followed them. They were a couple blocks away from the drop site, but Kat wouldn't be surprised if agents were on patrol nearby.

The shops were closed down, and the only establishments open were restaurants and bars. It was getting darker as they got closer. Not too many people were outside on a Tuesday night, which made it easier to avoid getting noticed by bystanders.

The building they needed to get to was in the middle of a long strip of connected buildings. Emrah had figured they could approach from the other end of the street and go in through the walls of the other buildings.

There was no convincing Héloïse out of it. She needed to save Serena. Even if they couldn't succeed, at least she would've tried. They'd spent the rest of the day getting used to Héloïse's powers. Thankfully, no extra clients showed up. Kat locked the door and shut all the blinds just to be safe while

Héloïse practiced. She'd taken both Kat and Emrah through the walls. Emrah had wanted Héloïse to practice more with Kat before he felt comfortable trying it himself. Eventually, he did, and thankfully nothing went wrong. Even after all the practice, Kat couldn't get used to the tingling sensation of dissolving into a blurry silhouette of herself. But at least it became more manageable and less disorientating.

Héloïse hadn't brought her cane. It would only slow her down, and since they were using her powers rather than trying to suppress them, she had no need for it. Kat had bandaged up her leg before leaving. They had all dressed in dark clothing, and they blended in with the shadows outside as the last bits of sunlight faded over the horizon.

"Last chance to back out," Emrah whispered as they approached the edge of the building strip.

"I'm not leaving her," Héloïse said. "I have to do this."

Emrah looked in Kat's direction. She could barely see his face in the dark, but she found his eyes. He wasn't making eye contact, and he kept blinking. "Are you going to be okay in the dark?"

"Made it this far," he said. Kat glanced around, but there was no sign of anyone. Granted, if someone was hiding in a dark window watching them, they were screwed. "The longer we wait, the more likely we'll be noticed."

Héloïse held out her hands. "You are ready, yes?" she whispered. Kat took Héloïse's hand.

Emrah stared down. "If this goes south, we get out of here. Don't hesitate." He took Héloïse's other hand.

Héloïse began to blur and, in the dark, it was nearly impossible to notice her at all. They had more of an advantage than Kat had realized. The tingling hit her hand, and her heart rate spiked. Hopefully, this was what the compact had meant she'd needed to do.

Héloïse wasn't visible, and soon Emrah wasn't either. Kat couldn't see anything in the darkness, but she felt a pull toward the building. She pushed against the bricks. It wasn't as easy as with the walls in the offices. The thick material compressed her. The bricks were rough and coarse, like sand blowing into her. Thousands of sharp grains scraped against her face. She recoiled at the sensation of the dust slicing across her skin. Kat couldn't inhale. Her reflexes wouldn't let her take in a breath. She'd suffocate, choking on the dust. The pressure was building.

Her hand broke through the other side of the wall. Then her arm. Next her shoulder, and the rest of her came through. The pressure vanished, and she stumbled forward. She grabbed her face, running her hands against her cheeks. Smooth skin, not dusty.

"Which building was it?" Héloïse asked. They stood inside an empty laundromat. The front windows provided enough light to see the rows of machines.

"It's the fourth one down," Emrah whispered. "We've a few more to go through." He held his hands out and glanced around the room. Kat reached out to him, but he didn't react. She gently touched his wrist, and he latched onto her with both hands. "Can you see?" he asked.

"Yeah, it's dark, but I can see," she said. "Come on." She gently guided him around the washing machine and down the aisle. He clung to her, taking small steps and trailing behind.

The back wall was lined with a wall of dryers. Kat took Emrah's hand and held it out for Héloïse to hold on to. Kat took her other hand, and the tingling returned as soon as Héloïse vanished in the darkness.

Passing through the machines was easier than expected. It felt like walking through the flower fields back in California. But instead of leaves and flowers, whatever mechanical parts composed the dryers were brushing up against her. The wall came, and it was thick like pudding.

They passed through the other shops. It was dark, but Kat

and Héloïse held Emrah's hands and guided him through the next few buildings. They came to the final wall.

"Héloïse," Emrah whispered. "This next one's it."

"What if I look first?" she whispered.

"They could be inside too," Kat said.

Héloïse let go of their hands. "I'll be right back. They can't see me like this." She dissolved into the air, and the blurring cloud disappeared through the wall.

It was quiet. All they could hear was the faint sound of their breathing. Kat and Emrah waited in some office space, Emrah holding on to Kat's sleeve in the dark. They were far enough away from the windows that anyone on the street wouldn't be able to notice them from afar. The agents were probably hiding too so as not to spook the Necromancer.

"I'm back," Héloïse's voice sounded, and Kat and Emrah straightened. "It's a big office, but I don't think anyone is inside." She took their hands and pulled them through.

It was much darker. Even without night blindness, Kat couldn't see much. The faintest trickle of light shone from outside the room they were in, but it wasn't much.

Kat reached into her pocket and took out a lighter. They were in an office. There was a pristine desk with a chair and filing cabinets, plus a closet door and the exit to the rest of the space. Kat slowly pulled open the filing cabinet drawer. It glided silently, like it had never been used before. It was empty. She checked the rest of the drawers. All of them were empty.

Kat walked to the closet and opened it. Empty. Nothing on the desks. Nothing in the drawers.

"What is it?" Emrah said, somewhere behind her.

Kat glanced around the room. "Everything's staged," she said, then took Emrah's hand and guided him toward the door.

The layout was huge. No wonder it had taken Héloïse a few minutes to return. A massive sea of cubicles was laid out in a grid. A wall separated the bullpen from the front lobby with an archway entrance. The moonlight from the lobby windows filtered through the archway and made the bullpen more visible than the private office. As long as they stayed out of the archway's line of sight, any agents looking in through the front windows wouldn't see them.

A few private offices lined the walls. "Stay here," Kat said. She slowly moved against the wall to the next office. The door was ajar, and she held her lighter inside. Her heart was pounding, but she kept her breathing quiet. She half expected a face to emerge from the darkness and grab her.

The orange flame from her lighter barely illuminated the room. Another pristine office with nothing inside. Filing cabinets for show and nothing of use in the desk. Stapler with no staples inside. Pencils in a cup but all of them unsharpened.

Kat stepped back into the main area where Emrah waited with Héloïse. He had a lighter out too, and they stood against the wall. "What now?" he asked.

The fake office likely wouldn't offer any clues leading them to the Necromancer. They needed the vials to be at the site. Hopefully, whoever had collected the briefcase payment had dropped off the vials too. Kat held her wristwatch to the flame. 10:55. "We have a bit before the meeting time, but let's get out of here well before midnight," Kat whispered. If they got back early, then maybe she could use the compact tonight to figure out how to find Serena's body. "We can split up to search faster." Héloïse nodded. Emrah looked at Kat, actually making eye contact with her. "Can you see?" she asked.

"More than I could before," he whispered as he gestured to the lighter.

"Good, good." She smiled. "As soon as we find one of the vials, we're getting out of here."

"And they said Sparrow on them?" Héloïse asked.

"Yeah, or pan sear."

Emrah laughed under his breath. "Well, I don't know if I

can see well enough to read, so if I feel anything like a glass vial, I'll have you verify for me."

"Héloïse, help Emrah search these offices," Kat said. "And stay out of the line of sight of the entranceway."

"What if the vials are on the other side?" Héloïse asked.

Kat glanced across the office bullpen, where there were a few other rooms lining the walls. But they'd have to cross over. "I'll take care of those. Check the offices on this wall in case one of them has anything."

Emrah went into the next room with Héloïse, and Kat started ahead. A few of the cubicles extended out and could cover her from the line of sight of the archway. Hopefully, no one outside would notice her.

She went to the back of the office and crawled into the cubicle. Inside was a small desk with a wooden chair in the station. Nothing on the desk that looked like anyone worked there. The drawers were also empty. She closed her lighter.

The walkway had a gap to get to the other side of the office. Kat was in the back and concealed by the dark. She had dark clothes on and dark hair. No one would see her if she was quick. She took a breath and darted across the gap to the other cubicle. Her heart pounded in her ears. Most of her cases weren't this nerve-wracking. For her blood pressure's sake, she was glad.

The other side of the wall didn't have as many private offices. Only two doors on opposite ends of the wall. Kat flicked her lighter open and approached one of the doors.

The abyss of darkness consumed the room. Her little lighter didn't do much. Hair rose on the back of her neck when she stepped inside. Héloïse said no one was in the building. No one was inside. Yet it felt like someone was in the room with her.

This room was bigger than the other offices. Kat slowly took another step forward. It wasn't an office but a conference room. On the other side of the room, another door connected back to the hallway. She held the lighter up and could make out the silhouette of a large oval table in the center of the room. Chairs were sparsely scattered around the table. A staged conference room for fake meetings too? She approached the edge of the table, and the smell hit her. The hospital.

The smell of bleach was unmistakable. Not the summertime smell of pools. Not the household kitchen cleaner. Industrial medical bleach. Pungent chemicals soaked into the mops she'd used to clean the floors in the surgical suites. Between the caustic smell of bleach and the glaring fluorescent lights, she had always felt sick after her shifts at the hospital. The smell was the worst part. The smell lingered. It never washed off her skin.

The scent was faint, but she knew it all too well. The closer she got to the table, the stronger it got. The table reeked of it. Kat held the lighter to the surface, where the varnish had been eaten away. The rims still had their luster, but the top was splotchy with exposed, stressed wood. Like the table had been cleaned over and over, and the coating had been scrubbed away.

The Necromancer was a WWII medic. He had probably maintained his surgical sanitization standards. Bad guys had standards. Murder wasn't off the table, but germs were. Then again, he had probably seen the results of shoddy disinfection and knew it was worse than murder. And yet he worked with Edmund Clark, who chose to live in that dumpster?

Kat scanned the perimeter of the room. Something loomed in the corner. She backed up. It wasn't moving. What was that? Big and bulky. Boxes? She inched around the table, holding on to the backs of the chairs in front of her. Not boxes. A weird filing cabinet. She hopped behind the next chair and held on to it as if it would protect her. A fridge? In the conference room?

Kat inched closer. It was a full-sized fridge. Was this

supposed to be their fake break room instead of a conference room? Kat pulled on the handle, but it didn't budge. Metal jiggled. She moved the lighter down. Someone had drilled a chain into the side of the fridge. Thick and heavy chain links with a bulky padlock to secure them. The chain wrapped around the bottom of the handle three times and held it shut.

Was this where the vials were kept? They needed to be refrigerated? Everything else in the building was fake, but this room was real. The bleach on the table. The lock on the fridge. This had to be where the vials were kept.

Kat yanked on the lock. The thick steel didn't budge. Didn't even wiggle. She needed the key. Or Emrah. Or Héloïse.

Kat set the lock back down and peered out of the conference room. Where the hell were they? She went to the back wall and darted across the bullpen, then poked her head in one of the rooms. Emrah's silhouette froze when he saw her. Kat flicked on her lighter. "It's me," she whispered.

"It better be," he said in a low voice.

Kat walked over to him. He was in the room alone. "Where's Héloïse?" she asked.

"We split up to look faster," he said. "Any luck?"

"I think I found it."

"You did?"

"But it's locked. I need help." Kat reached out and took his hand.

She led him back to the conference rooms quietly. Emrah gripped her hand as they crawled through the bullpen, and she guided him through the darkness.

Once they were in the conference room, she took out her lighter. "There," she whispered, pointing to the fridge in the corner of the room.

They walked over to it, and Emrah patted it down with his hands. He grabbed the lock and felt it. "Yeah, I can do that," he said, then dug into his pocket and took out his tools. "You think the vials need to be kept cold to work?"

"Maybe?" Kat whispered. "We can store them in my fridge until we know what to do next." Emrah tried getting his tools into the lock but missed. Kat tried to hold the flame closer without setting his hair on fire. "Can you see?"

He leaned his face inches away from the lock. "Eh, not really," he muttered. Kat took his wrist and aligned his hands properly. "Thanks."

"Are you able to open it?"

"Don't need to see anymore." He slowly maneuvered his fingers as he wiggled the tools deeper. "It's a touch-and-feel game from here."

"Good, because I can't do that part for you," Kat said. Emrah closed his eyes while he angled his hands back and forth. "Maybe we find Héloïse instead—"

"Wait," he whispered. He furrowed his eyebrows together and tilted his fingers down. Kat held her breath as Emrah lowered his hands. The final pin clicked. "Got it." He turned the tool, and the lock popped open.

"You're the best." Kat put the lighter back in her pocket.

"Don't forget that," Emrah said while he put his tools away.

Kat grabbed the chain and untangled it from the handle. The links clinked together, so she pressed them against her stomach to muffle the noise. She could barely see her hands, but she kept untangling the chain as quietly as she could. Emrah tapped his fingers on the handle. Kat unwrapped the last loop, and the door was free. "Now," she said. He cracked open the fridge.

The door sprang open and whammed into Kat. "The hell!" she cried out as she dropped the chains, which crashed against the fridge and rattled.

She stumbled backward and held her shoulder where the door had struck her. The chains kept rattling, shattering the silence. A gush of frosty air rushed into the room and chilled her ankles.

"Emrah?" She fumbled for her lighter.

The only sound she could hear was the clinking of the chains slowing to a stop. And then a raspy gasp from the ground. "What the fuck," Emrah whimpered.

Kat flicked on the lighter. It wasn't a fridge but a box freezer. Layers of frost buildup coated the inside, but it was empty. No shelving units. No trays. No vials. Emrah lay face down on the floor.

Kat reached down to grab his arm, but it was frozen solid. Kat jolted back as a frozen body lurched to the side. Emrah wheezed from underneath it.

Kat grabbed his arm, and his skin felt warm and soft. She dragged him to her, but he scampered back. The body rolled off his legs as he swatted at his face, hyperventilating. "It's okay, it's okay," Kat whispered in his ear. She wrapped her arms around his chest.

He twitched, and his legs kicked out. He smacked his face. "Something—my mouth." His voice cracked as he released a guttural groan. "Touched my mouth," he hissed.

"Quiet, quiet," she said, holding him tighter. It was too loud. Between the chain dropping, her yelling, and his flailing, it was too loud. Her ears rang with adrenaline.

He curled forward and frantically scrubbed his mouth with his sleeve. Kat held out the lighter. The other body lay stiffly on the floor where Emrah had shoved it. *That* had been in the freezer? Was it . . .

Kat let go of Emrah and crawled toward the body. Her hands were shaking as she turned it over. The body was rigid. It didn't feel like a person but a steel mannequin. Stiff and lifeless. The cold burned her fingers.

It was a woman. Her skin was discolored and frostbitten. Her dark hair was brittle but secured in a bun. Her eyes were closed, but Kat recognized the heavy brows.

"Is that what I think it is?" Emrah whispered.

"It's Serena," Kat said. She was wearing a dark women's pantsuit and black flats. It looked like her work outfit. They'd taken her right after she was killed? "At least we know where she is."

"What good's her body if we don't have the vial?" Emrah asked.

The room was getting colder as the freezer spilled out more frozen air. Kat glanced at her watch. 11:18. They were cutting it too close to the meeting time. She had hoped they would be leaving by now. But they'd searched most of the area. Nothing else was in the room. "Where else would they be?"

"What if they're not here?" Emrah asked. "What if the Necromancer hasn't brought them yet?"

"Then we're screwed," Kat whispered. This wasn't the plan. The compact had said there was a way. The begonias. What else could they have meant—

The front door opened in the lobby.

Kat darted to her feet and hauled Serena's body up. The cold corpse was rock solid, like a sculpture. The cold numbed Kat's fingers as she shoved Serena back inside the freezer. Thankfully, her body had been frozen in a curled position that was easy to fit.

Footsteps scuffled from afar, faint and distant. They were in the lobby. Had ERA heard them? Or was it the Necromancer already?

Kat grabbed the chain. The links clinked once, but she stopped moving to silence them. Three times. The chain had been wrapped around the freezer handle three times and locked in place. Nobody could know they were there. Slowly, Kat looped the chain around the handle without making a sound. One.

The lights came on over the bullpen. They were coming, but at least she could see what she was doing. Two.

Emrah scrambled next to her and grabbed her arm, but she didn't budge. Kat stiffly switched hands again to pass the chain through one more time. Emrah's lips pressed against her ear. "Let go," he hissed.

Kat pulled it through. Three. Emrah grabbed the lock and looped it through the chain link. He pressed it firmly against his stomach to muffle the sound as he clicked it closed. Footsteps shuffled closer, as did the sounds of sniffling and heavy mouth breathing. ERA wouldn't be so obvious. It was the Necromancer.

# CHAPTER 20

# THE NECROMANCER

Emrah set the lock down and grabbed Kat's waist. They dove behind the conference table and crawled under. Emrah scooted the chairs to conceal them from the doorway.

Kat curled up next to Emrah and prayed the darkness would cover them. Her heart raced so fast in her chest it made her dizzy. Granted, being under the table, the potency of the bleach smell was even stronger. The chemicals clouded her mind.

A shadow stretched on the floor, and black boots emerged in the doorway. He flicked on the conference room lights and shuffled inside. Kat held her breath and shut her eyes.

He trudged into the room, his heavy boots scraping against the carpet. They were supposed to have more time. It wasn't supposed to be until midnight. He must've arrived early to set up for the meeting. But that wasn't written on the calendar. How was she supposed to know? ERA was coming, and they'd do a sweep of the whole building.

Kat and Emrah and Héloïse wouldn't be able to get out. They were trapped. Tears seeped from her eyelids. A foul smell struck her nose.

Over the smell of the bleach, the scent of death wafted into the room. It wasn't the Necromancer. Clark. Kat opened her eyes. Serena's corpse had smelled better than Clark.

The chains rattled against the fridge as he fiddled with the lock. It popped open, and he yanked the chain off. The chain clamored against the fridge as he opened the freezer.

Wisps of cold air spiraled over the floor as he dug Serena's body out and hauled her over to the table. Emrah lowered his head, and Kat grabbed his arm. A heavy thud pounded above them as Clark dropped her frozen corpse on top. Her whole body was a solid block of ice. And the vial of who knows what would be able to restore her to life? Her body scraped against the table, and it boomed in Kat's ears.

11:21. There was no way she'd make it back in time to use the compact tonight. At least she had found out where Serena was, so her question had been answered anyway. Granted, right now the compact was the least of her worries. They had almost half an hour left before all hell broke loose. Assuming ERA even waited until midnight. They needed the Necromancer, and only Clark had shown up. Was there even a chance they could make it out? Héloïse was still out there somewhere. Maybe she could save them. Maybe there was a chance.

Clark sniffed and groaned as he locked the chain back up. He trudged over to the table and pulled out one of the chairs. Emrah coiled his legs back as Clark plopped down. His feet protruded inches away from Emrah. Clark rustled in his jacket pocket and unscrewed a lid. He slurped loudly.

Kat leaned against Emrah and held her watch out for him. He rested his head on top of hers as they stared at the watch face. The faint ticking sound couldn't be heard above Clark's heavy mouth breathing.

The second hand marched on. Minutes passed. Maybe they could sprint. Maybe they didn't have to worry about not being seen—just about being recognized or captured. If they could run quickly, they just had to make it to Héloïse and dart through the walls. But how fast could they get out from under the table and run past Clark?

It was a quarter till. Kat's heart sank. She wished she had Telepathy so she could get a plan out to Emrah and Héloïse. Granted, if she could read Emrah's mind, he'd probably be scolding her right now. He'd be right. Trying to bring one person back from the dead might end up putting three more in the grave.

A back door clicked open. Clark turned and slid away from the table. Low voices murmured outside the conference room. Nothing discernable. Just the low vibrations and the scuffling of boots on the carpet.

Clark got out of the chair and left the room. Kat looked at Emrah. It was their only chance. Kat crawled out from beneath the table, but Emrah grabbed her calf and tugged her back. They were coming in. Kat ducked back under.

"Just hurry up already," a gruff voice said. It was Clark's.

"I'm here for my patient first. You come second," a second male voice said. It was smooth, but he didn't have the same city accent. Was that the Necromancer? "You can wait."

A cluster of heavy boots crowded around the table. Kat pulled her knees into her chest and clenched her jaw. Maybe half a dozen men had entered the room. They were surrounded.

"Can't you give it to me first?" Clark grumbled.

Something thudded on the table. Not Serena. Something else had been set down. "Depends on if you learned your lesson," the man said.

"I get it, I get it. You won't hear from me ever again," Clark said.

"If I hear one rumor, one whisper—"

"You won't," Clark snapped. "We're done."

"Then it's been a pleasure doing business with you, *Mr. Smith*." The man spoke with a sarcastic cheeriness. He had to be the Necromancer. Something scraped against the table. He must be sliding Serena's body around. "What exactly happened to her?" he asked.

"How should I know?" Clark scoffed. "Clumsy bitch fell down the stairs." Her body rolled like the Necromancer was angling her around to examine her. "You got all the money, right? We're done."

"Yeah, speaking of her payment," the Necromancer said. His voice turned sharp. "Over triple what the charges should've been."

"So?" Clark grumbled. "They had money to burn."

"Funny how it was the exact amount for your quota."

"What difference does it make?" Clark huffed. "They paid it off. You got your money."

Serena's body thudded back onto the table, and the Necromancer stomped toward Clark. Clark stumbled back, but the other men didn't let him get far. "Did you kill that young woman?" the Necromancer asked.

"I—what?"

"The bruising on her neck is too clean." The other men blocked Clark from the door. The Necromancer hadn't wanted Serena killed? Clark had done that of his own accord?

"What difference does it make? You got your money."

The Necromancer sighed bitterly. "Oh, it's not about the money," he growled. He stepped closer to Clark, and Clark shuddered.

"Did you hear something?" a different man asked.

The room fell quiet. Kat closed her eyes. She didn't move a muscle. Emrah sat rigidly still next to her. "What?" the Necromancer asked, a hint of concern in his voice. Pressure built in Kat's head as she held her breath. This was it. It was over.

One of the men shuffled out of the conference room. "Did anyone follow us?" a nasally guy asked as he poked his head into the hall.

"Are you sure you're not just hearing the voices again?" someone else laughed. A few others chuckled.

"Clam it," the Necromancer snapped. He walked toward the doorway. The silence rang in Kat's ears. She pressed her palms into her mouth as tears welled in her eyes. Nobody moved.

The back door exploded open. Everyone in the room scuffled. "You rat!" the Necromancer shouted.

"The hell? I didn't do this!" Clark hollered.

Gunfire broke out. Shock seized Kat's body, and her limbs locked up. Glass shattered, and the lights went out one by one. Darkness flooded the room. Everyone ran out of the conference room, and flashes from gunshots lit up the hall like lightning. A plume of black smoke erupted in the hallway. The bullets and shouting and screaming. It reverberated. It was deafening.

Kat flew backward. Emrah dragged her out from under the table. "Now or never," he whispered. Kat's legs locked up, and she staggered to her feet. Serena's corpse was thawing on the table. Next to her was a briefcase. That was it.

Emrah hauled Kat toward the doorway, but she slipped away from him. "There's no time!" he hissed.

She grabbed the briefcase and flipped the latches, but it wouldn't open. Locked. Gunshots rang out, and she curled in on herself. She shook the case violently, but it wouldn't open. She couldn't get the lock.

Emrah yanked the case from her hands and stared at it. "It's locked!" Kat cried. "There's a lock—" He smashed it to the ground, and the case exploded. That worked too.

Blue light emerged from the splinters. Two small vials. Corked inside was a cerulean liquid that illuminated the room. Time stood still.

Kat picked up the vials, and they were chilling to the touch. This . . . this was life? Life was cold? The color was so vibrant. A sense of tranquility washed over her. She couldn't hear the bullets anymore. A soothing hum encompassed her. Liquid sky trapped behind the glass.

Emrah's voice was muffled as he said something about Maiki and pan sear. Black ink scrawled on the glass. Both said *"Panacea."* One had *"e clark"* and the other *"s line."*

Emrah snatched one of the vials from her hand and ran in slow motion. The light reflected off his glasses and illuminated his face. He poured the liquid through Serena's parted lips, and the light disappeared. The frost on her skin dissipated, and the ice thawed rapidly on the table. She was coming back to life.

Kat stared at the vial in her hand. The aura hummed louder. Choirs of angels serenaded in her ears. She could bring anyone back to life. She could do anything she wanted. It was hers.

Emrah shook her, and she snapped out of the haze. The gunfire echoed, and her adrenaline resurged. "I said run!"

Shots concussed in her ears. Half the lights were out. Opaque black smoke crept into the room. Gunpowder lingered in the air, but not the smell of smoke. It was dark. She couldn't breathe. Screams echoed across the room. It was dark. It was too loud. It was dark.

Emrah pulled her toward the doorway. Into the darkness. Where they'd be shot up. Torn apart by bullets. Like the man who'd tried climbing the fence. "No, no," she whimpered.

Emrah gripped her wrist and looked at her. "On three," he said. Kat shook her head. "Yes. One, two—"

"Em—"

"Three."

He yanked her, and they sprinted into the hall. Bullets flew through the smoke in front of them. Kat ducked her head and ran. Left foot. Right foot. She couldn't see through the smoke. She couldn't hear over the gunfire. She only felt Emrah's hand. And it ripped out of her grasp.

Someone collided into her. She crashed into one of the

cubicles. Her head smashed into the wooden desk. Sparks crackled in her vision, and it all went black and blurry. She slumped down and crumpled to the floor, head pounding. Someone was on her. Crushing her. Limp. "Em," she murmured. Her vision returned with static. Not Emrah. The man wore a suit and had a shaved haircut. An agent. His vacant eyes stared into hers. Dead.

Kat gripped the vial in her hand and crawled over the dead body. The side of her skull throbbed where she'd hit the desk. Her hands trembled as she crawled. Her elbows threatened to give out. The gunfire kept echoing. She couldn't see Emrah through the smoke. He was gone. Maybe safe. Or dead. Well, if he was, he wouldn't stay dead. She had the spare vial.

Kat bolted off her feet and ran with her head down. She clutched the vial in her fist and held it against her chest. They weren't going to die. They'd saved Serena. They could escape. A body charged out of the smoke. It slammed into her. She flew backward and hit the ground. Her brain jostled in her skull, and she winced. The room undulated. She couldn't tell which way was up. If she hadn't had a concussion before, she probably did now.

She teetered forward. The man landed a few feet away from her. Clark. Between the two of them was his gun. It was him or her. Kat lunged for it.

She snatched it before he could grab it, then shuffled backward and aimed it at him. The metal rattled in her shaking hand. Her finger froze against the trigger.

Clark locked eyes with hers. Bullets sprayed between them. She shrieked and rolled out of the way. The bullets sank into the cubicle walls. She covered her head, gripping the gun and the vial. Had Clark been hit, or was he still behind her? Did he know she had his vial? She dragged herself under one of the desks.

She clutched the gun in front of her and held it ready. She

didn't want to kill anyone. She just didn't want to die. Footsteps stomped closer to her. Clark was coming back. She held the gun up. She didn't want this. He ran toward her. Her finger curled around the trigger.

The gun exploded and her arm flew back, her wrist smacking into the desk. Emrah plummeted onto her.

"What the hell!" she cried.

He grabbed her shoulders. "You've shit aim." The cubicle wall had a bullet hole in it.

"Well, thank God."

"Hajmo." He hauled her to her feet and yanked her along.

Emrah gripped her wrist tighter this time. She couldn't feel her feet. Stars floated at the edges of her vision. He ran faster than she could keep up with. Her throat went dry, and she couldn't breathe. Emrah jumped over something, but she tripped. Another agent sprawled on the ground in a pool of blood. Bright red blood soaked into the carpet. Emrah dragged Kat along, and the body disappeared in the smoke.

He hauled her into an office and tossed her against the wall. The room had less smoke, but there was still a faint haze. Kat slumped against the floor, her head spinning. The throbbing worsened with each gunshot.

"Found her!" Emrah called out. Héloïse popped her head out from behind the desk, and she ran to Emrah. He reached for her. A dark figure bolted in the room.

"No!" Héloïse screeched and lunged forward. Emrah whipped around, and the man aimed a gun. He fired.

Three shots cracked in the air.

Emrah's face dissolved as the bullets flew into his head. Kat shrieked. Emrah's body collapsed and disintegrated before he hit the ground. A blurry haze flew across the room and disappeared through the wall.

The man pointed the gun at Kat. She gritted her teeth and stared at him. A black mask and hood covered his head.

She could only see his eyes. And the barrel of the gun. Tears trickled down her cheeks. He pulled the trigger.

Click.

He pulled the trigger again, but it only clicked again. Kat clenched her jaw. Enough bullets to finish Emrah but not enough for her, huh? She raised her gun.

The man put his hands out. "Hey, let's make a deal, doe eyes." His voice was silk. The Necromancer. "I didn't kill you, so you don't kill me."

"You shot him," she growled, her voice raw from screaming.

"I think I missed." He dropped the gun and backed away.

"You killed him!" Kat stood to her feet and shook the gun at him.

The Necromancer backed up against the desk. "Little disappearing act might've saved him," he said. "Neat trick."

Kat squeezed the vial in her left hand. The cold glass numbed her palm. The humming crept into the back of her mind. Emrah wouldn't stay dead. But it might feel good to kill this guy anyway. She fired.

The edge of the desk exploded into splinters. The Necromancer flinched and then stared back at her. Why had she done that? "You don't want to shoot me, doe eyes. It won't stick." He jumped on the desk and pushed a ceiling tile to the side.

Kat's hand shook even after the recoil. Why had she shot? She didn't want to hurt anyone. The Necromancer pulled himself into the ceiling. Emrah wouldn't stay dead. But no one else had to die. The humming buzzed in her brain. Gunshots rang out. Bullets tore into the Necromancer's body. A red mist plumed into the air.

"Fuck!" he shouted as he fell from the ceiling and crashed onto the desk. His silky voice turned to gravel. He groaned and convulsed on the surface. A woman ran into the room. Agent Esqueda. Kat sank to the floor and tossed the gun away.

Esqueda yanked the Necromancer's arms and dug out her cuffs. Blood was already pooling over the surface of the desk.

The Necromancer pounced on Esqueda. His hands latched on to her throat, and she screamed. Kat ran to her, but the humming returned and immobilized her body. Time stood still.

Wisps of sky-blue light spiraled from Esqueda's face and into the Necromancer. The humming segued into a lullaby. Esqueda's knees buckled, and she sank under his grasp. When the Necromancer let go of her, she crumpled to the ground. The last bits of blue light twirled around his arms and neck, piercing into him. He climbed back up and disappeared through the ceiling. The song faded. Gunshots and screams echoed from the hall. The Necromancer was gone.

Esqueda lay on the ground, taking shallow breaths. Kat crawled toward her. Esqueda clutched her abdomen, blood smeared all over her hands. Her shirt was intact, but blood was seeping through her clothes like she had been shot repeatedly.

Blood soaked her entire shirt. "You—What are you . . ." Esqueda whined. Her Southern accent had lost its sweet melody. Her voice was filled with terror. "Hurts. It hurts." Tears trickled down her face. Her sienna skin had turned a sickly pale color. Kat's chest tightened at hearing her whimper. "I didn't . . . How did . . ." Esqueda choked up. She grabbed Kat's hand. Her palms were slick with blood, and it streaked on Kat's skin. There was so much blood.

The tingling sensation spread through her shoulders. Esqueda's hands fell through hers. Kat whipped back toward Héloïse, who was a blurry silhouette. Kat could barely see her face, but her eyes were frantic. "Emrah?" Kat whispered. Her voice was disembodied. Literally.

"He's alive," Héloïse said.

"He's safe?"

"I got him in time. Let's go."

Relief washed over Kat. She cackled hysterically and then started crying. Material Phasing made people immune to bullets after all.

Héloïse pulled her toward the wall. They were all alive. "Wait," Kat said. She pried out of Héloïse's grasp, and her body solidified. Esqueda closed her eyes as her breathing faded. Emrah was alive. Serena was back. No one else had to die.

Kat unclenched her left fist. The blue light glittered in the room, and the humming returned. She could do anything she wanted. *Who cares if one more stranger dies?* Kat recoiled at her thoughts. What was it doing to her?

Kat turned away, but the melody called to her. It sang louder. She uncorked the vial and cupped Esqueda's face as she poured the liquid into her mouth. Esqueda whined as she drank. The blue light glistened on her lips. Beautiful light draining away on a stranger.

The humming reverberated in Kat's ears. The soothing melody morphed into harsh discord. *What a waste. She could have saved anyone, and she'd chosen a stranger? She could have done anything she wanted. She could have fixed everything. A waste.*

Kat shook her head. She stroked Esqueda's cheek with her thumb and wiped away her tears. The last drop of blue disappeared, and the sound ceased.

Esqueda took a deep breath, and the warm color returned to her face. She moved her hands off of her wound and slowly sat up. Blood still covered her chest, but it wasn't gushing anymore. She stared at Kat in disbelief. "Why?" Esqueda asked.

The tingling returned to Kat's shoulders and spread down the rest of her body. Even with distorted vision, Kat saw Esqueda smile. Héloïse pulled Kat through the wall.

# CHAPTER 21
# THE FRIEND

Héloïse let go once Kat was through the wall. The tingling stopped. The muffled gunshots were barely audible. Kat's ears were ringing from the silence.

"Is she okay?" Emrah asked.

Kat tackled him into a hug, and he coughed.

"I'm so glad you're alive," she sighed, squeezing him tightly. Hot tears spilled from her eyes and dripped onto his shoulder.

"Yeah, me too," he laughed and hugged her back.

She trembled against him and sniffled. "I'm sorry," she whispered. "I'm sorry. You were right."

"Nah, you were right," he said. He patted her back twice, and she let go of him. "Let's not stick around."

Héloïse took their hands and led them out of the rest of the building. They stayed in the shifting form for several more blocks. It didn't feel like they were running. Kat's feet hit the ground but with less impact. Air rushed through them. It felt like speeding down a hill in a wagon. Nothing could slow them down.

It was maybe another mile before they stopped running. There was no way they'd be caught here. Héloïse let go of them, and they solidified. The tingling faded, but Kat's skin still prickled with the lingering sensation from her overstimulated nerves.

"Listen," Kat whispered, "if anyone asks, you know nothing." Héloïse nodded at her. "You were home the whole evening. You know nothing."

"And Serena?" Héloïse asked.

"Let ERA think she came back during the commotion," Emrah said. "You're surprised by all of this."

Héloïse nodded. She looked at Kat and then threw her arms around her. "Thank you," she whispered. "For believing me. And everything else."

Kat hugged her tightly. "Thanks for going back for me."

They said their goodbyes and split up. Emrah walked Kat home. They walked much slower. No need to run anymore. And two people going for an absurdly late-night stroll were less suspicious than two people sprinting in the dark.

The streetlamps and half-lit moon illuminated the sidewalks. A gentle breeze rustled through the trees. The night air soothed Kat's eardrums. The ringing faded away. But her head still ached, a bruise already forming.

"You can go back to your apartment," Kat said, her voice still raw. "I can make it from here."

"It's on the way." Emrah's voice was much calmer. Like they were returning from a mundane night at the bar and nothing more.

"Thank you for what you did," Kat said. "I . . . I didn't think I'd freeze up like that."

"Figured you didn't know what you were getting into."

"How did you stay so calm?" she asked. "Well, except for when that body fell on you."

"Hey, there's a very big difference between having a corpse fall on you and getting shot at," he said. "I'd take getting shot at any day of the week."

Kat smiled. "I'd rather have the corpse fall on me."

"Easy to say until it touches your mouth." Emrah shuddered and shook his head at the thought. "Second day in a row there's been a health code violation. We could do with less excitement for a while. Don't need you putting your life on the line for the rest of the month."

"Deprive me for a whole month?" Kat scoffed in fake pain. "I can't live like this."

Emrah rubbed his sleeve over his mouth. "Well, too bad. I doubt we'll be so lucky the next time we're getting shot at."

Kat's smile faded, and she glanced at him. "Back there . . . He would've shot you?"

Emrah adjusted his glasses, stretching his jaw out. "Felt it go through," he said, his voice becoming uneven.

Kat's stomach twisted. "What did it feel like?"

Emrah stared ahead. The light from the streetlamps reflected off his glasses and concealed his irises. "Strange. Like scratching an impossible itch." He shook his head. "I don't know. Don't want to think about it."

Intestines were no longer in the lead for the worst possible organ entanglement. Hopefully the bullets hadn't stirred anything around in Emrah's head. "I'm glad you're alive," Kat said.

"You sure?" He smirked at her. "You weren't trying to finish me off with the gun back there? Wanted to get out of paying me overtime?"

Kat bumped her shoulder into him. "I didn't know it was you."

"You could've killed me. You owe me," he laughed. "So now I forbid you from dying."

"Because you'd miss my money?"

"Obviously." Kat could hear the smile in his voice. Emrah cleared his throat as they crossed the street. His voice was softer when they made it back on the sidewalk. "Look, I, um . . . I don't blame you if you still don't trust me," he said, "but I'd like to consider us friends. Not just because you pay me."

Kat looked at him, but he stared ahead and clenched his jaw. A nervousness crept into her throat. It'd been a rocky start, but they had moved past it. The jokes, the meals, the drinks shared. It had taken a while to learn how to be comfortable around him. But the comfort had come like a thunderstorm after a drought. "I forgave you a while ago," she said. "I'd like to be friends."

Emrah nodded a bit forcefully. His glasses slid down his face, and he shoved them back up. "That's good. Me too. I . . . I don't have many friends. Actually, don't have any friends," he muttered.

"I don't either," Kat sighed. "We have each other from now on?"

"I'd like that," he said. "Next time you have a stupid plan, know that I'm calling you out because I care."

"Well, I'll keep that in mind. Maybe I'll listen better."

Emrah laughed, and the lightness returned to his voice. "Don't listen to me too much though. This somehow worked," he said. "We got her back. And you got a spare?"

Kat pursed her lips to the side. "Eh, not exactly. I . . . used it."

"What?" He grabbed her shoulder and pulled her back to face him.

"No, no, I'm okay." She brushed his hand away. "Remember Agent Esqueda?"

Emrah stopped walking. "They know you were there now?"

Kat glanced back at him and brushed her hair out of her face. "If it wasn't for me, she'd be dead. I'd like to think she wouldn't rat me out." Emrah stared at her, shifting his jaw to the side. The streetlamps illuminated his blond hair but cast a shadow over his face. He stared at her, and her stomach twisted. Esqueda had better not make her regret it. "I was trying to be a good person," Kat mumbled.

Emrah strolled along with her. "Didn't need to save her to prove that."

Kat's face heated. "Well, it's too late to get it back," she said, brushing her hair behind her ears. "Besides, they can't prove I was there if I don't have it. And I didn't really want to keep hearing the humming."

"Humming?"

"From the vial. The blue light," she said.

Emrah stared at her, tilting his head. "Light doesn't make a sound."

"What? No, I know that, but the magic part was humming."

"You got tinnitus?" he asked.

She huffed at him. "No, did . . ." Emrah raised an eyebrow. The sinking feeling crept back. "You didn't hear it?" she whispered.

"What'd it sound like?" The edge had returned to his voice.

"It . . ." How was she supposed to describe it? Like the sound of someone clearing her mind and twisting her thoughts? "I don't know. Like a soothing voice?" She pulled the front of her shirt so the collar would stop rubbing against her neck. "It made everything quiet, and it felt like the ocean. It . . . it felt like nothing bad could happen when I looked into the light."

"Are you a moth?"

Kat's jaw fell, and she glared at him. "How dare you."

He smiled but furrowed his eyebrows. "I was wondering what had gotten into you," he said. "You looked a bit empty in the eyes. Figured it was shock."

"I definitely was in shock too," Kat said. A knot pulled in her stomach. Why hadn't Emrah heard the humming? What was wrong with her? Despite solving the case, she had more questions swirling in her mind. And it was well past midnight. She'd have to wait until tomorrow to use the compact. "Well, thanks for not letting me get killed."

"Hey, what're friends for?"

Emrah dropped her off at her house. The lights were still on like she'd left them. "Take a half day tomorrow," Kat said as she hopped up her front steps. "I don't want to see you until lunch."

"You sure?" Emrah asked, lingering on the sidewalk.

"Yeah. I'm sleeping in, so don't show up. I beg of you," she said. "I'll see you later, as long as I'm not arrested."

"I'll bail you out of jail."

Kat laughed nervously. "Jail and prison are a bit different." She unlocked her front door.

Emrah cracked a grin. "Then I forge your new identity, and you go to California with your cousin."

Kat grumbled and opened her door. "Go to bed." Emrah shuffled backward on the sidewalk and blended into the darkness.

Kat's head pounded by morning. Movement made it worse. Sound made it worse. Light made it worse. The side of her face was bright fuchsia and swollen. Her left eye had trouble opening. Her headache blocked out the soreness from her scabbing thigh. She had forgotten about it until she'd seen it in the shower and nearly passed out from dizziness.

It was a toss-up for what made her feel more nauseous— the dizzying headache or her empty stomach. She barely made it downstairs before eleven. The only reason she bothered eating was to placate her stomach so it would stop digesting itself. She didn't bother making toast, just slathered a glob of strawberry jam onto the soft slice of bread.

She was so out of it she barely noticed how pathetic the jam was.

Emrah found her slumped over the table, lazily chewing her breakfast. He came by at a quarter after noon and then brought her painkillers. Either her concussion had gone away, or the drugs had done the trick. She was in better spirits and could at least work.

Kat reviewed the background checks for Jerry while she had Emrah propose a cover story for Héloïse's case summary. He'd gone through Kat's journal and listed the findings about Serena's coworkers, Peter Line, and the memorial. He'd omitted the parts about ERA and Edmund Clark. If ERA came by, they would have the paperwork to help with an alibi. They backdated the forms to Tuesday.

The front door opened around three o'clock. Kat glanced out and saw Maiki in the foyer. Her heart sank with a bittersweetness. Maybe it was the last time she would see her cousin. At least for a while. "Hey," she said and walked over to her.

Maiki's face dropped. "Oh my—what happened to your face?"

Kat touched the bruise with her fingertips. The swelling had gotten worse. "It's not as bad as it looks."

Maiki moved Kat's hand away to look at it. Kat tried not to grimace in front of her. "Did you get hit with a bat? What happened?"

"I tripped in my office," Kat said. "Smashed into the edge of the desk. But I'm fine now." She pulled Maiki over to the living room. "I'm fine. I promise."

Maiki gawked at her. "Are you sure?"

"Don't worry about it. Let's just hang out while we have time." Kat hugged her tightly. "How long do you have? We can get dinner or—"

"Actually . . ." Maiki pulled away and glanced at her wristwatch. "I got maybe half an hour."

"What?" Kat deflated. "What time are you leaving? Maybe I can . . ." Maiki shook her head. "What?"

"I'm . . . not going anymore." Maiki smiled. "I'm actually looking for apartments around here. My dad reached out to someone for me. I'm going to tour one in a bit."

Kat blinked at her. "So, I can still see you?"

"I'll be around for a while," Maiki said. Kat smiled so brightly the tension made her bruise ache. Maiki fiddled with her golden pendant. The plum blossom sparkled in the sunlight. "I thought about what you said. I'm not going to find what I'm looking for in San Francisco. And I have plenty of reasons to make this place home. Or at least start."

Kat hugged her. "I won't mess it up this time. We can see each other more and talk. We can hang out. I promise. I mean it."

"I'll hold you to that," Maiki said. "I'll have some free time until I can find a job. But I'm sure that won't be hard. Everyone needs a secretary these days." Maiki pulled away from Kat and laughed. "If you need more temp work done in the meantime, let me know. I wouldn't mind doing that again."

Kat tilted her head to the side. Maiki had seemed to have a nicer time with Jerry than Emrah ever did. And Emrah had been too important out in the field for her to leave him at a desk. An extra set of hands would help a lot. "You know, I might take you up on that offer."

Maiki smiled at Kat and fixed her hair. "Do you still have a lot of work—"

"No, no," Kat said. "The case is over. I just want to hang out with you." Maiki smiled. Kat felt relief for the first time in a while.

# CHAPTER 22

# THE STENOGRAPHER

After another day, the swelling on Kat's face had gone down. A dark purple bruise was all that was left. She could conceal most of it with makeup, and she parted her hair down to hide it. Hopefully, it'd be gone before next week.

Kat swirled her spoon idly in her chocolate tea while she reviewed the summary report. The new desk for the lobby had arrived. Emrah was with Maiki in the front trying to assemble it. They had insisted they would be able to manage without her supervision. But after hearing their squabbling and overzealous hammering, she doubted their claims.

As tempting as it had been to use the compact for herself last night, Kat had refrained. She'd wanted to ask if she would be arrested, but there was no point. Knowing what would happen wouldn't change anything. Though Emrah had proposed a rather convincing escape plan. It had seemed like a joke at first, but the plan was too sound. Like he had thought about it before. But it had been a day and a half, and Kat hadn't been arrested. She took that as a sign the coast was clear. Instead, she'd used the compact to verify Jerry's background checks. They came back clean.

Emrah knocked on her door. "Miss Okazaki, you've people here to see you."

Kat packed up her files neatly in the folder. "Send them in," she said.

The floorboards creaked, and Héloïse came through the door with a bright smile. She wore a vibrant yellow sundress, and her hair was curled beautifully. Instead of holding her cane, she was holding Serena's hand. Serena stood with rosy cheeks and a warm smile.

Kat stood up. "Hello, glad to see you," she said.

"It is good to see you," Héloïse said. "Kat, I'd like to introduce you to my wife."

"Hi." Serena waved.

A flutter surged in Kat's chest. "Wife? Congratulations!" She grinned.

"We didn't want to wait anymore," Serena said. Even with the city accent, her voice was melodic. "We'll have a ceremony when we're ready to plan, but we couldn't put it off any longer."

"That's a wonderful idea." Kat smiled at Héloïse. "You look so much brighter."

Héloïse beamed at her. "I have much to look forward to in life," she said, her eyes falling on Serena. "And it seems my condition . . . is not as critical as it was previously. I don't need the cane anymore."

"From . . . Because?"

Héloïse smiled. "I may have familiarized myself with my condition. And it has become easier to control." Kat maintained a smile. While she was glad Héloïse had found control, it angered her that it was illegal. How Maiki had put up with this nonsense for as long as she had, Kat would never understand.

Kat slid the folder over to Héloïse. "These were meant to be signed on Tuesday morning, when we discussed everything. If you could date it accordingly?"

"Yes, yes, thank you," Héloïse said. She walked over and took a seat to read everything, never letting go of Serena's hand.

"If anyone asks . . . this is the official story we'll be going with," Kat said.

"I think we'll be in the clear," Serena said, swaying Héloïse's hand in hers by her waist. "They let me go after I couldn't answer their questions. I didn't know what they were talking about. When I got home, Héloïse told me everything."

Kat nodded. "And your parents?"

"My parents are out of ERA's custody too," Serena said. "They're just glad I'm alive. Now they're busy spreading the news that I'm not dead anymore."

Kat tilted her head. "How's that going?"

Serena rolled her eyes and sighed with a smile. "We're telling the family that the doctors prematurely announced my death," she said. "Some brain injury that other doctors considered hopeless. However, my parents were trying to find someone better to help me. That's why they were avoiding everyone. And their miracle doctor managed to save me after all."

Was this the cover story ERA had come up with? They didn't want the Necromancy leaking to the public. "How's your family taking it?"

Serena shrugged. "We'll find out at the celebration party, I guess. Hopefully the wedding can distract everyone."

Kat nodded. "Do you know if they caught the Necromancer by chance?"

Serena shrugged. "It sounded like they got everyone. That's why they let us go. We can all put this behind us now."

Kat pressed her lips together. The compact had implied there'd be disappointment. Perhaps ERA truly wouldn't have brought back Serena. But now that she was back, they were likely taking credit for doing the right thing. Not that it really mattered. Serena was back, and ERA couldn't prove Kat had committed any crimes. "Hopefully, you don't have to worry about this any longer," Kat said. Serena smiled at her. Her dark hair fell to her waist. A few strands framed the sides of her face, matching her dark eyes. "Did you know at all?" Kat asked.

Serena smiled softly. "About what?"

"Edmund Clark?"

Serena's face went grim, and she sighed. "That he was alive? No," she said. "That he was my father? Also, no. But as far as we're concerned, he stayed dead in the war." She tried to smile, but it didn't reach her eyes. "I did want to thank you for everything." She used her other hand to dig through her purse. "Héloïse told me that you're the only reason I'm here." She pulled out an envelope.

"I'm glad I could help," Kat said, taking the envelope. "And Mr. Stojanovic is the one you should really thank. He was the one that brought you back."

"The young man outside?" Serena asked. "I have one for him too." She gestured for Kat to open her envelope.

Kat glanced down and opened it. Inside was a check with an exorbitant amount of money. "Oh my God," Kat breathed, taking a step back. Her eyes fixated on the row of zeros. "You can't be serious."

Serena smiled at her. "I quite literally owe you my life." She glanced down at Héloïse and smiled. "It's the least I could do."

Kat stared at her in awe. This would offset the cost of the new desk. And fund another renovation project. And build her savings with the money left over. Kat held the check against her chest. "Thank you."

"If I ever need a private detective, I know where to go."

Kat smiled at her. "You know where to find me. As long as ERA doesn't find out we got involved."

Serena smiled. "Your secret's safe with me. I'll take it to my next grave."

Héloïse shook Serena's hand. "Do not say such things," she grumbled as she flipped through the rest of the forms.

Serena laughed. "Hopefully it won't be for a very long time."

An unsettling feeling crept into Kat's stomach. "Could I ask?" she whispered. "Um."

Serena looked back at her. "Anything."

Kat tucked her hair back and gave a nervous smile. "What was it like?" Serena tilted her head. "Being, um, dead. Did you . . . see anything?"

Serena sighed and thought back. "I can hardly believe that I was dead. It was like falling asleep."

"Sleep?"

"Yeah, a dreamless sleep. The ones where morning comes quicker than you thought."

The unsettling feeling didn't go away. "Huh. I don't know if that's comforting or not."

"I guess it's the same as remembering before you were born."

Kat grimaced. "I find that . . . worse."

"Ah, la vache, ma chérie," Héloïse said. "Don't frighten her." Héloïse looked up at Kat. "Do you have a pen?"

"Yes, right here." Kat slid one over to Héloïse. She signed all the documents, and they finished.

Kat led them out to the lobby, where Emrah and Maiki sat in front of a half-built desk. Pieces of wood were piled in the corner of the room, half put together. "That doesn't look right," Maiki said. Emrah stared at it, tilting his head. "You did it backward."

"I don't think . . . Is it backward?" Emrah asked and adjusted his glasses.

"Do you know what you're doing?" Maiki asked.

Emrah tilted his head to the side and scratched his temple. "Oh, I did it backward."

"You broke my desk?"

"I did not. It was just backward."

"You broke my desk!"

"I cannot break what was never made in the first place." He looked at Kat with wide eyes. "You said some assembling acquired? This is all assembling."

Kat resisted the urge to grin. "This is Mr. Stojanovic. He is the one that helped you."

Emrah dropped the tools, and they clattered to the floor. "Hi, good morning." He stood and smoothed out the front of his shirt.

Serena laughed as she handed him the other envelope. "Thank you for all that you did."

He took the envelope and looked at it, then back at her. "Come back if you ever need help," he said.

"You are the first ones we go to," Héloïse said. She looked at Kat and gave a soft, sad smile. "I hope you find your happiness again."

Kat's eyes stung, and she looked down. "Me too," she whispered. "But I'm glad you got yours back."

Héloïse gave her a side hug, then smiled. She held Serena's hand as they went out the front door.

"What was that about?" Emrah asked.

Kat cleared her throat and took a deep breath. "What?"

Emrah narrowed his eyes on her. Her face still felt hot, her eyes still stinging, but she forced a smile. "You alright?" he mouthed.

She pressed her lips firmly together and nodded. That feeling of cement weighed down her tongue. Emrah's eyes scanned her face, but she looked away.

"Katsumi, he broke my desk," Maiki said. She was kneeling in the pile of wood, staring at the queen-sized sheet of instructions.

Emrah glanced back at her. "It's not your desk. Kat got it for the front."

"Well, it'll be her desk if she's greeting clients for us while we're out," Kat said, her voice back to normal. She walked over to the pile of wood. "I thought you said you could handle this."

"We disassemble and then reassemble," Emrah said as he opened the envelope. "Not broken—Whoa . . ." He stared at the check. "This for payment?"

"No, that's your bonus," Kat said.

"All of it?" He glared at her, his eyes bugging out. "This is mine?"

"You earned it."

He stared at her in shock. Then back at the check. Gears turned behind his eyes, like he was calculating something.

"Are you retiring now?" Kat asked. She was half joking, but the fear of him leaving crept inside her.

Emrah shifted his jaw to the side, then nodded. "Yep," he said. "Buying a private castle. And sheep. Lots of sheep." He smiled at her.

"That's your retirement plan?" she asked.

He folded the check and tucked it into his wallet. "What? What's wrong with sheep?"

Kat shrugged. "I'd prefer chickens," she said, kneeling next to Maiki. The raw and unlacquered side of wood faced outward on the bottom panel. "That's not correct."

"I—" Emrah grumbled something to himself, not in English. "I need more coffee."

"Can you make me more tea?" Kat asked. He clicked his tongue twice, and she clicked back. Emrah went into the kitchen. Maiki carefully started pulling the nails out of the bottom panel. Another panel was connected backward that they hadn't noticed yet. This would take a while.

# CHAPTER 23

# THE INFORMANT

Half a package of bandages later, and the desk was assembled. It only took the entire day, but no clients showed up to interrupt them. The desk came together nicely in the end. As long as no one looked too closely at the nail holes where they didn't belong, it was fine. It made the lobby more cohesive and professional, which was the goal. For the first time since she'd bought the place, Kat had a sense of pride in her business.

Maiki went home for the evening to sign the lease to her new apartment, but Emrah stayed late. He was finishing up the last of the background checks while Kat set up the lobby. She had bought fresh flowers in a turquoise vase and arranged them in a better display than the store had. Perhaps she could find some artwork to hang on the wall. Cover up some of the water damage. Maybe get a rug. Would a rug muffle the terrible squeaks? She had enough money to splurge now. Maybe she could paint the kitchen cabinets pastel. Her face grew sore from how much she smiled while admiring the lobby.

Emrah appeared in the kitchen. "Reports are on your desk," he said.

"Thanks," she said. She could proof them later. He went over to the sink. "More coffee?"

"Found another splinter." He flicked open his pocketknife and dug into his palm.

Kat's stomach flipped at the sight. "Heugh. I don't want loose fingers in my kitchen."

"But then you can make finger sandwiches," he said, keeping his hand steady while he wiggled the tip of the blade around.

"Oh, well, when you put it like that, why don't you leave some behind?"

"Will do, boss."

The front door opened. A woman wearing a dress lingered in the threshold.

"Hi, how can I—" Kat froze. Her heart skyrocketed into her throat. Agent Esqueda. It was over. She had snitched. No good deed went unpunished.

Esqueda's hair was down. Dark curls framed her face and rested past her shoulders. She wasn't wearing a suit either. Her salmon blouse tucked into a circle skirt. "Is it a bad time?" Her Southern accent sounded surprisingly gentle.

"To arrest me? Yeah, it's actually incredibly inconvenient," Kat said. Emrah glanced at her from the kitchen, but Kat didn't look at him.

Esqueda narrowed her eyes. "I'm not here for work," she said. "I want to talk."

Kat raised an eyebrow at her. If talk was code for getting a confession, she'd have to try harder. But Kat could play this game. "If it's just talking, fine. Come in," she said. Esqueda shut the door and took a few steps. The floorboards crackled, and she jumped. "Yeah, it does that. It's fine."

Esqueda followed Kat to the offices. She glanced into the kitchen, where Emrah was spinning the tip of his knife in his palm. "What's he doing?" she asked.

"Making dinner," Kat said.

"Huh?"

Kat went into her office and plopped into her chair. Esqueda followed her, gently shutting the office door. "Leave it open," Kat said. Esqueda stared at her but complied. If she was going to try something, Emrah would at least be able to hear it. "So, what's there to talk about?"

Esqueda took a seat in the chair across from her. She stared at her fingers, picking at her nails. "Why did you do it?"

Kat reclined in her chair with her knees propped up on the edge of her desk. "Do what?"

Esqueda pressed her lips together. "I know that you—"

"I have nothing to confess," Kat said.

Esqueda nodded and leaned back in the seat. "I'm not trying to trick you. I just want to understand." She looked down at her hands. "You had . . . life. You had it. Why did you waste it on me?"

Kat maintained a neutral expression. "It's interesting you find your life to be a waste."

"That's not what I mean," Esqueda leaned forward in the chair. "You don't know me. You could've saved it for yourself or your family. Or sold it for any price. You wasted it on a stranger. No less someone that could've had you arrested."

"Do you plan on arresting me?"

Esqueda shook her head. "No, you don't deserve that." She brushed her hair back. Ringlets of curls spiraled over her shoulder. Kat envied the effortless shape her hair held. Not that hair styling was relevant, but she couldn't take her eyes off the cascading curls. "I told my boss I tried helping one of our agents and his blood got all over me," Esqueda said. "No one knows I almost died. Or that you were there. And everyone thinks Serena was brought back before we arrived."

"Oh, Serena's back?" Kat exclaimed. "How'd that happen?"

Esqueda glared at her. "You know how."

Kat threw her hands into the air. "I couldn't possibly. She's really, truly alive?"

Esqueda shifted her jaw to the side and laughed. "Yeah."

"Well, how interesting," Kat said with a cheery grin. "How is she?"

"Newlywed."

"Well. My, my. I'll have to send the couple some crystal."

Esqueda rolled her eyes. "I know you did it."

"I have no idea what you're talking about." Kat swiveled side to side in her chair and maintained eye contact. She waved her fingers out. "I don't have magic."

Esqueda smirked bitterly. "We have Edmund Clark in custody. Everyone else managed to escape."

Kat's smile dropped off her face. "What?" She grabbed the arms of her chair. "What about the Exalter you were trying to catch?"

Esqueda shook her head. "Didn't get him. We didn't account that . . . shooting them would backfire." Esqueda looked away, her expression hard.

Serena said they got arrested. Though ERA had probably given Serena false information to avoid public paranoia. Then why was Esqueda being so forthcoming? How much more would she divulge? "Well, maybe Clark will be useful," Kat said. "Or perhaps the Lines? Surely, they know something. How else would they have gotten involved?"

Esqueda leaned back. "Apparently, Clark's been black-mailing them for a long time," she said. "He and Cynthia were an item right before she got with Gerald Line. But it turns out she was already pregnant. Gerald couldn't risk a scandal. They had a rushed wedding before anyone realized, but Clark caught on. They paid for his silence for years."

So, Gerald knew the whole time? And that was where Clark's money had come from. No secret illegal business deals. Edmund had just held that secret over their heads for years? Until they thought he was dead.

"How did Clark come back?" Kat asked.

Esqueda leaned back in the chair. "We're still working on that. He's not saying much," she said. "The Necromancer brought him back while Clark was overseas. During or after the war. I don't think Clark knows for sure. His memory's shot from drinking."

Great. Of course the only one in custody didn't have the best memory. "So he's been alive all this time? Working for the Necromancer?"

Esqueda nodded, but a look of unease lingered in her eyes. "Clark was in debt to the Necromancer for being brought back." She brushed her hair away from her face. "The vial you gave me," she whispered, looking up at Kat. "Did it say Sparrow or Panacea?"

Kat tilted her head. "I don't know what—"

"Please," Esqueda said. "Was it Panacea?"

The desperation in her eyes couldn't be an act. "Yes," Kat whispered. Esqueda took a breath of relief. "Why does it matter?"

"Sparrow requires refills," Esqueda said. "It's how the Necromancer keeps his people on a short leash. It's why Clark got sloppy."

All those refills every two weeks were so he could stay alive. "So Clark needed his quota met before he could get his life back fully?"

Esqueda nodded. "Clark confessed that he killed Serena so the Lines would do business with him. He broke her neck and spilled water down the stairs to cover it up. He arranged a meeting with the Necromancer once the payments went through. But Clark's not talking anymore. And he won't be around for much longer without the vial."

Kat pulled her knees up in her chair and leaned back. "Why are you telling me this?"

Esqueda looked down. "I need your help." She scooted her chair forward and leaned on the desk. "I don't know how you did it, but you figured out a lot in a matter of days." Her sweet Southern accent turned heavy, and she stared at Kat with a coy grin.

"It was a lot of luck," Kat said. "And ERA intervening was a big clue."

Esqueda shook her head and smirked. "No, you're smarter than you let people think."

"So what?"

"The Necromancer's in the wind. We're hoping Clark can help us, but if he doesn't talk soon, then we're back to square one. And the longer we wait, the further he gets away."

Kat raised an eyebrow. "And you want my help?"

"Off the records."

Kat scoffed. "So you can get all the credit from my work?"

Esqueda's face twisted. "He's an egomaniac that's profiting off of playing God. He shouldn't be on the loose."

"Sounds like a dangerous guy," Kat said. "Why are you coming to me when you have all those fancy resources and manpower at your disposal?"

Esqueda grimaced. "They're taking me off the case."

Kat raised her eyebrows. "Really? Even after you gave them the meeting time?"

"Look, you were right." Esqueda's shoulder jostled as she bounced her leg. "They don't take me seriously. But we can't let him keep slipping away. Our way's not working. So, I figured to try it your way."

"Oh, well, I'm flattered. But what makes you think I'd help you?"

Esqueda stared at Kat with heavy eyes. "Because the Necromancer knows your face."

The hairs on the back of Kat's neck rose. Her feet slipped off the edge of the chair, and she stared at Esqueda. "Am I in danger?" she whispered.

"Possibly."

Kat shifted her jaw. Maybe he wouldn't recognize her. It

had been dark and smoky. But what if he did? What if he'd seen enough to target her?

"We can work it off the records," Esqueda said. "I can give you updates."

Kat laughed under her breath. "You're putting a lot of trust in me."

"You saved me when you didn't have to. That's earns as much trust as anything could."

Kat refrained from smiling, but it delighted her more than it should to hold control over a federal agent. "What's in it for me?" she asked.

Esqueda rolled her eyes. "We don't have a maniac on the streets, and you don't have to constantly look over your shoulder."

"A fair point, but unfortunately, that's not enough." Her heart pounded in her chest, but she kept her voice steady. Indicating fear would void any potential leverage. "If I spend time working this, that's time I'm losing from other clients. Money keeps the lights on, and my employee doesn't stick around for fun either. And since this is off the records, I doubt I'll get an invoice." Esqueda glanced down and furrowed her eyebrows. "So, I'll need something else."

"What if I helped you with your other cases?" Esqueda asked.

"Keep talking."

"If you need a stronger background check or maybe a get-out-of-jail-free card." Kat's eyes widened, and Esqueda smiled. "Do we have a deal?"

Kat could probably take on some higher cases with this pull. She could also solve cases a lot faster. "How long is this deal good for?"

"As long as you're helping me catch the bastard." Esqueda stared at her. The desperation in her eyes returned. "Deal?"

"You really want this guy," Kat said. "Is it personal?"

"He made it personal when he tried to kill me," Esqueda said. "Deal?"

Kat hopped up and walked over to her. As tempting as it was, she had promised to be less impulsive. She couldn't accept without consulting Emrah first. Or the compact. "Let me sleep on it."

"You really have to contemplate?" Esqueda asked, her eyes following Kat.

Kat ran her fingers along the backrest of Esqueda's chair and tapped her shoulder. "Up." Esqueda grumbled and slouched back. "Up."

"What more do you have to think about?" Esqueda asked, crossing her arms and staring up at her. "Either you're in or you're out."

Kat leaned over Esqueda's face. "I'll let you know tomorrow," she said.

"What happened to Miss I-Need-Closure?"

Kat hooked her feet around the back chair legs and slid her hand along the top of the backrest. "You're not my client." Kat shoved the chairback forward. Esqueda catapulted to her feet and thumped into the desk. Emrah popped through the doorway, and Kat waved him away. He silently spun back into the hall.

Esqueda brushed herself off and stared at Kat. "Do you enjoy being irksome?"

"Only to federal agents that refuse to leave," Kat said. She snagged Esqueda's wrist and hauled her out of the office. The floorboards crackled as Kat dragged her to the lobby. Emrah wasn't in the hall but loitering innocently in the kitchen. "Come by tomorrow," Kat said and opened the front door.

Esqueda pulled her hand free and stepped outside herself. She turned back to Kat and narrowed her eyes. "Are you going to make me regret this?"

Kat leaned against the doorway and stared at her. "Only

if you make me regret it." Esqueda didn't look satisfied, but she nodded. Then finally left.

Kat shut the door and flicked the blinds closed. She stared out the window. Esqueda walked down the block. No one else was watching the house.

"So?"

Kat jumped and spun around. Emrah stood behind her. "You need to stop that," she muttered and took a breath. His hands were covered in bandages. "Still got ten fingers?"

"Missing two," he said. "If you see them lying around, let me know."

"I'll keep an eye out." She looked up at him. "What do you think? Is she trustworthy?"

"I doubt this is some setup." He adjusted his glasses and shrugged. "Don't like that we won't be paid."

"She can help us with other cases that will pay us," Kat said, leaning against the window. "But the Necromancer might recognize us."

Emrah shifted his jaw. "Yeah, that puts a damper on the evening, huh?"

"Yeah," Kat sighed. Even if the Necromancer hadn't seen their faces, he would find them if he wanted to. If he was smart enough to have escaped ERA multiple times, what else was he capable of? How far would he go to hunt them down? "Am I crazy for wanting to take the deal?"

Emrah shook his head. "As long as no one finds out what we're doing."

Kat nodded and stared up at him. "Keep this between you and me. Not Maiki. She'll stay with our regular clients."

"Fine by me," he said. He leaned against the door next to Kat and sighed. "Good thing we have her help considering our workload just increased."

"Any of our clients take precedence over this," Kat said. "We only work on it in our downtime. And perhaps we can establish a schedule with Esqueda when she meets with us."

"Sounds like you're taking the deal then," Emrah said.

Even with Emrah's approval, she needed to verify. If this was some elaborate trick for ERA, or if it would only get them killed, then it couldn't be worth it. "We'll see." Kat took Emrah's wrist and pulled him off the door. "Come on."

"Where we going?" he asked.

Kat opened the door and pulled him outside. "You can't cook with those hands." She locked up the building, and they headed to DeLacey's.

Kat was snuggled in her bed at midnight. She held the compact in her hands. The swirling white light shimmered. "Should we investigate the Necromancer?" she asked. The light turned into a blush pink, and she smiled seeing her favorite flower. A peony bloomed inside. A blessing from her grandmother.

Peonies were good fortune to those brave enough to pursue it.

End of Book One

# Acknowledgments

The lockdowns happened while I was in college, and I spent most of my time with my roommate while we did our homework. Often we worked in silence as any conversation broke our focus. I couldn't talk while graphing animations and she couldn't listen while reading her political science textbooks. Eventually, she started reading aloud and I listened to her like a podcast. Somewhere between animating stylized light and hearing about trials at the Hague, the story came to me.

Thank you to Daisy Lupa for taking all the political science classes for your major but telling me about your lectures and readings. And thank you for proofreading my creative writing assignments, which inevitably turned into this book. You're the best critique partner, royal advisor, and trusted confident, especially eight P.M. on Sundays. And to my old library coworkers Hailey and Duncan for all the banter and shenanigans during the night shifts that inspired Kat and Emrah's humor.

To my mother for obsessively watching crime shows and my father for obsessively watching WWII documentaries. Both of you have thoroughly supported me creatively even when I was extremely classified about what I was making.

Thank you to my alpha reader Veronica Trunzo for helping me take the leap in sharing my work and all your encouraging feedback. Thank you to Maisy for beta reading through the rough patches. Thank you to Odette Locke for your unwavering support during the publication process.

Thank you to my wonderful and talented editor Allison Erin Wright who helped this story become the best version of itself. Thank you to my other editor Stefanie Molina-Santos for her consultation. Thank you to my cover designer Holly Dunn who found the perfect vision for this book.

# About the Author

A.K. Ikezoe is a fantasy author from Chicago, where she grew up with a love for books and magic. She graduated from Northern Michigan University in 2022 with an animation degree and English minor. She spent six years working as a librarian and currently works as an animation lighting compositor. In her free time, she enjoys writing fantasy stories, traveling to new cities, and spending time with friends and family.